Also by Linda Broday

Texas Redemption

Bachelors of Battle Creek
Texas Mail Order Bride
Twice a Texas Bride
Forever His Texas Bride

Men of Legend
To Love a Texas Ranger
The Heart of a Texas Cowboy
To Marry a Texas Outlaw

Texas Heroes
Knight on the Texas Plains
The Cowboy Who Came Calling

to MARRY a TEXAS OUTLAW

LINDA BRODAY

Published by Sourcebooks Casablanca, an imprint of Sourcebooks, Inc.
P.O. Box 4410, Naperville, Illinois 60567-4410
(630) 961-3900
Fax: (630) 961-2168
sourcebooks.com

Printed and bound in the United States of America.
OPM 10 9 8 7 6 5 4 3 2 1

I dedicate this book to all the forgotten and abused children in the world who have no voice, no one to stand up for them, no one to care. I put these children into all my stories because they lend such immense depth, emotion, and enrichment. I urge you not to close your eyes and hearts to those in need. Be their advocate. Each of us has an obligation to shine a light wherever and however we can.

One

North Texas
Spring 1879

ALONE. HUNTED. BONE-TIRED OF RUNNING. SOME DAYS HE almost welcomed death so he could rest.

Trouble stalked Luke Weston from one end of Texas to the other. Being a wanted man with a price on his head and a large target on his back stole any hope of going home.

The black gelding's hooves struck the rocky floor of the narrow canyon, sounding like shots from a tracker's gun. Luke shifted in the saddle and tried his best to pretend that the nervous jitters crawling up his spine weren't whispering a warning. But he couldn't afford to. Men in his profession who ignored their gut usually ended up as a meal for the coyotes or buzzards.

A large flock of nasty scavengers silently circled above him now, watching with their greedy eyes—they waited as well for the bullet that would end his life.

He tucked his long black duster outside his Colt and removed the narrow leather loop anchoring the weapon to the holster. The warning whispering in his ear, he rested his hand on the wooden grip into which he'd carved one word—*Legend.*

The trouble stalking him wasn't anything new. Except this time, he knew one name.

Munroe O'Keefe.

The young jackass, desperate to make a name for himself, had bragged from Austin to Fort Worth that he would kill Luke Weston and that he'd be a hero for it.

Luke had broken camp as the sun rose and spotted the young gunslinger high up on a ridge. Since then, he'd thought he'd lost him in the rugged landscape littered with gullies, ravines, and desert mountains.

But had he? Was he underestimating his adversary?

"Stupid fool," Luke muttered. O'Keefe didn't have the brains of a stuffed goose, or he'd realize that killing Luke would only draw a wide target on his own back. Luke's death wouldn't bring the kid any fame, and for damn sure wouldn't bring him glory. The only thing it would accomplish would be to put O'Keefe on the run for the rest of his life.

Knowing one name didn't cover it all, though. Munroe O'Keefe was only one of many on his trail. Others included lawmen from Texas and beyond, bounty hunters anxious to collect the price on his head, outlaws wanting to recruit him.

And that was only a partial list.

A low, angry growl rumbled in Luke's throat and he cussed a blue streak under his breath.

The sudden rustle of sagebrush that rimmed the rocks behind sent alarm rushing through him. His Colt cleared the holster as he swung around.

A coyote froze for a second, staring back at the gun pointed at him before loping off into the brush. Shadowed by the low brim of his Stetson, Luke's gaze swept the narrow trail. Finding nothing, he finally holstered his Colt.

It took a minute to force his nerves to settle. He dragged the cool Texas air deep into his lungs. Such was the price he had to pay for past mistakes. Now, his face was plastered on every wanted poster across the state, and the reward was growing higher by the day.

Luke forced a bitter laugh and smoothed the withers of his mount. "Major John, you might find yourself in the company of a new owner soon. You're a good friend, but another man might not take kindly to a beer-drinking horse, so try to refrain and mind your manners."

Major John snorted and tossed his head high as though to say "you mind your business and I'll mind mine."

"Keep your attitude to yourself. I mean every word." Sudden pain pierced Luke's heart. One of the hardest moments of his life so far had come six months ago, when he'd had to bury his nameless black gelding. He'd searched high and low for one equal in looks and temperament, and the minute he'd gazed into Major John's eyes and seen the animal's heart, he'd plunked down the money. He hadn't regretted it. So far.

A bead of sweat rolled into Luke's eye and he swiped at it impatiently to stop the sting. Damn, he'd be glad to rise up out of the steep, narrow confines of this canyon. Only six horses wide, it reminded him too much of a coffin. He longed for a breeze on his face. The morning was only a few hours old, but the moisture left by the sudden spring shower had already burned off. He'd have to remove his duster first chance he got. The sun's heat would be relentless soon, bouncing off the rocks. He had important business in Dead Horse Creek, just south of the mighty Red River that separated Texas from Indian Territory. Dead Horse was known as a dangerous outlaw hideout.

Finally, he had his first real chance to find the man who'd framed him for a cold-blooded murder. The man who called himself Ned Sweeney was like some damn ghost. Even his name was stolen from a Beadle's Dime Novel. Who knew what his real name was. Luke had heard rumors that Sweeney never stayed more than one night in the same place. If he didn't catch him now, no telling when he'd surface again. Convincing a desperate man on the run to do the right thing might pose a problem. A tight smile curved Luke's mouth.

If he could get his hands on the rotten bastard, he'd wring the truth out of him. The question of why Sweeney'd framed him had haunted Luke for two years.

Luke readily took responsibility for the things he'd done, but the blood of federal judge Edgar Percival was on Sweeney's hands, not his. It was strange how many crimes landed at Luke's door these days—another downside of having a reputation for a fast draw and a price on his head. It was easier to pin everything on a man already known as an outlaw than look for the real criminal.

Anger and frustration left a sour taste in his mouth.

Minutes ticked by slowly, until at last he exited the canyon. Dead Horse Creek wasn't more than a half hour away. A friend, Brenner McCall, had given him the tip, assuring him that Sweeney would be there. He urged Major John into a trot.

Luke's thoughts were still on Ned Sweeney and on clearing his name when he spied a lone wagon near the only tree of any size within miles. He drew his Colt.

Nothing moved, and he rode closer. No one would leave a wagon and team of horses in the middle of nowhere by choice. Then he spied tools on the ground that suggested someone had been fixing the wagon. But where had they gone? The hair tingling on the back of his neck was a warning. Could be an ambush.

Every nerve taut, he drew near and his mouth tightened in a thin line.

Bound and gagged, a woman slumped under the tree, her head sagging on her chest. She appeared to be dead. Her blue dress was covered with dried blood.

A noise alerted him and Luke swung around as two men scrambled toward cover.

"Stop where you are!" Luke ordered. When they kept running, he fired, but they jumped into a ravine, the bullet missing them.

Alert to the slightest movement and sound, he slowly dismounted with his gun drawn. The woman's eyes suddenly flew open. She made muffled noises that he couldn't make out through the gag in her mouth, but he did read her fear. As he strode toward her, she kicked her legs, defiance flashing from her eyes. She leaned her weight against the tree trunk, ready to kick the daylights out of him.

"Ma'am, I don't mean you any harm." He raised his hands as he advanced. Rage spread through him. Why would those men do this?

The bound woman showed no sign of calming.

"I only want to untie you. Nothing more." He crept a little closer, and even though the two varmints were probably watching, he slid his Colt back into the holster. It was within easy reach. Maybe the woman would see him as no threat with it out of sight.

"If you're going to hurt me, I won't come closer. Nod if you agree not to kick."

Several heartbeats passed. The woman finally nodded once, although fury flashed in her eyes as Luke knelt to remove the gag. Why level her wrath at him? He was trying to help.

When he took the obstruction from her mouth, she let loose. "Damn you! You better run, you bastard, because when I find my damn gun, I'm going to put a bullet right between your eyes."

The language shocked him as much as the anger.

"Hey, lady, I don't know what you think I've done—"

"What you've done? How about tying me up like a Christmas goose!" She released a string of cuss words.

"Now wait just a cotton-pickin' minute. That wasn't me. I've never seen you before." Was she an escaped lunatic? Maybe he'd had it wrong and those two men he'd rode up on were taking her to the asylum. But then why would they run?

For a second, he was almost tempted to stuff the gag back into her mouth. Her withering glare could have stripped a layer of hide from his chest. "I was riding by, minding my own business, when I saw you," he said hotly. "In case you haven't noticed, I'm all you got, lady."

Unless he counted the two men who'd vanished into the ravine. Since he hadn't seen any more of them, he figured they must've ridden away. He needed to decide what to do with her before they returned.

"I sure could use a drink of water, if you can spare some, handsome," she said sweetly through gritted teeth. She blew a strand of hair the hue of a summer sun from her eyes.

The gesture reminded him that he hadn't untied her. On second thought, he had some control leaving things as they were, but on the other hand, she could be hurt, in shock from blood loss. When he caught the quiver of her chin, he knew she wasn't as rough as she appeared.

"I'll get some water once I free you. Are you injured?"

"Everything hurts." She stared down in a daze at her ruined skirt. "I don't know where this blood came from."

He quickly cut the ropes binding her arms and legs, then stalked to his horse, his long, black duster slapping against his legs, and jerked out his canteen. He returned and squatted next to her. "Take it slow."

After drinking her fill, she handed it back. "Thanks."

She looked at her hands with a stricken gaze, staring at a ring set with a small emerald. Then she glanced down at her dirty dress, paused at the long rip up one side, and began digging in the folds, probably for the gun she'd threatened him with before. Giving up her search, she leaned to touch her scuffed boots as though she'd never seen them before.

"My name's Luke. What can I call you?"

"I'm..." She glanced up in anguish, putting a hand to her head. "My name is... It's..." She stopped, her forehead wrinkling in clear confusion. She let out a sharp whimper. "I...I can't remember. Oh God, I don't know my name! Why can't I remember? Wait. I have a ring. I'm married." Her troubled eyes pierced him. "Are you my husband?"

If he was, he wouldn't wait for her to shoot him; he'd do it himself. "No, ma'am. I'm one hundred percent certain you're not my wife." Correction. He upped the percent to a thousand.

Her lost, frightened look deepened. "Then you can't... you can't tell me who I am?"

"No, ma'am. I've never seen you before." Luke had limited experience with lunatics. Not even the pretty kind with curves and long legs that could make a lonely man think about sultry nights and slow, rainy days.

Crazy or not, she was a looker. But then, lunacy didn't always attack the ugly ones.

"I don't know who I am." Her voice was small and quiet, all the bluster gone.

It would be a hell of a thing to forget your name. Although he had—on purpose. Completely different.

"Maybe you can tell me how you got here and who those men were who tied you."

"Men? I haven't seen anyone except..." She frowned. "Once or twice, I sort of saw shadows in the darkness."

"Two men ran from here when I rode up."

Misery sharpened her features. Her voice was barely louder than a whisper. "I don't know anything about them. I just don't know anything about anything. I want to go home but I don't know where that is. Where *is* my husband? Did he leave me here? Maybe...maybe I'm not married. Or...oh God, maybe..." A strangled sob rose as she clawed at the blood staining her dress, her eyes wild. "Maybe I killed him."

After witnessing her scalding temper, the latter *was* entirely possible. Her dress bore witness to something bad. Luke touched her slender shoulder, wanting to offer some bit of comfort. With forced confidence, he stood. "I don't believe you're a killer and you shouldn't either. I'm sure there's an explanation."

"Who am I, then? Where did I come from? Maybe I'm a woman of ill repute."

"Look at your clothes. They're not the sort a loose woman would wear. Aside from the stains and rips on your dress, it's nice—modest. I'd say you've been well cared for."

Hearing a noise, Luke pulled his Colt and whirled. He

scanned the area but saw no threat and returned the gun to his holster. "I've got to get you out of here, *amiga*, before those men come back. Can you walk to the tail end of the wagon?"

"I'm really woozy, but with your help I can." But when she stood, she collapsed in his arms. "My legs are too numb. I can't. And my head is splitting open."

Luke lowered her back to the ground. "Just sit here a minute. I'll keep watch."

"Move, please," she cried, hurling herself away from him.

He'd barely gotten clear before she spewed vomit. He reached for the canteen and wet his bandana, putting it on the back of her neck. He knelt, rubbing her back. At last, she emptied everything from her stomach and rose. Luke wet the bandana again and gently washed her face.

"Rinse your mouth, *amiga*." He handed the canteen to the woman, who appeared at least five years younger than his thirty. "Do you mind if I feel your scalp for a lump? You have blood matted in your hair."

A blow to the head appeared a logical conclusion. He'd once seen a man forget everything except how to pull on his boots after a wallop by a stout length of wood.

Though she felt poorly, the mystery lady rallied to shoot him a lethal stare. "Go ahead, but touch me anywhere else and you'll regret it, mister."

Lord, he already regretted a great many things where the morning was concerned.

"Not 'mister.' Luke," he gently reminded her. "And you don't have to worry."

He slid his hand into the mass of honey-blond hair spilling onto her shoulders and down her back. He ignored the silk strands wrapping around his fingers and gently worked his way across her scalp.

"Does it hurt when I touch this area?"

The woman drew a sharp breath. "Yes."

"You have a large lump. You could've fallen and hit your head, or else someone struck you before they tied you up. That's likely why you can't remember anything." Despite the lady having tried his patience at first, he fought rising waves of anger. If he could get his hands on the two men who'd done this, he'd make them very sorry.

Unshed tears bubbled in her eyes. "Will it come back?"

"I'm about the furthest thing from a doctor as you can get, *amiga*."

"Why do you keep calling me that?"

"'*Amiga*'?"

"Yes. That's not English. Even I know that much."

"It's Spanish for a woman who's a friend."

Her forehead wrinkled in thought. "So, you're Spanish?"

"Just half. My mother was Spanish; my father is white."

"Oh. I wonder if I'm a mix." She glanced down and gave a little cry. "If I do have a husband, I'm going to chew him out up one side and down the other." She peered closer at her ring. "Any fool knows this isn't a wedding ring and the size of that emerald makes him a cheapskate. I sure didn't mean much to him."

The lady might've forgotten her name, but she sure knew her jewelry. He covered a grin with the back of his hand.

She suddenly wobbled, digging her fingers into his arm. "I'm going to be sick again."

Luke quickly got out of the way, but only bile came up. When her sickness passed, he wiped her face again and let her rinse her mouth. "I'll carry you to the wagon, *amiga*, where you can lie down."

He swept her up in his arms and strode to the back. He'd get her situated, then drive her to the nearest woman who could look out for her. With his conscience cleared, maybe he could still manage to overtake Ned Sweeney if he rode hard.

"Just a moment." He propped her against the side of the wagon while he lowered the heavy wooden gate. Her face had turned the color of cold ash. The wagon bed was empty except for a pail, a shovel, and wooden crates at the front covered with a dirty canvas. Damn! No blankets back there. It wasn't going to be a very comfortable ride to find help.

"Wait a minute." He went to his horse. Bringing back his bedroll, he spread it out.

"Let's get you inside where you can rest." Carefully, Luke lifted her onto the bedroll. Someone had to be searching for her, wondering why she'd vanished. He should've chased after those two men he'd seen running, but the lady had seemed more important at the time.

She murmured, "I don't mean to be trouble."

"You're no trouble." Though every bit of softness in him had disappeared long ago and his heart had long since turned to stone, he could no more leave her out here than become a priest.

He crawled up and took her hand. "Try not to worry. Just think about shooting me and that should perk you right up."

"I just wish I didn't feel like I'm not a...a person anymore. I need... I need..."

She needed an identity, something to ground her. He understood that perfectly. Until a short while ago, he'd shared that problem...except he'd never forgotten his name for one second. Though he'd tried hard, he'd found it hopeless to forget. To pretend he was someone else. To wish for things he could never have.

Luke stared at a row of little roses around her collar. "How about I call you Rose? Just until you get your memory back."

"Rose." A little smile curved her lips. "I'm Rose."

It was funny how such a simple thing could brighten a lost lady. It had been a long while since he'd brought cheer to anyone. Fear was the only thing he seemed to be able to spread and that was measured in spades.

Except...there had been one—Angelina—who'd thought he hung the moon. But she was gone. He'd laid her to rest with the angels three years ago and rode off without looking back.

He cleared his throat, dragging himself back to the woman he'd called Rose. "I'm going to check those crates to see what's inside, then we'll get going."

Rose's brow wrinkled. "Wish I knew."

Crawling to the cargo, he threw back the canvas. Three small crates held whiskey, and it wasn't the rotgut stuff. Then he stared in disbelief at the contents of the rest: at least a half-dozen brand-new rifles rested inside.

Two

Now what in Sam Hill were Rose and those two men doing with a load of rifles and good whiskey? Luke pushed back his hat and thought of asking, but what was the point when the question would only upset her.

Maybe her husband was a saloon owner? But that didn't explain the Winchesters. Could the two thugs have waylaid Rose and her husband? But where was he? Lying dead in the ravine?

"Rose, do you know how long you've been out here?"

She pushed back a golden strand, wrinkling her forehead, clearly struggling for some speck of memory. "I didn't fully wake up until you came. I thought you were one of the men in the dark shadows who talked of digging a grave and putting me in it. Sorry."

"Don't apologize." He laid a hand on her arm. "Just rest. I'm going to take a look around."

"What's under the canvas?" Hope filled Rose's hazel eyes.

Luke replaced the cover. "Nothing useful. We'll be on the road when I get back."

He told her to think good thoughts before he jumped out. He walked around the wagon, checking its condition, and looking for anything to identify it. He noticed nothing distinctive. Not until he moved to the team of horses.

They looked to be a pair of three-year-olds. Very nice

horses. The brand froze him in his tracks. That spoked wheel with a star in the middle was impossible to mistake. The horses belonged to Stoker Legend, of the Lone Star Ranch. It was the largest spread in North Texas.

Memories poked him like the bristly thorns of a prickly pear cactus. Deep yearning surged, so powerful it stole his breath. If only he could claim what was his.

But he couldn't.

He knew he'd have to return the horses—plus get a few answers as to who'd taken them. But first things first. Luke slammed the door on those bygones. As he strode toward his horse, his mind raced. They were only about a two-day ride by wagon from the western edge of Lone Star land. But the ranch stretched over four hundred and eighty thousand acres, and reaching headquarters and the doctor that Stoker Legend employed would take three. Lost Point was closer, but they had no medical help there and Rose needed answers.

The wagon was travel-worthy, at least. Luke had noticed signs of a repaired axle. He must've ridden up on them right as they finished. Fortune had smiled on him for once.

A skyward glance found the black buzzards still circling, still waiting, still a bad omen. A harbinger of evil.

When he was two steps from the gelding, gunshots rang out and a bullet splintered the side of the wagon where Rose lay.

He raced to take cover beside the wagon. "Are you all right, Rose?"

"I'm not hit. Who's shooting at us?"

"My guess is the two cowards I saw running." Maybe they were friends of hers. The finality of missing his appointment at Dead Horse Creek sank into the pit of his stomach. Heavy disappointment swept over him. How long would it be before he got another chance at Ned Sweeney?

Luke dropped to the ground, slid underneath the wagon, and scanned the small ravine to his right. He waited. Thoughts and speculation rambled around inside his head like a bunch of marbles clanking together. All the while, hot anger grew. He didn't know what the hell was going on, but of one thing he was certain: when he caught the ones who'd tied Rose and left her to die, he'd get some answers or else fill them so full of lead their kith and kin wouldn't recognize them.

A slight movement drew his gaze. The sun's rays glinted on gunmetal. When orange flame burst from the end of a rifle and bullets kicked up the dirt near him, Luke fired two rounds toward the spot.

As he pondered his next move, something touched his leg. He jerked around. Damn! The fool woman had climbed out of the wagon and was crawling up beside him. "Stay down," he ordered.

"What do they want?" she whispered. "We don't have anything."

Nothing except shiny new rifles and whiskey.

"We're about to find out." When a head poked above the rim of the ravine, Luke squeezed the trigger again.

"Damn you!" a man hollered. "You shot my ear off."

"There's more where that came from," Luke grated out. "What do you want?"

"You got something of ours."

"Yeah, what's that?" Luke kept his gaze on the ravine.

"My woman and our stuff in the wagon. Hand 'em over and we'll let you live."

Rose sucked in her breath and clutched Luke's shirtsleeve with trembling fingers.

"You mean the woman you left tied and gagged while you ran?" he asked.

"She's simpleminded. Didn't want her wandering off. You scared me, so I ran. You got a lot of nerve stealing her."

"I am *not* simpleminded," Rose whispered furiously.

"What's her name?" Maybe Luke could get her some peace of mind before he concluded his business with them.

"Well, it's…it's… Hell, what difference does it make?"

"That's what I thought." The anger that had simmered

upon finding Rose erupted in a boiling fury. "Here's what I'll do, boys. You can have the rifles and liquor but the woman stays. Best offer you'll get."

"There's two of us and only one of you."

"You might not be too smart, *compadre*, but at least you can count. Before you get in over your head, you might want to know who's holding this Colt on you. I killed my first man at fourteen and I haven't stopped. Two more won't make any difference."

When the piece of cow dung answered back, he seemed to have lost his confidence. "Who might you be?"

"Luke Weston. Show yourselves and I'll face you both. Might even give you a fighting chance." His voice came out as hard as steel, and as unforgiving as the wild Texas land.

A deafening silence followed. Then after a few seconds, one spoke up. "You said we could have our crates?"

"Dillydally and you'll get a big goose egg. I'm tired of dickering."

"No, no! We'll take them off your hands. You ain't gonna shoot us when we come to collect the crates, are you?"

"Luke," Rose whispered. "Don't trust these sidewinders."

Like he was about to. "Stay here." He crawled from under the wagon and took cover at the side. He swung his attention to the pair who deserved to die. "Toss your weapons. I said I wouldn't shoot you, but don't tempt me."

"We're coming." Guns flew out, landing on the hard ground.

Two men, one tall, wearing a black leather vest, and a shorter one in a wide-brimmed sombrero, climbed from the ravine. Vest Man had blood oozing down one side of his face from his missing ear. The two slowly moved toward the wagon, leading two horses and a mule.

Gripping his Colt, Luke stepped forward, his eyes catching every twitch they made. The short, stocky fellow in the sombrero nervously scampered into the wagon and started handing down the crates to his partner on the ground.

Luke didn't notice Rose behind him until she touched the back of his long duster. He almost jumped out of his skin. "I told you to stay put."

"I had to get a good look at these low-down skunks," she grated out. "I am *not* simpleminded."

He let out an exasperated breath. The lady was going to be the death of him yet.

When the pair had unloaded the last one, Luke spoke. "I ought to shoot you where you stand for tying up the woman."

The short weasel didn't have one drop of Mexican blood, and he refused to meet Luke's gaze. "Had to. She saw everything."

"Which was what?"

A strangled cry sprang from Rose's mouth.

"She didn't tell you?" asked Sombrero.

"Been a little busy and she wasn't in the best shape when I found her, thanks to you."

"We thought she was dead." The one in the vest told his partner, "I said we shoulda finished her off."

"Does it sound like I'm dead, you ugly piece of worm puke?" Rose yelled, scratching and clawing to get past Luke. "I'll finish you off!"

Dios mío!

"Settle down, *amiga*," he ordered quietly. "I'm trying to get some answers for you, damn it."

Rose's mutinous glare didn't ease his worry.

The rifle-runner brought his bloody face around. "We didn't do all of that. It was Reno Kidd and if we ain't back with our loot, he's gonna come lookin' for us. He's the mean one."

Yeah, Reno would kill his own mother without batting an eyelash. Luke hated the yellow-haired outlaw. He'd sell his soul for two bits. Rose was lucky he had only bashed her head in.

"I oughta come over there and kick you both half to death!" Rose yelled. "Just for letting him do this to me!"

"Hush, Rose," Luke grated. Tamping down his irritation, he brought his focus back to the men. "Where is Reno anyway?"

"He rode on ahead to make a deal, leaving orders to meet him this afternoon."

"How does the woman fit into all this?"

"Damn it!" yelled Sombrero. "Reno took her for insurance in case we were trailed." The man's wide hat shielded his eyes, but Luke felt their hard glare.

A tic developed in his jaw. He'd seen his share of men like these.

"Look, can we just have what we came for?"

"Where did you cross paths with the woman?" When neither answered, Luke's bullet kicked up the dirt at Sombrero's feet. "Where?"

"Doan's Crossing." Vest shifted uneasily. "That's all we know. Gotta long way to travel before night."

"You'll leave when I say. Which one of you hit her?"

"Yeah," Rose hollered around Luke. "I'm going to kill whoever cracked my skull."

"Reno Kidd." Vest shifted again, crossing his arms. "I thought he plumb killed her. She was throwing a wall-eyed fit, screaming at the top of her lungs, and hitting. She's a wildcat. He had to shut her up somehow. Every time she came to, Reno hit her again. Her father ain't gonna be happy about that either."

"I'll show you what a wildcat is!" Rose tried again to get loose.

Luke's thoughts whirled. The gang had evidently waylaid Rose and stolen the contraband. Why had she been traveling with it? "How did she get all this blood on her?"

"The dead man, I guess—he might've been her husband. Leastways, she was with him. The other fellow could be dead too. Or shot up."

"You're a real prince."

The outlaw wasted no time in denying murder. "Hey, weren't us, mister. We just rob."

Luke wouldn't lay odds on the shifty man speaking the truth.

The tall, vest-clad man wiped at the blood running down his neck. "Weston, we gotta go. We ain't got all day."

Luke hoped some of this was jogging Rose's memory. He breathed deep to calm his anger. "One more thing. What's her father's name?"

"Look, we've told you all we know," Sombrero snapped. "Reno has the answers. We don't know squat. He only said her father is a mean hombre, someone you don't want to mess with."

"You're a lying sack of shit!" Cussing a blue streak, Rose again tried to fight her way around Luke. He managed to grab her around the waist, lifting her off the ground before she made her break. One thing for certain, she wasn't a preacher's daughter. He never expected to hear any decent woman giving profanity such free rein.

"I'm not one to mess with either, *compadres*," Luke snapped. "Load the contraband onto your mule and get gone. But if I ever see either of you again, I'll fill you full of lead and leave you to rot under the sun."

"You don't have to worry none," promised Vest.

"Give Reno a message. Tell him Luke Weston is coming for him. Time and place is my choosing." Luke wanted a lot more but he doubted they had the answers he was after. These two were nothing but low men on the totem pole. And he needed to get Rose safe before anything else went wrong.

Without so much as a grunt of acknowledgement, the two strapped the crates onto the mule. Only the rifles and half the whiskey would fit, so they took the bottles from the extra crate and stuffed their saddlebags full. In their haste, several bottles dropped onto the hard ground and shattered, soaking the thirsty earth. They snatched up their pistols, jumped on their horses, and galloped toward a ridge.

Rose broke free and raced toward them. "Who am I? Damn it, tell me! Who am I?"

The anguish in her chilling cries echoed in Luke's head as he chased after her.

With heartrending sobs, Rose collapsed into a heap, her forehead touching the ground. Luke gently lifted her up, clutching her against him. He rubbed his hand up and down her back.

"Who am I?" she whispered brokenly.

Three

Rose sagged against Luke, safe inside the circle of his strong arms. Even if no one ever claimed her, she desperately needed to know who she was. Where she belonged. Anything was better than this emptiness inside her head that maybe had once held memories of a childhood, a family, a father.

Luke lifted her in one smooth motion and eased her down on the bed of the wagon. His pale-green eyes held kindness as he wiped her eyes. The man who'd spoken with a hard edge had a tender touch.

Though she didn't know her own name, where she came from or who her family was, she didn't want to die. From what those men had said and the throbbing pain in her skull, she'd come close.

"Did any of what we learned from those two rifle peddlers jog your memory?" Luke prodded.

"No. I wish they could've told me who my father is." Rose met his eyes, wondering how an outlaw and killer could be so kind. "They said my father wasn't going to be too happy for what Reno did to me. Was he in cahoots with them? They seemed to know him." Her stomach roiled and she thought she might retch again.

"Look, don't read too much into what they said. Men like that lie at the drop of a hat."

Warmth spread through her. He was only trying to spare her feelings, but she appreciated that. Most men probably wouldn't give her state of mind a thought.

Rose gave him a wry smile. "At least I know I'm not an orphan." But would a father like hers be a step up? Something told her it wouldn't.

"That's the spirit." Luke winked. "Hang with me and I'll get your answers, but right now it's too dangerous to stay here. Do you want to lie in back or ride up with me?"

"I'll ride on the seat." Where she could see trouble coming.

With a last look at the only place on earth she knew, Rose let him help her into the wagon box. After tying his horse to the back, he removed his black duster and stowed it under the seat then took his place next to her. Propping his foot on the wood in front in a careless pose, he set the horses in motion.

She cast a sidelong glance at this man who'd saved her. He had a rugged profile that seemed to have been carved over time by the wind, sun, and weather, with raven-black hair and green eyes that could harden to silver. He'd killed his first man so young. He should scare her, but she felt just the opposite. Luke could've easily given her over to the two jackasses back there. Instead, he seemed willing to risk his life for a stranger, and that was something she'd never expected.

Though she couldn't say with certainty, she imagined few people had ever stuck up for her before. Her throat tightened. "Luke, do you think I'll ever know my name or where I belong?" She bit her quivering lip to still it.

"We have to have hope. If we don't have that, we have nothing."

His reply hinted at something bad he was trying to fix.

They stopped at a narrow spring and refilled the canteen. Luke plucked some leaves from a plant growing next to the water and handed them to her. "Chew on these mint leaves to get the bad taste out of your mouth. Plus, it'll ease your stomach."

His thoughtfulness caught her by surprise. Even when it didn't look like it, he was thinking of her. She chewed on the leaves, enjoying the fresh feel they gave her mouth, and watched him care for the horses. This man who could probably kill with ease had a soft spot in his heart. Soon they got on the road again, the sway of the wagon soothing as they rocked along. Luke put some mint leaves into his mouth and chewed.

"Were you going anywhere important when you found me?" she asked.

He was silent a moment before finally saying, "It'll keep."

Something in his quiet tone told her that she'd cost him a great deal, but at least he didn't seem to be holding it against her.

"I don't know who you are, Rose, and I'm no expert, but I can say one thing. You didn't learn to cuss like that in church." Luke stared straight ahead with a somber face. A slow grin formed and she was struck by his handsome features.

Suddenly, the day seemed a little brighter. Rose pushed back her hair. "The words just slipped out so easy without me even thinking." She made a face. "I must have a terrible temper."

"I'd say so. You scared five years off those two lowlifes."

"What kind of person do you suppose I am? If you could take a stab?"

Luke swiveled to face her. His pale-green eyes seemed to stare deep into her soul. "With your temperament and rough language, you could be a mule skinner. Only I've never seen one as pretty as you. Or maybe you're a lumberjack. Except you're a long way from any trees." He paused, his grin fading. "I'm sorry. I shouldn't make light of your predicament."

"It's okay, Luke. Getting all down in the mouth only makes me feel worse. I appreciate your efforts to make me laugh."

"It takes a strong woman to face your situation."

Rose shrugged. "I don't have much choice. With a father who's apparently a crook and an outlaw, I just wonder what else the rotten bastard taught me?" She released a string of blistering cuss words, hating to think of what she had become. She probably wouldn't like that person very much.

"Can you try to curb the profanity just a bit? I can't get used to such words coming from someone who looks like an angel."

His quiet compliment made her heart skip a beat. For him, and those eyes that could melt the layers of ice inside, she'd do most anything.

She sat up straighter. "Where are we going?"

"Normally I'd ask where you want to go, but since you haven't a clue, I'm heading toward the Lone Star Ranch."

"Why go there?"

"Nearest doctor. I know the owner. Good man. Stoker Legend will take you in. And besides, these horses carry their brand and I need to return them."

Rose raised her chin a trifle. "I don't need a sawbones."

That ranch would only mean more people she didn't know. What would happen to her if she couldn't ever find a familiar place again? Find *someone* at least she recognized? Her chin quivered. Even if it was a bad person, it would be better than no one at all.

Luke took her hand and his voice was gentle. "The only way to find answers to your questions is to go to someone who knows. A doctor can tell you about your condition. And I'll get on the trail of finding out the truth of what happened at Doan's Crossing. I'll help put you back together."

"Why would you do that for someone you've never met before?"

"Because it's the right thing to do. I'd want someone to do that for me." He turned her hand over and studied her palm.

For a man who killed people, he had a gentle touch. Heat spread through her as though she stood too close to a smithy's forge. "What are you looking at?"

Eyes the color of spring pasture land lifted and the intensity she saw in his gaze made her fidget. "I once knew an old woman in New Orleans who seemed to tell a good many things by the lines of a palm."

"Like what?"

"How long you'll live, how passionate you are—stuff like that. Of course, I didn't buy into it, but lots do."

"Can you tell if I have a husband, a mother, children?" Her voice broke with longing.

Luke suddenly tensed, dropped her hand, and stared into the distance with narrowed eyes.

"What did you see?" she asked.

"Movement ahead."

"No, on my palm." She knew he'd seen something. "Tell me."

"It's riders," he insisted. "Move closer and try to hide the damage on your skirt as best you can."

He shifted, putting his reloaded Colt within easy reach and striking a lazy pose with his hat tugged low. He was ready to shoot his way out if needed.

Pulling his duster from under the seat, he told her to drape it around her. She covered her bloody skirt then pressed against his side and slipped her arm through his. She wasn't going to let them take the only friend she had.

No matter what she had to do. Nor could she let him kill on this fine day.

Minutes later, lawmen surrounded the wagon and forced them to stop.

"Morning, gentlemen," Luke drawled. "Mind getting out of our way?"

"We're looking for a woman." The speaker was an old sheriff with a crooked nose that had been broken countless times.

"The only one I've seen is—"

"Me. His wife," Rose interrupted. She gazed with what she hoped was adoration up at Luke. "Don't be shy saying it, sweetheart. But it's still sort of new, I reckon." She cupped his jaw and turned to the riders. "You see, we were married two weeks ago and we're on our honeymoon. My darling sugarplum promised to take me to Fort Worth."

She pressed her lips to his in a long, searing kiss. He didn't respond for a moment, then shock and thrilling tingles rippled over her as he kissed her back. And when she parted her mouth, he slipped his tongue inside as bold as you please. His hand curled just under her breast and sent waves of aching hunger through her.

"Ahem," one of the lawmen said. "We need a word, if you don't mind."

"Oh, dear sir, but we do mind," she murmured against Luke's mouth. "Very strenuously."

"Damn, woman," Luke whispered. "Aren't you overdoing it?"

"Me?" she argued low. "What was the tongue for?"

"Added effect." His eyes held a devilish gleam.

"Sorry, ma'am," another of the posse tried. "Please give us a quick word and we'll be on our way."

With his arm around her, Luke raised his head. "My wife Rose is very...passionate. Why are you looking for this other woman?"

"She murdered her husband last night, mister."

Rose gasped, reeling from the shock. And the fact that they stared right at her. "My heavens, how horrible. Did she shoot him?"

"Oh no, ma'am, nothing that tame," said the lawman with the mole. "She gutted him."

"Where did this take place?" Luke asked, nuzzling Rose's neck.

"Doan's Crossing."

Rose stiffened in panic.

"Careful," Luke whispered. "Just a little longer."

"Do you know her name, by chance?" Rose asked quietly.

"Josie. Josie Morgan," the man answered. "From the description, she's the spitting image of you, ma'am."

She shivered even as Luke's arm tightened around her. Could she have done something like that? Was she a murderess? Oh, dear God, she'd rather be a mule skinner. Please let her have been that—or a lumberjack.

"If we happen to spot her, we'll report it to the first lawman we run across," Luke promised. "Now, if you don't mind, we have somewhere to be and my wife, bless her sweet soul, is a very impatient woman." He winked at the posse. "You fellows remember what it was like to be newly married, don't you?"

A murmur of agreement came from the nearest rider.

Rose glanced down and her heart pounded to see the duster had slipped, exposing a big portion of her bloody skirt. Slowly, so as not to draw the lawmen's gaze, she tried to tug the shield back into place.

"Say, don't I know you, mister?" One of the lawmen in the back, a younger man, moved forward, staring at Luke. "What's your name?"

Rose held her breath as Luke's hand inched slowly down toward his Colt. Desperate to draw the riders' attention, she loosened the top buttons of her dress and moved the fabric aside. "My goodness, it's so hot today!" She touched her cheek with a fingertip and drew it painstakingly down the long column of her throat, past her collarbone until it disappeared into her cleavage.

The young lawman's Adam's apple moved up and down as he swallowed hard.

"Name's Jones," Luke drawled. "I come from Tascosa in the panhandle. A wild, wooly place, but it's where I met my beautiful Rose and tied the knot."

"I never thought I'd ever find such a handsome man to give me a second look. I'm truly happy," Rose added hastily. "Ours is a match made in heaven."

"I must be mistaken." The young man turned aside, mumbling to himself.

The hawk-nosed marshal leaned over. "There's a lot of blood on your dress, ma'am. What happened?"

Panic raced through Rose. She could feel color drain from her face. "Blood? Oh, good heavens, no!" She forced a giggle. "This is nothing but red mud. My mama always complained about the North Texas red dirt and was never able to get it to wash out of anything."

The sudden lifting of the marshal's white brow in apparent skepticism must've been what prompted Luke to quietly add, "My wife likes to make love in the...uh, creek. It's really embarrassing to talk about."

Of all the stories he could've made up and that was the best he could find? Rose was mortified. She couldn't have gotten the blood from a deer they'd killed. Oh no. It had to be from making love in the mud. And blame her for it, no less.

She patted his vest. "Sweetheart, these men don't have time to be gossiping like that! They simply have to find that Morgan woman before she kills again."

Several of the men shook their heads, chuckling, but one had leaned forward to get a better view.

"Sorry to have held you up." The old sheriff touched the brim of his hat and the group galloped off, kicking up a cloud of dust around the wagon.

Luke jiggled the reins and the team began to move. "What the hell was that back there?"

Her spine stiffened. "What do you mean?"

"Attacking me like that."

"Wait one minute. If I recall, you didn't appear to object." The nerve of him to play the innocent!

"You enjoyed every second of that," Luke accused.

Maybe a little too much, but she wasn't going to let him know. His body's definite response said he had too.

"And you didn't?"

Luke glanced back to check on the lawmen. "How did you even think to do that? Where did that performance come from?"

"I don't know. I noticed a spark of recognition in that young one's eyes and I knew I had to save you. He was a step away from arresting you." Rose scooted back to her original position. She thought he'd at least be grateful for her efforts.

"Don't ever try to save me again." Luke's voice held a sharp edge. "I'll only get you hurt—or dig you a grave."

His words slapped her. "Well, pardon me. Next time you can save your own damn hide, mister." Yet she'd seen his hand move for his gun; she knew how close he'd come to killing those lawmen. How could she have stood watching him hang, seeing the life drain from his body?

The brittle silence stretched her nerves. Too late, she hated her angry words and wished she could take them back.

"I deserved that," Luke finally said in a quiet tone. "I'm an ungrateful bastard."

"No, it was me, Luke." At last, Rose unknotted her twisted stomach. "I really did kill my husband. I wasn't that serious before when I wondered if I had." She covered her mouth with her hand to stifle a sob. "But I really did. They said so. And nothing pretty like a gunshot—I gutted him. Oh God!"

"We don't know you did any such thing," Luke said firmly. "You could've gotten that blood on you any number of ways."

Except those two gun runners had said that she'd gotten it from the dead man who may or may not have been her husband. But she wasn't going to remind him of that.

"Yes, maybe I slaughtered a deer." She brightened. "I'm not Josie Morgan. I can't be. I'm Rose. Thank you for marrying me—for making me your wife."

Luke jerked around. "Hey, you know that was only pretense, right?"

"Oh, sure." She raised innocent eyes to his. "It meant nothing." Nothing at all. Only she wanted it to with all her heart.

With one fingertip, Luke pushed back his hat to study her. "Scratch my previous suggestions about what you did before. With the way you handled those lawmen, you're a born actress."

"You think so?"

"Several times you had *me* almost believing we were

newlyweds. You can sure kiss, lady. And when you unbuttoned the top of your dress and teased those men… they forgot all about who we were. A lady of the evening couldn't have done any better."

"Yeah. I wonder if that means I really am one?"

"Nope. You didn't charge."

Rose giggled and watched his mouth curve in a slow grin, revealing rows of white teeth. She sighed and imagined being married to him for real. Kissing him whenever she felt like it. Sleeping in his arms. Making love until dawn.

But for now, they were both outlaws and on the run.

Both killers?

Her fate appeared tied to his.

When, if ever, her memory returned, what else would she discover about herself?

Four

Five miles down the road, Luke pulled up next to a little spring. Underground water sprang from the rocks, providing cold, sweet refreshment.

"We'll leave the wagon and go on horseback from here, make faster time." He placed his hands around Rose's waist and lowered her to the ground. "In case that posse backtracks."

"Do they lynch women?" Rose's changeable eyes filled with unshed tears. "I can't get hung before I know who I am—and what I did."

Luke gathered her trembling body close. "I'm not going to let that happen. When I have you somewhere safe, I'll get to the truth. Trust me?"

Rose stared deep into his eyes. "With my life."

That she stated the words with such strong conviction dropped a heaviness over him. He didn't want to feel responsible for her. Damn it! The lady needed someone better than him to look up to. Didn't she know that? He dragged in slow, steady breaths before thrusting the canteen at her. "Can you fill this while I move the wagon into some thick brush?"

"You won't be gone long?"

Panic lining her face tightened his chest. He was all she had and to lose him would probably be more than Rose could take. He ran a finger across her cheek. "I'll be back before you even miss me."

At her nod, he climbed into the wagon and drove it a short distance into a tangled mass of mesquite and scrub oak. It took no time to unhitch the team and ride the horses back. Rose's eyes lit up when she saw him. Could she be Josie Morgan? While he liked the solid ring to the name, he preferred his simple Rose—for now, anyway. Especially since Josie seemed to be a wanted woman. Not that there was anything a bit simple about her. He let out a troubled sigh. Answers to the riddles were out there somewhere—for both of them. He just had to try harder.

"See? I'm already done," he said. "One of us will have to ride bareback. That'll be me. You can ride my gelding."

"What's his name?" She moved to the horse's side and murmured soothingly as she stroked his long neck.

"Major John."

"I like that. He'll let me ride him?"

"Long as you don't let him smell beer, he'll be docile."

She giggled. "Beer?"

"Loves the stuff. If I don't tie him good outside a saloon, he clops in just like he owns the joint and I can't get him out until he gets good and ready."

"That's the funniest thing I ever heard."

"Glad you think so. You're pretty when you laugh." He watched a blush stain her cheeks and his heart fluttered strangely. The lonely part of him wished he could have a woman like her. She had spirit and grit. He had a feeling the safe, easy path would bore her. Rose seemed the sort to dare anyone or anything to try to put a bridle on her or a bit in her mouth.

"Ready to ride?" he asked. "We're burning daylight."

Her forehead wrinkled. "I know I've heard that saying before. Just like spouting off to the lawmen about my mama and difficulty with this red dirt. I don't know where that came from." She stared into the distance as though trying to conjure up ghosts to fill in the holes.

"Maybe your memory is fighting its way back." He put his hands around her slender waist and helped her onto Major John.

"I hope you're right. I hate being lost inside. You don't know what it's like to be a stranger to yourself."

Luke swung onto the back of one of the roans. He couldn't imagine having his head scrubbed of all memory. His safety depended on knowing who were his enemies, and who were friends. Where could he take Rose? Now that he knew she was wanted by the law, the Lone Star Ranch was out. He'd promised himself never to bring trouble to the Legend family's door.

As they trotted away from the watering hole, Luke made sure Rose stayed beside him. His eyes were constantly scanning the rugged terrain for signs of a dust cloud made by the posse when the perfect answer sprang to mind.

"I'm taking you to Deliverance Canyon," he told her. "No one will find you there."

The women there would protect Rose while he sought answers. Tally Shannon and her small, ragtag army of survivors had sought safety there after escaping a mental institution. Their families had stuck them in the Creedmore Lunatic Asylum to get rid of them for one reason or another, despite their being as sane as anyone. From them, Luke had learned the ease with which people could put someone into a place darker than prison—death without blood on their own hands. Tally and her ladies would care for Rose until Luke could get back. She was in need of safety. They'd not turn her away.

In fact, she'd fit right in with the gun-toting women. They could help each other. They'd furnish her a gun and she could teach them to cuss—a perfect match.

"I thought we were going to the Lone Star Ranch."

"Changed my mind. Deliverance Canyon is safest. It'll delay getting you to a doctor, but with the posse looking for you, it can't be helped."

Over the next half hour, he told her about Tally

Shannon and the others and assured her that she'd be safe with them.

"How horrible that they have to hide like animals! I'd like to put a damn bullet into the people who made them suffer. Hell, why would someone do that?"

Luke still couldn't get used to Rose cussing. She looked like a beautiful angel until she opened her mouth.

"Any number of reasons. Greed, hate, jealousy, fear—take your pick," he said.

"The women sound real nice. I already like them."

"They'll have clean clothes for you. I'm sure wearing those bloody ones is none too pleasant."

"Makes my skin crawl. It's like I'm carrying around a dead person on me and I don't even know who he is. How did you learn about Tally and her girls?"

"They saved my life once after I got shot-up bad."

"I'm glad they fixed you up," she said softly. "How long will it take to get to the canyon?"

"Another day, barring trouble. How is your head?"

"The pounding is letting up some. Thank you for caring. And the mint settled my queasy stomach."

"When my mother was so ill, mint was the only thing that made her feel better." He handed her more from his pocket.

As they traveled, Luke let Rose talk and he found out a lot about her from what little she didn't know she was revealing. Her words indicated some education and she was always mindful of trouble on their heels, glancing back and staring at the brush. He tested her skill at arithmetic and from her ease with ciphering, he discovered she excelled in numbers. She had one of the quickest minds he'd ever seen.

And that was dangerous for him.

They'd played a game where he tossed out a word and she came up with a response.

"What do mountains say to you?"

"Lonely."

"Darkness."

"Death."

He scowled at her odd answer. "Why would darkness mean death? Care to think on that?"

"I don't know. Except that bad things happen in the night. Mean people come out to prey when we can't see them." She gave a frustrated groan. "What do I know? I'm a mess with a head full of nothing. Let's go on."

"Saloon."

"Home." She wrinkled her brow. "Now why did I say that, Luke? Odd. Maybe I worked there? Did I entertain men upstairs? Why would I call such a place home?"

He didn't know but he filed it away. They played on with nothing much new coming to light. Then she'd taken her turn with him. He was careful not to let her know too much.

By nightfall he felt a kinship with Rose. She wasn't just a woman he'd rescued. She'd become a real person and he admired her quick wit. They took shelter in a small sandstone cave where no one could see their campfire. A tiny stream was just outside. He tied the horses in a large clump of mesquite and juniper where they could get to the water before riding off on Major John a short distance to hunt for food. He soon returned with two plump rabbits that he'd caught in a snare he made.

To his surprise, Rose had used the time to wash the blood from her hair and her body as best she could.

Rose's skill at skinning the rabbits said she'd performed the task many times. While she prepared the meat, he patted down Major John and left the beer-guzzling horse with the others, bringing the saddle inside the cave.

As the meat cooked over the flames, they talked.

"You're a man of mystery, Luke Weston." Rose's blond strands, cleaner now, glistened like pure gold in the firelight.

"Why do you say that?" Luke recalled the silky way her hair had wrapped around his fingers. The way she'd kissed him earlier—hot and hungry. Whether she was Rose or Josie, the lady held deep passion in her eyes. Right now, that green-gold had turned liquid brown in the flames. It had seemed perfectly normal to kiss her, to taste the sweetness of her mouth. To curl his hand beneath a full breast.

"All day you've let me rattle on and not revealed anything of your life story. I'd tell you mine if I knew it. I sense there's more you're not saying between you, the Legend family, and the Lone Star Ranch." She rotated the skewer Luke had whittled from a small limb. "You have so much heaviness inside when you mention them. Makes me wonder who they are to you."

Luke turned away. Rose wasn't supposed to have seen that. He had to be more careful. But she was easy to talk to, and he'd already spoken of things he'd told few people.

"You'll probably learn soon enough." He propped himself against his saddle, stretched his long legs in front of him, and tugged his hat down farther to hide his eyes so she wouldn't see his pain. "They're family. I didn't know until a few years ago that the big, powerful Stoker Legend was my father; Sam and Houston Legend are my half brothers."

"That must've been a shock." She studied him, trying to draw out his secrets. Damn if she wasn't good at that.

"In a whole lot of ways. My mother kept the secret until she lay on her deathbed. She begged me to forgive him." Luke snorted. "That was near impossible. I boiled with anger, the kind that scars your soul, and I stayed that way until two years ago when I finally went to the Lone Star. Then I learned the truth. Stoker never knew about me. He hadn't left my mother and ridden off to marry someone else as I'd always believed."

He stared into the flames, remembering how devastated Stoker had been to learn what had happened to his beautiful Elena Montoya. After Stoker had left her bed that final morning, Elena's brothers had come and forced her into a wagon. They took her to San Antonio and Stoker never knew what had happened to her.

"Stoker accepted me right off as his son, giving me a portion of everything he owns. He said it's my birthright." Luke shifted and rotated the skewered rabbit.

"Why aren't you there?" came Rose's hushed cry. "Why are you so unhappy?"

"I'm a wanted man with a price on my head. I won't bring trouble to them. At least I can do that much. Do you want to know what I was doing this morning when I ran across you?"

"I know it was something important."

"After all this time, I'd finally gotten a solid lead on the man who framed me for the murder of a federal judge. He's like a damn ghost and I had a short window of opportunity to catch him."

"Only I got in the way. Oh, Luke, I'm so sorry." Rose touched him. Warmth seared his flesh through the fabric.

He longed to hold her in his arms again, but the danger had passed and she didn't need comforting. "I'll find him eventually, and when I do, I'll get what I need to clear my name. Of that charge, at least." Luke let out a troubled sigh. "My...Stoker offered to help. Sam and Houston too."

"But you won't let them."

"I created this mess and it's mine to fix. I told them I won't take the Legend name until I can do it with honor. No matter how long it takes." They'd argued with him until they were blue in the face but it hadn't done any good. Once Luke made up his mind about something, he wasn't changing it.

"Did you know this judge?" Rose asked.

"Sort of. I went that night to pay him. He said five hundred dollars would buy my amnesty. I had warrants out for me for some other things and he vowed to get them erased. I had won that much money the previous night in a poker game. When I got there, I found the judge bleeding on the floor. As I knelt over him, someone struck me from behind. I must've only been out for a minute."

Luke paused, wondering for the thousandth time how the man he now knew only as Ned Sweeney had gotten wind of his whereabouts.

"When I came to, I was lying on the judge with my Colt in my hand. I was still groggy but saw a dim figure over me. He thrust his hand into my pocket, took the five hundred dollars."

Took his freedom from him. The killer had made sure Luke would never know a moment's peace.

"You didn't recognize him?" Rose asked.

"My head was pounding and everything was blurred. But he muttered something about how easily I fit into his plans, thanked me for taking the blame for his crime."

"So, someone saw you before you could get away?"

"The bastard ran out the door, yelling that the judge was dead. I staggered to my feet, almost made it to a door that led to a garden, but not before men poured into the room and saw me." Luke turned abruptly. "Time to eat."

"I'd like to hear more," Rose said softly. "Whenever you feel up to talking again."

"I've said too much and you have problems of your own. You don't need mine too." He poured a cup of coffee and settled back to eat.

"Not having a memory seems both a blessing and a curse. Maybe I'm on wanted posters too." Rose put a piece of meat into her mouth and chewed. "This is really good."

"I'm sure you were starving."

"I was. Who knows when I last ate." She licked her fingers.

They finished the meal in silence, sitting side by side. The flickering flames added the only cheer as Luke stared out into the darkness through the cave opening.

At last he spoke. "I apologize for going on about my sorry-assed life while you have no clue about yours."

Rose shifted, getting comfortable, and gave her blond curls an impatient shove. "Just because I have no past to talk about doesn't mean you should keep silent. I like hearing about you, and your problems take my mind off mine." She lapsed into silence. They sat listening to the crackle of the fire for several moments. Finally, she spoke quietly. "I wonder if I have children somewhere. If they're crying for their mother. If they're being cared for."

"It'll come back to you." Luke's shoulder brushed hers and the contact sent a jolt through him. He realized he loved being with her. Rose had to be scared and lost but she tried not to show it. Reno Kidd and his gang had stolen everything from her. Yet, she still had this amazing fight in her.

Despite that she'd caused him to lose Sweeney, he felt more at peace with himself than he had in a long time. And it was because of her.

Somehow, someway, he'd not stop digging until he found her missing self.

Doan's Crossing seemed a logical starting place, since it was where Reno and his men had abducted her. Surely someone had seen something. Jonathan Doan, who ran the trading post there, was an honest, hardworking man. It was a popular place for fording the mighty Red River, so there were always people milling about. If Doan hadn't seen her, Luke knew others would have.

Or they'd know Reno Kidd.

The hired gun drew a crowd wherever he went. Reno was a braggart and a bully, a dangerous combination that left lots of bodies in his wake.

Luke blew out a huff of frustration and turned his thoughts back to making plans. Get Rose to the canyon first, then since the crossing was near the Lone Star, he'd ride over and return the horses and find out if they were stolen. Maybe Stoker and Houston could shed light on who'd taken them. He knew she needed a doctor, but it didn't seem as urgent now and getting answers did—before the posse found her.

Yep, he breathed a damn sight easier with a plan. But Rose's situation reminded him that happiness was fleeting at best with anyone.

Life could seem almost perfect until it suddenly wasn't.

Until darkness blocked out the sun.

Until violence touched safe little corners of Texas and reminded him evil existed everywhere.

Five

THE FIRELIGHT CAST GHOSTLY SHADOWS ON THE SANDSTONE walls of the cave. Leaning against the saddle, Luke stretched out his legs and crossed his feet at the ankles. Rose inched closer until she could rest her head on his shoulder and shivered against the night's chill. Though hesitant, he put his arm around her.

"Cold?"

"A little. It's more than the night air, though. I keep thinking of those lawmen out there."

"You're safe."

"Do you mind holding me? Just for a while?"

She sounded lost and afraid. During the word game, she'd let slip that darkness was as good as death to her, and her bravado had faded away. "As long as you need." He folded his other arm around her as well and created a safe cocoon. She snuggled against him, her softness molding to the planes of his chest.

Each unforgettable curve promised heaven…even for a man bound for hell.

Luke inhaled softly, savoring the contact. Sometimes loneliness dug into him clear down to his soul. He breathed, ate, and slept—but he didn't live.

Didn't dream.

Didn't hope.

Those feelings were useless for a man who simply existed. This life of his didn't allow room for the softness of a woman. He'd made that mistake once and he'd not repeat it. He took out his pocket watch. His Angelina had given him a silver timepiece to mark their first year of marriage. It was worth more to him than everything else he owned combined.

He closed his eyes, reading the engraving from memory.

Mi corazón, mi amor. AGW.

Angie Guzman Weston.

My heart, my love. He winced as piercing pain shot through him. Only she had seen the good in him. Hers had been a beautiful soul. Why had she stepped in front of the bullet meant for him? He wasn't worth saving. The violence of his life had ended hers, and he'd have to carry that guilt the rest of his days.

A rotten man like him should never have touched Angelina. And he knew better than to let Rose get too close.

Rose shifted to get comfortable. "I feel memories lurking at the edge of my mind, teasing, taunting me. I try so hard to pull them in but they scamper off before I can." Rose glanced up. "Waking up with no recollections... This is so hard, Luke. But maybe I'm going at this all wrong."

"What do you mean?" He tucked the watch away.

"I've been trying to figure out who I used to be, when I need to find out who I am now."

Rose's anguished words struck him. They held great truth. This rough beauty in his arms was like a stone in a rushing river. Each tumble on its way downstream revealed dozens of different sides. She could be as prickly as a thorn or as soft as goose down in a matter of minutes.

"I can tell you're a thinker," he murmured against her hair. "Sometimes people go their entire lives without knowing who they are. You've even got me looking at myself." He wasn't the same shiftless man who stood in his boots two years ago. He had a father and brothers now—a family. All he had to do was claim them. Dammit, if only he could! Before he'd learned about them, any consequences of the things he did touched only him. Now, he didn't want to sully the Legend name that stood for honor, integrity, and almighty strength. Now he wanted to be someone they could be proud to know, instead of someone to hide away in the shadows when friends called.

Now he wanted to walk as a free man in the light. To live.

Only it was too late. The killing wouldn't stop. No one would let him hang up his gun. The minute he did, he was dead.

"Oh, Luke, I haven't known you long at all, but even I can see the honor inside you." Rose rested her palm on his chest. "You have a caring heart and more courage than anyone we crossed paths with today. Probably more than anyone I know, but since I don't know who I know, how can I say that with all honesty?"

"Don't make me into someone I'm not. I know what I've done. And don't try to save me, Rose." He jerked to his feet and propped himself against the cave opening, looking out.

Behind him, he heard her slinging things and muttering. When he turned, her face had gone dark with simmering fury.

She planted her hands on her hips. "Don't, don't, don't. That's all I hear from you. I'll do and think as I damn well please."

"You don't know what I'm capable of." He tried to keep anger and disgust from his voice but he failed. "What I can be…when the blackness takes over. I can't stop myself."

Rose gasped. "Listen to me, Luke Weston. There's always hope. Hell, things can change in a heartbeat. Each sunrise can hold a brand-new future. You have a family if you don't throw them away."

"Stop, Rose. Tomorrow holds no promises, especially not for me." The pretty lady should get far, far away from the likes of him. He swung around to see her sling a tin cup against the stone wall, her teeth clenched. "Are you ready to turn in?"

Rose blew out a gust of air. "Reckon so. You pay me no more mind than a pesky bull gnat anyway."

Luke unfolded the bedroll next to the low fire. "Here you go. Sleep well."

"Where are you going to bed down?"

"I'll stand guard. Never sleep much any given night anyway." Grabbing his rifle, he sat down. The leather creaked against his weight as he leaned back against his saddle. The weapon lying across his lap, he stared out into pitch-black so thick he couldn't make out the horses.

"I feel bad," Rose said. "I'll share the damn bedroll. There's room for both of us."

Without turning, Luke answered gruffly, "It's safer this way…and I won't have to apologize come morn." Didn't she realize the temptation? He wouldn't be able to control himself with her body pressed to his. Bad enough that she lay on the other side of the fire. He glanced her way as she crawled onto the bedroll.

The crazy lady was as prickly as a roll of barbed wire and too smart by half. She should have to wear a sign warning others. She hadn't hesitated when the lawmen surrounded them. He recalled the feel of her soft lips on his, the minty taste of her mouth too sweet to ignore. He'd been like a man dying of thirst, crawling across a parched desert. Holding her in his arms offered a bit of peace for his ragged soul.

For a second back there today, he'd forgotten a posse of well-armed lawmen had cut off any chance of escape. The ease with which Rose had slipped into the role of seductress told him she'd done it before. Maybe many times.

Who was she?

Luke glanced at the bedroll, her golden hair fanned out like a swath of expensive French silk. Was she really the murderess the posse claimed she was? Or a woman of ill repute? Some rich man's secret kept pleasure? A genteel wife and mother?

With her ability to cuss like a lumberjack, he quickly ruled out the last. He grinned. Learning the truth about her would be interesting. So many possibilities lay in store.

But what if he discovered she had a life with others? That thought drew a frown.

He had to stop this. Damn it! Of course, she had a life with someone. Everyone did if they let themselves choose it.

Three heartbeats later, he went out to check the horses, something far safer than thinking. Wispy clouds drifted across the fingernail moon like gossamer curtains, and the crisp sage-tinted air bit at him playfully. From a distance came the mournful howl of a coyote, but the darkness whispered no warning here. Luke and the night shared a kinship. He could tell when danger lurked by listening to the sounds around him. All seemed well and the horses were fine.

At least some things were peaceful, if he didn't look too deep inside himself. Rose had turned him upside down and sideways. He'd never seen a feistier woman or one who amplified more fully the lonely man inside him.

Elena Montoya's face swam in front of him. His mother would be angry at him for the man he'd become. She'd scrubbed other people's clothing on a rub board until her fingers bled, for only a few cents a day. Yet she'd taken pride in who she was...and in her boy. Elena had strolled down the street with her head held high, even when her illness made walking difficult.

No matter how bad it got, *she'd* never stolen. Never said a harsh word about anyone. And no matter how angry she became, *she'd* never killed. Thank goodness he'd kept much of his life hidden from her. It was the only decent thing he'd ever done.

Luke came quietly back inside and sat down. He reached inside his leather vest for the black book he kept there and flipped it open. Each page held the names of everyone he'd robbed, and the amounts he owed. A good portion of that had gone for supplies, medicines, and clothing for the hunted hunkering down in Deliverance Canyon. But not all.

Some he'd crossed through, one at a time as he repaid the money, but even so, he'd barely made a dent.

Making things right would take a long time at this rate.

And who knew what circumstances lay ahead that might cause him to kill again.

With a troubled sigh, he put the book away and rested his head on the saddle. The fight to stay awake was a struggle and the last time his eyes drifted shut, he couldn't force them back open.

Slight movement at his shoulder startled him. He drew his Colt before he got his eyes open enough to see.

"It's only me," Rose murmured softly. "Sorry to disturb you."

"Anything wrong?"

"You look cold and I can't sleep."

Before he knew what was happening, she threw the bedroll over him and crawled against his side. "Hold me, Luke. Make my fears go away."

Luke shifted and rasped out a warning. "Don't care for me, Rose. I'll break your heart." Yet despite his warnings, he didn't have the strength to push her away. After a long moment, he put his arm around her and held her tight.

Her hot anger flashed. "Don't, don't, don't. What about the dos? Or are there any where you're concerned? I'm sick and tired of you warning me of pitfalls every time you open your mouth. Hell, I might as well be some snot-nosed kid. I'm a grown woman and I'll do as I want, think as I want, and say what I want."

"We're just people passing on the same road, Rose. Nothing more."

Though she didn't say anything, he heard a sniffle and felt wetness on his shirt. He didn't deserve her tears. Couldn't she see that he lived on borrowed time, that he had nothing left to give? He was as empty as her memories. He smoothed back her hair, pressed his lips to her temple. When dawn came, he'd put some distance between them and don the lonely mantle befitting an outlaw once again. But for now, he'd soak up the feel of her beside him.

And pray the morning came slowly.

"You're lonelier than I am, Luke Weston," she said quietly. "You're filled with pain and misery and regret. For just one night, forget who you are and wipe your memories clean."

"To forget is futile. This is who I am, so accept it, Rose. You can't change me."

"No, but you can. Stop pretending that everything is set in stone. I see what you try so hard to hide. You have a soft, caring heart, and don't deny it."

Before he could think of a reply, she lifted her head and leaned toward him. Very softly, she pressed her lips to his. That the kiss was a bit slanted didn't matter. What did matter was that she gave him a smattering of hope, hope that maybe he *could* become someone better. And hope that he'd find his way back from this hell he was in.

Their lips locked, he dragged Rose into his lap and clutched her tight. He slipped a hand into her blond hair, then slid down the silky curve of her throat. And lower.

What would it hurt if things went further? No one would ever know.

Hell and be damned! He cursed his conscience.

Luke broke the kiss and settled her back to his side. "We can't. I have to look at myself in the mirror. It's not right to take advantage of you and your situation."

Rose jerked away and blew a silky strand out of her eyes. "Why the hell do you have to be so damned noble? Right here, right now in this cave might be all either of us get."

Angry, Luke swung to face her. "Hold it right there. Lady, if things were different, if I knew you had no one waiting, I'd take what I want—what we both want—and not waste a second doing it."

"I know." Rose let out a sigh and pulled the bedroll around her shoulders. "Damn you, Luke Weston, I wish you weren't right. I need to feel alive and not something dead and buried. Hell, you're no better off than me."

"Maybe so, but at least I'm not blind to reality."

"Luke, what did you see on my palm when you were staring at it? And don't tell me nothing. I'm not buying it."

What was he going to tell her? He couldn't reveal that her fate line was broken, the same as his. She had enough to deal with. So, he would lie.

"You're right. I did see something." He took her palm and pointed. "See this line here?"

"The squiggly one? Does it mean I'm easy?"

"Nope, it indicates a huge trauma in your life. And see this other one running alongside?" Luke allowed a chuckle, hoping she'd buy his explanation. "It says that everything is going to work out. So, you see? It's nothing bad at all."

"Then you did only spot riders before?"

"Just like I said." Luke stared at her hand. It was so delicate, yet the same wasn't true of her character. She was one tough woman and as mean as a mama lion when she had to be. "Better try to get some sleep."

"Luke?"

"Yep."

"I'm glad it was you who came riding by and found me."

"It's late, Rose." He was glad about a good many things. If she hadn't been with him and planted those hot kisses on him when the posse came, he'd have likely died in a shootout. He'd once witnessed his brother Sam Legend swinging from a tree by the neck. Luke had managed to cut Sam down in time to save him but he'd never forget the sight. He was not going to his death dangling at the end of a rope.

"Do you think we could've been happy if you'd found me a long time ago?" Rose lightly touched his jaw.

"Yeah. I think we'd have been happy."

Thankfully, she lapsed into silence and he soon heard her breathing slow. When he was sure she slept, he lifted a strand of her hair and rubbed it between his thumb and forefinger.

Luke gently lowered her to the bedroll. For a long moment, he stared at the beautiful woman. Her dark lashes lay on her high cheekbones like the long fringe of a Spanish shawl.

A strong urge came over him.

He bent and brushed her lips with his.

For a single moment, time stood still and let him find a bit of peace and contentment for his ragged soul.

Six

Luke woke Rose just as the morning crawled out from under a blanket of light fog that clung to the low hills. He poured coffee into a tin cup for her. "Morning."

She stretched. "I was having the most wonderful dream. I think I'll go back to sleep and see what happens next."

He chuckled. "That never works. Want to tell me about it?"

"Nope. That'll ruin it." She squirmed from the bedroll and suddenly he couldn't feel the heat from the steaming cup of brew burning his fingers. Tousled golden hair framed her face and her barely restrained curves spilled from the ruined dress. He'd never seen anyone prettier. She was as far from a tobacco-spitting mule skinner as she could possibly get. Their hands touched as she took the coffee from him. For a split second, a shimmer of light danced around them and a jolt ran through him.

He'd had a similar experience once before and he'd married the lady. Whatever it meant now, though, he damn sure wasn't about to marry Rose.

Then she smiled and he forgot everything, including his vow just a second ago and his only hours-old determination to put distance between them. Deep hunger spread. He wanted the spitfire in his arms. How did a man fight something he desperately yearned for?

"I'll put out the fire and be ready to ride by the time you saddle your horse." Rose's low voice brought to mind a saloon girl after too much whiskey and smoke. She sipped her coffee and gave him a hesitant smile. "Luke, I shouldn't have pushed myself on you last night. Shouldn't have kissed you. It's just that I needed…a friend. You know?"

He met her gaze and saw the deep sadness. Before he made another mistake, he turned away. "I know. Don't worry yourself over it. I'll see to the horses."

Afraid of what he'd see if he glanced back, he strode into the early morning sunlight. He focused on feeding the horses the remaining grain in his saddlebags, telling Major John to share with the two mounts they'd picked up. By the time he'd gotten the animals ready, Rose strolled toward him with the coffeepot and tin dishes he always carried in his saddlebags.

"I only had time to give these a lick and a promise." Rose unloaded her hands. "I'll wash them better the next time we run across some water."

"There's a large creek not too far from here." He stuffed them away and helped Rose onto the black gelding, trying to pretend he hadn't seen her bare leg up to her knee. Those long, shapely legs that seemed to stretch to her neck were going to get him into trouble.

Oh yeah, lots of trouble.

He swung onto the back of one of the roans, lecturing himself. He needed to keep his thoughts *on* everyone who either wanted him dead or in jail, and *off* the woman beside him.

They rode east toward the ridge of barren buttes rising from the desolate plains. Rose chattered about various and sundry subjects, to which Luke only occasionally grunted a reply. He was lost in his thoughts and busy scanning the landscape for trouble. Ten miles down the trail littered with cactus, milk thistle, and broom weed, Luke pulled up at the larger creek. "I'll fill the canteen and that should get us there."

"I'll wash those dishes." Rose dismounted before he could get around to help.

Disappointment at losing another chance to touch her ran through him. While he admired her independence, he wondered if her eagerness to avoid his touch had anything to do with last night. He was the first to admit he hadn't handled that well. Hell! The only females he dealt with were saloon girls and ladies of the evening, and they were interested only in the coins in his pocket. Those kind were far safer.

Horses, guns, and outlaws he knew. But the kind of women like Rose seemed to be? Best to stay clear. They wanted far more than a man's money. They wanted his heart.

"Stop it," he mumbled to himself. He had to put distance between them as he'd vowed. It was the only way. He had to quit thinking with his body and listen to his damn head.

Luke dug out the coffeepot and dishes and handed them over, then grabbed the canteen and knelt beside the narrow creek.

Rose attacked the dishes with everything she had, splashing water all over her and him both. He scowled. "Do I stink or something? I know I can use a bath but not here."

Finally, she glared over at him. "You're acting like a bump on some damned log."

"Just thinking. That's what most folks do when they're *not* talking."

"Well, you don't have to do it so loud," she grated.

"What are you so all-fired mad about?"

"I don't know!" She splashed even more water.

He was tempted to dunk her in it to cool her off, except the creek was only five inches deep at most.

"Maybe I'm sore at you. Did you ever think about that?" She threw a clean tin plate onto a patch of grass. "You can't wait to get rid of me. You're going to dump me with those women and take off. I doubt I'll…I'll ever see you again." Her voice broke.

Had someone hit her on the head again while she was

sleeping? "Rose, you know why I have to ride out once you're safe. It's for you."

She jumped up and paced back and forth. "I may not ever have had one soul who wanted me. For all I know, someone cracked my skull because he wanted to be shed of me and considered it more humane than tying an anvil to my leg and drowning me. Or maybe my father couldn't stomach having a daughter like me. Or—"

Luke grabbed her and held her tight. "Stop it. This is crazy."

"I'm scared, Luke. Real scared," she whispered, clutching onto him.

He put his arms around her. "I wish I could give you back each memory you lost."

"I suspect it takes a lot to terrify me, but this has shaken me to the core." She clutched his vest with both fists. "I have nothing to relate to, nothing to call up that'll ease my mind. Nothing. I'm a nobody with no life before yesterday."

"It must feel like that now, but you are somebody." He smoothed the hair from her beautiful face. "We're partners and we're going to figure this out. Together."

"You must wonder what you got yourself into. An insane woman causing trouble at every turn." She smiled sadly up at him. "I physically attack you, force myself on you, and now try to drench you. Maybe you should take me to one of those places for loony people."

Luke hid a smile. "Nope. I'm not ready to give up on you."

"You probably should. Who knows? I may try to gut you next, like Josie did her husband."

"I'm not a bit worried." He dragged his thumb across her cheek.

"Then maybe it's you in need of an asylum," she said softly, stretching to kiss his cheek. "You can let me go now. I'm all right and we're burning daylight."

The brush of her lips on his skin carried the heat of a brand. He wasn't supposed to have the kind of feelings that twisted through him and settled in his heart.

A man like him couldn't care for any woman.

Especially Rose.

She pushed away and picked up the dishes. After Luke stowed them, they rode in blessed silence for an hour, putting them near their destination.

The sun hovered high in the sky when Luke picked up a sound that made the hair on his neck rise. He pointed to a large stand of mesquite and silently mouthed *Hide* to Rose. They'd barely gotten concealed when the sun flashed against metal.

He slid his Colt from its leather sheath and waited for what seemed an eternity.

At last, a lone rider came into view. His hat was pulled low, but something about his silhouette was familiar. The horseman approached slowly. The cowboy leaned from the saddle, staring at the ground, looking for signs. He was tracking someone.

But who?

When the rider raised back up and adjusted in the saddle, Luke noticed the silver star pinned to his vest. A lawman. Now that changed things.

Over in the brush, Major John snorted, giving them away. Luke set his sights on the lawman's chest. "I'll give you two seconds to toss your weapon, mister."

"I'm not looking for trouble." The man eased his gun from the holster and let it drop to the ground.

"Well, that's good because I don't reckon I am either." Luke quietly ordered Rose to stay hidden, then rode from behind the mesquite thicket.

The lawman turned, his face coming out of shadow. "Luke?"

Recognition finally dawned. "Sam? What are you doing?"

"Looking for you, brother."

"Any particular reason?"

"Felt in my bones that you needed me. Pa got a telegram from a U.S. Marshal about a murder at Doan's Crossing. He sent me to find you."

"Damn that Stoker. Every time he gets wind of something happening around here, he thinks I'm involved." That was exactly why Luke had to stay away from the Lone Star. They couldn't save him and trying would get them killed.

"He… *We* care. Why are you riding that strange horse?"

"My black's taken at the moment." When Rose came slowly from the thicket on Major John, Luke introduced her. "I found her tied up yesterday with no memory of how she got there. I needed something to call her so I came up with Rose. We crossed a posse yesterday searching for a woman matching Rose's description who killed her husband. We convinced them to ride on." He glanced at Rose and grinned, remembering the kiss that stripped him of the ability to form a thought.

"Do you think Rose is the one they're looking for?" Sam asked.

"I don't know at this point."

Rose stretched to shake Sam's hand. "Luke told me a lot about you last night. I'm real glad to meet you."

"Same here." Sam turned to Luke. "Where are you headed?"

Luke's gaze followed Rose as she turned back into the brush. Probably lost something. "Deliverance Canyon. Rose needs a change of clothes and I'm going to leave her with Tally while I get some answers."

Sam jerked his head toward the brand on the horses. "How did you happen to come by stock from the Lone Star?"

Luke thumbed back his hat and wiped a trickle of sweat. "That's another big mystery. They were hitched to a wagon there with Rose that had crates of high quality whiskey and brand-new rifles. I don't know anything more. Have you heard any scuttlebutt about rustled horses by chance?"

"Nope." Sam pushed back his hat and wiped his face with his sleeve. "Pa wouldn't have anyone working for him who'd be involved in anything concerning whiskey and rifles. They have to be stolen."

Sam studied Rose, and Luke knew what he was thinking.

Maybe she was up to her pretty little neck in rustling, murder, and God knew what else. But she hadn't been lying about having no memory. No one can act that well.

"Ever hear of Reno Kidd?" Luke asked.

"A wanted poster on him came in a week ago. He's a killer of the worst sort," Sam said as Rose returned. "Murdered an entire family over in Indian Territory. Before that, about a dozen people."

Rose sucked in a breath. "That family might've been my kin."

"All we have are possibilities and maybes." Luke covered her hand and found it a chunk of ice. "Don't borrow trouble."

She nodded and swallowed hard. "I'm trying."

Luke caught Sam's arched brow and knew what he was thinking. "I'm getting her to safety is all."

"Hey, no need to explain. Mind if I ride along with you to the canyon?" Sam asked.

"Suit yourself." Luke scanned the terrain. "You could prove useful if that posse doubles back. One reason I have to get Rose hidden as soon as possible." He turned toward the ridge of buttes and urged his roan into a trot, making sure Rose stuck close to Sam.

"Do you live on the Lone Star Ranch?" Rose asked Sam.

"No, my wife and I live in Lost Point." Sam pointed in the general direction. "I'm the sheriff. Before that I was a Texas Ranger."

"Doesn't that make being brothers a bit difficult?" she asked.

Luke let out a chuckle. "You can definitely say that. Before Sam knew we were brothers, he chased me all over Texas, trying to catch me."

"You led me on quite a merry chase," Sam admitted. "Never saw anyone so slippery."

"And now?" Rose asked softly.

Sam glanced at Luke. "Now, I'm trying to help clear his name."

"That's wonderful. Sam, do you have any children?" she asked.

"One adopted son and about to have a babe soon. My wife, Sierra, is excited to bring us another child and that could be any day now." Sam smiled. "I don't know about me with a newborn, though. I'll probably drop the little thing on its head."

"I doubt that." Luke felt a twinge of jealousy. He envied both of his brothers for being free to settle down and have families. He slowed, falling back. The trail widened, allowing the three of them to ride side by side with Rose in the middle.

"What do you hear from Houston?" Luke asked. "I haven't seen him since we came back from that cattle drive of his six months ago."

Sam pushed back his hat. "He's built a house on a section of land away from headquarters. Lara's loving it."

"I imagine things are more peaceful out from under Stoker's thumb." Luke thought of his powerful father, and his penchant for taking over everyone's lives.

"You can call him Pa, Luke," Sam growled.

"Nope. I can't." Luke met Rose's glance and he knew she was thinking about their conversation last night.

You have a family who loves you. Please don't throw them away. Let them help, she'd pleaded. Then afterward had accused him of being even lonelier than her.

It was hard for her to understand and no one but another outlaw would know this need to constantly move. Such a precaution kept him alive.

Rose rode closer until her leg rubbed Luke's. "I like your brother. He's nice."

"Yeah, he is." Luke was happy Sam rode with them. His younger brother made him feel warm inside, like he was welcome to visit anytime no matter what trouble came with him. Sam was the man Luke most wished he could be.

A Legend through and through. One filled with honor and strength.

But he wasn't. He was Luke Weston and he shouldn't forget that. Still, Rose had given him hope that he might one day claim the Legend name. Who's to say it was impossible? He would never bet against the lady.

They arrived at Deliverance Canyon in early afternoon and, after making sure no one was following, proceeded down the steep, narrow trail. Halfway down, Luke stopped and gave the loud caw of a crow. When an answering one came from below, he told Rose it was safe to proceed.

"Why did you have to do that?" she asked.

"If we don't, Tally Shannon will put a bullet in us without a second thought," Sam answered. "She's one tough woman."

"Has to be." Luke maneuvered through large clumps of broom weed and sage. "It's the only way they stay alive."

Rose smiled. "I'm sure she's not that bad. I can't wait to meet her."

A few minutes later, when Tally swung a rifle her way, Rose's face told a different story. She gripped Luke's arm so tightly he wasn't sure he could pry her fingers loose. Rose wasn't scared of Reno's men and would've whipped them to the Gulf of Mexico and back if he hadn't stopped her, but she seemed frightened of flame-haired Tally, with the gun belt around her waist and a brand-like tattoo on her cheek.

"I told you never to bring anyone here," Tally grated, raising the weapon. "I ought to shoot you."

"Don't you dare!" yelled a woman named Holly Beth as she flew toward them. "I'll never speak to you again. Luke and Sam are our friends. Besides, she's a woman."

Luke stepped forward. "Tally, we could sure use your help. Rose needs to hide. She's lost her memory and lawmen are looking for her."

"What did she do?"

"We don't exactly know. A posse says she murdered her husband but I'm not sold."

"If they followed you here, I'll kill you, Weston."

He pushed away her rifle with a forefinger. "Hell, Tally,

how careless do you think I am? Sam and I always make sure we're not trailed before we come down here." He lowered his voice. "We know what's at stake. We'd never jeopardize any of you."

"People grow careless over time." Tally glared, but she removed her finger from the trigger and some of the bluster went out of her.

His gaze flew to a newly dug grave with a pitiful little wooden marker. Everything stilled inside him. His chest constricted as he forced out the question. "Who died?"

"Estelle. She got sick and couldn't recover. Don't know what she had." Tally pushed back a strand of hair.

Damn it to hell! He'd known living down here came with risks but he wasn't prepared for death. If they'd had access to a doctor, Estelle would probably have had half a chance. He dragged air into his lungs.

The rest of the women pressed around them. A young girl about seven or eight caught his attention. She was new. Taking slow, measured steps, she went to Tally and slipped her hand into the leader's palm. Tally bent to speak in her ear. Judging from the way the child held her head, and walked as though afraid of falling, Luke suspected she couldn't see.

He had a hard time swallowing. "You have a new face among you, Tally. Who's your little friend?"

"Violet." Tally smiled down at her and smoothed her blond curls. "I couldn't leave her in that place. Being blind is no reason to stick someone in a hellhole."

Sam pierced Tally with a stare. "I've never asked and you've never said, but I suspect you have someone on the inside who lets you know about these things."

"I do." Tally narrowed her gaze. "You'll never get her name from my lips."

"My brother and I aren't fools. Whoever she is, she's a saint in my book." Luke drew Rose forward and made the introductions.

"You've lost weight. Go kill something." Tally shoved

Luke toward Sam. Sliding a protective arm around Rose and clutching Violet's little hand, she disappeared into one of several crude dwellings perched amid the rocks. The rest of the women followed.

Rose and Tally were so much alike it scared the spit out of Luke.

His chest tightened as he watched the small procession of courageous women. Rose was safe. They'd protect her.

After a few minutes, he and Sam moved the horses to the stream that followed the canyon.

"I'm glad Tally didn't shoot us." Sam squatted on his heels next to the water. "She seems angrier each time I come. I think this life is getting to her, and the group keeps growing. Violet's so young. What's going to become of her if anything happens to Tally?"

"Who knows? Being stuck down here has to be hard on all of them. They're barely existing and little better than wild animals at that. They can't even go into town because of the tattoos on their faces that give Creedmore Lunatic Asylum ownership over them." Luke knelt and scooped water into his mouth. "I just hope Rose doesn't talk them into giving her a gun. That would be a mistake." He let out a worried sigh. With her high-strung temperament, a gun in her hands would amount to bigger trouble than he could handle. "Wouldn't put a damn thing past that woman," he grumbled.

Sam punched his arm. "I swear. You shouldn't talk about her that way. I've never seen anyone with a sweeter disposition."

Yeah, about as cuddly as a rattlesnake. Luke smothered a chuckle, then quickly sobered.

Come to think of it, she'd been pretty damn nice in his arms in the dark of night.

A low fire flickering across her pretty features…

Her soft breath mingling with his…

His lips pressed to hers…

Seven

Rose glanced around Tally's makeshift home, and at the flowers in a can and the jars on a shelf that made the abode livable.

"We have several options for you to consider, Rose." Tally Shannon laid out two very different sets of clothing—a dress, or pants and a shirt.

Rose felt a kinship with this woman. Tally's brusque attitude had vanished when they'd entered the two-room dwelling. The survivors had fashioned it from rough mesquite and scrub oak plus whatever else they could manage to scrounge. A small rug lay on the dirt floor, probably to give it a homey feel. Little things did matter. The weathered door appeared made from the bed of a wagon. All the other shelters had only blankets hanging over the entrance, so the fact that Tally's didn't spoke of her standing as a leader.

Little Violet perched on the end of the bed. Rose couldn't imagine being blind. It was bad enough to forget her name, where she came from. If she lost her vision, she'd flat go crazy.

As sounds of the other women in the next room drifted in the air, Rose wasted no time making her choice. "The pants. I need the freedom to move."

A plan had already formed in her head. Luke would be furious, but she wasn't going to let that stop her. This was her life hanging in the balance. "I hate to ask because I know how badly you need to defend yourselves, but do you have an extra gun? And how about a hat?"

Without a word, Tally opened a trunk and removed a six-shooter. "I don't know how well this fires. I haven't tested it recently, but you're welcome to it. Out here, a woman being chased needs protection. You do know how to shoot?"

"I wish I knew. So much about myself is missing. I guess I'll find out." Rose closed her hand around the revolver. The weight seemed right in her palm, and there was a blue cast to the metal. "I think I was familiar with weapons, wherever I came from. This feels right."

Suddenly, an image swam in her mind. She saw a hand outstretched, holding a gun. Orange flame spat from the barrel. A hole opened in a man's chest and he dropped to the dirt. Before she saw the shooter's face, the vision faded.

Rose closed her eyes, trying with all her might to pull back the fragment. Had she seen herself? Or someone else?

"What's wrong?" Tally asked. "You're pale."

"I just had a flash." She shared what she'd witnessed with the copper-haired beauty.

"Maybe everything is coming back." Tally rested a hand on Violet's small back. The girl smiled up, her eyes full of adoration.

"I hope so," Rose murmured. "I may not have weeks or months to sit around twiddling my stupid thumbs waiting for a cure. I may die before I even know why this happened." Rose flipped open the chamber of the revolver and found it empty. "I'll need a few cartridges if you can spare them."

"Of course." Tally impatiently shoved back a copper strand of hair from her face. "I'd give anything if I *couldn't* remember the hellhole I came from. In the dark of night, I still hear the tortured screams echoing through that place." The pretty woman touched the diamond-shaped tattoo on her cheek.

Rose laid her hand on Tally's arm. "I can't imagine the pain of what you went through."

Violet whimpered and clawed at the quilt, trying to burrow underneath. The child didn't wear the mark, thank goodness, but hearing the talk must've triggered some deep fear. Tally pulled Violet into her arms. Tears bubbled in the eyes of the hard-shelled leader as she clutched the girl tightly, murmuring soft words in her ear. Violet soon settled.

Anger, frustration, and sorrow swept through Rose. "Luke said Violet is new. How did she get here?"

"A friend who works on the inside brought her." Tally rested her face against Violet's hair.

"I'm glad."

"An evil man runs that place. One day, I'll make him and everyone else pay." The gritty hardness in Tally's voice made Rose shiver.

No doubt she would. She'd never bet against Tally Shannon. Anyone who did would be a fool of the highest order, and not long for this world.

"I hope I can be there with you. I'm beholden for the loan of the clothes and the gun." Rose worked at the buttons of her dress.

"Wait a minute. Let us help you get that last stain from your hair. That can't feel very pleasant."

"That would be wonderful. I tried to wash it in a creek, but I had no soap so couldn't get all the blood out."

Tally called to one of the women to heat some water. While they waited, Rose studied her new friend. It was difficult to pin an age on her. Her mouth bore only a few wrinkles around it. A wild guess put the woman somewhere in her mid to late twenties, but she could easily be older. She appeared ageless and the hard glint in her eyes said she'd seen far more than anyone should.

Rose wondered about her own age. How many winters had she seen? She picked up a small mirror on a crate next to the bed and studied her reflection. Her mouth appeared too wide, her brownish-green eyes too large, but she had nice, straight teeth that gleamed white. She shifted her attention to her blond hair and marveled at the mixture of light and dark strands. Aside from her teeth, definitely her best feature.

"Tally, how old would you say I am?"

The woman cocked her head to one side in thought. "Somewhere in your twenties, I think. You've done some living and I would say you've borne sorrow. The lines in your face reflect that. Just pick out whatever age you want to be." Her mouth quirked up at the corners. "That's one advantage of no memory."

"I suppose. Still, I'd rather know things." Rose returned the mirror to the crate and twisted the emerald ring from her finger. She held it up, letting the light shine through the small, green stone. If only the ring could talk. "If you don't mind my nosiness, how did you come to be in that asylum?"

"My father's new bride threw me in there the day after my father's funeral. Lucinda hated me from the first but I knew as long as my father was alive, he'd protect me from her." Tally dragged her toe in the dirt floor, leaving a small trench. "My father was a wealthy landowner and left me thousands of acres in his will, in addition to money. Lucinda wanted everything. So, she tied and gagged me, drove me to the asylum, and gave the overseer a goodly sum never to breathe a word of my existence. Two weeks later, the man showed me my obituary in the newspaper that stated I'd passed in my sleep. Died of grief."

Rose sucked in a quick breath. How could anyone be that cruel? "How long before you escaped?"

"A little over a year, but I saw enough during that time to curl your hair. Things you'd not believe." Tally wearily rubbed her eyes as though to wipe away the memories.

"I'm sorry."

"Like I said, I'll find a way to get to them, and death plays no favorites. Whatever you sow, also shall you reap. I'll get the rest of those women out and burn that place to the ground as God is my witness. Then I'll claim what's rightfully mine." Rage flashed from Tally's eyes. Rose made a vow never to get on her bad side.

After settling Violet with her rag doll, Tally stood. "I'll see what's keeping the hot water."

Rose's gaze followed the woman through the opening, wondering what story awaited herself at the end of the journey. Had someone betrayed her?

Wrongs had to be righted. That was the way of things, no matter how long it took.

Luke Weston understood this, and now it seemed clearer than ever what she had to do. She tackled the buttons of her dress with renewed vigor.

As the last rays of the sun bounced off the walls of the canyon in a blaze of purple and orange, Luke sat with Sam, cooking over a campfire a large portion of a deer they'd killed. He was getting worried about Rose. She'd been with the women for hours.

Luke's gaze wandered to Tally's dwelling. "Sam, you're going to stay the night, aren't you?"

His brother glanced up at the sky. "I hadn't planned to, but it'll be dark soon and dangerous for travel. I just hate leaving Sierra too long, with the baby coming any day." With a solemn face, he turned to Luke. "I'll never forgive myself if I'm not there. I want mine to be the first face the little tyke sees, hear it cry." Sam's voice grew raspy. "Craziest thing you probably ever heard."

Luke squeezed Sam's shoulder. "A man needs to be there for the important things." Like hearing a cry from someone's heart when they didn't even know their own name. "What do you suppose is keeping Rose?"

"I learned long ago that it's best not to know." Sam turned the meat. "I'm sorry you didn't get to keep your meeting with Ned Sweeney."

"Makes two of us. I've got to find him soon. I can't

outrun the law forever, and with each sunrise my chances grow slimmer. Sam, I have these dreams where I hear a shot, feel a bullet ripping into me, taste blood on my tongue, and know I'm dying. I wake up in a cold sweat." Luke hated the panic and fear those nightmares brought.

Sam nodded. "I had bad dreams for a long while after the hanging, feeling the rope around my neck, and would wake up with my heart pounding clear out of my chest. I wish you'd let me do more to help."

"What kind of man would I be if I let Stoker and my brothers take care of me? I have to earn the right to claim the Legend name and a piece of the land that you've all bled for."

Sam shot him a look of admiration. "You're one fine man."

Luke reached into his pocket for the little book detailing his sins and pitched it to Sam. "I paid back some of the stolen money and intend to pay it all." Luke's quiet admission brought surprise to Sam's face. Clearly, his brother hadn't expected this.

"You will." Sam flipped open the book and glanced through the pages before handing it back. "I'm impressed."

"I find some honest work now and then. Redemption is slow in coming, I'm afraid." If his luck and time held out, he'd see the end of the darkness one day. He was short on patience but long on determination.

"For the hundredth time, I wish you'd let us help."

"You've beat that poor horse to death. Give it a rest," Luke growled.

In the growing shadows, the firelight played across a lower section of canyon wall, illuminating some scratchings. Curious, Luke got to his feet and sauntered over to look. Sam followed.

"Looks like pictures or something." Luke struck a match and held it closer.

"They're drawings of some sort." Sam struck another match. "People. Women."

Luke's match burned to his fingertips. "I'm going for something to give better light." He hurried to the fire and made a torch by wrapping a piece of cloth around a stick, then returned. He held the light to the wall.

As he made out drawings of each woman in the canyon with their names scratched below, his chest tightened.

"It's a remembrance wall," Sam said quietly. "To mark their time here so others will know they once lived."

Deep sadness enveloped Luke. He traced the outline of Tally, Darcy, Holly Beth, and the others with his fingernail, saw the faint drawings of tiny tears on their faces, felt their pain. Everyone had a need to leave their mark behind in some fashion or another. His was the carving on the handle of his gun that said *Legend*. This was these valiant women's efforts. They were hunted like dogs, despised for being in the way, eliminated as though they were worthless.

Luke's voice was husky. "I have to do something. I won't leave them here to rot." He felt the weight of Sam's hand. "Damn it to hell! They never expect to leave this place. They're going to die down in this canyon like Estelle. These drawings make it clear they've given up hope."

Somehow, someway, Luke would get them out. Not today, but soon.

The door to Tally's small dwelling finally opened and she stepped out with Violet in tow. The others followed. Maybe their powwow was over. As Luke and Sam returned to the fire, a young man caught his attention. He wore a large, floppy hat that concealed his face.

Just one thing wrong...*he* had curves.

"Damn it, Rose!" He jumped to his feet. The tall, long-legged beauty wore pants that hugged her hips and she'd strapped on a gun belt. As she neared, she pulled off the floppy hat and long blond hair tumbled down her back and over her shoulders. He sucked in a breath. The colors of twilight washed each strand in brilliant gold.

Smiling, she strode toward him. "Hell, Luke. Close your mouth or you'll catch flies," she teased.

"The answer is no."

"Had you fooled, didn't I? Just a little?"

He glanced at Tally. "You were supposed to give her a clean *dress*. Not pants. Not a shirt. And damn sure not a gun."

Tally shrugged. "Clothes are clothes. I let her choose and this is what she wanted."

"Yeah," Rose said. "Did you ever consider my thoughts?"

He thought about plenty where she was concerned. Too much, in fact. Things he had no right thinking. Things that would get him in deep, very dangerous water. Things that would make it very hard to say goodbye.

"You look...nice," Luke admitted. The scent of her freshly washed hair and skin swam around him, luring him as a bee to honeysuckle. He studied her closer.

Where were her breasts?

Could a woman just hide them like that?

Sam stood, grinning like he'd eaten locoweed. "Rose, I wouldn't have known you in those clothes and hat. I've never seen a lovelier woman. Next to my wife, that is."

"Thank you, Sam." She put her hat back on. "I'm ready to find out who I am. I think this disguise will fool anyone."

"No, you're not going." Luke found Rose's skill at going around him more than a mite unsettling. And she used a crowd in which to do it. Anything he said would find him in an enemy camp. He saw red. "You went to an awful lot of trouble for a get-up you won't need."

Rose put her hands on her hips and glared. "Is that so?"

"I'm not taking you and that's final."

"This is a free country last I heard," Rose huffed. "You don't get to tell me what to do, Luke Weston."

"Hey, brother. Think this over." Sam pulled Luke aside. "Maybe Rose *should* go along. It's her life that's at stake here. Treading familiar ground seems the best way to regain her memory." He lowered his voice. "Besides, you know she'll strike out on her own anyway as soon as you leave. Wouldn't it be better if she's with you? It'll save time trying to find her later."

"Sam, if we run into that posse…" He'd kill anyone who touched her, lawmen or not, jail or not, hangman's noose or not.

"They'll never recognize her with those clothes and her hair up under that god-awful hat. You should think about changing your appearance some too."

"I do, almost always when I go into a town. As fast as my beard grows, two weeks of not shaving and I'm the spitting image of a buffalo hunter. I keep some ragged clothes in my saddlebags." Luke rubbed the growth already on his jaw and grinned. "How do you think I managed to slip by you when you were a Texas Ranger and chasing me to kingdom come?"

Sam groaned. "I'm just now finding this out?"

"Yep." Luke listened to Tally's conversation with Rose.

"Luke is concerned for your safety," Tally said. "He's afraid you'll get hurt. He cares about each of us like we're his family. I think maybe we are, in a way."

"You're right, Tally," Luke said quietly. "You're my family. Rose, it's up to you. If you want to come, I'll protect you with my life."

Rose met his stare, raising her chin. "I'll never ask you to die for me. I only want you to listen to my side. I promise not to whip anyone or cuss them up one side and down the other."

He raised a brow. This he'd have to see.

"You'll be amazed what I can do when I put my mind to it," she finished in a rush.

Heat pooled low in his belly as he recalled her sultry mouth and the feel of her in his arms. And that was when she'd been at her worst, in a torn and blood-spattered dress. If that was *not* putting her mind to it, she'd have him twisted in knots before they made a full day.

His gaze lazily slid along her curves and down each long, shapely leg that the pants did nothing to hide. He let out a loud groan.

Eight

After a night spent tossing and turning, his mind planning every move, Luke finished saddling Major John. Now that Rose was coming, she'd need a horse of her own. He strode to where Sam was getting his buckskin ready to ride.

"Sam, I was going to ask you to take the two roans we found back to the Lone Star, but now that Rose is coming, we're going to need one."

His brother glanced up. "You can always return the other later. It'll give you an excuse to stop by. What will you do about a saddle?"

"Do without. Will you see what you can find out at the ranch about these horses and the wagon?"

"I'll talk to Pa and Houston." Sam scowled, looking like the lawman he was. "If there's corruption at the Lone Star, we'll find it. Most of the men have worked for us for a number of years but they may have hired someone new. You take care of yourself and Rose. Let me worry about stuff here. I'll ask around and see if anyone knows her."

"Thanks, *hermano*. Next time, don't come looking for me," Luke growled. "You're becoming too much like Stoker. I'm not a kid."

"To take a page from Rose's book—I'll do as I damn well please." Sam lowered the stirrups. "So will Pa."

"Do what?" Rose asked.

Luke whirled and found himself drowning in her wide eyes. "Just a brotherly disagreement. Are you ready?"

"I am." She put her hands on her hips. "Luke Weston, if you're going to start out as grouchy as an old mountain lion, I'll ride by myself. The morning's too young for us to get off to a bad start."

Sam winked at her and grinned. "You tell him."

"Can we go? Or are we going to stand around and talk all day?" Luke didn't want to admit that the tall beauty had him already unsure of which way was up. He had no idea how he was going to manage to keep his mind on the danger ahead. If the group of lawmen didn't get them, outlaws would. And if they didn't kill him, Rose might.

Tally, then each woman, gave Rose endless hugs and wished her good luck. They all invited her to visit again soon. Clearly the women had bonded, which would come in handy if he had to hide her here in the future.

"Bye, Rose," Violet said shyly. "I wish I could see you. Would you bend down and let me feel your face?"

Luke watched Rose get on her knees. Violet ran her fingers across Rose's face, feeling each curve and indentation.

"You must be real pretty," Violet announced. "You try to talk mean, but you're very nice."

"Violet, I think that's probably the best thing anyone ever said to me." Rose wrapped her arms around the little girl and held her for a long moment.

Tally moved Rose aside for a word. Though Luke tried not to listen, he heard the woman's advice. "Rose, don't avoid facing yourself to worry after him. You can't run away forever. Our problems always catch up with us. Take care and come to visit."

The words of wisdom slammed into Luke and he realized that's what Rose was doing. She couldn't fix herself, so she was trying to fix him. He'd have to set her straight.

Finally, Luke got her on the horse and they left, parting ways with Sam once they were out of the canyon.

"Luke, I want to come back here and try to help those women," Rose said, riding beside him.

"Like how?"

"I don't know. It's just not fair that they're being hunted when they didn't do anything wrong."

"You'll get no argument from me." He glanced ahead a hundred yards where the trail passed between two large boulders. It was a good place for an ambush. He rested his hand on the butt of his Colt. It paid to be ready.

"Luke?"

"Hm?" He listened closely for sounds that might indicate movement. A flock of buzzards circled high above. Damn those birds. They seemed intent on following him.

"What's wrong?" Rose whispered.

"Nothing yet. Trails like this make me a bit jumpy."

She slid her pistol from the holster at her hip. More unease settled over Luke. He didn't know if she could hit the broad side of a barn. Women with weapons made the inside of his mouth as dry as cotton. Besides, the one Tally gave her could blow up in her hand or go wide and hit him. In his opinion, a female with a loaded gun was a recipe for disaster.

"Put that away. Do you even know if it'll shoot?"

Rose's back stiffened. "Tally said it would and that's good enough for me."

"I figure she'd know, all right. When we camp for the night, I want to test it and see how you shoot, but for now, I need to listen for trouble."

When she didn't argue and returned the pistol to the holster, he breathed a sigh of relief. They lapsed into silence and rode slowly through the narrow passage. He kept Rose close beside him, so close their legs touched. The contact sent warmth rushing through him that he tried his best to ignore. On the other side of the passage, he relaxed, grateful to encounter nothing more deadly than a big, sticky spider web.

Luke shot Rose a smile. "Now, what did you want earlier?"

"I had a flash of memory while I was with Tally Shannon." She met his surprised stare.

He didn't know what this meant, but it made sense that her memory would return in little fragments instead of all in one big chunk. He waited for her to continue.

"It happened when Tally handed me this gun and my hand closed around the butt. I knew I'd done it before. I think many times."

"You don't seem very happy." He reached for her hand and found it as icy as before. He was starting to recognize it as a sign that she was scared. "What did you see?" he asked quietly.

Rose told him about seeing the gun firing and the man falling dead. "What does it mean, Luke?"

"Your guess is as good as mine. Do you think you were the shooter?"

She frowned. "I don't know. I only saw a hand." Her fingers curled inside his palm. "I can't explain how familiar it all felt the second I held this weapon. I know how to handle a pistol."

The unease was back, twisting in his gut. For argument's sake, if she was an expert marksman, it could mean only one thing—that she was probably someone who made her living with a gun. Maybe a female outlaw.

He'd know more when he tested her aim.

He just hoped she didn't shoot him—or one of the horses—before he had the chance to find out.

The sun had slipped low in the sky when they stopped to make camp on a rocky creek bank. Rose knew she'd jarred Luke with the scene from her past. He hadn't spoken more than a dozen words since. A man like Luke didn't seem to deal in guesses and suppositions. An outlaw's life appeared to depend on facts, to know straight out who was after him and how near they were.

He didn't understand her need to talk, for conversation. It eased her nerves.

Before she could throw her leg over the saddle, he was there. Instant heat swept through her the minute his strong hands closed around her waist. She slid slowly down the length of his body.

His eyes held desire. She didn't need to have a real name to know that much.

She loved how anger could turn those pale-green orbs to silver. She'd seen that when he'd faced down Reno Kidd's men, and later at the cave where they'd stayed. Luke Weston could instill almighty terror. But not in her. No matter how upset he got, she knew he'd never hurt her.

Rose clutched his sleeve and held her breath. Warmth swept over her as his eyes darkened almost to the color of emeralds. For a moment, she thought he'd kiss her. She hungered for his mouth, his touch, his rough, low voice that made her quiver. But her feet settled on the ground and the moment passed, much to her immense disappointment.

"This is the only water for miles around and known to experienced travelers, so we'll have to be on guard. Keep your disguise on."

"Sure, Luke."

"I'll find some game for supper." He grabbed the horses' reins and led them to the water.

A heavy ache filled her heart as she watched him stride away.

Don't care for me, he'd cautioned. *Don't try to save me.*

"Too late," she whispered. It was too damn late.

She cared and there wasn't one thing she could do to stop it.

"I'll get some wood and put the coffee on," Rose called and started for a large stand of scrub oak. She bent to collect some nice limbs when she heard crying.

Who on earth? She pulled out her pistol and scanned the area for horses or a wagon, but saw nothing other than

Luke with their mounts. The whimper of a dog caught her attention and drew her toward a thicket.

"Shh," warned someone in a whisper.

Rose crept forward until she spied a figure curled on the ground, covered by the tall brush. A dog growled low.

"Hello? Is anything wrong? Are you hurt?" she asked.

"Go away. I'm fine." The voice sounded young.

"Please, I won't hurt you."

Luke stole up beside her. "What is it?"

"Someone is hurt, I think." She pointed toward the forms. "I'm sure they're scared."

"I'll take a look." Luke moved toward them. Suddenly, the dog growled and lunged at him with the hackles on its neck standing. It sped around their legs, barking furiously.

"Watch out, Luke." Though the pet was small, it probably had razor-sharp teeth.

"Come here, Rowdy!" A thin boy who appeared to be somewhere in the vicinity of twelve scrambled for the mutt. "Don't kill him, mister."

"I don't kill dogs, son." Luke crouched and let Rowdy smell his hand, then scratched the pooch behind the ear.

The poor thing looked a sight with one half-chewed ear and dirty, wiry hair. Rose swallowed a sob. Rowdy seemed an appropriate name for the little scrapper.

She knelt beside Luke. "Hi, I'm Rose and this is Luke. What is your name?" she asked gently.

"Rose? Why are you using that name?" The boy looked puzzled; the poor thing was little more than skin and bones.

Her heart raced. "Do you know me?"

"You look like Josie. Josie Morgan."

Rose sucked in a breath. There was that name again.

Luke glanced at her then back at the kid. "Do you think you might be mistaken?"

"Possible I guess, but I don't think so. Josie's my friend. I've seen her lots of times," the shaggy-haired lad answered.

"Where?" Luke leaned closer.

"At our farm. Josie came with this other man to talk to

my pa." The youngster gave a sob and dragged his sleeve across his face to wipe a tear trickling down his cheek. "Leastways it was at the farm where I used to live. Before my ma and pa died."

"I'm sorry." Rose laid a comforting hand on the boy's thin arm. "How long ago did they pass?"

The boy scrunched up his face. "I sorta lost track of time. What month is this?"

"We're in May." Rose wondered how she could know that and not her identity. She shot Luke a questioning glance and he nodded to confirm she was right.

"My folks died when it was cold." The boy hugged his dog tighter, struggling to hold back a sob.

"Where do you live now, son?" Luke asked gently.

"Uncle Bert. He's mean." The youth had spoken the words so low Rose almost missed them but she had no trouble seeing the fear that filled his brown eyes.

"Mind telling us your name?" Luke asked. Panic filled the boy's eyes as he tried to rise only to collapse. "Just so we'll know what to call you."

"Noah."

"That's a fine name, Noah." Rose smoothed back hair so dirty she wasn't sure of the color. "Are you hurt?"

He nodded. "A little."

"Well, let's get you back to camp and tend to you. I'll bet you're hungry." Luke picked up the boy, who seemed to weigh nothing at all.

Noah squirmed around, apparently looking for his dog. "Rowdy's starving."

"We'll feed you both," Rose assured him. She snatched up a few pieces of wood and hurried after them and the mutt.

Luke sat the youngster down on a flat rock and went to get some water. No telling when Noah had last drunk. Rowdy jumped into his lap and licked his master's face. Rose attempted a smile but found it faltering. An ache filled her chest as she searched in the saddlebags for food.

She found two cold biscuits and three slices of venison left from breakfast. Precious little, but those would tide the boy over until supper.

Luke returned with a cup of cool water and squatted in front of Noah. Concern deepened the lines around his mouth and Rose could see anger building, the kind that would terrify everyone when unleashed.

Although Luke forbade anyone to care for him, he had no such rule in place for himself toward others. He rubbed Noah's thin back as the youngster wolfed down the biscuits, sharing the venison with Rowdy. The way both barely took time to chew said they hadn't eaten much in a long while.

Now that he was clear of the brush, she could see the full extent of Noah's injuries. Raw welts encircled his wrists and ankles where someone had bound him tightly.

Again, she went to the saddlebags and rummaged for a small tin of salve. She gently dabbed the thick ointment into the wounds.

"How did you get these?" Luke's rasped words told her he was struggling to keep a tight rein on his anger.

"He chains me in the barn at night. That's where I stay. I'm not allowed in the house. He lets me out in the day to work." Noah's soft answer was mumbled and low, as though someone would hear and punish him if he said it louder.

"Bert?" Luke asked tightly.

Noah nodded and released a loud whimper. The little dog whined and licked his face in sympathy.

Fury burned red-hot in Rose. If she beat Luke and got first crack at Uncle Bert, she'd definitely put a bullet between the man's eyes. Then one in his chest where no heart lived.

"I finally got loose yesterday and ran all night. He's going to come and take me back." Noah shook his shaggy hair from his eyes. "This time he'll kill me," he whispered. "Then he'll feed Rowdy to the pigs like he said."

A chill ran up Rose's spine. She watched Luke's eyes turn

icy silver. There was no need for words; they were in perfect agreement. Uncle Bert would find nothing but a cold grave waiting if he was stupid enough to come for Noah.

Nine

Rose had so many questions to ask Noah, but knew she had to bide her time. Feed the boy first and let him rest.

Then find out what he knew about her.

Why the hell had she gone to his farm with a man? Who was he to her? Somehow, she knew the answers would be key to unlocking everything. But they lay just out of reach, teasing at the edges of her mind. Taunting her. Just like the emerald ring on her right hand. She tugged it off and stared at it. Who had given her the piece of jewelry? Or had she thought it pretty and bought it for herself?

The puzzle was driving her crazy.

With a heavy sigh, she slipped the ring back on and made a fire. When the flames died low, she set the coffeepot amid the embers. Hopefully, Luke would return soon with fresh game, but if not, she'd let Noah and the dog have her portion. She glanced to them lying on the bedroll fast asleep. Not surprising seeing as how they'd walked all night, desperate to get as far from pain and trouble as possible.

Suddenly, Noah whimpered, begging his uncle to give him food and a blanket. "Please, I'll be good," he cried.

The ache in Rose's heart cut off her ability to breathe. No telling what he'd suffered. She hurried to him and laid a hand on his chest. Her touch quieted the boy. Rowdy glanced up at her with sad eyes before burrowing against Noah's side.

After a few minutes, she returned to the fire.

Josie Morgan. She turned the name over in her mind, trying to spark a memory.

From what Noah had said, she'd been to his farm lots of times. She had to have seen the boy, eaten at the same table. Yet, she couldn't remember, not for the life of her. Maybe when Noah got around to telling her more she'd recall something. If she truly was Josie, she should probably start using the name. She whispered it to test how it sounded. Thoughts rolled in her mind.

Josie killed her husband—gutted him with a knife.

A shiver crept up the back of her neck.

What else had Josie done? Who else had she killed?

Bathed in twilight, she sat there, watching Noah sleep.

Before she knew it, Luke returned with a turkey. They'd eat well tonight.

She hurried to take the bird from him. "You must've seen this big fellow right off. You haven't been gone more than fifteen minutes."

"The strangest thing." Luke dismounted. "He practically walked right up to me. Just stood there, waiting for me to grab him. Saved me a bullet."

"Luke, if you think I'm going to believe that, you're crazy." She marveled how the remaining sunlight struck his sharply angled jaw and high cheekbones, danced playfully in his midnight hair. A yearning to bury her fingers in it came over her. "But thanks. I needed a smile to brighten my thoughts. Noah's been asleep ever since you rode out."

"That's good." Luke's deep voice brought tingles. "The boy's exhausted."

"And hungry. Which we'll soon remedy."

Rose's gaze followed him as he unsaddled Major John and led the horse over next to the roan. Long and lean, Luke Weston cut quite a handsome figure with his broad shoulders and narrow waist. The pair of black trousers with the silver conchas up each side drew her attention to his long legs. Any woman would consider herself lucky to be with such a man—outlaw or not.

Besides, he had the biggest heart she'd ever seen, and he could kiss. Rose couldn't forget how those finely sculpted lips had settled on hers.

But would he want to kiss a killer?

Luke finished the last bite of turkey and leaned back against his saddle. He gazed at Rose, watching the firelight softening her pretty features. It became more and more apparent that her name was Josie Morgan.

Even so, no one would ever convince him that she could have killed anyone, unless it was for good reason.

Looking at her now, he had a hard time believing that she'd hurt a fly. But her fury at Reno's men when she didn't even have a weapon rushed back. And there at Tally's when she was mad enough to fight the ones who'd wronged them told him she could kill if provoked. Maybe that's what happened.

People who killed others without reason were cold, unfeeling. Dead inside. That definitely crossed Rose off the list. He'd never seen anyone with a bigger heart or as much life.

He shifted his gaze to the boy. He'd put a crimp in Luke's plans; he'd meant to find out just how well Rose could shoot. Besides, he needed to fire that pistol at her side first to see if the thing was even safe.

He'd make sure of it before they left at sunrise.

What was he going to do with Noah? He wouldn't leave him. But could he, in good conscience, take the boy into even more danger?

Luke watched him hand his little dog a hunk of meat he'd pulled from the bone. Both had eaten until they were about ready to explode, yet couldn't stop. Maybe Noah feared they wouldn't get any more.

"How old are you, Noah?" Luke asked quietly.

"Fifteen," the boy mumbled, keeping his head down.

"Maybe you oughta try again, son." Luke noticed the red streaks climbing up Noah's neck at getting caught in the lie.

"Ten." Then he threw in quickly, "And a half."

A flicker of a smile crossed Luke's face. He saw a lot of himself in Noah and remembered when he was at that in-between age, badly wanting to be older.

Rose leaned forward. "Now that you've eaten and rested, I'd like to know more about you and how you might know me. What is your last name?"

"Jordan," he answered. "My folks were Abel and Ester Jordan. We had a farm outside of China Lake."

"What happened to your folks?" Luke asked.

"Someone shot 'em. I heard the shots and found 'em. Never saw the shooter."

After explaining her memory loss, Rose asked, "Why are you so sure I'm Josie?"

Noah picked up Rowdy and sat him in his lap. "Because you brought me Rowdy. And gumdrops. We'd sit under a tree while the men talked. You told me how much you missed your mama. She died and you were sad. You were real nice and I liked you."

"I'm glad I showed you kindness."

"Most grown-ups pretend us kids are invisible, but you spent time with me...like you really wanted to."

"I know I did want to." She touched his hair and Luke could see how much she cared for this child. But then, she'd be drawn to him anyway because Noah was the only link she'd found to her past.

Noah pulled a length of braided leather from his pocket. "You taught me to make this."

Luke sat in silence as Rose took the handiwork that showed painstaking care. She fingered it slowly and let out a soft gasp, riveted by something only she could see.

"What are you looking at?" He touched her shoulder.

"A picture—a memory, just now. I was leaning over Noah's shoulder, showing him how to weave three narrow strips of leather together into this braid here. Before I could grab hold of the memory, the image vanished." She met Luke's gaze. "I *am* Josie Morgan. Of that I'm certain."

He swung to Noah. "You said she came with a man. Can you describe him?"

Luke held Rose's icy hand and watched her in silence, seeing her desperate need for answers—even if they brought pain. He found himself praying she'd drop her search. Somehow, he knew that when the truth came out, the answers would destroy her.

"He was kinda old," Noah said. "He had gray hair and a beard. Not as tall as you. He didn't smile or anything. My pa called him Captain. I wish I knew more so you could find yourself, Josie. I hate being lost. It's scary."

"You're not lost anymore," she said. "And I'll find my way too before long. What did I wear when I visited?"

"A dress. It was real pretty, like my mama's."

"Did I wear a gun?"

"Nope. But once I saw you unbuckle a gun belt when you dismounted and put it in your saddlebag. That man—Captain—got real mad. He said you had to wear it."

A frown deepened the lines around Rose's mouth and on her forehead. Luke couldn't tell what she was thinking, but the more the boy talked, the more troubled she became.

"What kind of horse did I ride?" she asked.

"It was a black-and-white Indian pony." He grinned. "I wanted a horse just like it. Once you said that you dreamed of riding him to Galveston. You told me you wanted to live there where bad people couldn't find you and you could wade in the water."

"I don't think I was very happy." She glanced at Luke. "I'm more confused than ever."

"None of this is sparking anything?" he asked.

She shook her head. Night settled around them and with the black shadows came fear.

Worry darkened the kid's eyes and Luke suspected he was thinking about his uncle. "You have us, Noah. I won't let him take you."

"But what if he kills you?" Noah shivered. "He's real bad."

Josie laid a hand on Noah's arm. "Honey, your uncle doesn't have the skill it takes to shoot someone like Luke. But if he does somehow manage, I'll put a bullet in him myself. You're never going back there. Tell him again, Luke."

"It's like Rose said. If he comes for you, it'll be the biggest mistake of his life." Luke almost wished he would. He ached to put the piece of scum in the ground.

"I'm not Rose," she said softly, returning the braided leather to Noah. "From now on, I'll answer to Josie. I only borrowed Rose for a while anyway. Denying the facts won't change them."

Pain in her eyes bruised something deep inside him. Right now, he'd give anything to have back that brash, bold woman who'd threatened to whip Reno's men to within an inch of their sorry lives. The pretty lady with a mouth that begged to be kissed.

Still, he had to give her hope, even if it was false. "I'm having a devil of a time knowing what to call you. It's not a hundred percent fact that you committed any crime, most of all murder."

"You're only fooling yourself." Resignation dripped from her words. "I *am* Josie Morgan. And I am a k-k-killer." She clasped her hands over her mouth to stifle a sob.

Luke pulled her up and folded his arms tight around her. "Don't think that. I don't care what anyone says or what name you take. You didn't murder anyone. Get that through your head."

She glanced up. "How can you be so sure?"

"I've ridden with cold-blooded outlaws who took lives for the thrill of it for more years than I care to count, shared their fire, eaten with them. I know their sort and you're not one of them. You were horrified at that blood on your dress and couldn't wait to be rid of it."

Noah spoke up, "You were real nice to me. And kind. I always liked you, Josie."

"You're sweet, Noah. I'm glad I wasn't mean." Her gaze shifted back to Luke. "You're not one of those men either."

A cutting hardness snuck into Luke's voice. "Make no mistake—I've killed and I will again. I have darkness inside me that likes dispensing justice. It's time you faced that. Some say I'm nothing more than a rabid animal. You'll regret trying to find anything good."

He set her apart and strode toward the horses that were bathed in darkness just like his rotten soul.

When the black shadows swallowed him, he turned. Josie was standing where he'd left her, staring toward him. Golden hair curled around her shoulders and spilled down her back. She was the most beautiful woman he'd ever seen. Not just on the outside. She had a kind, sweet spirit that drew people to her. Noah saw it and Luke for damn sure did.

Far too clearly.

For a moment, he cursed this hunger for her that gnawed at him, growing stronger with each sunrise. How long could he keep fighting the urge to take what he wanted? At last, he cursed his conscience that wouldn't let him ride away while she and the boy slept. Who was he fooling? It was too late for him to try to right all his wrongs. Some of his victims had died, others had disappeared without a trace, and yet others refused his money, saying it was stained with blood.

He had nothing to offer any woman, most of all Josie Morgan. She had problems of her own. She didn't need his too.

Boot heels struck the ground as Luke moved near the fire. Josie heard him but lay still on her bed, a cushion of juniper and mesquite. Noah slept on the bedroll a foot away.

Without moving a muscle, she opened her eyes. Luke added some wood to the fire and sat down beside it. Weary lines deepened around the outlaw's mouth. Flames flared, illuminating his chiseled features. Though he appeared somber, his eyes no longer held that hard anger.

Josie ached to make him whole. To help him find a purpose to his life. Yet that was up to him.

She could live without a past, but Luke couldn't live without a future. If she could, she'd heal all the dead places inside and help him feel again. She'd teach him to laugh and dance. One problem with the world—there was too little dancing, she decided.

She hadn't heard him laugh since they'd pretended to be married.

With her eyes closed, she pictured herself in his strong arms, the silver conchas on his pants flashing as he twirled her around a dance floor. She could almost hear his heart beating next to hers. Feel his kisses, the sort that could make her breathless and her pulse race like a herd of stampeding horses.

In a flash, a memory replaced her daydream. She was dancing with a gentleman who wore a green brocade vest. She was laughing—happy and carefree.

Where had that woman gone? Who was her partner?

Why had she begun living with a gun?

Josie rose and sat down beside him. She needed his strength. "I'm cold," she whispered.

Luke put his arm around her and she scooted closer. "You're going to be sorry for taking up with the likes of me," he murmured into her hair before dropping a kiss on her forehead. "You should heed my warning," he said with a growl rumbling in his chest.

She laid her hand on the side of his jaw and glanced up with a mulish tilt to her chin. "I'm not afraid of you."

"You should be. I'll destroy you like I have everyone else I've touched."

Not so, her heart whispered back. "Save your warnings

for those who'll listen. I'm wise to you, mister. You don't frighten me. You know why?"

"I'm too tired to play games." He drew her closer. His breath ruffled the hair next to her ear.

"Humor me." She leaned back and jabbed a finger into his chest. "Why do you think I'm not intimidated?"

"Because your memory was wiped clean and you've forgotten the dangers of tangling with a rattlesnake?"

Josie snuggled into the folds of his shirt and vest, inhaling the scent of wild Texas sage. "I can still recognize rattlesnakes just fine." She took a deep breath. "I see the man you really are—the one you don't *want* people to see. You love your brother Sam and those women in the canyon. You care deeply for Noah. Hell, Rowdy too. No one can fool a dog."

As though hearing his name, Rowdy trotted over to lick Luke's hand.

"The mutt just knows which side his bread's buttered on," Luke muttered.

"Oh, hush." Josie patted his chest. "You'll risk death for any of us. So stop pretending you're this mean, bad person. I'm not buying it."

Luke didn't move, didn't reply. She listened to the crackle and pop of the fire, hoping he would say something at least, even if it was to tell her to stop talking or go pickle some cactus.

Long after she'd given up, he murmured, "Go to sleep, Josie. Don't worry about anything—or anyone. I'm watching."

Ten

The sun shone bright the next morning as Luke took Josie's pistol, testing the weight. The balance was good. He flipped the full cylinder open, stared down the barrel, aimed at one of the red fruit on a prickly pear, and squeezed the trigger. The bullet hit it dead center and the red fruit flew apart, juice spraying.

"How is it?" Josie asked.

"Pulls just a hair to the right but not so much as you'd notice. It's a good, solid weapon." He handed it to her, trying his best to ignore the graze of her hand, and soft curves encased in denim that left nothing to his imagination. Josie was danger with a capital *D*. "Now show me what you've got."

She wasted no time, taking aim at another cactus fruit. Again, the bullet shattered it.

Luke whistled through his teeth. "Damn, lady! That's good shooting." In fact, she handled a weapon almost as well as he.

"I told you I could." Josie holstered it, drew again and fired. The target burst into pieces. "It just felt right when Tally handed it to me. What do you suppose this means?"

"You're definitely an expert." But at what? Had she killed people as well? Say it was true she gutted her husband, why hadn't she just shot him? If she hadn't wanted anyone to hear, she simply could've slit his throat.

Josie was too open, too honest for that. She wouldn't care who saw. Or apologize either.

"Can I shoot the gun?" Noah asked, squinting into the sun.

"No!" Josie and Luke yelled at the same time.

"You're too young," Luke said, draping an arm around the boy's shoulders. "When you get a little older, we'll see."

"Then I'm staying with you and Josie?"

Luke's heart twisted when the goofy kid looked up at him with a grin. What the hell was he doing? He didn't need a ten-year-old to look after. A ten-year-old didn't need the responsibility of burying him. It wasn't right.

"You can stay for now. Not promising anything else," he said in a quiet tone. "You might still find some kin to take you in."

"I won't. I want to stay with you. Don't ride off and leave me when I'm sleeping. Promise?" Panic filled Noah's brown eyes. "I won't be any trouble. Please."

He ruffled the boy's shaggy hair. "I'll never leave you to fend for yourself as long as I'm alive." As he was speaking, Luke remembered his yearning to do just that last night. Josie was silently watching, and he met her gaze. She crooked a brow as though to remind him she saw the man he was.

Lord, how he wished he could be the man she thought she saw.

"Target practice is over," he said in a brusque tone. "Hide your hair under that hat, Josie. Gotta ride."

She scowled but did as he asked, for once without a fuss.

From a distance, he supposed she'd pass for a man. But any closer and those rounded hips would give her away. He silently groaned, remembering the feel of her in his arms. Even though he tried to push the thoughts away, they always lingered in the back of his mind. Damn! She *was* going to be the death of him.

He strode to the blanket and got out his knife. Moments later, he had a serape. "Put this on."

Josie grinned and slipped it over her head. "Thanks, Luke. I look more like a man now."

Heat arced through him. There was no disguising those lush curves. Without a word, he hurried to put distance between them.

They broke camp, then he boosted Josie into the saddle with a hand to her backside that rattled him. The feel of her firm flesh encased in denim had fed his dreams until now. Now he didn't need to imagine in the darkness. Josie drew her brows together in a scowl, which he ignored.

"Ready?" he asked Noah.

Giving his long hair an impatient shake, the boy nodded. Luke lifted him up behind Josie and handed him the dog. Rowdy yipped twice then snuggled contentedly into the crook of Noah's arm. Luke's chest tightened. Boy and dog were meant to be together and he'd make sure they stayed that way. Anyone touching them or Josie—especially her—would find themselves in a hell they didn't want.

She'd been right. He would protect them all with his life.

He swung onto the roan and they rode. He kept a sharp eye out for trouble. An hour later, the hair on his neck stood. Someone was trailing them.

But who?

Munroe O'Keefe, the boy who wanted to make a name for himself? Reno Kidd, the cold-blooded killer? The posse of lawmen hunting Josie? The list seemed endless.

When they stopped to let the horses rest at a spring, he warned everyone to stay close.

Noah glanced up and gave a nod.

Josie swung around. "Who do you think it is? I felt them, too, a while back."

"Don't know. Got a feeling I don't like, is all." He led the horses to the water coming from the rocks. "I'm going to scout around. Noah, keep Rowdy near. He'll warn you."

"Yes, sir."

Using the horses to shield his movements, Luke slipped into the tall brush. He kept his head down and began a slow circle around the spring, never letting Josie and the kid from sight.

Slow.

Easy.

Silent.

He barely made a sound. Halfway through the circuit, he spied a rider approaching. Moseying along like he was, the man didn't appear a threat, but Luke had learned to never let down his guard. He glanced toward the spring but found he'd lost sight of Josie and Noah.

Where had they disappeared to? Worry niggled in his head.

"Hold it right there," Luke ordered, stepping from cover with his Colt pointed at the rider's chest. "Who are you and what do you want?"

The man halted, his slouchy hat covering his eyes. "Need water for my horse. Any law against that?"

The horse excuse provided a good reason for being there, but Luke didn't like the way the traveler's hand inched toward his holster.

"What's your name?"

"Dutch Moody. Can I get some water or not?" His hand had reached his pistol. "If you're thinking of robbing me, you'll be sorely disappointed, mister."

"Lift your fingers from your weapon or I'll blow your hand off, Dutch Moody." Luke's rasp carried a cold, hard challenge. If Moody didn't comply, he'd be dead in a heartbeat.

Just as he thought Dutch would draw, the man gave him an insolent smile and raised his hand, his palm open.

"Why are you following me, Moody?"

"Who says I am?"

Luke's eyes narrowed. "Luke Weston. Get down off your horse."

A tense moment ticked by. He could see the rider taking his measure, no doubt wondering who would be faster.

Behind him, Josie's angry words rent the air like shots from a gun. "Get away from that boy or I'll blow you clean in half!" A sudden gun blast roared. Josie screamed and Rowdy barked frantically.

Luke knew he had to get to them, to see who was

trying to hurt them. But before he could move, a gunshot exploded.

A hot whoosh of wind swirled, the chaos surrounding Luke. Every nerve went taut. Luke covered the short space to the rider and yanked him from the horse. But the moment the man's feet touched the ground, he drew his gun and jammed it against Luke's side. "Now, we'll see how well you take orders," the bastard snarled.

Like hell. Luke was done taking orders.

Not wasting a second, he whirled and fired. Moody was dead before he hit the ground.

Luke sped for the spring and reached it in time to see a man drive his fist into Noah's stomach. The kid bent double and collapsed, whimpering, in a heap. Josie's gun lay nearby in the dirt, evidently ripped from her hand by the assailant.

"Damn your rotten, low-down hide!" Josie leaped onto the stranger's back as Rowdy got close enough to sink his teeth into the attacker's ankle. But then a kick sent the little dog flying into the brush surrounding the spring.

Luke didn't know if Dutch Moody had been in cahoots with the attacker, but it stood to reason. Moody was probably supposed to distract him so his partner could move in. Luke would sort it out later.

The other attacker struggled with Josie. Before Luke took two strides, the attacker slammed her to the packed dirt. She landed with a thud, her hat flying from her head. She lay unmoving, her blond hair fanning out around her, her beautiful eyes closed.

Alive or dead, Luke couldn't tell. Fury blinded him. The yearning to kill—the hunger for revenge—rose so fast that it shook him.

The piece of filth stood over her with his .45 pressed to her head. "I'll teach you to meddle. Say your prayers, lady."

"I think you need to say yours," Luke growled and stuck his Colt into the stranger's back. "Put down the gun. Nice and easy."

"And if I don't?"

"Let's just say, my finger is awfully heavy on this trigger. The buzzards will have quite a feast this day. Maybe they'll even leave a few scraps for the coyotes."

Noah writhed on the ground. "Don't, Uncle Bert! I'll be good. Don't hurt my friends."

Shock flashed through Luke at the name, fast as orange flame would come from his Colt. He stood next to the devil. Whatever Uncle Bert did next wouldn't matter. The cruel man wasn't walking away from here.

Bert Conley raised his .45 in the air and slowly turned. He wore a twisted grin. "The boy belongs to me."

Luke had never seen such cold, dead eyes.

"Not anymore," Luke answered. "He wants to come with me. It's less painful."

"You got no right to meddle in family business. I'm all the kin the dirty little maggot's got. Besides, he steals food."

"I heard how you starved him. Chained him in the barn."

"Had to. His ma and pa didn't teach him to mind his manners, respect his elders. The task fell to me."

The gloating set Luke's blood boiling into a frenzy. "You're a real caring bastard." He heard Josie moaning—she was alive!

In a sudden move, Bert Conley swung his gun down to Josie's head.

Icy fear swept along Luke's body as he fired. The explosion from his Colt sent a bullet spinning into the man's chest. Acrid smoke stung Luke's nose and blocked his vision for a second. Bert crumpled at Luke's feet.

Sparing only a cursory glance to make sure he was dead, Luke holstered his weapon and knelt over Josie.

"Don't try to move, *mi corazón*," he murmured as he pushed a strand of hair from her eyes. That he'd unwittingly called her "his heart" in his mother's native language brought a frown. He didn't need to complicate things more than they were. Josie Morgan wasn't his darling, his sweetheart, his anything. She was simply a friend. Like Noah. His scowl deepened. The two were completely different.

Hell! He was a fool.

"Keep your damn mind off her," he murmured to himself. He'd help her get someplace familiar and that was it.

Her eyes fluttered open and she stared up at him in panic. "Noah? Did his uncle kill him?"

"No. The boy's only hurt. You, on the other hand…you worried me, *amiga*."

A smile teased the corners of Josie's mouth. "You were worried about me? How much?"

He moved quickly to change the uncomfortable subject. "Are you hurt? You landed hard enough to knock you out."

"My back aches, and my head."

"I'm not surprised." He helped her stand, her legs shaky. She hauled off and kicked dead Uncle Bert. He'd expected no less from the high-strung filly. It probably made her feel better. "Rest here and get your bearings. I'll check on Noah."

He squatted beside the kid. "How are you, son?"

"Is he dead?" Noah whispered.

"Yep. He can't hurt you ever again."

Noah whimpered and moved closer to Luke. "I hated him, you know. Is that wrong?"

"No, not when it's deserved. When I saw him hit you, I, too, got this black hate in my heart. At the time, I didn't know who he was. I just knew I wanted him dead." He smoothed the boy's hair. "When you start to think about him, close your eyes and picture your ma and pa. Don't waste another thought on your uncle."

Noah suddenly jerked his head. "Rowdy! Did he kill my dog?"

"I'm sure Rowdy's all right. He's probably hiding in the brush." He wouldn't place any bets, though, recalling how hard Bert kicked him. "You rest here and I'll go find him."

Before Luke could move, Josie plopped down next to Noah and put her arms around the boy.

Luke strode to the thicket where he'd seen the dog land

and called to him. Everything was eerily quiet. Not even a breeze ruffled the wild sage and mesquite.

"Here, Rowdy! Come on, boy."

Again nothing. Luke kept walking through the tangle of weeds and thorns, calling Rowdy's name.

Finally, he pushed aside a wall of briars and there lay the little dog.

"Hey, boy." Rowdy raised his head and whimpered. Luke squatted down and ran his fingers across the dog's back and down each leg. Rowdy rewarded Luke's gentle touch with a lick. Feeling nothing broken, Luke picked him up and walked back to Noah.

"Rowdy!" The kid smiled. "Thank you, Luke."

"Any time." He put Rowdy in his master's waiting arms and the reunion did his heart good. But Noah's ashen face and the fact that he hadn't stood up yet drew worry. Something wasn't right.

"Noah, are you in pain?" Luke knelt at eye level.

"Yes. And dizzy."

"What's going on, Luke?" Josie asked. "Of course the kid's in pain. He got the whey knocked out of him." She shot the dead man a look of utter contempt.

Luke touched Noah's chest. Maybe broken ribs? "What hurts? I need to know."

"My stomach." The kid grimaced and let out a moan when Luke touched his midsection.

"Anywhere else?"

"My back, kinda. I don't think I can walk," Noah whispered.

"That's fine. You don't have to." Luke stood and drew Josie aside. "I think he might have some damage inside. We need to get him to a doctor."

"I agree." Her gaze moved to Dutch Moody's body. "Are we going to take time to bury these two?"

"Can't spare it. Leave both of them for the buzzards. It's all they deserve anyway." Luke eyed the two extra horses. Now they had one for Noah and saddles.

After dragging Bert away from the watering hole and leaving him with his partner, Luke collected their weapons. Tally Shannon and the women could use them.

Worry filled Josie's eyes. "Where can we find a doctor?"

"A place I swore to avoid when I have trouble dogging my trail," he murmured low, "the Lone Star."

He was going home.

Eleven

"Glad to see you, son." Stoker Legend shifted his weight in his hand-tooled saddle.

In the twilight, Luke took in the heavy Colt hanging from the large man's hip, hoping he never had to face that—or the man wearing it—in a fight.

Stoker's gaze drifted to Josie and Noah before returning to him. "My gut told me you were coming, so I saddled up and rode down to the gate."

"Hello, Stoker." Luke stared right into those piercing green eyes, so like his own. Stoker's size and bearing intimidated him more than a little, but he knew him to be a fair, honest man. Stoker hadn't thrown him out on his ear when Luke had come to him two years ago, even though he'd given the rancher one hell of a shock. Maybe one day Luke could tell him what his heart longed to say. But not now. He couldn't let Stoker get too close. For both their sakes.

A wry grin curved Stoker's mouth, then faded. "It's become a habit riding down here these days, especially after Sam brought back that stolen horse."

Luke glanced up at the huge crossbar overhead that proclaimed the land the Lone Star Ranch, then back at Stoker. His chest tightened. He was home. His gaze swept to the proud Texas flag fluttering high above headquarters a short distance away and his throat narrowed. He loved that flag—and Stoker's welcome. Even if he couldn't tell the man how much it meant.

"The law is trailing us," Luke said bluntly. "I told you I wouldn't bring trouble to your door, but I need a doctor for the boy. If you'll take him and Josie, I'll ride off."

"I won't hear of it. That was your rule, not mine, son." The usual thunder was strangely absent from Stoker's voice. He glanced at Josie then Noah, riding close beside Luke.

Luke introduced them, adding, "Noah's hurt bad."

Though slumping in the saddle, the kid tried to offer a smile but couldn't quite get the energy to make it form.

"You know I'll do anything I can. This is your home, part of this land belongs to you. It always will."

Land he couldn't claim. But the words meant more than his father knew. Outlaws needed a safe place to rest.

"Doc needs to take a look at Josie too. She took quite a beating herself." Luke ignored the scathing look she gave him.

"Sam already told me about this pretty little lady's memory problem." Stoker swung to her and introduced himself. "I hate to hear that you're also banged up, ma'am. Doc will give us some answers and fix you up in no time."

"Thank you, Mr. Legend," she murmured sweetly before shooting Luke a look of death. "I'll be fine. Just tend to the boy, please."

"We can argue about that later," Luke said. "Let's get Noah to the doctor." He set Major John into a trot.

The four of them rode side by side up to headquarters. Stoker grabbed a passing cowboy. "Go down to Doc Jenkins's house and tell him he's needed."

Luke was glad for the evening shadows to cloak his arrival. Only a few at the ranch knew he was Stoker's son, even now. The less who knew, the better for all.

The large clock in the entrance chimed seven times as Luke carried Noah inside the immense stone structure that served as both ranch offices and residence. He quickly moved past the lavish furnishings and up the wide staircase to one of the bedrooms. Josie, wearing the serape, followed with Rowdy in her arms. From the corner of his eye, he caught her gaping in amazement. He didn't blame her for being overwhelmed. Few people lived as large as Stoker Legend. Luke's brothers, Sam and Houston, had grown up amid such wealth. Luke often wondered how it would've been to live here and how differently he'd have turned out.

He'd lived in squalor, and watched his mother work herself to death. All while the Legends had everything.

For years, he'd let bitterness eat at him. Then he'd finally met the man who'd fathered him, and brothers who didn't know he existed.

Memories swirled so thick in the air he could reach out and touch them.

Josie's grip on his arm brought him back to the present. "Are you all right?"

"I'm fine." Or he would be when he rode out again. This visit would be short.

"You're probably tired to the bone, son" Stoker declared. "You look like you're about to keel over."

"I'll rest when I'm dead." Even then, Luke doubted there would be rest for the likes of him. Satan would probably poke him with his pitchfork every time he closed his eyes and tell him to add wood to make the fire hotter.

While they waited on the doctor, Luke removed Noah's clothes and noticed the kid's discolored, very swollen stomach. The light from the lamps in the room fell on the mass of vivid purple and green bruises. Josie's loud gasp came from behind him. He longed to put his arms around her, to tell her things would be all right.

But would they?

Stoker leaned closer. "What the hell happened to this boy?"

"Evil happened." Luke drew a blanket over Noah, who had yet to utter a word. He shared what little he knew about Noah's past and how they'd found him on the prairie. "I killed his uncle back there."

"Killing's too good for the varmint," Stoker thundered. "This is unforgiveable. I wish I could bring the bastard back to life and administer some Legend justice for myself." He narrowed his eyes at Luke. "Though that's exactly what you did, son. You gave him a helping of Legend law. It seems you inherited my burning need to right wrongs—however I have to do it."

Giving a quick nod, Luke glanced away. He didn't know what to say to this man who'd fathered him. Maybe he never would.

"Noah's a sweet kid who got a bad break," Josie said softly, removing her serape.

Doc Jenkins bustled through the door, all business in his three-piece pin-striped suit. His gaze landed on the kid and stayed there. "I heard you brought in someone injured, Luke."

The highfalutin doctor lifted the fancy cane from his arm where he'd hooked it and set his black bag on the bed. Seeing Noah startled him. "No one said it was a child. Or one who's been beaten."

Luke told him about the fight and Bert driving his fist into Noah's stomach. "The boy has felt poorly since."

Doc grunted and felt around Noah's belly, then rolled him over to prod his back. Another grunt. Near as Luke could recall from being under the doctor's care in the past, two grunts meant things were pretty bad. The physician might be a pretentious dresser, but he was the best doctor Luke had ever seen.

Jenkins asked Noah some questions, then turned. Luke put his arm around Josie. Stoker moved closer. "He's got internal damage. Some bleeding. Bruised pancreas."

Josie gripped Luke's arm. "Can you fix it?"

"We'll see what strict bed rest will do." Jenkins closed his black bag. "A lot of times these things fix themselves."

"And if they don't?" Luke asked.

"Then I'll have to cut the boy open, but don't buy trouble. Bed rest might do the trick. I'll check on him in a few hours." He turned to Luke. "I hope you're staying awhile this time. Folks here worry about you."

"Not sure." Luke scrubbed the back of his neck, trying to avoid Stoker's look of disapproval. "Doc, I want you to take a look at Josie. She got hurt in the same skirmish as Noah, but before that she was struck on the head and knocked out. Can't remember a blessed thing."

Josie scowled at Luke before flashing Jenkins a smile. "I have this teensy little problem of not knowing my name, where I came from, or my family. I got hit on the back of the head two days ago, and that's when Luke found me. He's been going around the countryside collecting strays like he has nothing better to do. Noah was the one who recognized me and told me my name."

"Come with me," Doc Jenkins said. "Noah needs his rest. I want to examine you where we won't be disturbed."

"I'll speak to Mrs. Ross, my housekeeper, about getting some rooms ready." Stoker brushed Luke's arm. "When I get back, we need to talk."

Luke cleared his throat, wishing he had some whiskey to brace him for what he had to say. "I'd rather not stay in the headquarters, if it's all the same. I'll find a bed in the barn."

The doctor attempted to usher Josie out the door but the tension rippling in the room evidently made her hang back. She stared between Luke and Stoker. "Is everything all right, Luke?"

"Go with Doc Jenkins. I'll sit with Noah for a bit. Or would you like me to come with you?"

"No, I'll speak to him alone, let him poke and prod and have his fun." She shrugged. "Who knows? He might even find a brain up there."

"Be nice, Josie," Luke growled. "He's never met anyone like you."

No one had. They broke the mold when they made her and probably because the world was shocked enough by one. He hid a grin. At some point, he'd have to get her out of his head, but not today.

Still, exactly how bad did he really want to? The lady brought fresh air and promise to his life.

Suddenly, Josie froze and braced herself with a hand to the doorjamb. She seemed to be somewhere else.

Luke strode to her. "What is it, Josie?"

She stood there silent with unseeing eyes for a long minute. Finally, she turned to him. "I saw a man's face. He shoved it into mine and curled his lip." She shivered. "He's filled with hate. I think he wants to kill me."

Stoker joined them. "Describe him."

Doc Jenkins wormed his way between them. "Later. Let me do my job first. Besides, this young lady is tired. Needs rest and food. A hot bath. You're way down the list, gentlemen."

Luke protested. "She has information that may be helpful. Someone is trying to kill her."

"I said later. That's it for now." Jenkins took her arm and led her to the stairs.

Frustrated, Luke slapped his palm against the wall. Who had she seen? Someone he might know? Being on the run had allowed him to cross paths with a lot of men, most of them dangerous.

"Doc is right." Stoker laid an arm across Luke's shoulders. The weight of his father's touch soothed Luke's nerves. Any contact in the past had been very brief, but this was a real touch, his first, of affection from the man. Luke closed his eyes, letting the sensation seep into his thirsty soul.

He could get used to this. To what end, though? How much good would it do to bring his sorry mess to his father? Stoker Legend deserved far better than a son who'd lived outside the law. Luke had sown nothing but toxic weeds. What else could he expect to reap?

Nothing. If you danced to the music, you had to pay the fiddler at some point.

"I believe you were going to tell Mrs. Ross to ready a room for Josie." Luke severed the contact, and immense loss flooded him immediately. He strode to the bed without a backward glance, listening to his father's heavy footsteps moving down the hall.

Luke steadied the emotions running through him and glanced at Noah, now sound asleep. Poor kid. Luke reached for his hand and held it. Maybe Noah would feel his caring. Everyone needed to feel the warmth of genuine love. He prayed that God, if He took a notion to listen to the likes of him, would spare the boy.

He'd never been more alone than he was at this moment. Yet the silence of the house whispered the word *home* in his ear, offering a sliver of hope.

The dapper doctor—a well-dressed man who looked to be in his fifties—opened a downstairs door and Josie entered a brightly lit room. While she didn't know her circumstances, she doubted she'd ever seen anything like the ranch headquarters. Expensive things surrounded her. A thief could make a fortune by lifting just a few items that no one would probably ever miss. And a thief is probably what she'd been, or the thought of stealing never would've entered her head.

The evil face she'd seen so vividly in her mind scared her. Who was he? How had she known him? She prayed he was the man she'd gutted, because she didn't like him. Fear shot through her at mere recollection of the brief glimpse.

"Have a seat and get comfortable," Jenkins said, setting down his cane and the black bag.

Trembling, Josie sank onto the cowhide sofa. "How much do you know about memory loss, Doc?"

"I've seen two cases in my time. One man's didn't last but a short while."

"And the other?"

"Last I heard she never regained her identity."

Doc's quiet words struck dread in Josie's heart. She couldn't go the rest of her days this way. She couldn't. What kind of life would she have, to be forever lost?

He sat down next to her and patted her hand. "I believe in keeping positive. As long as the sun rises each day, we have hope for change. Now, let's get busy."

Though she thought Jenkins was a bit uppity, he projected genuine warmth. Over the next hour, he examined first her sore back, then her head. Finally, he lifted a lamp and stared into her eyes, asking endless questions. How often did she have headaches? Dizziness? Ever see double? Have hearing trouble? Other than today, had she ever had other flashes of memory?

Finally, she asked, "How much longer is this going to take?"

"We're through." He peered at her strangely. "Unless you have anything to add. Perhaps you've held something back."

"I've told you everything and I'm very tired." She wearily brushed back her hair. "So, Doc, what's the verdict?"

"Since you've had three memory flashes already, I'd say the prognosis is good for a full recovery."

"That's wonderful!" Josie couldn't wait to tell Luke.

"However, I can't say how long this process will take. Your memory could come back in an hour, a week, or a year." He put everything back into his bag. "Something is going to trigger it. What that word, place, or some traumatic event will be, I can't say. I believe when it happens, everything is going to flood back in a rush."

"Thank you, Doctor." She moved to the door, anxious to find Luke. She knew the tension between him and his father would send him running. Panic gripped her. If he'd already hightailed it without her… She closed her eyes and sought to still her racing heart. Without him, she couldn't face tomorrow's sunrise. She needed him like she needed food and water and air. The tall, black-haired outlaw settled this turmoil inside that threatened to engulf her.

But a very tall woman who introduced herself as Mrs. Ross was waiting outside the door. "I'm taking you upstairs for a hot bath and some food."

"I appreciate the care, but can't it wait, Mrs. Ross?"

The kindly woman took her arm. "I promise this won't take long."

Josie smiled. "How about if I come find you later?"

"You'll get lost in this monstrous place."

How true. Josie sighed and followed Mrs. Ross, fretting the whole way. She needed to find Luke and sink into the comfort of his arms.

Breathe the special scent that was Luke Weston, the man with kisses like fire.

Nothing would be right again until she did.

Twelve

After a quick meal and a bath, Luke accepted a heavy crystal glass from Stoker and sank into a leather chair in his father's spacious office. He pressed the glass to his cheek and glanced around. What he saw froze the air in his lungs. There on the wall hung an oil painting of Elena Montoya when she was young and full of life. The artist had captured his mother's rare beauty. She looked as though she could open her mouth and speak.

"Your mother had my heart from the first time I laid eyes on her, son." Stoker filled the chair beside Luke's.

Luke pointed to the wall. "When? How did you accomplish this?"

"I commissioned the painting right after your return from the cattle drive to Dodge City six months ago. As for how…I gave Elena's likeness from her locket to the famous artist, Harvey Creed." Stoker released a gratified sigh. "This room is my favorite in the entire house. I sit for hours in here, staring at her, wishing I could turn back time. Dear God, I loved that woman. She lit a fire in me that still hasn't gone out. Did she find someone else, someone who'd take care of her?"

"No. There was no one else. Men came with offers of marriage, but she sent them all away." Each time Luke had begged her to at least consider one, but she'd just smiled and shaken her head.

A cry tore from Stoker's lips and his shoulders sagged as though he were an old man.

"What do Sam and Houston have to say about this being in here?" Luke imagined they didn't like it any.

"They were the ones who told me to hang the portrait. Their mother's pictures are all over the house. They wanted me to put up yours too."

Surprise shot through him that his brothers showed no jealousy. But then, they were unusual men. Luke's gaze flickered to the huge, mahogany desk and memories spiraled like a rampaging tornado, gobbling up everything in its path.

His mind flew back two years, to a time in this room under very different circumstances. He'd been worried about his brother Sam then. Rustlers had strung him up from an oak tree, and Sam would've died if Luke hadn't cut him down in time. The trauma of the event messed with Sam's head and his captain sent him home to straighten himself out. Afraid Sam couldn't make the trip, Luke hadn't rested until he'd made sure his brother made it safely.

Unaware that Luke was his brother back then, Sam had chased him for over a year for stage robberies. But there was never a moment, even when he thought he hated them, that Luke didn't watch over Sam and Houston from afar. His brothers were as innocent in this as he was. Still, they were Stoker's heirs. And Luke was a bastard child, a wanted man. All the secrets had come to light in this very room.

Stoker, Sam, and Houston had been less than thrilled at first. In fact, they'd been downright bull-snorting mad.

For certain, Luke's notoriety had caused problems for them, especially with the reward jumping higher and higher. The last poster he'd come across, tacked in the train depot in Austin, had set the reward at two thousand dollars. *Dead or alive.*

He muttered a curse and tossed back the whiskey, feeling the liquid fire burn a path down to his stomach.

"Still chased by demons, I see." Stoker rose to refill their glasses and returned to his chair. "I don't suppose you're any closer to clearing yourself?"

"Thanks for the whiskey. I needed it. To answer your question—not by a long shot." Luke stared into his mother's eyes, shining down on him from the portrait on the wall. "I almost had Ned Sweeney."

He told his father about coming upon Josie bound and gagged on the open prairie. "I couldn't leave her."

"Of course not. Who would've done such a thing? She's a sweet young lady and needed help."

"The two men I found with her claimed the outlaw Reno Kidd bears the blame." Hardness filled Luke. "I'll ask before I kill him."

"The bastard deserves it. I'd like to help." Stoker took a big gulp of liquor from his full glass. He gripped the bottle in his other hand, keeping it near for refills. His father seemed as much in need of the bracing liquid as Luke.

"I've paid back some of the money already." Why he'd said that, he didn't know. Possibly in hopes that his father would say he was proud of him?

Hell hadn't quite frozen over enough yet.

Stoker leaned forward in surprise. "It's a start, son. I could pay those off for you in a matter of days but for your god-awful stubborn pride."

"Sometimes money can't solve everything." He met Stoker's piercing eyes with his own steady gaze. His mother had loved Stoker Legend to the day she died. Luke suspected she'd be happy to see them sitting here like this, together at last.

He shifted his gaze to the desk, remembering how Sam had caught him in the early dawn. He'd hoped to put his mother's locket in Stoker's desk before anyone saw him. But it hadn't worked out that way; instead, he'd faced down a brother convinced that he'd been stealing. Luke still recalled the shock and how the color had drained from Stoker's face when he opened that locket and saw Elena Montoya's face staring back.

That morning, Luke had fulfilled the promise he'd made

to his mother on her deathbed. Now, two years later, things still weren't resolved on his side. Would they ever reach a point where he could let go of the past?

"Luke," Stoker said, "my respect for you grows each time you come. You've never taken the easy road—you shoulder responsibility for everything you've done like few men I've ever seen. I wish I could take your burden. I've spent sleepless nights worrying if you're dead or alive—or in jail somewhere."

"I don't want you losing sleep, not over me."

Stoker drained his glass and a mist filled his eyes. "When Sam rode with the Texas Rangers, he was the reason I installed a telegraph here. He was the one I watched for at each sunrise and sunset. Now it's you. That's why I rode down to the crossbar this evening. That's why I want you to sleep in the house. Just once, I want to know you're near." His voice broke. "You're my son. I love you, Luke."

Everything stilled inside of Luke. He wasn't ready to hear this. It wasn't time. Why the hell hadn't he stayed away? He couldn't accept what his father hungered to give. Not yet. Maybe not ever.

"I know." The raspy words squeezed from Luke's tightened throat, barely louder than a whisper. He rose, set his glass on a small table, and strode out the door.

Moments later, he found himself outside, gulping the fragrant night air as if none remained in all of Texas.

It was a mistake to come. He didn't fit here.

He'd made so many mistakes.

Maybe *he* was a mistake. He'd brought his mother nothing but pain.

Luke hurried past the row of sleeping businesses. The place was more like a small town, houses and stores all put in so Stoker's ranch hands and their families wouldn't have to travel days by wagon to shop or see a doctor. The latest was a telegraph. He vaguely recalled Stoker telling someone to take care of their horses, so he headed to the corral.

Why there, he didn't exactly know. He wanted to saddle

Major John and ride back out, but he couldn't just dump Noah and Josie on Stoker this way.

Hell!

Still, he kept walking. Maybe he sought comfort that the horse could give. Or maybe because Major John was the only thing in the world that he owned outright.

Stoker's words kept rumbling inside his head. Luke shouldn't have let him speak of love. His father didn't realize how deeply Luke would hurt him. Not by choice. But he would.

A shot rang out and the dirt kicked up around his boots.

"Stop it right there, Luke Weston, or I'll drop you. Don't think I won't."

The familiar voice kept him from reaching for his Colt. He whirled to see Josie racing toward him, smoke curling from the end of her weapon. The crazy lady had her gun drawn and appeared ready to kill him on the spot. What had happened? Something the doctor said? Or was it Noah?

Cowboys poured from everywhere, some in nothing but their long johns, all clutching weapons.

"Where's the trouble?" one asked.

"It was just an accident," Luke hollered. "No cause for alarm." Or at least he hoped not.

The men grumbled, holstered their guns, and retreated into the various dwellings.

Josie arrived out of breath.

"What the hell's the matter with you?" He took the gun from her cold fingers before she fired again and waited for some answer that would make sense. The racing pulse in the hollow of her throat alarmed him. "What's wrong?"

"You're a lowdown, double-crossing sidewinder if I ever saw one." She spat the words like they were snake venom. "I'm not going to let you leave, even if I have to shoot you. Not tonight. Not like this. Hell, you're exhausted and so am I."

"What are you talking about?"

She put her hands on her hips. "You're heading straight

for the stables, aren't you? I'm guessing you and your father had words. Saw it coming. I knew something would send you running."

"I'm going to check on Major, but to clear my head, not to leave." He tried to keep the anger from his voice but it sneaked in anyway. "I'm not riding out. Yet. I needed some fresh air."

Josie leaned back to stare up at him. "I thought you were leaving me. Mister, when you head out, I'm going with you." Her chin stuck out at an obstinate angle. "This is a fine place to rest—in fact, there's none nicer—but if you're thinking to dump me here, you'd best think again."

The fragrance that belonged only to her filled his senses. She stood before him bathed in the silvery moonlight. Her nearness messed with his mind. Her lips were too perfectly curved, too tempting, too close.

"You're one crazy, mixed-up woman, Josie." He put his hands gently around her neck, lowered his head, and claimed her mouth.

The kiss was hot and needy, and he didn't apologize for the sudden roughness.

Hunger for her consumed him with all the fierceness of a summer storm. He stood unmoving in its path, facing the furor. Not since Angelina had he felt this way about any woman.

Josie was imperfect, like him. She knew exactly who she was and made no excuses for any lack. The lady never pretended to be more than she was—not even when she played a role. But she didn't have to. She could do whatever the situation called for, whether it be a tender touch or a bullet from her gun. Luke had never seen another like her, even in all his wandering. Maybe she'd come into his life to make him see that his life had purpose.

When he broke the kiss, he nibbled slowly across her lips, teasing, wanting to make her yearn for more as he did. As her breathing became ragged, he gently tugged her plump bottom lip into his mouth with his teeth.

He pulled her against his chest with a low curse, and gave himself over to the passion or lust or whatever the hell it was. He slid his hands into her hair and wrapped the silk around his fingers.

She thrust her arms around his neck and melted into him, her breasts pressed flat against his chest.

What they had seemed right. Yet if it turned out to be all wrong, he couldn't stop. Not this time.

This time the hunger was too raw and consuming.

He couldn't think. Couldn't speak. Couldn't move away as he should. All he could do was feel, and the need to banish the constant loneliness for a little while drove him past the line he'd drawn. He wanted to feel whole again and only Josie could make that happen.

Luke deepened the kiss and slid his hands down the sides of her breasts, following the line of her body to her hips. Josie Morgan was made for loving, her curves designed for a lonely outlaw to hold in his dreams.

The way Josie clung to him told of the desperate desire she, too, felt. She melted against him and made little mewling sounds in her throat. She tightened her grip on his vest as though he were fighting to get away.

She didn't know he'd move heaven and earth to spend just one night in her arms. Better for her that she didn't. Better for everyone. That way, no one would get hurt when he said goodbye.

Even though he knew it to be a lie, he told himself that this meant nothing, just slaking a thirst for both of them. But he wasn't a good enough liar to convince himself of that.

Truth be told, she'd wiggled her way past every one of his defenses and planted herself in his heart. Maybe admitting that would buy him some favors when someone's bullet sent him to the fiery pits of hell.

He ended the kiss when he realized she needed air. With a final brush across those swollen lips, the closeness driving him insane, he rested his forehead on hers.

"*Dios mío.*"

"Luke." Her breath came unevenly.

"Lady, someday when I get all this mess straightened out and I know for sure you're free, I'll take you somewhere private." His voice was hoarse and raw. He rested his hands at her small waist above the low-slung gun belt and vowed, "I'll light a fire inside you and make slow, steamy love until the stars fall right out of the sky and the world disappears."

"So maybe there's hope for us?"

"Who knows?" It depended upon a lot of things—her past for one. His past for another. "Don't get too accustomed to this."

"I swear, Luke. I've probably never met a man with so many don'ts." Josie twisted the silver button of his black vest. "You're far too serious. It doesn't hurt to be a little bit more positive, you know. Try putting a few more dos *somewhere* in your vocabulary. You'll love how it improves your outlook." She glanced up. "Maybe I can help you."

"Help me how?" he growled.

"To smile more. To laugh. To appreciate what you have instead of seeing everything you don't."

Damn if she didn't make a good point. He already knew how much lighter he felt being with her.

Sliding his arm around her, he changed the subject. "What did you learn from the doc?"

"My back is fine. It'll take a while for the soreness to leave."

"And your memory?" he prodded.

"Jenkins thinks it'll all come flooding back any second." She waved her arm wide in exaggeration. "It could take a day, a week, a month, or a year. He said the right thing will have to trigger it."

"That's encouraging, Josie."

"I suppose, but I'm tired of waiting. I want it now. I need to know things." She lowered her tone. "That face I saw as I left Noah's room bothers me. I think he's going to try to kill me and I don't even know why."

"Let's go where we can talk." He put an arm around her

waist and they strolled to the huge barn. They sat on some hay bales. "Now describe what you saw."

"I'll never forget that face, not if I live to be a hundred. He had this long, dirty-yellow hair that looked like straw. Brown, rotted teeth. Light-colored stubble along his jaw. But the most frightening thing was his smile." She shivered. "His smile was evil, like he just wanted to reach into my chest and rip my heart out."

Luke put his arm around her and she leaned her head on his shoulder. "I've seen men like that. Anything else?"

"I noticed a scar on his cheek."

"What kind? Straight, wide, jagged?"

"No. It was a small circle."

Everything inside Luke stilled. "A circle?"

"Yes. I know that sounds crazy but that's what I saw."

"That's Reno Kidd, Josie. I put that scar on him during a fight, and not that long ago. I had on this ring that had a sharp, raised center. My fist cut a circle. Reno has yellow hair like you described and rotten teeth. No question. He's the one you saw."

Josie shivered. "How did I survive him? How?"

"Being unconscious must've saved you."

"No," she objected. "You saved me. You came along before they had time to…do whatever they planned."

Luke tightened his arm around her. "Try not to think about could'ves and would'ves. It didn't happen. You're here, safe where their evil can't touch you."

"Reno wants me dead," she whispered. "He'll hunt until he finds me."

Thirteen

Josie's anguished cry tore at the fabric of Luke's heart. The sounds of horses nickering close by, the barn cats' meows, talk between cowboys outside the doors faded until all he could hear was her frantic heartbeat.

"I won't let him near you." Luke mentally kicked himself. Why had he let Reno's men just ride off like that? If he'd known the whole story, he'd have made them lead him to Reno.

Except Josie had been in bad shape and he couldn't have left her.

She nestled against him. "I'd hate to go through this alone—without you. You give me hope and courage."

That seemed pitiful little, but he was glad he could at least offer that much. Maybe this time his gun would save someone, not take their life. He clung to that bit of promising redemption. Each tiny piece helped heal his soul.

She twisted around. "Luke, is everything all right between you and your father?"

He was silent a long minute. When he spoke, his voice was low. "He wants things I can't give and I don't know if I ever can."

"Like what?"

"Dammit, Josie, don't pry. Some things a man can't talk about. Stoker and I…our relationship is complicated."

Two weary cowboys came in, leading their mounts. They nodded politely and moved down the long row of stalls.

"Luke?" she said.

"Yep."

"Promise you won't sneak out and leave me behind."

"I never sneak," he said. "When I leave, you'll know it. But I do want you to stay here. Where it's safe."

"No. This is my life we're trying to get answers for. Make no mistake. I *will* be at Doan's Crossing, either with or without you."

The hard grit in her voice told Luke she wasn't going to stand for any shady tricks. Josie yawned and stretched.

"I think I need to get you to bed, Miss Sleepyhead."

"Luke, please sleep in the house. I won't get a bit of rest if you don't. I've grown used to having you near and I need it now. Noah does too and would say so if he could speak." She lightly grazed his cheek with a finger. "Please. I've never begged you for anything." A frown formed. "Well, only a few times."

"Stoker put you up to this, didn't he?" The question held frustration and anger but he couldn't help it. He knew Stoker's skill at manipulation. After all, how far could you trust a man who'd deceive his own son and marry him off to a woman sight unseen? Thankfully, Houston had fallen in love with Lara and had become the best father he could be to Lara's daughter, Gracie. Still, Luke didn't want Stoker trying to meddle with anything in *his* life.

"I haven't spoken to Stoker. I swear. I peeked in on Noah and your father was asleep in the chair beside the bed. Luke, he was holding the boy's hand and Rowdy had curled up in his lap. I think he's taken quite a shine to them."

Now that he had to see. The tough man who laid down the law with an iron fist didn't seem the type to get close to shaggy-haired runaway boys and scruffy mutts.

"All right. Enough. But I refuse to sleep in a bed." To do so would be too hard. The only single way he could stay here was to separate himself however he could.

For their sakes, he'd do whatever he had to in order to keep this part of his life from touching his family, as he'd kept it away from his mother all those years before her death.

Even if it meant appearing to be an ungrateful bastard.

As they walked back past the row of businesses, Luke told her what he knew of each. "Over there is the schoolhouse for the ranch kids. Sam's wife, Sierra, taught there until they married and moved to Lost Point. I wish you could meet her. She's something."

"How far away is Lost Point?"

"About five hours, more or less. Stoker likes having Sam nearby. My other brother, Houston, lives out a mile or two on the ranch. I'm sure we'll see him tomorrow morning."

"You like your brothers," she stated.

Luke didn't have to mull that over. "Yes. Yes, I do. I like having people to belong to, knowing if I need them they'll come running, no matter the time or place."

"I'm glad. Everyone needs someone. Even me," she said softly.

"Yep, and for now I guess I'm it." He took her hand. "I want to show you something."

He led her on past the town and around the side of the headquarters.

Josie gasped and stopped. "Oh, Luke. It's beautiful."

Ahead of them, near the tall flagpole where the Texas flag would fly come morning, stood two tall poles, a huge bronze star suspended by heavy chains between them. Moonlight shone through cutouts in each star's tip and reflected on the ground in a lacy pattern.

"I've probably never seen anything so breathtaking in my whole life." Josie moved closer. "It's just unbelievable."

"The first time I saw it I stopped and stared for a good bit. I've learned a lot about my father from the things that mean so much to him—the Texas flag he flies, this bronze star that represents what he cherishes, and his boys. Family is everything to the man."

"As it should be to you too, Luke Weston." Josie glared

at him. "I just don't get you. If I had a place like this to go to, I'd never leave. But no, you'd rather be riding off to God-knows-where, dodging hot lead and getting shot half to death."

"When and if I ever get my life straightened out, I'll claim this land. Until then, I'll only be passing through." It was nice to know he had some reason for living. He'd never take any of this for granted either. The Lone Star was special.

Josie playfully tugged him forward. "Come on."

Luke watched as she lay down, positioning herself over the lacy pattern on the grass. She stretched out with her arms high over her head, her golden hair fanning out around her. She had to be as crazy as a loon, but she was his crazy lady. She was wild, adventurous, and bold, and everything that he wasn't.

And he wanted her. Oh God, how he wanted Josie Morgan.

When he lay down next to her, she reached for his hand and threaded her fingers through his. He loved the feel of her velvet skin, the softness that reminded him of Angelina.

"My brothers told me of a legend associated with this land."

"What kind of legend?"

"Some kind of old saying. They claim that if a man sleeps beneath the Texas star he'll learn his true worth. Of course, my brothers don't put much stock in it."

Josie stared deep into his eyes. "The legend is nice, Luke, but you already know your worth. You're a good, honorable man."

"And you got this sage wisdom in all of three days?"

"In the first hour we met. If you weren't a man of honor, you'd have left me tied to that tree and kept on riding to catch Ned Sweeney. Some things you instinctively know right off. Like a certain smell. I knew Reno's men and Noah's uncle were no good because I could smell their putrid breath, all rancid, like they're rotting inside. Sometimes you just know."

"I have to agree." He raised himself up on an elbow and pressed his mouth to her soft lips.

He knew that no matter how this thing with Josie went, he'd be forever lost without this wonderful, maddening, crazy woman.

She was everything he wanted—temper, six-shooter, and all.

But fate had a way of snatching things from his grasp.

Fourteen

Boot heels struck a hardwood floor like shots from a Sharps .50 caliber buffalo rifle. Luke jerked awake and grabbed his Colt, tossing aside a soft wool blanket. For a second, he struggled to remember where he was, but a quick glance at his surroundings assured him he was in the office at the Lone Star headquarters.

The memory of Stoker covering him during the night flooded back. Luke had feigned sleep, only raising an eyelid enough to see the huge man tiptoeing into the office. The sight lingered in his mind. But it was the care with which Stoker had spread the blanket over him that would stay with him forever.

Luke had slept under the watchful gaze of his mother in the portrait above. And also, it seemed, that of his father.

The backs of his eyes burned. He'd missed her gentle touch and hadn't realized exactly how much until this. His mother had stopped her tender nurturing when he was twelve and he'd told her he was too big for that. The hurt in her eyes swam in his vision. He'd been so very foolish, thinking she'd always be there.

"*Estúpido*," he muttered angrily.

The knob on the door turned. Luke rolled from the sofa to his feet and slid his Colt back into the holster as Houston Legend strolled in.

The large form of his brother blocked the morning light spilling through the doorway. "Thought I saw that black gelding of yours, Luke. I was hoping you'd come to visit."

"Not by choice." Luke tucked in his shirt and strapped on his gun belt. "Needed a doctor and no time to waste."

"Who's hurt?"

"A runaway boy I found. He's bleeding inside."

"I sense a story there. Most likely someone's dead." Houston twirled the dove-gray Stetson in his hands. "Which you can tell me about over coffee. Had any yet?"

"Nope." Luke picked up his hat. "Know where I might get some?"

"Just might. 'Course, if you've gotten Pa riled, we'd be safer building a fire in the corral and making our own." After scanning the room and taking in the blanket, Houston faced him squarely. "Our beds not good enough for you?"

"Your beds are fine for civilized folk." Luke let a grin form. "You know, you and Sam sound more like Stoker every day. I expect you'll soon start to act like him too. He's not the only one who tries to meddle."

"Well, you haven't done that good a job tending your life lately. We think you could use a hand." Houston adjusted Luke's hat like he was a kid and patted his black vest.

"You do, do you? Want to take a walk in my shoes?"

Houston chuckled. "Nope. They won't fit. Besides, my body can't take all those bullet holes."

Luke's chest swelled with gratitude at the simple banter, at having such a home to come to. He clasped one of his brother's hands and pulled him into a quick hug before releasing him.

Houston stepped back to study him, as though stunned by Luke's uncharacteristic show of affection.

A few minutes later, they walked into the cozy breakfast room. Stoker gave Luke a knowing nod and handed him a cup. Luke reached for the coffeepot and filled both his and Houston's. Settled at the small table, Luke finished explaining the last few days to Houston.

Stoker blew on the hot liquid and took a sip from his cup. "Doc just checked on the boy. He said the bleeding inside shows signs of stopping. So far, no more swelling."

Relief swept through Luke. "That's great. The boy's been through pure hell. I have some more good news. Josie also told me that Doc is sure her memory will return. At some point. It sounds promising."

"What are you going to do with them, son? I mean when you ride out, as you and I both know you will." Stoker pinned Luke with a piercing stare.

Luke squirmed. He hated the way his father had of looking down into places he didn't want him seeing. The secrets he hid were buried deep, along with fledgling hopes and dreams, too new to stand any scrutiny. At least not Stoker's meddling kind.

"Stop it, Pa, don't badger him. Just be glad he's here," Houston said firmly. "I'm sure he has a plan. Right, Luke?"

Steam from the hot brew wafted up into Luke's face. "It's asking a lot of you to take care of the boy for a while but I don't see any other way. Doc won't let me move him. Would you—"

"Of course I will." Stoker leaned toward Luke, his elbow on the table. "I'll be happy to look after the boy. I don't know how much clearer I can make it that I welcome you, son. Anytime, day or night. What about the woman?"

"Josie laid down the law." Luke chuckled. "Threatened to put a bullet in me if I leave without her."

He'd never forget the sight of her standing there spitting mad in the moonlight like some golden-haired angel warrior, smoke curling from her pistol, anger flashing like daggers from her eyes. He had no doubt she'd come within a hair of leaving a few bullet holes in his hide.

Then he'd showed her the bronze star, and that moment changed everything. Including him.

"She hit you?" Stoker refilled his cup, his mouth twitching.

"Nope." Luke reached for a hot biscuit. "The bullet kicking up dirt around my boot gave me a new direction."

"Smart woman." Stoker took a plate of bacon and eggs from Cook and grabbed the salt. "I like her thinking. Maybe I'll take a page from her book." He shot Luke a cutting glance that made him want to find a hole to crawl into. Luke had seen his share of fearsome men, and none of them held a candle to Stoker Legend.

Curling a hand around his cup, Luke silently watched his bear of a father. Last night's talk stood between them like a fragment of a shattered life that a man couldn't claim. He wished he could tell Stoker he loved him, wished he could be the kind of son Sam and Houston were. And dammit, he wished he had his brothers' easy way of talking to the man. But too much water had washed under the bridge and eroded the supports. Nothing was left but silt and rock.

Putting aside all his bluster and thunder, Stoker Legend was as tough as a piece of dried boot leather, and he took no grief from any man. Part of Luke still couldn't help thinking the money and land Stoker offered him were too little, too late.

In spite of everything, the bitterness of doing without lingered. The nights he went to bed hungry and cold, the days of watching his mother toil over tubs of scalding hot water, then when ready to drop, ironed and folded the laundry.

If his mother wouldn't go to Stoker for help, maybe he shouldn't either. In a way, Luke felt he was betraying her.

What would she say if she saw him sitting at Stoker's table? Eating his food? He imagined she'd be happy he was finally home. At least he hoped so.

Luke pushed aside the nagging thoughts and reached for the coffeepot. "You and Josie could've been cut from the same cloth. That's one determined woman."

"Nothing wrong with a strong filly." Stoker gave a hard nod. "And nothing wrong with wanting to keep my sons within eyesight."

Luke's spine stiffened. If he didn't watch it, his father would bulldog his way over the top of him as he'd done to both Sam and Houston, and sweep him up in the tumult.

"Glory to Pete, Pa," Houston growled. "You've turned into a regular mother hen. Might as well put an apron on you and be done with it. I thought you learned a long time ago to let us be. You can't keep Luke tied here any more than you can Sam and me."

Glowering, Stoker shoveled a bite of eggs into his mouth. "Are you calling me weak?"

"Nope." Cook set down Houston's plate and he dug in. "Just saying you need a project, something to occupy you. Maybe something with ruffles."

"Of all the fool things to say. I have work to keep me busy." Stoker pointed his fork at Houston. "Namely, making sure this land stays as strong as the day I plunked down roots forty-three years ago."

Deep emotion flickered across the faces of his father and brother. Luke watched them closely. Despite their gruff words, subtle displays of affection rippled between them that were as hard to miss as the width of the mighty Red River. They shared a deep bond that was borne from being family.

The price of Luke's mistakes had never been clearer than at this moment.

Maybe he would always be the outsider, the black sheep...the one any decent family would have to hide.

Cook brought in a fresh pot of coffee and went back with the empty one.

Stoker wiped his mouth with a napkin. "Luke, I never noticed how much you resemble your mother until now. You have the same black hair and high cheekbones. You're almost the spitting image."

"Those who knew her often remarked on it," Luke mumbled.

Houston glared. "Don't say that too loud, Pa. We don't want to give the people who make the wanted posters any ideas. So far none have Luke's picture on them, and that's a relief."

The air stirred and Josie strolled into the breakfast room carrying Rowdy. She looked rested, finally, clad in a pretty lavender dress, her golden hair curling around her shoulders. All three men jerked to their feet. Luke finally dragged his eyes from her and pulled out her chair.

"My goodness, this is a fine morning. Thank you, Luke." Her hand met his and sent warmth coursing through him. The dog growled at him and bared his teeth as though warning Luke to keep his distance.

Luke gave the mutt a steely-eyed glare and introduced Houston as the men returned to their seats and their breakfast.

Houston reached across the table to shake her hand. "Nice meeting you, Josie."

"Same here. I'm glad to know Luke's family." She lowered Rowdy to the floor. "This poor little fellow's hungry, but still didn't want to leave Noah's side. I had to coax him to come with me."

Luke wondered if she'd threatened to shoot the dog too.

"Cook will fix him something. She does it for our mutts every morning; no trouble to throw in a little extra," Houston said, rising. He went to the door and spoke to Cook then returned. "Be ready in a moment."

"I trust you slept well, my dear." Stoker slabbed butter onto a hot biscuit so thick it dribbled off onto his plate.

A smile twitched at the corner of Josie's mouth. "I think I died. I can't remember when I've slept so soundly." She frowned. "I shouldn't keep saying things like that when my memory only goes back three days." Her gaze met Luke's and softened. "I owe Luke my life. Even though finding me threw a kink in his plans, he never hesitated one second. I was in bad need of help and he showed me such extraordinary kindness. Saved me from the men who tied me up too. He even named me Rose right off because he saw how much I desperately needed to be someone."

Stoker roughly patted her hand. "My son knows how to treat a lady, especially a pretty one like you. It doesn't matter what name you go by. Both fit you."

Luke watched a becoming blush color Josie's cheeks. It was clear how much Stoker's compliments meant to her.

"Thank you, Mr. Legend," she murmured.

"Nope." Stoker shook his finger at her. "I'm Stoker. And I want you to know that you have a home here anytime you want to claim it." He pointed his fork at Luke. "Maybe you can talk some sense into my son."

"Now, Pa," Houston said. "I thought you were going to stop pressuring Luke."

"Ain't pressure I have in mind. Just want my long-lost son close by to share in the running of this spread. I have more than enough to go around. This is Legend land run by Legend men, and by God that's the way it's going to be," Stoker thundered and slammed his fist down.

Rowdy yelped and ran to Josie. She murmured soothing words to stop his quivering.

Unperturbed, Cook pushed through the door with a bowl filled with some kind of meat. The hefty woman must've heard and seen everything over the years, since nothing seemed to faze her now. Josie set Rowdy on the floor and Cook plunked down the bowl.

After getting Josie's breakfast order, Cook disappeared back into her domain.

Josie grinned at Luke. "Is it always this way?"

"Yep. Pretty much." He glanced at her hand resting on the table, memories swirling in his mind like colorful autumn leaves. Last night, lying in the moonlight beneath the huge bronze star with their fingers intertwined, had been one of the most special times he'd ever known. Not since Angelina had he felt this much peace.

God, Josie had looked so beautiful, bathed in the moon's silvery rays. But she looked even more breathtaking now in the breakfast room with the sun striking her hair, creating a halo around her head.

Not that he would ever call her saintly. He suppressed a grin. But that's what appealed to him. She was real and you got exactly what you saw, without any apology for shortcomings. The lady stood nose to nose with him, daring him, not afraid to voice her opinions even when he glared.

"Luke?"

He jerked his head toward Houston. "What?"

"Just wondering about your plans," Houston said. "I'd like to talk before you ride out."

"I have to check on the boy and get the horses ready. I need to cover some ground today, but I can spare a little time for catching up while I wait for Josie to get ready." He remembered Houston's little girl. "How's Gracie these days?"

Houston chuckled. "Still ruling the roost and laying down the law. She's quite a general at one and a half years old."

Luke shook his head. "I pity you. Just think how bossy she'll be by the time she's grown. And that pretty wife, Lara?"

"Sam doesn't know this yet, but she's in the family way."

"Congratulations. That's wonderful."

"Maybe you'll have a son this time, Houston." Stoker laughed. "He'd better be a tough one—Gracie will make everyone toe the line."

"That she will," Houston agreed. "I won't have to keep my shotgun handy when suitors come courting. She'll handle them."

His brother's glow told Luke how much having a son would mean to him. Houston was as driven as Stoker to keep the Legend name and Lone Star Ranch going for generations to come. A huge part of Luke yearned for that too. Somehow, he had to make his mark, leave something lasting. Much more than a life of crime and a .45 that had seen far too much use.

A sudden yearning rose with a surprising realization.

He wanted a piece of this land.

To be a part of this legacy.

To be a Legend and wear the name proudly.

Fifteen

LUKE HAD THE UNCOMFORTABLE SENSATION THAT HIS CHAIR had been struck by a jagged bolt of lightning. But the hunger rising up was for more than just land and a name. He had to leave something lasting that his family could speak of with pride. He had to matter to someone. Luke glanced at the faces around the breakfast table. Lord knows he hadn't yet given them anything to brag about.

Them or any children he might have.

Josie folded her hands in her lap and her pretty, hazel eyes took on a faraway look. "Houston, you're one lucky man. I often wonder if I have children waiting somewhere. I love kids. Maybe one day I'll find out what I left behind."

"You will," Houston said with a wink. "There's no one better than my brother to help you."

"I couldn't agree more," she said. Cook brought her food and she picked up her fork. "What time will we leave, Luke? I want to talk to Noah and change clothes before we head out."

"How about two hours? I want to visit with him too."

"It's perfect." She flashed him a smile that quickened his heartbeat before turning back to her plate of food.

Stoker gulped the last of his coffee and rose. "I have some work to do but I'll be back to see you and Josie off."

Houston shot Luke a glance. "How about we talk?"

Josie seemed to sense Luke's hesitation. "Go on, you two. I'm a big girl. I'm sure you have things to discuss."

Luke nodded. "All right. I'll be down at the corral if you need anything."

He and Houston strode out. They didn't speak until they left headquarters.

"You old rascal! What's this between you and Josie?" Houston bumped him with his shoulder. "She's pretty, but she must not be too smart to take up with someone like you."

"Hold it right there. If we did have something going, which we don't by the way, she'd show uncommon good sense." Luke loved the teasing, the lighthearted moments with his brothers. The fact that they included him filled something deep inside.

Luke sobered. "I ran into Clay Colby a month or two ago."

"How's he doing? I think about him from time to time and wonder if he's hung up his gun." Houston tugged his hat lower against the early morning sun. "Even if he was an outlaw and gunslinger, he made a hell of a drover for me on that cattle drive to Dodge City last year."

Luke nodded. "I'd ride the trail with him any day. He didn't make it, Houston. Sure, he bought that little spread he wanted, but men looking to make a name wouldn't let him work the land or put in crops. He's drifting again."

They reached the corral and Luke propped one booted foot on the bottom rail.

Houston stared into the distance. "I was afraid of that." Deep sadness dripped from the quiet words.

"You know it'll be the same for me. How can I ever hope to make a life here? These people on the ranch don't know what it's like to live a life that's only violence. I shudder to imagine their reaction to having an outlaw in their midst. Tell me that, brother."

"Wish I knew, Luke. Dammit!" Houston leaned against the rail. "You know Pa, Sam, and me will fight them for you and send the devils right back where they came from with their tails between their legs."

Quick anger flared. "I don't hide behind my family. Not behind anyone. I fight my own battles, head-on like I always have. Nor have I ever run. Although a few times I should've."

The day Angie died flashed into his mind.

The same anger flashed from Houston's eyes. "That's not what I meant and you know it. We'll fight alongside, not take over."

Luke snorted. "Stoker not taking over? I've gotta see that." The man had his finger in everything.

"Okay, not a good choice of words either." Houston pushed back his hat with a forefinger. "We'll help you build a life, but you have to want it. Want it way down deep in your soul. You have to want it so damn bad you don't care if you eat, sleep, or breathe."

"I never cared much before when it was just me. I accepted trouble as coming part and parcel with the kind of life I chose." Luke let out a weary sigh that seemed to rise all the way from his toes. "But now—now that I have you, Sam, and Stoker, I need more." So much that it scared the bejesus out of him.

Because now he stood to lose the family he'd never had if he failed.

That vulnerability instilled fear so deep inside it made him tremble.

But should he expect anything less?

He'd charged headlong into his fate the first time he'd taken a man's life. There was no question Jarvis Niles, a customer Elena Montoya washed and ironed for, had deserved to die. He'd humiliated Luke's mother in a way no one ever had a right to do. And all over shirts! Angry that she hadn't laundered his shirts exactly the way he wanted, that rich, arrogant bastard had made her crawl across the floor on her hands and knees and lick his muddy boots.

Only a kid then, Luke hadn't realized the high price of taking a life.

Now that he was grown, he saw he might've handled things differently. Then again, maybe not.

Sixteen years later, Luke's blood still boiled.

His mother never licked another man's boots again.

Next to him, Houston leaned against the rail. "Don't let anything stand in your way. By God, you have to fight like a demon, Luke."

"I do that every day just trying to stay alive. There's a man out there somewhere looking to kill me right now. Munroe O'Keefe has sworn to put me six feet under by any means necessary. Bragged about doing it. And he's just one in a hundred." Luke scrubbed the back of his neck and let out a weary sigh. "I get so damn tired of looking over my shoulder, listening for the sound of the bullet that will send me to hell. Waiting for it to rip into me."

"That's no way to live, Luke. Gotta be something better. Has to be. How is the search for Ned Sweeney going?" Houston asked. "We've sent out hundreds of telegrams. One person says he's here, another there. Nothing has panned out."

"I was an hour away from catching him when I rode up on Josie. Two of Reno Kidd's men were there with a Lone Star wagon and team of horses."

"Sam told me. They were stolen," Houston said. "A ranch hand named Max disappeared 'round the same time. I sent someone out there and they found his body riddled with holes. Sam and I think Reno Kidd and his men probably killed him. Maybe for the horses and wagon. Might've intended to sell them."

The likelihood had also entered Luke's head. Reno was an outlaw of opportunity. He stole everything he came across and killed the same way. No point to it, no rhyme or reason.

"Was Max hauling anything of value?" Luke asked.

"That's the thing. Max was taking a load of posts to the southwest section of the ranch to build a holding corral for some wild horses we're trying to catch. Nothing to kill anyone over. Never found the posts, though."

Luke's thoughts tumbled like rocks down the side of a

mountain, gaining speed as they went. The remote land was the perfect place for an ambush. "I'm thinking they saw Max alone. Finding nothing of value to steal, they decided to take the wagon and horses. They probably didn't think beyond that moment. Reno Kidd is rotten clear down to the soles of his feet."

Houston swung around. "Why did they have the whiskey and rifles in the wagon when you found it? Where did they get those?"

"I'm sure they robbed someone else that day. Or the merchandise could've belonged to Josie and her husband. They could've been hauling those crates and Winchesters to a mercantile they owned." Luke wouldn't know for sure until Josie's memory came back. "The gang was probably liquored up real good. Reno and his gang appear to have gone on some kind of murdering, stealing rampage."

"Why take Josie? Why not kill her?"

"For insurance, is what Reno's men said. In case they were caught, they had her to bargain with." A thought flashed through his head. "The posse claimed Josie killed her husband. But who told them that? Josie was out cold. I have to get to Doan's Crossing. I need to find Reno and his gang and beat some answers out of them."

"Don't we all," Houston said dryly.

"Yeah." Luke prayed he could wring the truth out of someone. He had something special in mind for Reno. He'd dispense some more Legend justice. Luke liked making wrongdoers pay.

He liked it a whole lot.

Sixteen

Noah opened his eyes and slowly looked around before he focused on her. "Where am I, Josie?"

She leaned forward from her chair beside the bed and took his hand. His voice was weak but that was probably natural after being so sick. Relief swept through her that he knew her. Maybe he was going to make it.

"We're at Luke's father's place—the Lone Star Ranch. You've been very sick. I was real worried about you. Luke too."

Rowdy crawled up on Noah's chest to lick the boy's face. The little dog appeared to have been mighty worried too. Sorrow still filled the dog's large, brown eyes.

"Uncle Bert can't get me?"

"Nope. You're safe. Luke killed him, remember?"

Noah drew his brows together. "Everything's all jumbled up. I'm glad he's dead."

"Me too." She felt his forehead and found it cool. "Are you in any pain?"

"My stomach kinda hurts."

"It'll get better. You're a survivor, Noah. Like me. We've been through a lot but we're still here."

The door opened and Luke sauntered in. She loved the slow, loose-jointed way he moved, a steadiness that could change to lightning-fast when the need arose. He met her gaze and her heart pounded. He'd stopped shaving so he could disguise himself after they left here, and the dark growth along his jaw projected danger—the lethal kind. He reminded her of a coiled snake, lying silently in wait, ready to strike with little warning.

His brow lifted and he scowled as he took in her pants and shirt. Disappointment that she'd changed out of the dress?

Maybe.

Probably.

Of a surety.

All of a sudden, she yearned to be a lady. To take a bath every day and fix her hair—to be more feminine. Not to have to worry about a killer with dirty-yellow hair and brown teeth. Or her stolen memory.

"Hi, Luke," Noah said, breaking the spell.

"Noah, I'm glad to see you come around." Luke moved to the bed, and Josie found herself struggling to breathe. His large presence seemed to consume all the air in the room. "How do you feel, boy?" he asked.

"Better." Noah glanced down and mumbled, "Sorry I made trouble. Didn't mean to."

The bed sagged when Luke sat down next to Noah. "Never apologize for what someone else does. Your uncle bears the blame for the problem. Understand?"

Noah nodded.

"I don't know if Josie told you, but we're riding out," Luke said gently.

"Where are my clothes?" Noah tried to rise but Luke held him down. Josie's eyes stung. Even hurt, the boy wanted to come with them.

"I'm afraid you're too banged up." Luke patted the lump in the covers where Noah's leg was. "For now, I have to leave you here. It's too dangerous anyway. My... Stoker Legend is a real nice man and he'll take good care of you until I get back."

Josie's anger rose that he hadn't included her in the coming back part. He had to be thinking he could get rid of her. "I'll be back too, Noah. You belong to us now."

She wasted the glare she shot Luke because he totally ignored her, smoothing out the quilt with his long, elegant fingers. Those fingers that had traced the line of her jaw and brushed her cheek as though she was worth something. At least in the dark of night. In the daytime, he appeared to think differently.

A silly grin covered Noah's face. "Belonging—I like that."

Stoker entered the room and had evidently overheard the conversation. He walked to the bed. "You don't have to worry, son. You also have a home here if you want it. We need each other, you and me. My boys are grown now and I'm told I need something to occupy my time."

Josie watched Luke meet his father's piercing stare and something passed between them. Maybe the glance said things they couldn't put into words. Maybe it was a start for both father and outcast son. The longing on both their faces held promise.

Take this morning over breakfast. She'd noticed subtle gestures and glances that spoke of Luke's thirst to claim his father's love. The almost touch of his hand when he passed Stoker the coffeepot. The way Luke had stared at his father from beneath lowered lids when he thought no one was watching. And the quiet respect in Luke's voice when he spoke to Stoker.

Noah appeared to be the bridge they needed and it could lead to healing. Maybe for all three.

Damn Luke anyway! Why he kept putting up walls around himself she didn't know. He was a god-awful stubborn cuss. He'd dug in his heels so deep she doubted a team of mules, twenty men, and two boys could pull him out.

But his hungry kisses had lit a raging fire inside her.

The memory of last night in the moonlight when he took her in his arms and lowered his lips to hers flooded her mind. He'd vowed to one day take her somewhere private and make passionate love to her.

He'd said he wanted her and she damn sure wanted him. She silently cursed the missing past that barred her from finding heaven in Luke's bed. But she knew he was right. They couldn't give in to passion. Not yet.

Of one thing she was certain. Even if the murdered man at Doan's Crossing was not her husband, even if she found out that she was married to another man, that couldn't quench her love for Luke. The handsome outlaw wasn't the sort of man a woman could forget.

She saw how much he loved kids. For example, now he was plumping the pillow, making sure Noah was comfortable.

The boy squinted up at Stoker. "Mr. Legend, thank you for the offer. I'll help you until I get well, but I can't promise to stay here after that."

"Noah, call him Stoker." Luke's hand slid down the boy's hair before stepping back.

"My son's right. I'm not mister anybody. I understand that me and this place don't much feel like home yet, but maybe that'll change one day." Stoker draped an arm across Luke's shoulders. "Cook has a burlap sack of food ready for you and Miss Josie."

"Thanks. I didn't want you to go to any trouble." Luke appeared uncomfortable next to his father.

Stoker sighed. "It's a sad day when a father can't provide a little food for his son."

The sadness etched on Stoker Legend's face made Josie's chest hurt. "Thank you so much, sir. It'll come in handy down the trail." She stood, told Noah to be good, and hugged him. Unshed tears blurred her vision. She turned away before she made a blubbering mess of herself.

The boy was the only person who'd recognized her. He'd given her back her name and told her she'd been kind to him. She wouldn't forget that. True that he was the link between her and her past, but also the living proof that she was a good person. She needed to know that.

Luke told her to wait downstairs and disappeared into another room with a bundle under his arm. When he stepped out onto the porch where she sat with Stoker, she barely recognized him. With his long hair, dark stubble, buckskin pants, and fringed shirt, he had transformed into a rugged buffalo hunter. She took in his lean form hidden beneath the baggy clothes, and his eyes crinkled at the corners from the smile he wore. His grim, dark scowls were gone. He'd changed before her eyes and she understood why. A buffalo hunter didn't invite second glances, wasn't a man who had to worry about a bullet ending his life at any second.

Few would know the outlaw in this disguise.

Or her either in the serape Luke had made.

A ranch hand brought their horses and she noticed a thick bedroll tied behind the roan's saddle, compliments of Stoker, she assumed. She stuck her foot in the stirrup and Luke placed his hands on her backside and boosted her up. The heat of his touch burned through the layers of clothing and she felt a yearning rise up so strong she trembled.

Did he feel this way too?

Or was she simply one more obligation? Maybe she'd read too much into those magical kisses under the beautiful Texas stars.

"You'll go near Lost Point." Stoker handed a burlap bag full of food to Luke. "A good place to stretch your legs. Sam and Sierra would love to see you. And keep dodging those bullets, son."

"I plan on it. I'll try to stop and see Sam if I can." Luke tied the bag to the saddle horn. "Take care of Noah for me."

"That kid might just be the best thing to happen to me lately. He needs me and I damn sure need him. Maybe he'll even grow to appreciate what I can do for him, unlike some." Stoker turned to Josie and winked. "Lots of luck to you. You'll always be welcome here, pretty lady. Don't forget that."

She thanked him for his warm hospitality. "Tell Houston that next time I come, I want to meet Lara. We'll have a cup of tea and solve all the problems of the world."

Suddenly Houston galloped up and reined to a stop. Neither he nor Luke spoke. The look that passed between them and the simple clasp of hands said it all.

They shared an unbreakable bond.

Josie had probably never witnessed such love. Her throat tightened. Luke's standoffish attitude with his father didn't apply to his brother. With Houston, everything seemed easy and free.

This Legend family had what she wanted. They didn't know what a special thing they shared. Wherever she came from, she knew it was far from this. She'd already learned her father was involved in something shady and God only knew what else waited for her when her memory returned.

A question crossed her mind. Did her father love her? If not in the way Stoker did Luke, she hoped he did a little at least. Luke didn't know how lucky he was.

She prayed he'd come to understand Stoker before it was too late.

Before someone put a bullet in him.

Before there would be no more second chances.

Making better time than they thought they would, they did stop in Lost Point after all. To rest the horses, Luke said, although Josie suspected he needed to see Sam.

She looped the reins around the hitching post in front of the sheriff's office. A glance at the businesses showed some newly built, and the older ones—some looking old enough to have been there since the town was founded—had fresh coats of whitewash.

Lost Point was a town full of promise.

An old woman sat on the boardwalk, pressing yellow flowers into the moist dirt of a planter. A crutch lay beside the bench. Josie's gaze went to the missing foot beneath the hem of the woman's dress and she had trouble swallowing. She couldn't imagine how many difficulties the woman faced being unable to walk.

A thought struck Josie. Everyone seemed to be missing something. For her, it was her memory. For this woman, her foot. For Luke, the missing part was even greater. He didn't have the ability to let anyone care for him—other than his brothers.

Why not her and why not Stoker? The answer eluded her.

"Howdy." The old lady smiled. "It's nice to see visitors." She peered closely at Luke. "Ain't I seen you before?"

The buffalo hunter disguise probably threw her. Josie grinned. It would throw a lot of people, she suspected.

"Yes, Miss Sally. I'm Sam's brother, Luke." He introduced Josie and sat down on the bench. "This town is sure thriving. I wouldn't have given you a plugged nickel for your chances when Felix Bardo and his gang took it over. How long has it been now?"

Sally grinned. "Two years. We've been sprucing it up a mite. We couldn't have gotten shed of that riffraff if not for Sheriff Sam, you, and the rest of the Legends."

Josie gained a lot in simply listening. Whatever had taken place here, Luke and his brothers had played a huge part.

"One thing you have to know about us, Miss Sally. We can't let lawless men hurt people. There's justice and then there's Legend justice."

"That's the onliest kind," Sally agreed.

"How are you getting on, ma'am?"

The woman shrugged. "Ain't complaining."

The office door opened and Sam strode out. "Josie, I'm glad to see you. Sierra had the baby last night. A boy." He stared at Luke for a long minute before recognizing him.

"Congratulations, *hermano*." Luke slapped his back. "Just what you wanted—a boy to carry on the Legend name."

"Yep." Ten freshly sharpened razors couldn't have scraped that grin off Sam's face.

"I'm very happy for you, Sam," Josie said. "What did you name him?"

"Sierra insisted on Sam Jr." He rubbed the back of his neck. "I don't know if that's so good, especially if he gets some of my wild notions. Me and Pa butted heads like two billy goats."

"It's a fine name, brother," Luke said quietly. "You turned out all right, and I suspect Junior will too. He comes from fine stock. When can we meet him?"

"Is now too soon?" Sam asked. "I can't wait to show him off. Hector wanted to stay home from school today but Sierra made him go anyway. The boy is crazy about his new brother."

"I hope he always feels that way." Luke's comment sounded kinda odd to Josie, but Sam didn't seem to notice.

Walking a short distance, Sam stopped at a pretty, white-washed house with a white fence in front. An explosion of flowers of all kinds and colors filled the yard, creating a beautiful rainbow. Josie gasped in delight. Someone had taken a great deal of pains with the house and yard.

The rooms inside showed the same attention to detail. Sam seated them in the parlor while he went to speak to his wife.

"I hope I find a house like this waiting for me," Josie said. "It makes my heart smile."

Luke nodded. "My mother loved flowers. We used to walk in the cemetery each Sunday and remark at the pretty roses and whatnot. I was going to plant her some, but never got to it."

"I'm sure she didn't find you lacking, Luke. Mothers love their sons no matter what. Any failure is only in your mind." Josie laid her hand on his. If only she knew how to brighten his mood. He'd slipped further into a black hole with their visit to the Lone Star.

Sam returned. "Sierra can't wait to see you. Come on back."

Josie was struck by the dark-haired beauty holding the new babe. She'd likely never seen a more serene woman. Sam introduced them and Josie shook her hand. "I'm very happy to finally meet you. I love your name."

Sierra laughed. "My parents named me for the mountain range. Everyone else finds it odd. Hello, Luke."

He bent to kiss her cheek. "Hi yourself, *dulce*. I see you've been busy."

"Just a little." Sierra quirked an eyebrow. "When did you become a buffalo hunter?"

"When I found the possibility of getting hung a tad too painful."

Josie listened to their teasing banter, finding that she didn't like the soft way he spoke to Sierra Legend. Whatever the two had shared was like a silent, ghostly presence in the room.

Had they once been lovers?

She couldn't rule that out. Whatever the bond between them, it had been formed by something deep and lasting.

"Shoot, I was about to haul you into a cell for being a vagrant until I heard your voice, big brother." Sam motioned to some chairs. "But then I recalled you saying you sometimes disguise yourself as a buffalo hunter. It sure works."

"I'm glad." Luke stood until Josie sat down. "This getup has saved my life many a day."

Sierra handed Luke the babe. "Time to get started on your uncle duties. Just don't get any lice on Sam Jr. or you and me will have problems. And I'll not have you teaching him to use a Colt either."

"Yes, ma'am." Luke spared a grin. "I do believe I've had the law laid down to me. I won't start him on his lessons until you give the word."

The babe could've been a basket of eggs for all the undue pains Luke took. Josie watched him settle the tiny bundle in the crook of an arm, his large hand bracing the child's bottom. There was something about the hardened outlaw, this man who wouldn't let anyone care for him, gently holding so fragile a life. She blinked hard and swallowed. He didn't hide his feelings about those he protected, so why did he push away others' feelings for him?

Did he see himself as so unworthy?

His words flooded her memory. *Make no mistake—I've killed and I will again. I have darkness inside me that likes dispensing justice.*

And yet he'd protected her, and had tucked Noah and

a ragged dog with a chewed-off ear into his heart. A sigh rose inside her. Luke Weston's moods would challenge the smartest minds in the land. She doubted someone like her would ever figure him out.

Even so, Josie knew he was something special. She couldn't deny the fire that blazed inside her, scorching a path straight to her heart. She yearned for him, to know this tall outlaw. He carried himself with such honor, and the need for justice burned fierce inside him. No matter the danger to himself, he'd plow into any situation with his gun blazing.

What she'd found—the kisses and sweet caresses that made her heart pound—meant more than this fool's journey she'd embarked upon. Who was she kidding? Even if she did find where she came from, it didn't mean she belonged there now.

Suddenly, she had an overwhelming urge to abandon the search for her past. To find answers could mean she might lose Luke Weston forever...and he was not something she could ever give up.

Not now. Not in this lifetime.

Seventeen

Both Doan's Trading Post and Jonathan Doan's house were dark by the time Luke and Josie arrived.

The two structures were the only ones within sight, though dozens of campfires dotted the rocky area all around. Most belonged to men and women either waiting to cross the river or ones who'd arrived on this side too late in the day to go on. Sounds drifted toward Luke—quiet voices in conversation, a baby's cry, a barking dog.

The crossing was little more than a temporary camp. Maybe someday someone would build a town, but for now, the fires of weary travelers and the trading post were all that anyone needed.

A mile farther down the road lay the ferry that carted folks and their animals across the Red River during daylight hours.

A slight detour to lose Munroe O'Keefe, who'd picked up Luke's trail at Lost Point, had put their arrival later than anticipated. The brash, young gun must've had Lost Point staked out after somehow learning that Sam was Luke's brother. How, Luke didn't know, but it posed a problem.

They now hid in the dark shadows of a large oak, watching the scene. Suddenly, Luke spied the man weaving through the tents, leading his horse. He yanked Josie deeper into the shadows and bit back a curse.

Munroe O'Keefe.

"What now?" Josie pressed close.

"That man walking toward us. His name is Munroe O'Keefe. Take a good look. Stay away from him. He wants me dead so he can become famous. The fool. He started trailing us after we left Sam's. Thought I lost him, though."

"Him?" Josie snorted. "He's nothing but an ugly, sawed-off runt. You can handle him."

Maybe so, but he didn't want to do it here. Luke peered around the tree trunk at a large group of Texas Rangers sitting next to a low fire. His job had just become more dangerous. He'd give anything to know what they discussed.

Behind him, Josie nudged his elbow. "Well? What do you see?"

"Lawmen. The man they claim you murdered must've been someone awfully important to draw this much attention." Someone rich, maybe, or of high rank. He couldn't figure it out. The law was scarce in this part of Texas, but it seemed this crime had drawn men from across the state.

What had Josie stumbled into?

"Wish I knew who he was," she said barely above a whisper. "Luke, what have I done? I don't look good in prison stripes. They're not one bit flattering. In fact, they're really hideous. I'll be so ugly I'll have to sneak up on a drink of water."

He struggled not to laugh. She clearly had never seen female inmates or she'd know they didn't wear stripes. Even so, to worry about clothing or her looks at a time like this struck him as funny. But then this was wonderful, fearless, crazy Josie.

"Or they could hang me." Josie grabbed him. "Do they take women to the gallows?"

"Let's not get ahead of ourselves." She was worried enough. He didn't want to tell her that, though rare, sometimes they did hang women. Luke turned back to his post in time to see a rider on a beautiful palomino materialize from the shadows.

Brenner McCall, his old outlaw friend. What was he doing here? Brenner spied the Rangers and quickly shifted course, disappearing into the trees and brush that flourished thick along the banks of the river.

Luke needed to talk to him. Maybe after he found a safe place to make camp, he could leave Josie for a short while. It wouldn't do to have those two meet. He had to keep her away from McCall.

From all outlaws, friend or foe.

Trust didn't come easy to Luke and was even harder now. Money—or a woman—could turn a man into an entirely different person, even those men he knew well. Brenner McCall had changed from the man he used to know. He'd become shifty-eyed and dishonest.

Josie jostled his elbow again. "What are we going to do?"

He turned to face her. "I'll find a place to make camp for the night. We'll have to be quiet, and we can't risk a fire."

"I can do that. Whatever we have to do to stay alive."

Just then O'Keefe yelled in the midst of the small campsites, "Anyone seen the outlaw, Luke Weston?"

Josie sucked in a breath and pressed against Luke.

Hell and be damned!

"Who wants to know?" a voice yelled back.

"Just the man who's gonna become famous for killing him." O'Keefe stood with his legs braced apart, his twin guns shining in the flickering light.

One of the Texas Rangers got to his feet. "It'll take someone better than you, mister. Weston is lord-almighty fast with a gun and doesn't need to go around bragging about it."

"Men inflicted with the bragitis are sure to find the cure—in a bullet," said an older ranger.

"He's a killer with a price on his head," O'Keefe huffed.

"You're not telling us anything we don't know," answered the first ranger. "Even so, he's a sight better than you in our books."

Josie gripped Luke's arm. "Damn that little bastard! He's no match for your gun."

"Or yours either," Luke answered.

Her anger was apparent in her reply. "Those Rangers should just lock the fool up."

"Unfortunately, there's no law against stupidity. Let's find a place to sleep." Luke put his arm around her narrow waist and gathered the reins of the horses. He had to get her away from here fast, before she took it in her head to stride out there and give Munroe O'Keefe a piece of her mind. And then proceed to kick his scrawny butt.

He led her away from the yelling match that ensued. The last he heard was the rangers warning O'Keefe to ride on or they'd find something to arrest him for, even if they had to make it up. Apparently, the man had gained no friends.

Not too far downstream, Luke ran across a shoal where huge roots of salt cedar and oak stuck out of the ground like the fingers of a fat giant. Nearby was a small squatter's cabin. The hinges squeaked when he pushed open the door.

He took her hand. "It's not the Lone Star but—"

"It'll do just fine, Luke." She smiled up at him. "And we have water near."

"Always a selling point." He returned her smile. "I'll stash the horses somewhere close and scout around some, try to see what I can learn. I'm afraid supper is whatever is in the food bag Stoker sent."

Josie planted her hands on her hips. "Stop apologizing. I'm not complaining. I can handle harsh conditions just fine."

So said the woman who'd just railed against wearing prison stripes.

"Humph," he said instead of teasing her, and laid the saddlebags on the dirt floor. Josie went out and removed the bedrolls while he lifted off the saddles. They made quick work of lightening the horses.

Luke placed his hands on her shoulders, staring into her eyes. "An old outlaw once told me that the expected never happens on the trail. If I don't come back, walk to the trading post. It's not far. No one will spot you in those clothes with your hair under the hat. Ask for help."

"What would I say?"

"You're a good actress. With your skill, making up a story will be child's play."

Her lip suddenly quivered. "But, what about you? I can't just leave and not know if you're alive or—"

"Dead," he supplied softly. "You can say it. Make your way to the Lone Star. Stoker will know what to do."

"If that horrible man at the trading post kills you, I'll make him pay. You can count on that." Fury filled her voice. "The low-down skunk won't get away with it."

"That's my girl." A smile came despite his efforts to hold it back. Josie made him happy to be alive. For however long he had.

Thick clouds had blocked the moonlight. He draped an arm across his golden-haired angel's shoulders. Though most wouldn't give her a second glance right now in her boy's clothes and serape, he'd never seen her as anything except a woman. Not even when bloodstained and waving a gun at him.

Josie was a rare beauty with a heart full of caring, and a spirit that wouldn't be broken.

He pulled her against him, so close he could feel the wild beating of her heart. The firm binding beneath her shirt told him she'd tightly wrapped her breasts.

More's the pity.

He wished for time to remove the strips that flattened her. The desire to feel her fully against his chest rose up inside him, carrying scorching heat and driving passion.

"Leave me something to remember you by," she murmured.

The simple request was all he needed.

With the roar of the river behind them, Luke slid his hands down her body, crushed his lips to hers, and took his pleasure. He'd spent the last few days thinking about this kind of kiss, dreamed about it, waited patiently for the moment.

Unlike the others they'd shared, he held back nothing.

He kissed her all out, with aching desire pushing him past every boundary he'd set. When she softly parted her lips, he slipped his tongue inside, tasting her need. Thrusting in and out.

He burned with uncontrolled hunger.

Unbridled passion.

Thirsted for what she wanted to give.

A blacksmith's forge was cool compared to the heat consuming Luke. The flames seared clear through to his weary, godforsaken soul.

His hands slid down her flat stomach, traced the curve of her hips, her firm bottom.

Josie clung to him as though being swept away by a raging river and he was a piece of driftwood. "Never let me go, Luke."

Good God, what he'd give to be able to promise.

"Help me make new memories to fill the emptiness in my head," she begged against his mouth.

His groin tightened with need. He wanted to forget she had no memory. Forget the danger lurking so close he could reach out and touch it. And he wanted to forget he was an outlaw with nothing to offer. But he couldn't. To do so would put Josie in harm's way.

If only he could be Luke Legend, for just one night—someone with integrity, who stood tall on the side of the law.

She seemed to sense the direction of his thoughts and stepped from his arms. "Cowboy, I'll remember that kiss long after I'm dead."

So would he.

He lifted a strand of her hair and rubbed the silk between his fingers. Lord, how he hated to leave her. "I'm kicking myself for it, but I won't apologize. I don't regret the kiss." Then before he lost his mind and pressed his lips to hers again, Luke knelt to pull a bottle of whiskey from his saddlebag. It didn't pay to visit an outlaw's camp without sharing something. He strode to the horses and lifted the reins. "Keep your eyes and ears open. I'll be back."

Or not, depending on any number of things.

Scanning the area for trouble, his Colt in hand, he led their mounts into the thick brush. After hiding the animals in a little wash in a tangle of undergrowth, Luke focused on finding Brenner McCall.

Downwind of the trading post, he sniffed the air for a campfire and listened to the sounds around him. Finally, he heard a man's ragged cough drifting on the breeze. Could be his old friend.

Within moments, he spied a cold camp. McCall had nestled in a small wind cave with barely enough room for one man. The white-haired old outlaw had to be in his fifties by now and had seen his share of bad times. McCall wasn't a hardened man—just one with a lot of skeletons in his past. He'd killed his share of men, but as far as Luke knew, it had never been for the sport of it as it was with outlaws like Reno Kidd.

Brenner McCall, under the alias Cash Starr, had once pulled off the largest, most brazen bank robbery in Texas and the price on his head had made Luke's look like pauper's pennies. McCall didn't have a cent of the stolen money left. He'd lived to gamble, any game of chance, and he'd played his games from Texas to San Francisco and back again.

A man's vices almost always did him in. That had been a hard lesson learned, one not everyone managed before they succumbed.

Most others' involved women and gambling. Something to make them feel alive as never before. Luke's was far worse. At eighteen he'd fallen in with a rough bunch and they'd introduced him to opium. He'd become addicted, loving how the powerful drug blocked his pain and the nightmares that came with darkness.

Luke winced with the shameful memory. He owed his life to Brenner. The man had helped him find his way back from hell. Last Luke had heard, Brenner had opened a law practice. Talk was that Brenner now did his robbing on paper. He swindled farmers out of their land to pay his gambling debts. Something about men who walked on both sides of the law didn't sit well with Luke.

"Brenner," he said low, clutching the bottle of whiskey. "It's Luke Weston."

The old outlaw yanked his gun awkwardly from the holster with his left hand. "Show yourself."

Luke stepped forward with his hands raised. "Satisfied?"

"I always said you could track a beaver in a river." Brenner put his gun away and gripped his upper arm. He was badly hurt. "Wish I had half of your skill."

The best tactic was to play dumb. Luke had learned a lot over the years that way. He considered Brenner McCall the closest thing to a friend, but that didn't mean he trusted him. How could you trust someone who played both ends against the middle? Which of Brenner's two faces was talking to him tonight?

Still gripping his arm and grimacing, Brenner McCall dragged himself from his one-man cave. "Can't be too careful. The law is crawling all over these parts like a bunch of red ants."

"Why do you care? I thought you'd turned into a respectable lawyer now."

"I have. Got my eye on a judgeship. Or maybe governor if things go right." Brenner rubbed his leg. "I'm too old for this life. I need comfort now. Got bad knees and my joints hurt."

"Outlawing is hard on a man," Luke agreed. "How'd you get hurt, Brenner?"

"Gunshot. Don't want to talk about it."

"I'll take a look at it," Luke offered.

"I've seen to it myself. Bullet went through."

Who shot him? Luke wanted to ask, but Brenner didn't seem to invite those kinds of questions. At least not yet. Luke passed him the bottle of whiskey. "So why are you hiding out, sitting on the cold ground, when you could walk right up to any campfire?"

After taking two long swallows from the bottle, Brenner said, "I have my reasons."

Clearly, he was hiding something.

"Know why the Texas Rangers are here?" Luke dropped to the ground next to him.

"Yep." Brenner muttered a curse and wiped his mouth with the back of his hand. "Hell, I'd give a hundred dollars for a cup of coffee."

The short gray bristles of his neatly trimmed beard told Luke that Brenner had gotten accustomed to regular barbering. A far cry from the old days.

Luke cast Brenner a sideways glance. "Someone get killed?"

"Folks found Walt Preston gutted here at the crossing a few nights ago."

Luke let out a low whistle. "No wonder this place resembles a lawman convention."

A few pieces fell into place. An ex-congressman and powerful rancher, Walt Preston had been considered a shoo-in for state governor in the next election. Preston was a blowhard known for throwing his weight around, expecting everyone to follow blindly like a bunch of dumb-ass sheep. His egotistical attitude had turned Luke's stomach.

How was Josie involved? Luke pondered that. Preston already had a wife. Unless...Josie was his sweet little plaything on the side?

A muscle in Luke's jaw quivered. That possibility brought thoughts he didn't even want to consider.

"Did anyone see who twisted the knife into Preston?" Luke asked.

With a groan, Brenner rested his back against a boulder and turned up the whiskey bottle. He didn't offer to give it back. "Fingers were quick to point to a woman by the name of Josie Morgan, but she didn't do it."

It appeared Luke had come to the right source. Still, hearing the name spoken like that was a bit unexpected. He slowed his breathing. "I happened upon a posse looking for someone by that name. They said she killed her husband, but you and I both know Preston already had a wife. Wonder why they said that."

"Shoot, who knows. Folks are always getting stuff wrong."

Luke studied Brenner's face. "You sound awful sure of the facts."

Brenner grunted. "I oughta know. I was there."

Surprise shot through Luke. Was Brenner McCall a witness, or the killer? He had to be sure. "So, you know this Josie?"

McCall let out a string of curses a mile long. "You might say so. The Morgan gal's never tied the knot and I know that for a damn fact."

Relief swept through Luke and eased his conscience. If Brenner wasn't pulling a fast one, then Luke could quit kicking himself for stealing those passionate kisses. "Tell me this—why were the pair of you there that night?"

Brenner narrowed his eyes. "Boy, you're sticking your nose where it don't belong."

"I have a vested interest. Someone asked me to look into it. To borrow a page from your book, I'd rather not say who."

Brenner grimaced and clutched his shoulder. "You do learn well." He took another drink of whiskey.

"Did you kill Preston, Brenner?"

"If I'd wanted him dead, I'd have shot him instead."

Luke digested this, wondering if Brenner spoke the truth. "Then who did?"

"Reno Kidd. He's why I'm here. The arrogant, murdering bastard took something from me and I mean to get it back. Even if I have to put a bullet between his beady little possum eyes to do it."

Luke's gaze narrowed. "What did Reno take?"

"Recall how I always told you the expected never happens on the trail?"

"I do."

"I was here with Walt Preston that night. On...*business*. Reno and a couple of dirty gringos jumped us from the shadows, intent on robbing us. Preston refused to hand over his cash. He and Reno scuffled, and then Kidd got him with a knife. Josie—Miss Morgan—started screaming at the blood. Preston was dead. I drew my pistol and fired. Next thing I know, I'm shot in the shoulder and bleeding. Couldn't even chase after the bastards. Hell."

"What happened to Josie Morgan, Brenner?"

"Not sure, but I think Kidd took her. That's why I'm looking for the bastard."

That part of the story matched. Luke was on the right track. "That wound must pain you something awful. Let me take a look at it."

Brenner ignored Luke's offer, instead seemed far away, still reliving the murder. "Gotta find Josie. Reno Kidd is a dead man when I catch him."

Everything was making a little better sense.

Though the night was darker than the inside of Sam Houston's tomb, Brenner McCall's silver hair shone. Sorrow twisted through Luke. He wanted his friend to be one of the good guys—to have tried to turn his life around. He'd become a lawyer, sure, but he was still the same shady outlaw, looking for an easy way to line his pockets.

Looked like he was right to mistrust the man, even though Brenner once had saved him from certain death. Luke remembered how Brenner sat by his side for days on end, bathed the face of that eighteen-year-old kid that Luke had been. How the man had held his hand and staved off the opium demons, pulling Luke from their grip.

Luke owed him, no question. But he also had a vow to fulfill. "Brenner, I need to know. Just who is Josie Morgan to you?"

Eighteen

THE COAL-BLACK NIGHT HID MANY THINGS, BUT IT COULDN'T hide Brenner McCall's wary eyes. Luke watched them shift.

The man growled. "Careful, boy. Questions will get a man killed before you can blink twice. Thought I taught you better."

"You also told me to listen to the things that *aren't* said as much as the things that are."

Brenner's hand inched toward his gun. Luke didn't take his eyes off the man he'd once considered like a father. He realized now how very far from that ideal Brenner actually was. Stoker could teach this man a thing or two about the subject.

"Do you really want to do this?" Luke asked. "Whiskey and age have slowed your reflexes. I'm guessing you probably can't see so well either. Do you want to die tonight?"

A sudden, easy grin erased the thick, tension-laden air. Brenner reached into his pants pocket and pulled out cigarette papers and a sack of Bull Durham. "The girl didn't have any place to go and I took her in. She's a good person." Brenner gave him a one-eyed squint. "You remember how I took you in and put your legs back under you, boy?"

"Sure do. I'll owe you for it for the rest of my life."

"You got a funny way of showing loyalty." Brenner tapped a line of tobacco onto a thin paper and changed the subject. "What are you doing at Doan's, anyway?"

"Looking for a few answers for a friend. And trying to keep Munroe O'Keefe from putting a bullet in my back," Luke said. "He just showed up too."

The old outlaw grunted. "Heard he was gunning for you."

"The fool is worse than a crazy badger. He's determined to kill me to make a name, however he has to do it." And if he kept coming, he'd eventually succeed. The truth soured in Luke's stomach. "Back to Reno Kidd. Where do you think he might hole up?"

"Wish I knew. I'd be sitting on his doorstep right now." Brenner rolled a cigarette and licked the paper to seal it. With a heavy sigh, he rustled up a match. "The young ones today don't have the brains God gave a turnip. It's not like when I came to Texas. I had sense enough to blend in and not draw suspicion. I damn sure wouldn't taunt lawmen like Reno does. I think he's messed up in the head."

Luke had stopped listening. If Kidd found out Josie had survived, would he come to silence her once and for all?

If so, Kidd would find himself in Luke's crosshairs.

What was Josie's role in Preston's death? That part had Luke scratching his head. Had she been in on whatever plan Brenner and Walt Preston had going? Or maybe she saw what Kidd had planned for the politician and tried to stop it. He liked the second idea better.

He thought back to what Reno's men had said and done, the day he'd found Josie. They'd said that her father was a mean hombre, and someone you didn't want to mess with.

Who the hell was her father? Did they mean her natural father, or Brenner, since he seemed to have been taking care of her? She wasn't his by blood; Brenner'd never had children of his own.

Brenner probably could tell him, but as Luke had already seen, it was dangerous to ask too many questions.

So, if not Brenner, then Walt Preston? Did Josie belong to him in some other way? Maybe she was like Luke—a child born on the wrong side of the blanket.

Luke stretched out his long legs and put his hands behind his head. "What do you hear about any trouble these days?"

Brenner blew out a line of smoke rings. "What do you mean?"

"Uprisings, county wars, blood feuds—that sort of thing."

"It's a strange question."

"I'm just trying to figure out what parts of the country to shy away from. I don't want to get caught up in the middle of a big mess."

Brenner inhaled on the cigarette, making the end glow fiery red. "The Texas Rangers ended the Horrell-Higgins feud down in Lampasas County, but I know for a fact Mart Horrell is still looking to even the score. He lost five brothers in that squabble."

"Blood feuds never die. They go on and on until there's no more kin to bury," Luke said. "Anything else?"

"The Lincoln County War is going on, but I doubt you'll be heading to New Mexico Territory. A bloody fight. I'd steer clear of there if I was you, Weston."

"That trouble isn't for me," Luke said. "How about you?"

"Hell, I'm getting too fat and old."

Luke glanced at the man he'd ridden with. The glow of the cigarette lit up the deeply lined face, his hair and beard.

Suddenly, Noah's words filled his head. *He had gray hair and a beard. Not as tall as you. He didn't smile or anything. My pa called him Captain.*

Josie had visited Noah's farm with the gray-haired man. Was Brenner "Captain"? He'd admitted he knew her. It fit.

"I was glad I missed the war. That was bloody," Luke said casually. "Did you ever see war, Brenner?"

"Too much of it." Brenner grimaced and held his shoulder. "I served with the Johnny Rebs, saw too many of my men die. It hurts extra bad when you promise to keep them safe, extra bad when you're their captain and leading them into battle. Rips your guts out."

Though Luke had been suspicious, hearing the rank sent shock through him. "How come you never told me?"

"It was a long time ago. Better to forget." Clutching the half-empty bottle of whiskey, the old outlaw yawned. "It's gonna be a long night. Where are you camped?"

"I don't know yet," Luke lied. "Wherever it is, I'll have to keep one eye open for O'Keefe."

In the silence that drifted around them, they could hear a mournful coyote and the rush of the nearby river. Thoughts of the golden-haired woman waiting for him filled his mind. She needed answers to take back her life, and he'd move the moon and stars to get them for her. So, he'd keep digging as far as he could.

At last, Luke said, "I can't seem to shake that question about Josie Morgan. How does she figure into all that went on with Preston here?"

Brenner jerked up straight, dropping his cigarette in his lap. He quickly flicked it off. "You'd best leave, Weston. I warned you to stay out of it."

Luke got to his feet. "I never did listen too well. Better get that gunshot seen about." He took two steps and paused. "About that tip you gave me concerning Ned Sweeney. I never got there, but my gut tells me he was nowhere near that creek."

He turned and melted into the brush, satisfied with what he'd learned. He was slowly putting all the pieces together of what happened that night. Brenner and Walt Preston had met for God knew what. Some kind of shady deal, to take place under cover of night. But why here? This was an out-of-the-way spot and quite a distance for Walt Preston to go, seeing as how his spread lay a good way south.

The closest thing nearby of any note was Dead Horse Creek, Luke's destination when he first found Josie. But that was neither here nor there.

So, Reno and his bunch had seen Brenner and Preston, figured them for some easy money, and tried to rob them. Josie raised hell, and Reno knocked her cold.

Everything fit together—except her. She could've been

up to her pretty little neck in whatever happened before Reno arrived.

Who the hell was he to throw stones? He'd done far worse. Trying to survive made you do things you wouldn't otherwise consider. But one thing eased his mind—she hadn't killed anyone. At least not that night. The blood on her dress had been from Kidd's doing.

He made it back to the abandoned cabin without incident. Josie was waiting outside the door, gripping her pistol. She swung in the direction of his footsteps.

"It's only me, Josie."

"I'm glad you're back. I was ready to go looking for you."

"I told you to wait."

She stood so near. So tempting. So full of sass. No one would ever tame this woman. The clouds suddenly parted, allowing the moonlight to caress her with its silvery rays. His mind flew back to the previous night at the Lone Star, lying beneath the huge bronze star with their fingers intertwined.

The hot kisses they'd shared.

He knew at that moment he'd be lost and dead inside when the time came for them to part ways.

And it would probably be sooner than he thought.

No matter what she'd done, or who she'd been involved with, he still burned with hunger for her. When he moved closer, she put her arms around his neck and kissed him like the bold woman she was.

"I missed you, cowboy," she murmured.

Her warm, lush body pressed against him, making it near to impossible to remember the warning in his head not to let her get too close. But Josie squirmed against him and he immediately forgot everything except the willing woman in his arms.

He cupped her sexy bottom, holding her fast. His need jutted against her stomach but he didn't apologize. For that, or for the raw, dangerous kind of craving that could make him forget the price on his head and the waiting rope.

Luke ground his mouth against hers. Giving. Taking. Branding her with a passion so hot it made a raging wildfire seem like nothing more than a match. All the ferocity he'd kept restrained exploded.

There would be no turning back.

His hands slid up her body to the slope of her breasts. Thank goodness she'd removed the god-awful wrappings. Her nipples distended, seeming to strain for his touch. He brushed them with his flattened palms then rolled them hard between his thumb and forefinger.

Her breath hitched and a low cry came from her mouth. "Yes."

Tomorrow he'd go back to the real world. But tonight he'd take his pleasure with the only woman who excited him and made him feel whole. Now that he knew she wasn't married, he didn't have to hold back. Depending on how the cards fell, they might have only one night. He'd make it count.

He swept her into his arms and strode through the open door of the shack. It was darker than the inside of his boot. He stumbled over one of the saddles and almost sprawled across the dirt floor.

Josie's lips on his smothered his curse. She clawed at his shirt. "Make love to me, Luke. Love me like you want to. Make me forget I'm a killer."

"You're not one." He jerked his shirt over his head. "You're not married either."

Josie gasped. "Are you sure?"

"Yep. Just talked with a man who confirmed it." He backed her against a wall, unfastened her gun belt, yanked her shirt and chemise over her head and flung them aside. His ragged breath burning his lungs, he knelt to remove her boots then her trousers.

Desperate to quench the burning fire sweeping along his body, Luke stood and buried his mouth in the long column of her throat. His hands slid to the soft swells of her breasts and he kneaded the flesh that seemed to crave his touch. Lowering his head, he pulled a swollen nipple into his mouth.

She yanked at his gun belt, unbuckling it. Letting it drop, she found the opening of his trousers and slid a hand inside to grip him. He gasped for the sudden loss of air, fighting for control as her hand tightened around him.

Dear God! She was driving him out of his mind. Two dozen lawmen could have them surrounded and he wouldn't care, wouldn't even hear them.

He'd promised her at the Lone Star that if he found she was free, he'd light a fire inside her and make slow, sensual love. He had the match. Only the slow part was out. At least this time. His need was too great, and judging by the way Josie ripped the seam of his shirt getting it off, he suspected she shared the same feeling.

Her hands moved up and down his erection, faster and faster.

He propelled her against the wall, anchoring her there. Grinding his mouth against hers, he slid a hand between them to her throbbing center, which was hot and wet.

Blood surged into his head and he could hear nothing except Josie's heart crying out for him.

Lifting her up, he slid her down onto him. Hot tightness surrounded him and he knew right then that there would be no forgetting the wild and brash Josie Morgan.

Luke closed his eyes and soaked up the feel of being inside her, her breasts pressed against the hard planes of his chest.

The memory she'd begged him for earlier was nothing compared to what he'd leave her with come dawn.

She gave a soft cry and thrust her hands into his hair. "Love me, Luke. Give me all of you. I want to have it all with nothing held back."

Her body pulled at him, her tight muscles wringing every ounce of strength from him.

Stroke after stroke sent him finally tumbling over the edge. His heart pounding, he shuddered with a powerful release as Josie's muscles contracted around him.

She took his face between her hands and kissed him long and deep. They leaned against the plank wall, gasping for air, their ragged breaths mingling.

Luke picked her up and laid her on bedrolls she'd already spread out. "I want to take my time with you, lady."

"Promises, promises," she murmured in his ear.

He wished for moonlight in order to fully appreciate her beauty. But there were no windows for it to shine through. More's the pity.

The rest of his clothes landed somewhere in the dark within seconds. He sank down beside her and propped himself on an elbow, his head at her feet. Lazily, he ran a finger down each long, shapely leg.

"Have I mentioned that you have the most beautiful legs?"

Josie sucked in a breath and quivered. "Don't stop, Luke."

Like he had that ability.

Some men were drawn to different parts of a woman's body, but Luke had always preferred the legs. Josie's were gorgeous. He kissed his way along each then finished crawling up the rest of her luscious body.

Josie sighed, running her hands across his chest. "If this is a dream, I never want to wake up. I want to stay here forever. With you."

"With the bugs and scorpions?" he teased.

"You'll protect me."

That he would. Until death claimed him.

They talked, lazily touching each other, and rested. Josie turned onto her belly. Luke's fingertips followed the sensuous curve of her back, his hand drifting to firm buttocks that filled out every inch of those trousers. Making love to her would number among the most memorable moments of his life. She loved how she lived—full-out and dangerous.

A short while later, he rose to ready her for more. With his hands and mouth, he rubbed, flicked, and kissed her nipples, lingering over each one, making them harden and beg for more.

At last he claimed her mouth in a kiss that stole his

ability to think. The fire blazing inside him wasn't content to simply flame up. It wanted to devour him, burn through his sanity, and make him crazy with hunger for her.

"*Mi princesa*," he murmured into her hair.

"Make me cry your name," Josie whispered, stroking the muscles in his back. "Make love to me until the stars fall from the sky."

That had been another one of his promises that night at the Lone Star. No windows meant he couldn't see the sky, but he was pretty damn sure those stars had already fallen earlier.

He poised above her and slid inside again, feeling her muscles clench around him.

Slow, sultry heat swirled in his belly. It was the kind of good that made a man ante up everything he owned. For an outlaw on the run, his possessions didn't amount to much, but he'd gladly fork it all over for just one night with Josie Morgan in a real bed.

Just the two of them locked away with no cares in the world.

The release he sought poured over him like warm honey and he found himself spinning in a golden, shimmering sea of contentment.

Nineteen

Josie lay facing Luke, savoring the feel of his naked body against hers. He caressed her face with his long fingers as they drifted in the afterglow of making love, touching, whispering sweet words. They'd found a little slice of heaven here in the humble squatter's shack, a chance for them both to find peace, an island of perfection.

It had to be around midnight, but Josie couldn't sleep. She ran her fingers lightly over the fine hair on Luke's wrist and hand that rested on her belly. The same strong hand that could draw his Colt faster than the eye could blink had caressed her so tenderly.

"Tell me again that I'm not married. Are you sure?"

"Yep. The man I met with seemed dead certain. He was here the night of the murder, and he said Reno Kidd bears the blame for killing that man, not you. You're not a killer, Josie."

"At least not this time." She kissed his chest.

"Don't buy trouble," he warned.

"Who? Me?" She giggled. "Name one instance."

"Well, let's see. You fought like a tiger to claw out the eyes of those two men of Reno's and would have if I hadn't grabbed hold of you. And then you persuaded Tally Shannon to give you a gun and insisted I bring you on this dangerous trip against all my best advice."

Josie glanced up at her outlaw's dark shadow and grinned. "That's only two instances, barely worth mentioning."

A growl rumbled in his chest and his voice was husky. "I haven't even reminded you of Noah's uncle, Bert, and the fact that you tried to take him on all by yourself."

She could hear the things he couldn't bring himself to say: the fact that Bert Conley had almost killed her, and that shook him. She knew how much that terrified him, and that was enough.

"I declare, Luke, what is the true purpose of this score-keeping you insist on, anyway?"

"To try my hardest to corral you, *bella dama*."

Pretty lady. Josie smiled at the touching Spanish phrase. It was more than just spouting the phrases. They were a part of him.

She rose, propping her elbows on his chest. "I don't know very much about you other than your father's side. Tell me about your mother."

"Not much to tell. She raised me by herself. We were poor. She died. End of story."

"Nope. That's not all. That's not even a beginning. Now do it right."

With the music of the rushing river outside their door, he began to talk, hesitant at first—a trait of outlaws, she was beginning to learn. After explaining how he was conceived in Galveston when Stoker was young, he relaxed and opened up.

Her heart broke to learn how Elena Montoya's family had abducted her, taken her away where Stoker couldn't find her, how Luke had grown up with such bitterness. When he'd discovered his father's name, the bitterness had multiplied. Josie could understand how it would, watching the Legends in their privilege and wealth, while he had nothing. She pictured the lost little boy who had become an outlaw, the only way he had to cope with the pain of watching his mother slowly work herself to death.

When he stopped talking, she prodded gently. "Tell me

what happened when you were fourteen. What turned you into the man you are?"

"A killer," he corrected. "I killed a man—for his cruelty to my mother."

Josie gasped at the story he told about the rich man's brutality. "I would've killed him too!" she cried. "The bastard deserved to die." Her blood boiled and she hadn't even known Luke's mother.

"But then I didn't stop." He caressed her cheek with the pad of his thumb. "I'm good at what I do. I enjoy ridding the world of scum. Still do."

"One might argue that taking those lives was justified."

"Not in the eyes of the law. That first time, my mother made me turn myself in." He inhaled sharply. "The judge gave me four years in prison."

"That's horrible!" She tried to picture a scared fourteen-year-old boy locked up with hardened criminals, but the image was too painful.

"To teach me a lesson, the judge said." Bitterness filled Luke's quiet voice.

"I wish I could give that judge a piece of my mind," she said angrily, running her palm across his chest. Roughened, raised skin alarmed her. "What is this? What happened?"

"Which scar?"

Josie sucked in a breath. "There's more than one?"

"Afraid so."

"What caused them?" she asked.

"Gunshots mostly. Two are from stab wounds."

The darkness didn't allow for her to see. She could find her way only by touch, but what she discovered as her fingers traveled across his chest and stomach told an agonizing story.

The fishy odor from the river outside the door, coupled with the horrors she was discovering, made her stomach turn. Sour bile coated her tongue.

"How many scars do you have?" she asked.

"Too many. I'm likely to earn a lot more in my future, depending on how long it takes the lucky bullet to find me."

His scornful tone revealed more than he'd probably intended. Clearly, he didn't plan on a long life, likely didn't plan on anything beyond the next sunrise. Luke Weston was a man expecting death at every sound.

Josie wanted to cry. No wonder he didn't laugh or dance or rarely cracked a smile.

"Well, your damned attitude about it makes me fighting mad," she said. "Really, really chewing-nails furious."

His reply was soft. "I warned you not to get too close, about caring."

The cautions didn't make one speck of difference. Her heart already had ideas of its own. Josie trailed a finger down his neck. "Tell me about prison."

Luke's muscles suddenly tensed under her palm. "No."

"Please," she said gently, kissing the throbbing pulse in the hollow of his throat. "I want to know how you wound up in this dark place."

A muscle in his jaw quivered. "Prison—I wouldn't wish it on anyone. At night, the earth opened up beneath the floor and demons climbed from hell." Luke brushed away the tear trickling down her cheek.

"You were just a little boy," she cried in anguish. "A frightened little boy."

"I wasn't by the time I came out." His voice hardened to granite. "You do what you must to make it to another sunrise."

"Your poor mother. What it must've done."

"She often came to visit but I sent her away. I didn't want her"—his voice caught—"seeing me in a place like that."

"Of course not." Josie stroked his face, surprised to find wetness. This strong outlaw who tried so hard to pretend he didn't care about anyone or anything, that he didn't have a heart, did. A big one that hurt. She knew without asking that he'd never told another living soul about this part of his life. Not even Stoker or his brothers.

"After I got out, I discovered a way to cope with the pain

and entered another type of hell. Opium. I don't know why I'm telling you. I've never told anyone. It's my shame."

"Because I accept you as you are and don't ask for more. I'll never judge you," she answered simply. "We've all failed in some way. When I regain my ability to recall, I have a feeling I'll have similar things to share."

"I hope not." He sighed. "At any rate, I got off the devil's coattails before my mother found out. At least I spared her that."

She drew lazy circles on his forearm. "Where did the name Luke Weston come from? No mother of Spanish birth would give you that."

"After I got free of my addiction, I was coming down Trammel's Trace, an old Indian trail in eastern Texas, when I came across a dead man. Someone had bashed in his head. I found the name Luke Weston on a deed in his pocket. I figured he no longer had a use for the identity."

"Poor man. And the one you were born with?" she prodded.

"Rafael Montoya."

"I like that. It's beautiful. It suits you, especially when you wear your black trousers with the conchas." She grinned, remembering how snug they fit his lean body, showing his nicely formed behind and long legs.

Josie kissed him, marveling at this outlaw who'd found her. So many things had to fall into place for that to happen. If any one of them hadn't occurred, they'd never have met.

By the time daylight came through the cracks in the wall of the squatter's shack, she had the full picture of Luke Weston. He was much more than the simple killer he claimed to be. So much more. Whatever happened next, she knew that he'd always have a very special place in her heart.

An unbreakable bond had formed during the dark hours when her outlaw had shared his painful secrets.

Luke rolled to his feet and reached for his trousers, and Josie got her first glimpse of the horrible scars on his body, each telling a tale of violence...and survival.

One wound was pretty fresh. She got to her feet and put her arms around him. She laid her face against his back.

"Thank you for telling me about your life. I know what it cost you to let me see," she said.

Luke turned and folded her inside the circle of his arms. Her place of safety. Of comfort.

"Stoker and my brothers don't know about any of what I've told you. I trust you to keep my secrets."

"If that's what you want. But you know that nothing will change the way they feel about you. Quit expecting everyone to shun you, Luke. Get that through that thick skull of yours. They're your family, and family has got to love you, no matter what. It's a rule. I think." At least she hoped so. When she regained her senses, if she had family, she hoped they'd take her in.

"I won't take that chance. I'm already embarrassed enough. But if they knew the whole..."

He'd left the rest unspoken because fear his family would reject him hurt too much.

"Only in your mind, Luke. After we get dressed, I want you to tell me about this person you met with last night."

He kissed the tip of her nose. "After coffee."

"You said we couldn't build a fire."

"Not outside, but a small one in here won't hurt. Even so, I doubt anyone will pay any mind to a little smoke in daylight, and the Texas Rangers likely moved out this morning."

"That's good. Even if I didn't kill that man—"

"He was an ex-congressman," Luke interrupted. "From all accounts, due to be the next governor."

"Oh no!" Why couldn't he have been some crook or outlaw? "As I was saying, even if I didn't kill him, the law *thinks* I did. They're still going to come after me. And haul me to jail."

Those ugly prison stripes were not going away anytime soon.

"True. I'll just have to keep you safe." He placed his lips on hers.

The gentle kiss he probably intended turned into one of searing passion that drove her past the point of sanity. She had to have his skin touching hers. His hand slid down her throat to her breast, and when his fingers raked across the sensitive tip, the banked embers flamed tall.

Josie pulled him down to the bedroll and they spent the next half hour in a most pleasurable way.

By the time they finally got their clothes on, it was clear to her that she had to stay at least ten feet away from Luke, or they'd spend every second in each other's arms.

But moving even an inch from him brought cold loneliness.

She wondered if he'd come visit her in jail. Maybe her outlaw would ride in and bust her out. She glanced at him from the corner of her eye. Yes, he'd gallop in, hold the sheriff at gunpoint, and help her escape.

If not that way, she pictured him strolling in disguised as a nun and giggled at the image. He'd have to shave, of course.

But no, that wouldn't work. He had a dark shadow along his jaw even freshly shaven. And a holy sister with a shadow on her face would give him away.

Josie drew her brows together, searching for a different disguise. A saloon girl? But his legs and chest were too hairy. She burst out laughing.

Luke raised a questioning brow. "What's so funny?"

"Nothing really. Nothing at all."

She finally gave up on her idle musing. The only thing he could pass for was the disguise he had on now. And the warden wouldn't give a mountain man or a buffalo hunter access to her.

Oh, shoot!

This life of crime required too much thought. No wonder Luke had a few streaks of silver at his temples.

Tingles raced through her as last night's and this morning's memories swirled. She didn't know if she'd ever made love before, but she imagined she had. There was no soreness, not even any flecks of blood that something told her would be present if she was new to a man's touch.

Just a heart that beat with love for Luke Weston Legend.

Luke lugged back the abandoned washtub, made a fire, and now sat with a cup of coffee in his hand. Josie seemed quiet, a contrast from her usual habit of chattering like a magpie.

A very pretty magpie, he added.

The light caught on her hair just right and the strands looked like pieces of gold in a miner's pan.

He had no trouble remembering being inside her—at first fast and furious, consumed by a kind of hunger he'd never felt before. Then progressing during the night to steamy, sultry passion to savor, like Stoker's finest aged bourbon, letting the fire wind its way through his body.

One thing he knew—Josie was no virgin. She was accustomed to a man's touch. Luke frowned. A large part of him found that notion very unsettling. Who had caressed her, kissed her, tasted her sweetness?

"You seem so far away. A penny for your thoughts, Luke."

He took a long sip of coffee. "Not worth sharing."

Josie rested her empty cup in her lap. "Luke, I've decided I don't want to find my past. Whatever is there can stay hidden."

"You're just scared."

"No, that's not it. I sense there's nothing good. Maybe I'm the kind of person that no one would want. I can't live that way—I have to matter to someone."

He met the misery in her changeable eyes and reached for her hand. "*Princesa*, you matter to me. Don't ever, ever think you don't."

"Let's find a place and settle down. Just you and me," she begged. "Maybe accept that land on the Lone Star."

"How long do you think that'll last? A week? A month? I have a two-thousand-dollar bounty on my head now, and it's going to rise even higher. Men often kill for mere cents. We wouldn't make it six months before lawmen and bounty hunters would overrun the ranch. Do you want to live like that?"

"You know I don't. Jumping at each sound, waiting for the bullet to end your life—or mine—would kill me."

"Exactly." He brought her hand to his lips and kissed each fingertip. "I won't put you through that."

"We can try somewhere else where no one knows you. Don't you want me?" The question came out bruised, as though the words had been squeezed, fighting their way from her narrowed throat.

Luke wanted her worse than anything on earth. More than land, clearing his name. More even than claiming his place as a Legend one day.

He'd give up everything for her if he could. But he wouldn't ask her to share his dangerous life.

She would not watch him die or—heaven forbid—take a bullet meant for him.

"When I find a place where you'll be happy, our paths must part. It's what must be," he said softly, closing his eyes against the torment in her gaze.

Pain ripped through him to think of never seeing his beautiful Josie again. Never holding her. Never sleeping beside her, her fragrance binding them like a silken rope.

Dear God, how much agony should one man suffer?

Riding on without her would plunge him into a living hell.

Houston's words echoed in his head. *You have to want it so damn bad you don't care if you eat, sleep, or breathe.*

Of course, his brother had been talking about land, but it might as well apply to Josie Morgan too.

What was the solution?

He was back to finding Ned Sweeney. Maybe doubling his efforts, hounding the man night and day would produce results. Or have another chat with Brenner McCall.

But Josie?

"I'm going to see what else I can uncover here," he said. "With luck, I might be able to give you a family or a birthplace."

At least he could do that much for the woman who'd stolen his heart. She'd made him feel like he was worth something. He shook his head. He'd told her the very worst, things he'd never uttered to another living soul, and she still hadn't run. By believing in him and trusting so fully, she'd given him a reason to hang on to her with all his might.

But how in hell could he do that?

Josie Morgan didn't know the danger he'd brought her.

Twenty

"And if that life isn't one I wish to claim?" Josie jerked to her feet. "You can't give me a family I want, or a home—or respectability—if none exists."

Luke suspected fear of what lay ahead made her voice tremble. He'd once heard someone say that three things made you vulnerable—risk, uncertainty, and an emotional stake. All three were at work inside Josie.

In him also.

Each time he faced a new day or a man's gun at twenty paces, he was at the mercy of the unknown. Of fate waiting like a salivating beast, ready to pounce if he faltered.

In his experience, it seemed that getting something you wanted meant you had to give up something else in return. What more could life take from him? From her?

Luke stood and moved to her. "I understand how you feel and I know the fine line we have to walk with family." He tucked a loose strand of sun-drenched hair behind her ear. "We can't let them get too close or they'll see the things we hide. I'll make you a deal. When I—we—find yours, if they fall short, I'll take you away. Trust me?"

"With every ounce of my being. Only you." She leaned in to kiss him and he needed no urging to respond.

When she ended the kiss, he stepped away before they

spent the day engaging in guilty pleasure. He had to make use of the daylight while he could.

❧

Doan's Trading Post saw a brisk business, with cowboys arriving on one of the frequent cattle drives. A large herd of bellowing cattle stood near, waiting to cross the Red River. The stench from them went up Luke's nose.

From the cover of a low-hanging, leafy elm branch, Luke scanned the area. The group of Texas Rangers were gone. Must've ridden out. Maybe that meant Munroe O'Keefe had too. He saw no one else who posed a danger. There was no sign of Brenner McCall either. Not here, or at the wind cave where he'd slept. Luke had gone by earlier to check on Brenner and pry more information from him only to find him gone.

"Is it safe?" Josie whispered.

"As far as I can tell. We'll go into the trading post separately. Let me do the talking." He gave her a stern look. "All right?"

The mutinous angle of Josie's mouth did nothing to reassure him. Not one dadgum bit.

"All right?" he asked again.

"Fine," she finally answered. "But I go in first."

Adjusting her serape, she strolled inside. Luke counted to twenty before pushing away from the tree trunk.

He took a dozen long strides before a voice halted him. A man emerged from a group standing at the side of the trading post.

Munroe O'Keefe. Dammit!

Luke's pulse pounded in his temples.

"Luke Weston! You think you're better'n me and I'm fixin' to show everyone what a sorry excuse for a gunfighter you are."

Luke forced his heartbeat to slow. He casually fished a match stem from his pocket and stuck it in the corner of his mouth. "What took you so long? Someone should tell you that you're no good at tracking a man. I even left a wide trail for you to follow."

Red-faced, O'Keefe strutted toward him. Good. Luke had made him mad. He'd always found anger to be an ally. Boiling-mad men rarely shot straight.

"If you want to be me so bad, you need to smarten up," Luke said calmly. "You'll never fill my shoes being stupid."

A crowd had begun to gather. He saw Josie run from the store, her eyes wide. Dammit! He knew without a doubt that if O'Keefe got lucky and shot him, she'd kill O'Keefe on the spot and to hell with the consequences. Her temper wouldn't let her see that far.

Or…fear gripped him as his heart raced. This couldn't happen all over again. Please, not again. He saw Angelina's face frozen in death as he'd knelt over her that day. Blood oozed from the wound in her chest…from the bullet meant for him.

And now Josie appeared poised to put herself between him and O'Keefe. Just like Angelina.

Dear God, don't let it happen again. Don't let me lose Josie too. Not this way.

"I'm going to put a bullet right through your rotten heart, Weston. And then everyone will know I'm the fastest gun in the whole damn state." O'Keefe glanced at the onlookers, the crowd growing to about two dozen or more. "Place your bets, folks. Here's a chance to make some money."

Luke watched the fool posture and preen. O'Keefe's ego had outgrown his stature. He was nothing but a little man and always would be, no matter if his bullet found the mark today.

"You know, O'Keefe, somehow I always thought you'd pick a larger crowd than this to watch you become famous." Luke's narrowed gaze moved to the man's eyes. Always the eyes. Never the hands.

Right now, he saw the overconfidence of a cocky challenger.

"I would've preferred a big town if I had my druthers. So I could claim the money faster," O'Keefe crowed. "But here will do fine. Make me rich and famous, Weston."

"You're a low-down, no-good jackass," Josie hollered. At least she was staying put. For now. He didn't know how much longer she'd wait, though.

Please don't do this, Josie. For once, don't let your heart overrule your head.

"Well, since you seem to know what you're doing, let's get this over with," Luke answered with a shrug. "Wouldn't want to hold you up or keep these fine folks waiting."

He stood with his legs apart, barely breathing. Everything seemed to stop, as though the world was waiting. Even the herd of cattle settled down and ceased their bellowing. Maybe they smelled death in the air.

Minutes seemed to tick by. Though Luke had never fired first in his life, he was tempted to, just to end the delay.

"Don't let him do this, Luke!" Josie yelled.

He heard the cusswords flow from her mouth in a stream. He spat out the match stem, his hand hovering above the handle of his Colt. His nerves stretched thin.

Come on, O'Keefe. You wanted this, you bastard. Draw.

A flurry of movement came from his right but he didn't glance away from O'Keefe's eyes. *Keep still, Josie.*

"I hope you rot in hell, Munroe O'Keefe," Josie cried.

The man blinked hard, then again, and drew.

When O'Keefe's gun cleared leather, Luke pulled his Colt and fired.

Thick smoke blocked his vision for a moment. He felt no pain, nor tasted blood on his tongue.

He'd survived another bullet. He slid his Colt into the holster and shot a glance to where Josie had stood.

She was gone. Now she'd seen what he really was for herself and it had turned her stomach. An ache throbbed inside that nothing would ease.

Someone asked him if he was all right. He'd never be all

right. His soul was too pitted and scarred. Each time he put a bullet into someone, it added more.

He glanced at the braggart lying in the dirt, a boy so sure he was going to become famous. Another challenger, another senseless death, another day alive to fight again.

Where would it end?

Luke stalked over to O'Keefe. He picked him up, slinging the man onto his shoulder. He left the dead man's gun lying in the dirt and strode to the trading post where he dropped his load in the shade of the tree. No one spoke or even glanced his way as the onlookers went about their business.

A man brought O'Keefe's hat and stuck it on the braggart's head. "What will you do with him?"

"Bury him. That is, if Doan will loan me a shovel."

"Nice shooting. It was a fair fight. We all saw it. This man didn't leave you any choice." The stranger said goodbye and ran for the ferry.

Luke went inside.

A graying man who'd seen the better part of his life glanced up. "Howdy, stranger. I'm Jonathan Doan. Can I help you?"

"I need to borrow a shovel." Luke waved toward the door. "Unless you want to draw flies."

Doan's droopy mustache followed the man's head as it wagged from side to side. "I can't figure you out. I saw the gunplay and every bit of it was that young upstart's fault. Most anyone would leave him where he fell. That was a nice thing you did. Mind telling me why?"

"I'd want someone to do that for me." Luke's voice was quiet.

"Well, it was more than the fool deserved." Doan went to the back for a shovel and handed it to Luke. "You have some of the best reflexes I've seen, Weston."

The store owner leaned to yank Luke's wanted poster off the wall and wadded it up. "A U.S. Marshal put that up. He'll get nothing from me."

"Appreciate it," Luke said. "I'll bury the dead man a good ways off."

"Obliged. Anything else?"

"Information. Did you see what happened to my partner, about this tall?" Luke indicated Josie's height by a hand to his chin. "He was among the crowd but has disappeared."

"He?" Doan looked puzzled. "Oh, you mean the boy." Below his shaggy eyebrows came a knowing wink.

"Yes."

"A little girl about five or six years old ran up and yanked on *his* hand. The child said something and the two of 'em took off toward the ferry."

"Thanks, Doan. I'll return the shovel."

"No hurry. Glad to help."

Luke's thoughts whirled as he left. Where could Josie have gone? He was fairly certain she didn't know anyone here. He frowned. Unless her memory had returned and the child was someone familiar. Doc had said it could all come back in a rush.

Or maybe she went back to the squatter's shack. But why would a child take her there? Since they'd packed up everything that morning, there was nothing there that Josie would need. It didn't make sense.

Dark foreboding filled him.

Lawmen at work could be the answer. They could've used a child to lure Josie away from the crowd where they could arrest her without a scene.

He patted her horse—the roan—and prayed he'd find her. Though he'd been alone for much of his life, this time was different. This time the loss shattered everything inside him. He suddenly realized how truly broken he was. Somehow Josie had kept him glued together.

He needed her. The sweet, funny, temperamental Josie was his light in the darkness. And she had vanished.

His hands were unsteady as he lifted O'Keefe and slung him across Major John's rump.

A short while later, he reined to a stop in front of the

shack. Everything was eerily quiet. There were no signs inside that Josie had been anywhere near the place since this morning. He'd throw some dirt on Munroe O'Keefe and search for her.

After picking a spot, he plunged the shovel into the packed dirt. Sweat poured. He didn't know how much time had passed but it seemed like he'd dug for hours and the grave still wasn't deep enough. It would do, he decided. O'Keefe wouldn't complain.

Luke was drenched by the time he covered the would-be fast-draw with dirt. He tied the shovel to his black gelding and grabbed the roan. He scoured every bit of the area, turned over every rock, and even inquired at the ferry if she'd boarded. Everywhere he turned, he was met with a dead end.

Finally, he returned to the trading post.

Doan greeted him with a smile and a shake of the head. He still hadn't seen Josie.

Luke thanked him and moved toward the door when he suddenly turned. "Just curious...five days ago when that man was murdered, did you hear or see anything?"

"That I did. I had just closed up and was heading home when I heard the awfullest commotion. Two men—one in a wagon, the other on a horse, were talking. Looked pretty serious. Not one to buy trouble, I went on toward my house and had about reached the door when three riders showed up. One man leaped from his horse into the wagon, then all hell broke loose. There was even a woman there, yelling and cussing up a storm. I've never seen the like."

Had to have been Josie. But where had she come from? The wagon, or one of the horses?

"You didn't see her there before that?" Luke asked. "What did she look like?"

"Nope, I didn't see her until then, there in the wagon. She was real pretty, best I could tell, with long blond hair. I started down there to ask the troublemakers to ride on when the woman screamed, then suddenly went silent."

Doan paused to wait on a customer. When he came back, Luke prompted, "Tell me the rest."

Doan rubbed his bristly jaw. "I'm still trying to figure out in my mind what happened next. Everything was a blur and it was nighttime, mind you. The thin moonlight made it hard to make things out."

"Please try. This is important," Luke said. Before he could help Josie, he needed to know the facts, and Jonathan Doan was unbiased.

"Everyone started moving at once—the riders, the wagons, and two pack mules."

Luke frowned. "You didn't mention the pack mules or a second wagon."

Doan scratched his head. "I just now remembered them. Strange that I forgot. They came out of nowhere, maybe from one of the camps down by the river."

"And then what?"

"I didn't see hide nor hair of the woman anymore. There was a gunshot and everyone lit out of here, and that's when I saw the dead man lying in the road next to his wagon."

"The ex-congressman?"

"Yes. So they tell me. Very gruesome. Someone had stuck a knife in his gut, and there was no saving him. By the time I got there, he was already dead."

"What happened to the rider who was talking to him? Was he shot?"

Another customer entered and took Doan's attention. While the store owner took care of the drover, Luke went over everything in his mind.

Brenner hadn't told him the truth about Josie. She hadn't ridden in with him at all. What was he hiding? If she hadn't been on a horse, that meant she was in the back of Walt Preston's wagon, out of sight.

Odd that he hadn't seen Brenner McCall today. He wondered if the stove-up outlaw had moved on, or just changed hidey-holes.

Brenner was the least of his concerns right now, though.

Josie could be in trouble, could be headed to a filthy jail cell. In his mind, he could hear her calling his name, begging for help. Wondering why he didn't come.

When Doan returned, he said he hadn't seen where the fellow with Preston had gone and didn't know if the bullet hit anyone or not. Luke thanked him and left. He swung into the saddle and headed toward the ferry with the roan in tow.

Twenty-one

When the little girl had tugged on Josie's hand in the crowd and begged for help, Josie hadn't hesitated. Now she hurried with the child—who said her name was Lucy—and worried. She didn't know how much aid she could give, but she'd try.

The thought that this could be a trap entered her mind. Lawmen could be using Lucy to capture her. She rested her hand on the butt of her pistol. Her heart ached with a need to know if O'Keefe had killed Luke. What if the man who'd suffered more than any person she'd ever seen lay dead in the red Texas dirt?

She didn't think she could bear that torment.

Even if he'd killed O'Keefe, he had to be wondering what had happened to her. Damn! She should've told someone. She had to hurry and get back.

"How much farther to your mother, Lucy?"

The red-haired girl glanced up. Her tight pigtails had bent and stuck out at odd angles and she sported a row of freckles that marched across her cheeks and nose like little soldiers. "We're almost there."

They'd turned right about half a mile north of the trading post and trudged downstream through high grass and brush. She should've taken time to get her horse. Only she hadn't known how far they had to go.

"Good. Tell me again what's wrong with your mother."

Lucy faced her and turned both palms up. "She's having a baby."

"Oh." When Lucy had run up at the trading post, she'd simply said her mama was ailing bad. What did Josie know about childbirth? Probably enough to fill a thimble. Maybe not even that much. "Where's your pa, Lucy?"

"Don't know. He left a long time ago and didn't come back. He might be dead. He promised he'd be back when the baby was coming, but he isn't." Lucy wrung her hands. "I didn't know what to do and Mama doesn't want a man touching her. She said for me to get a woman. You were the onliest I found."

They pushed through the overgrowth on the river's edge and stood in front of a house that appeared to be made of sticks. The place blended into the landscape so well she could have missed it.

"We're here!" Lucy ran through a door. "Mama, I brought help."

Yeah, only the woman might be in worse shape when she saw how little help Josie would be. She squared her shoulders and went inside the dim dwelling. Light through the doorway revealed only one spotless room that consisted of a bed, a small wood-burning stove, a table, and little else. She wondered where Lucy slept. Apparently with her mother or on the sloping wood floor.

Lucy took Josie's hand and pulled her to the bed. "Make it come out," she pleaded. "It's been too long."

Josie took the word "it" to mean the baby. How did someone make a baby come out? Did you push or pull?

The sweat-soaked woman tried to smile but it ended up a grimace. She suddenly screamed and reached behind to grip the iron bedstead. Josie stood, unsure of what exactly to do.

Water. She needed water. At least she could bathe the mother's face.

"Do you have water?" she asked.

Lucy pointed to a bucket. "You know what to do, don't you?"

Josie chewed her lip. "Not exactly."

"You're a woman. Women should know about babies 'n' things." The girl's hands planted on her hips didn't make Josie know more than she did.

The realization that she hadn't been a midwife or even anything resembling one in her past crossed her mind. Nor had she been a mother, and that brought a deep pang.

"I think it's something you sorta have to learn." Josie gave Lucy her sunniest smile, picked up a cloth, and dipped it in the bucket. She grabbed hold of resolve that was cowering inside and asked, "How old are you, anyway?"

"Six and a half."

How could she be this young? Miss Bossy Butt acted and talked much older than Josie.

The little girl propped her elbows on the mattress. "At first I thought you was a boy. But then someone knocked into you and your hat came off." Lucy's eyes were round. "Why do you want to dress like a boy? My pa said boys have cooties. Do you have cooties?"

Josie bathed the woman's face. "No, absolutely not."

Lucy frowned. "How come you wear that gun? Do you kill people?"

"I wear it to feel safe." As for killing people? The girl would get even more confused if Josie said she didn't know. Maybe she could just ignore that part. Thankfully, the suffering woman came to her rescue.

"Lucy, quit pestering," the woman said. She smiled at Josie. "Sorry about all this. I'm Ada. You'll have to excuse my daughter. I'm obliged for your help."

"I'm Josie. And I don't know how much I can offer, but I'll do my best. I follow directions really well." She pictured Luke's stern look through narrowed eyes and amended, "Pretty well. So, if you'll tell me what to do, I'll do it."

Lucy crawled up next to her mother and laid a hand on the swollen tummy. "Don't worry, Mama, I'll tell her what to do." She cocked her head, fixing a stare at Josie. "You gotta find a sharp knife."

Josie felt the blood drain from her face. She couldn't kill this baby. Lucy might not want a new brother or sister but she'd just have to learn to accept the little thing. "They're not so bad once you get to know them," she squeaked. "You'll come to love this little person if you give it a chance."

Ada panted as more pains came. "The knife is to cut the baby's cord."

"Oh."

Lucy's face screwed up in a frown. "Don't you know anything?"

"It so happens I do." Some things. A few things. Apparently, not a whole lot about this. "How did you know to get a knife, anyway? Kids aren't supposed to touch sharp objects."

"Mama told me all about it just in case I couldn't find help. 'Sides, I helped last week to get Mrs. Faraday's baby out." Lucy patted her mama's huge belly, giving Josie a look that said she wished she'd found someone with more smarts.

So did Josie. After fumbling around in the small kitchen, she located a knife and scrubbed the blade clean. Her hands trembled. She had to find a way to somehow manage. Behind her came grunts and anguished cries.

"You can do this. You can do this," she said to herself in hopes of bolstering her courage.

By the time she returned, Lucy was gripping her mother's hand and telling her to hurry up. Then Ada screeched, "It's coming! Get down there. Tell me what you see."

Fear dried the spit in Josie's mouth. With her heart pounding, she quickly followed Ada's request. Her heart thudding against her ribs, Josie did everything the woman told her and the minutes crept by. Then amid the loudest screams and grunts she'd ever heard, Josie found herself holding a newborn. A little boy.

He was slippery and blue. And silent.

Damn her ignorance! What was she supposed to do now? And Ada had passed out.

"Now you hafta put your fingers inside the mouth and take some stuff out," Lucy instructed. "Hurry. Then you gotta spank the baby real hard."

Oh, heaven above. Why? It seemed cruel to spank the little thing simply for being born.

She glanced at Ada's pale face for confirmation. But the woman was unconscious. The outcome was up to Josie.

She was out of her element but she knew she had to act fast. She could do this. A life depended on her. With fear of failing washing over her, she laid the baby down and slid trembling fingers into the newborn's mouth to clear his throat.

"Now, hold the baby upside down and give it a good swat," Lucy said. "You gotta make him cry. Hurry."

"Yes, Lucy. I pray you're right." Josie did, but not very hard. She couldn't. Still no cry.

"Hit it harder!" Lucy yelled.

Josie delivered another slap on the buttocks, harder this time, and the newest member of the family gave a pitiful cry that sounded more like a lamb's bleat. Joy filled her. She grinned. She'd saved a life rather than taken one. Her. And quite possibly for the first time.

She wrapped the tiny boy and laid him next to his mother. She wished Ada would come around.

Lucy pursed her lips and passed her some string and the knife. The girl was as cool and calm as a blue winter sky. She'd make a good general. "Gotta tie it off and cut that cord. Jesus, it's sure long!"

"Don't use the Lord's name in vain, Lucy," Josie scolded, panting. She licked her lips and stared at the line connecting the baby to Ada. She gulped. "Where?"

"Tie a piece of string here and here." Ada indicated where with her fingers. "You cut in the middle."

Miss Bossy leaned close to observe and keep her on task. Josie felt as though she'd face dire consequences if she didn't pass the test. And who's to say what failing would do? She didn't know enough to argue.

Minutes sped by until finally she breathed a sigh of relief. Miss Bossy Butt handed her a towel to catch the blood. Then a whole bunch of other stuff came out of Ada, which required several more towels.

Ada finally came around and took the baby in her arms. "I'm sorry for conking out on you, Josie. I'm glad you were here."

"We almost lost him, Mama," Lucy announced, quite the voice of authority.

Josie slumped to the floor, totally exhausted. After a short rest, she rose and busied herself making Ada comfortable. She fed her and Lucy a light meal and began the cleanup. She knew how to do that.

Miss Bossy of course oversaw everything. When Josie asked her to help, Lucy informed her she was just a kid.

Yeah, a very spoiled kid at that.

With the chores finished, Josie took the baby boy from his sleeping mother's side and gently cleaned him. She didn't think she'd ever seen a more beautiful baby. Swaddling him, she held him close. A feeling of happiness and longing swelled in her heart.

She wanted a child—Luke Weston's child.

What kind of father would he make?

Watching him with Sierra and Sam's baby two days ago told her he wanted a child too, and he'd protect it fiercely.

Memories of their lovemaking filled her thoughts. A feeling of the familiar, such as when she'd held the gun, stole over her. She'd made love before. With someone.

Who? Had she loved him? Was he waiting for her?

Lucy plopped down beside her and gave her a nudge. "I want to hold my brother."

"That's an excellent idea." Josie made the transfer and sat back.

A change came over the bossy little girl. Lucy fussed and cooed and kissed on her brother, telling him she'd always look after him and they'd go fishing and digging for worms and steal away on a boat and have all kinds of fun.

Josie's throat tightened. This was love in its purest form. She hoped when she discovered her past she would find a brother or sister who'd doted on her the same way.

The sun was on the waning side of the afternoon. Luke would be frantic. She told Lucy she had to go and stood.

"No, wait!" the girl cried. Handing the baby to Josie, she told her to lay him next to her dozing mama and come outside with her.

"All right, but just for a minute." After laying the baby next to Ada, Josie followed Lucy to a lean-to in the back where her father probably kept his horse. "What is it?"

The girl knelt beside a box full of playful kittens. They appeared to be about a month old. She selected a cute solid black one and held it out to Josie. "Here. This is for giving me my baby brother."

"How precious." Josie put her face next to the soft fur. "But, honey, you don't have to give me anything. You did most of the work. If you hadn't told me what to do, I'd have stood there like an imbecile."

"Yep, I know," Lucy admitted. "But I saw you had promise. Mama always says that it's important to repay people for kindness."

"Your mama is a smart lady."

"I know. Besides, she'd switch my legs good if I didn't."

Josie leaned down to kiss the precocious child's freckled cheek. "You're going to grow up to be an important person, mark my words."

"That kitten was the runt of the litter and almost died," Lucy said. "He's the best one."

The words hit Josie like a blow. It was true that the weakest and most vulnerable were often the ones with the most heart. She could almost hear Luke's agony as he'd shared his secrets last night. Though he'd deny it, his heart had more depth than anyone's.

The brush rustled and Josie swung around, hoping she'd find Luke. But the approaching rider didn't bear any resemblance. Disappointment filled her.

"Pa!" Lucy cried. "We have a baby!"

"Oh no." He slid from the saddle in a panic. "I was supposed to have been back in time. I rode hard, hoping I'd make it, but the road had washed out and I had to take the long way around. I've missed you, punkin. How's your mother?"

"She's good. I have a brother," Lucy shouted, giggling. "And I helped get him out."

Josie smiled, introduced herself, and shook his hand. "You have a beautiful son."

"Call me Ben. Thank you for helping my Ada." The man pushed back his hat to reveal his red hair. "I'm so sorry I got delayed. Sorry I missed it. If anything had happened to Ada, I don't know what I'd do."

"She gave me a scare but I think she's fine now." Josie found his concern for his wife touching. How would Luke feel if something happened to her? Would his world tilt, knocking him off balance? Or would he go on as normal?

After Ben hugged and fussed over his wife and son, he loaded Josie on his horse and walked beside her back to the trading post. She thanked him, wishing him well.

The sun hung low as Josie looked around for Luke but she didn't see him anywhere.

Had he left her? Had he simply ridden on without her?

Or...oh dear God...had O'Keefe managed to best him?

A sob strangled in her throat as she adjusted her hat to cover her hair, and opened the door to Doan's Trading Post.

A gentleman with graying hair and a long, droopy mustache came toward her. "I was about to close up. Can I help you?"

She tried to lower her voice to sound like a male and said, "Looking for Luke Weston. Know where I might find him?"

"I'm sorry to say I don't. After he brought the shovel back, he left and I haven't seen him since."

Relief weakened her knees. He was alive. That rotten man hadn't killed him. "Shovel?" she said. "What did he need with a shovel?"

"Weston insisted on burying the dead man so I loaned

him one." Doan's faded blue eyes twinkled. "You're his missing partner. I've never seen a man more worked up when he couldn't find you. I'm sure he's scouring every inch around here for you."

Luke was worked up? That had to mean that she meant something, at least a little, to him.

Josie thanked him and left. Outside, she glanced in both directions. Where could he be? What was she going to do? She had no horse or anything except what she had on.

Deep loneliness swept through her as a sob tried to rise.

What if Luke had given up on her and decided to go back to the Lone Star? What if their lovemaking last night hadn't meant as much as she'd thought? What if he'd decided she was too much trouble?

The kitten mewed. She stroked the soft fur. "I guess it's you and me now." She held the kitten up. "You need a name. Lucy said you were a boy, so we need a boy's name."

She thought for several minutes and discarded everything that came to mind, finding none that fit. Finally, it struck her. "You're going to be Rafael. I'm going to find us a place to spend the night, then we'll start walking." She'd head out to the Lone Star at daybreak as Luke had told her to do in case they became separated.

The kitten would fill the immense loneliness. She scanned the travelers making small camps. Best to stay apart from them. She'd return to the squatter's shack. Maybe she'd find Luke there.

Before she could move, a solid black horse came toward her. The rider was tall in the saddle and moved as one with the animal.

"Luke!" She began to run.

The horse came at a gallop. Luke slid off before Major John came to a halt. He met her and lifted her up. Laughter sprang into Josie's throat.

She'd found him. Her world had righted again.

She was safe now.

Twenty-two

Frantic mewing dragged Luke's attention away from the feel of Josie in his arms. A cat? Where was the rascal? He hated cats with a passion—more than he hated buttermilk or persimmons. The animals always stared at him with hate in their little evil, glittering eyes.

When he lowered Josie, she thrust a kitten under his nose and announced, "Look what I brought."

"I see." He took a step back and returned the ball of fur's stare with one of equal dislike. In his opinion, all cats were devil-possessed, just waiting to steal someone's breath or put a curse on him.

He was cursed enough.

And this one was black—the worst kind.

"Oh, Luke, Rafael likes you." Josie beamed.

Great. "Where did you get him and where have you been? I've looked all over for you."

She told him about Ada and that Lucy had given her the cat to repay her.

"I'm glad you could help out but I wish you'd taken time to tell someone or leave a note or something." He raked his hands through his hair.

"I know, but I didn't think I had a moment to waste. I'm sorry."

Josie glanced up and he fell into the depths of her

brownish-green gaze. Heated desire in her eyes made him forget about the lost day and his search. He even forgot about the damn cat. All he could think about was getting her somewhere private.

"What are you going to do with...Rafael?" Why in the heck had she named the cat that, anyway? There were books full of nothing but names. Far better ones than his, for God's sake.

"Keep him, of course."

"Of course." Why didn't he think of that? He shifted his gaze to the cat and it hissed. The feeling was mutual, he thought sourly.

"I want to hear about the fight with Munroe O'Keefe," she said, dragging his attention back to her. "Tell me what happened."

"Nothing to tell. He's in a grave. That's all that matters."

Josie laid a hand on his chest. "It's not even a quarter of what matters. I see the pain your eyes. I know it cost you."

"Yeah, well, it's over and done. No need to dwell on it."

"We'll talk about it later. Where's my roan?"

"At the shack. I figure we'll sleep there again since it's getting late and head out tomorrow. I think we've learned all we're going to here." He helped her onto the gelding, bared his teeth at the cat in her arms, then climbed up behind her.

"Where will we go when we leave?" she asked.

"Back to the Lone Star. I want to see how Noah's doing. I need time to think and plan my next move."

She squirmed, grinding her bottom against him to get comfortable. Luke gritted his teeth and focused on his numbers. Two plus two equaled six. No, four. Five plus five was ten. Oh, dear Lord. Sweat popped out on his forehead. Josie Morgan was going to drive him straight into an early grave, he decided. He draped an arm across her chest and pulled her snug against him.

Luke nuzzled her neck and was rewarded with a happy sigh.

He wouldn't complain about the damn cat as long as Josie stayed near.

As night fell, they made a fire and cooked supper. Luke talked about the gunfight with O'Keefe.

Josie leaned against him, putting her head on his shoulder. "Why did you feel the need to bury him? He tried to kill you."

"Because one day, I'll want someone to do that for me." Luke drew in a ragged breath. "I don't want them to leave me for the animals to eat. It brings chills to think of them gnawing on my bones." He kissed her forehead. "I had a hard enough time leaving Noah's uncle and the other guy and riding off. If the kid hadn't been so sick, I would've put them below ground."

Josie glanced up. "You never let it show how you feel. You're a constant surprise, Luke."

"Before you drag more secrets out, tell me about this little girl, Lucy. She sounds like a corker."

He watched Josie's smile as she recounted the details. "That girl couldn't have been more than six or seven and smarter than God allows. She made me feel really dumb."

"Well, you're not."

Her smile faded. "Luke, I don't know what I did before but I know for sure what I wasn't. I wasn't a midwife, or even a mother, or I'd have known how to help Ada. Doc Jenkins told me that I'll automatically know and do the same things I did before without even having to think about it. He said amnesia won't change that. Still, some part of me wanted to be a mother."

"Josie, it's good that you're not." His voice softened. "You wouldn't want to find out that you left some little kids to fend for themselves or have someone else take care of them while you're gone. Would you?"

"I see your point, and no. It's just that my heart seems to go out to children—like Noah. He said I spent time with him and gave him Rowdy." She smoothed Rafael's black fur. The kitten mewed. "How do you feel about children, Luke? Do you want some one day?"

"I never let myself think about things like that. Not even

with Angelina. It makes me boiling mad when people hurt them, but as far as having one of my own…I block that from my mind."

"Why?"

"Men like me don't live long enough to raise a son or daughter and I don't want a kid growing up without a pa. Believe me, I know what that's like." He stood and pulled her up. "I need to check on the horses and then you and I need to call it a day. I'm beat." He grinned. "You kept me awake all night with your demands."

Josie gave him a playful push. "Just for that, you can sleep on your own damn bedroll. Don't come near mine."

As Luke let the night swallow him, he paused and glanced back at the woman standing by the campfire. The longer this journey took, the more they were learning. That she knew nothing about birthing babies was big. Seemed her mother would've told her a little about the process somewhere along the line. But she hadn't. Which led him to wonder what kind of mother Josie'd had.

And what about her father? The two gunrunners had said that Josie's father had planned the whole scheme and wasn't one to mess with. Luke didn't buy into much of the gunrunners' tale. Shiftless men like them played fast and loose with the truth.

Luke's gut said Brenner was the Captain. But how did he fit into it all? What was he hiding? And what had happened to him?

Luke's thoughts went back to the word association game he'd played with Josie following that first night. When he'd thrown out the word *saloon*, she'd replied, "Home."

Home in a saloon? Where? Why wasn't someone looking for her?

Luke shook his head. The questions still outnumbered the answers by a large margin.

Josie was terrified of what they'd find. That's why she wanted to quit. Part of him did too. Whatever he discovered could take her away from him. He didn't know if he'd find the will to live, to go back to his dead life once she was gone.

His feelings for her were strong and lasting. But it wasn't love.

He couldn't offer Josie that or the things she needed. Someone who'd be around to hold her, not someone hard like him.

Not an outlaw—a killer.

Luke was riding along a narrow trail that cut between large boulders. Everything screamed ambush. He wouldn't see the bastards until too late. Those damn buzzards circled overhead, their beady eyes searching. Waiting for him to die, waiting to peck out his eyes. He heard the roar of a pistol, felt the bullet ripping into his back, shredding the muscle and tissue. He didn't want to die this way. He wasn't ready. Please let him live a little longer.

Fire raced through his body as he fell from the saddle. Blood poured from him, soaking into the ground. Life ebbed from him until he no longer felt the pain. His breath became slower, his eyes heavy. His Colt lay inches away with the word Legend *winking at him. The last thing he saw before the blackness engulfed him.*

Luke jerked awake, drenched in sweat, gasping for air, his lungs burning. Tears ran down his face. He'd just seen his death. His stomach clenched at the premonition that he wouldn't have long.

Following the nightmare, he spent hours watching Josie sleep. He'd made love to her once because he'd been unable to resist her nearness, then let her sleep alone.

He had to let her go. How he could live with the loss, he didn't know. It, too, would be like dying.

He rose and stood in the open doorway of the shack for a while, staring out into the black gloom, trying to settle the decision in him. Once, Josie had come up behind and slipped her arms around him. They hadn't spoken. Maybe

Josie had known there was nothing to say. She had to feel him slipping away.

Muttering silent curses, he'd laid back down and must've dozed off because he'd woken to find the damned cat curled up next to him. He'd picked up the animal and plunked it down next to Josie.

When the first slim fingers of dawn poked through the cracks in the walls, Luke finally rose and put the coffee on.

Josie sat up and stretched. "Good morning."

"Morning," Luke answered. He took in her tousled hair, the color of ripe wheat, and the outline of her body. He swallowed hard and turned away, steeling himself.

Rafael left the warmth of the blanket to arch his back against Luke's boots.

Luke didn't know why, but he picked up the kitten and held it eye to eye. "You'd better behave yourself at the Lone Star," he growled. "You won't have the run of the joint. Stoker will feed you to the cows."

Rafael hissed and would've caught Luke's chin with his claw, except Luke was too fast.

"Don't scare him like that, Luke," Josie scolded, tucking in her shirt. "The poor thing is probably missing his mother."

"Humph!" Luke set him down and checked the coffee.

"I'm going out to take care of girl business," Josie said. "I'll check the horses."

"Don't be long. The coffee's ready."

Pulling on her boots, she left. Luke filled his cup and stepped to the door. The light of the rising sun caught on a spider's web covering nearby clumps of sage and milkweed, making it shimmer like pure silver. It danced in the morning breeze. He sipped on the hot brew, letting it clear his head, thinking how much he liked it here.

Josie suddenly ran from leafy cover. "Major John is gone!"

Luke rushed toward her. "He's not with the roan?"

"No." She wrung her hands. "I wonder if someone stole him."

He handed her the cup and strode through the waist-high

tangle of thorns and weeds. Only the roan remained. There was no sign of his black gelding. Just trampled grass where he'd once been. There was no sign of the rope either. Had someone untied the horse and left with it? Then why not take them both?

He untied the roan. "I'm going to see if I can find him."

"Want me to come too?"

"No. Have your coffee and get ready to ride."

Disappointment was etched on Josie's face. Luke tried to block it out but found it lodged in his mind as he followed Major's tracks. They led to the trading post.

A crowd had gathered around the front of the building. He wondered what they were looking at. Luke dismounted and tied the roan to the hitching rail. He stared in disbelief. Hell!

Major John had broken open two kegs of beer from an untended shipment being unloaded and was lapping up the last of the contents. The gelding raised his head, looked at Luke through bleary eyes, and snorted.

Jonathan Doan stood frowning, his arms crossed.

"Doan, I'm sorry about my horse," Luke said. "He somehow untied himself. I'll pay for the damages. Just can't right away, though. Give me a few days and I'll be back with the money."

"I wondered who that horse belonged to." Doan chuckled. "Never saw one with such an appetite for beer before. I once had a roan, though, that I couldn't keep tied or in a barn. It could unlatch any door or untie any knot. The damndest thing I ever saw. We'd find him in a cornfield, eating until he popped."

"Horses are sure contrary sometimes," Luke agreed.

"They sure are. Hey, don't worry about the damages, Weston. It's worth losing a keg to collect such a crowd. Business has never been so good." Doan glanced up. "If you ever want to sell him, I'll give you a fair price."

"Thanks, I'll keep that in mind. But I doubt I'll want to get rid of Major John." Luke caught the rope dangling from the horse and made a clicking sound in his mouth, the order to get moving. Major lapped up the remainder of the beer before he finally budged.

With a defiant shake of his head, the animal slowly moseyed after Luke.

A small boy laughed and hollered to his friend, "Joey, come see a beer-drinking horse."

A parade followed them, everyone wanting to see the spectacle. Luke cringed at the attention. Crowds never signified anything good, at least not in his experience. But they turned back as he and the two horses plunged into the thick undergrowth.

Blessed silence surrounded him.

Except for his hiccupping horse. The animal kept wanting to lie down and it was a struggle to keep him moving. Once Major John rested his head on the roan's rump and Luke had to stop and wait a minute.

Josie, playing with the kitten, glanced up with relief when she saw Luke. "I see you found him. Where was he?"

"At the trading post."

Major John gave a loud whinny, hiccupped, and nibbled at the grass. Josie walked around him, sniffing. "Luke, he smells like a brewery. Is he—"

"Sick on beer? Yep." Of all times to indulge in that bad habit. They needed to ride.

"What are we going to do?"

"Have no choice but to let him rest a while, make sure he doesn't get colicky." Luke tied the roan to the low branch of a willow. "If he gets colic, we're done for."

"How long does it usually take?"

"He should be okay to ride in a couple of hours. I hope." Luke gave his gelding a frustrated glare. "Guess we'll see."

"I confess, I thought you made that story up about him being a beer-drinking horse. I never thought it was true."

"Yep, it's true." Luke shook his head. "I always fear that he'll pull something like this when I'm in the middle of a mess and have only seconds to get away."

"That would be bad." A smile tugged at the corners of Josie's mouth. "Appears we have some time to kill. Any ideas?"

Luke couldn't miss the hope in her voice that he'd welcome her again in his arms. Honor wouldn't let him give her hope. "I have some playing cards in my saddlebag. Ever play poker?"

Josie knitted her brows. "I don't know."

"Won't hurt to find out. We can put more coffee on and make us a bite to eat first." Luke was curious to test her skill with the cards. If her home *was* in a saloon, then she probably knew how to play well.

He prepared to get his rear beaten by the prettiest lady this side of eternity.

The one he couldn't have.

Twenty-three

Josie rode next to Luke toward the Lone Star Ranch. Major John still wasn't quite right, even after waiting three hours, but at least the horse appeared to be all right. Not wanting to spend an extra day at the Crossing, they'd left before the animal was completely up to the ride.

Something was wrong with Luke and Josie didn't know what. He seemed out of sorts and had kept her at arm's length all day. He'd never talked much anyway, but he hadn't said two words since they'd left.

More than just the silence, his mood had changed and gone was the closeness they'd enjoyed the last two days. Everything between them had vanished, as though the kisses and the scorching heat of their naked bodies had been nothing more than a figment of her imagination.

Finally, she could take no more. "Dammit, Luke, something's wrong. Did I make you mad? Just because I beat you soundly at cards four out of six times—"

"Don't be ridiculous. But I did learn never to play with you unless I want to lose my reputation. I've only seen a few people with your kind of skill, and they were all men."

With a shrug, she said, "Maybe it was dumb luck. If you're not angry about that, what then?"

She couldn't see his eyes, hidden as they were in the shadow of his black Stetson. He'd exchanged his buffalo hunter garb for his old clothes, his form-fitting trousers with silver conchas trailing up both sides. He looked the same as when he'd untied her on the prairie.

Except he wasn't. Neither was she. They weren't the same people.

"Talking about it solves nothing."

"Aha! So it's not my imagination," she crowed. "Can you at least give me a hint of the problem?"

"It's me, all right? I was wrong to let you get close, for me to say the things I did. To allow us to make love."

Hurt pierced her heart. He didn't want her.

"Why? Just tell me that." Unshed tears filled her eyes.

Luke was silent for a good minute before he finally spoke. "You deserve someone better. Someone not toting around a past littered with bodies."

Anger crawled up Josie's spine. He'd decided all this by himself without giving her a chance to speak her piece. Dammit, she'd speak it now!

"Don't open the door to heaven if I can't come in," she snapped. "I won't stand on the outside with my face pressed against the glass like some poor little beggar child. Don't play with my feelings. I know I didn't invite men into my bed before like I did you. I didn't. I'm not that kind. Dammit, I'm...not." Josie turned away to hide her quivering chin.

"I never said you were." Luke moved the gelding closer to her roan and took her hand. "In a perfect world, and Lord knows that doesn't exist, I'd brand you with my touch and spend the rest of my life waking up with you. I never thought I'd find a woman like you. For a short while you made me feel almost normal. You made me forget that I have a date with destiny."

He paused then said gently, "I won't make you a widow."

A widow would be a lot better than being alone like she was now. Besides, who said he was going to die? On whose authority? Luke was going to live because she was going to make sure he did.

And he didn't have a say in the matter.

Without warning, five gunmen rode from a thicket onto the road, blocking it. Josie's horse reared and she would've slid from the saddle if she hadn't clutched the reins tighter.

"Can't let you pass. Turn around," one man ordered.

"What are you talking about?" Luke demanded. "I have a right to go down this road to the Lone Star."

"Not across Mr. Granger's land, you don't." The speaker swung his rifle around, pointing it at Luke. "I suggest you find another road."

Josie watched Luke's face darken. She knew he was thinking about challenging these men and had no doubt he could put them all onto the ground. Five against one was easy odds for Luke. And if he wanted to fight through, she'd help.

At last, though, Luke glanced at her and turned his gelding in the direction they'd come. She glared at the despicable armed men and followed. They didn't know how lucky they were.

Out of sight of them, Luke reined to a halt. "I don't know what's happening but I suspect Newt Granger just declared war on Stoker. We've got to get to the Lone Star, and we'll have to go the long way."

"How far is the long way?"

"Eighteen hours or more. If we ride through the night, we might make it in time for breakfast."

"I'll follow you," Josie said. All the way to the ends of the earth.

The sun had dipped low on the horizon by the time they rode down the dusty street of Medicine Springs. The town was a lively place, with rows of businesses. She counted three saloons and all were in full swing, light, music, and laughter spilling out into the street. One—the Lucky Lady—drew her as though extending a hand. Josie stopped to stare.

She'd been here. She was almost positive.

Maybe it was the sign outside, bearing a painting of a woman's head with bright-red lips and big, suggestive eyes.

Or maybe it was the music. She simply knew she needed to go inside.

Luke pulled up beside her. "What's wrong?"

"I've been here before," Josie answered, drawing her brows together in an attempt to remember. Something. Anything. She held Rafael to her chest for security. "It's familiar."

"In what way?"

Josie closed her eyes, letting the sounds penetrate, trying to pull up an image lurking in the shadows of her mind. "I've definitely been here." She grabbed his arm. "Luke, I was here."

"Is this your home? Or just somewhere you've been?"

"I don't know," she replied miserably.

"Move out of the street. I'm going inside to ask around." Luke grabbed her reins and led the roan to a hitching rail.

Josie dismounted, putting Rafael into a saddlebag. He'd stay put until she came back. "I'm coming with you."

She could tell by Luke's expression that he wanted to argue, but he kept quiet and a minute later pushed the batwing doors aside for her. She scanned the packed room. Every table was filled and men stood two deep at the bar.

Her glance swept to the stairs leading to the second floor. Oh, how she wanted to go up there. She moved in that direction when a drunk wobbled into her and pushed her sideways into another man. He emptied his mug down the front of her shirt.

Luke pushed him toward the bar. "Go get another, pardner."

"I believe I will." The man gave a goofy smile and staggered off, leaving Josie beer-soaked.

"Hey, mister." Luke grabbed a passing bartender and pulled him over. "Say, who owns this joint?"

The spindly man had to be around forty years of age. He'd parted his hair in the middle and slicked it back on both sides, the strands glistening with pomade so they couldn't move if they wanted to. "Sable."

"Sable who?" Josie needed a last name.

"All I know. I ain't worked here long." He glanced toward impatient customers pounding on the polished bar.

Josie sagged against Luke as the bartender rushed to stop a man from launching an empty beer mug at a very expensive mirror. Disappointment rushed through her.

"I take it the name isn't familiar." Luke tightened his hold on her.

"No." She'd been so sure that knowing would have triggered something. But she got no flashes of anything. Nothing except the blur of movement as a chair flew in the air toward them.

Luke barely jerked her out of the way in time. The chair crashed to the floor, breaking into pieces. "Let's get out of here."

His hand on her waist, Luke maneuvered her through the doors and onto the boardwalk. Josie turned for a last glance at the establishment that still felt so familiar. Why would she have been there? Why?

But the answer eluded her. She retrieved Rafael from the saddlebag, smoothing his black fur to soothe herself. She climbed on her horse and rode out with Luke. Her life was a shambles. She had no memory, no home, no family, and Luke didn't want her. Josie bit her trembling lip.

She owned nothing except a scrawny black cat.

What was she going to do now?

Dawn broke as they rode at last under the crossbar of the Lone Star. Luke breathed easier. Josie was safe.

Now to find some way to leave her. He had to find Brenner McCall. After their conversation at Doan's Crossing, it had become more apparent that Brenner held the key to both her situation and the deal with Ned Sweeney. Only, he had this mess with Newt Granger on his hands. He had to help protect the Lone Star and land he might one day claim. Luke released a troubled sigh.

An odd thing—Stoker wasn't there waiting, and Luke felt a momentary twinge of sad loss.

Stoker rode down to the gate every sunrise and sunset? His father had missed one. Hell, maybe he'd just said that and hadn't actually meant it.

The ranch was milling with people, even at this early hour. Luke spurred his gelding and he and Josie trotted toward headquarters and dismounted. Houston and Stoker stormed out and down the porch steps.

"Glad you're here, Luke. The ranch is under attack!" Stoker thundered. "Newt Granger's about to regret he's messed with me. The lying, no-good, cheating land grabber!"

"Calm down, Pa, before you have apoplexy. Doc warned you about getting overexcited." Houston thrust a hat in Stoker's hands. "Here, you forgot this."

Stoker yanked the hat from Houston and jammed it on his head. "I'll simmer down when Granger opens the damn road. I've wired Sam and he should be on the way, but he'll either have to come by river or go plumb down to Medicine Springs and back up." Stoker glared toward the western horizon. "Hell and be damned!"

"What exactly happened?" Luke had never seen Stoker so worked up and it was quite a sight.

"Pa got into another poker game with Newt two nights ago and won the man's prize racehorse," Houston explained.

"And now he's saying I cheated and demands I give it back!" Storm clouds didn't compare to Stoker's face. "I'll return that horse when I get my land back."

Only two things would get Stoker so worked up—land, or someone threatening his boys. Luke pushed back his hat. "So that's what this is about. Armed gunmen wouldn't let us through and we had to circle down and come the long way."

"Granger stole that western section from me and we've fought about it the last three years, but I never thought the two-bit land grabber would stoop this low." Stoker looked like he was itching to let the cusswords fly. Luke could tell by the way he shifted his glance to Josie and swallowed before shouting, "Hell!"

"I remember your warning about crossing that land when we had outlaw trouble in Lost Point a couple of years back. But when Houston drove those cattle up to Dodge City last year, he didn't have a problem getting through," Luke said. "Granger never bothered us back then."

Houston widened his stance as if bracing for a fight. He was as big and muscular as Stoker, except with a gentler disposition. Thank God. "Granger came over and talked Pa into another poker game, saying it was his chance to get that western section back. But then Granger changed his mind and bet his favorite racehorse instead. Pa won and now Granger is accusing him of hiding an ace up his sleeve, which are fighting words in themselves. He threatened to shoot us."

A blood feud. Luke's thoughts went to his conversation with Brenner about the subject. He knew how those usually ended—piles of dead bodies.

Josie yawned, clutching Rafael. "I hate to change such a serious subject, but how is Noah? I've been anxious to find out."

When Stoker assured her he was better, she asked, "Would you perhaps have some coffee and an egg? We rode all night. It seems I do my best thinking when my belly is full."

"Forgive my lack of manners, Miss Josie." Stoker took her arm, patting her hand. "I'll see you to the kitchen personally." He glanced back. "Luke, Houston, we can finish this around the table. We need to discuss our next move. But get some ranch hands out there so the bastards can't come across."

Houston held the door. "I'll take care of that and join you." He strode off toward the group of ranch hands at the corral, who already had their horses saddled.

"Sounds good to me." Luke followed his father inside. The prospect of hot coffee and food lured him too. The all-night ride had taken a toll.

At the door, Luke paused and glanced back over the hauntingly beautiful land. He'd fight to the last breath to keep anyone from taking it. He didn't actually own a piece of it yet, not really, but he'd made a down payment in a manner of speaking. Maybe loyalty and trust were good enough reasons to die trying to protect it.

He'd eat and help his father and brother decide the best course to take. If he had time, he'd catch a little shut-eye. Then he'd ride.

First to find Brenner. Locate him, and he'd find Reno Kidd. The two names kept popping up together even though Brenner professed to hate Kidd. And Josie was in the middle. Damn it! Something told him Ned Sweeney was involved in this whole ball of string too. How else would Brenner know where Sweeney was to give him the tip about Dead Horse Creek? Answers to all of it teased Luke's mind as Josie's elusive memory did hers. If he could just find the end of the string, he could unravel all the secrets and lies. He was so close he could taste it.

In all likelihood, Reno had hired out his gun to Granger. Kidd was drawn to violence—and gold—like flies to an outhouse. The man lived for the thrill of killing, and getting paid for it would double the incentive. If Granger was hiring guns to wage war on them, Kidd would be in the thick of it. And despite Brenner's avowal to stay clear of war, he would be too.

If Luke could just get the pieces to fit. He had to have a talk with Newt Granger.

Luke would—and could—do more than his share to protect this ranch that Stoker had established after Texas won its freedom. His gaze shifted to the flag flying high above the land that his father loved with all his heart. Stoker's sweat and blood had soaked into every inch of this ground. Now it was Luke's turn. He still had blood he hadn't spilled and he would make the time. It might be for naught but he'd give his all.

For the Lone Star and Texas.

For his family.

For a chance to ride as a Legend...if only for one day.

Twenty-four

Luke went upstairs instead of following Stoker and Josie into the kitchen. He needed to check on Noah. Even though he knew the boy was better, he still had to see with his own eyes.

Rowdy barked when Luke pushed open the door. The dog trotted over and sniffed his boots. Evidently, the mutt had taken a job as sentry but remembered Luke was a friend. He licked Luke's hand when he reached down to pet him.

The noise woke Noah. He smiled at Luke. "You came back."

"Of course I did. You didn't think I was fibbing, did you?" Luke helped the boy sit up and adjusted some pillows behind him, then sat on the side of the bed. He noticed a tray with remnants of Noah's breakfast sitting on a small table. "I expected to see you up, barking orders and running this ranch by now."

"Papa Stoker says I might someday." Noah grinned. "Do you really think he meant it?"

Luke grinned and ruffled his hair. "Papa Stoker?"

"It didn't feel right me calling him Stoker. Even though she's in heaven, my mama was frowning at me. Now she's happy and I think Papa Stoker likes me calling him that." Noah drew his brows together. "What do you think?"

The kid astonished him—to be so young and yet so wise.

But then, he'd had to grow up fast. Noah had probably lived several lifetimes when he was with his sorry uncle.

"The name fits. You call him whatever feels good. You know, you have quite a head on those shoulders," Luke said.

"But do you think I might run this ranch someday?"

"I know so. You've got smarts—you know how to count cows." Luke noticed the kid's clean hair. "Someone washed and cut your hair, boy. I can see that you *do* have eyes in your face after all."

"The housekeeper did it. Mrs. Ross is real nice. She smells like my mama." Noah seemed to sense Luke hadn't come to talk about the housekeeper. "I'm feeling better, Luke. Doc says he might let me walk to the porch and sit out there in a few days."

"That's good, kid. You had me worried. Anytime you want to go see what's going on outside these doors, I'll carry you. You don't have to wait until you can walk. Fresh air might be sorta nice."

The boy shook his head. "Papa Stoker offered too, but I'd rather wait until I can make it on my own. Me and Rowdy are fine up here."

"Noah, there's no shame in asking for help." His own words echoed inside Luke. If he really believed that, why did he refuse to do it himself? Stoker and his brothers had all tried to help. Luke squirmed, not liking the lesson.

"I know there's no shame," Noah said. "But I don't wanna be bothersome, for anyone to have to do everything for me."

"You couldn't be bothersome if you tried." Luke grinned when Rowdy wiggled into his lap. He stroked the little dog's head. "Guess what Josie found."

"What?"

"A kitten—a black one."

"Where is it? I want to see," Noah said.

"It's in the kitchen. I'm sure she'll bring the fur ball up after she eats." Luke eyed Rowdy. "What do you think this dog is going to do to find you with a kitten?"

Noah shrugged. "Guess we'll have to see. Rowdy's awful jealous. How come you're not eating, Luke?"

"Because I wanted to look in on you first, partner. I can eat anytime."

"Well, I think I'm getting tired, so you might as well go on and do it now." Noah forced a yawn and snuggled down in the covers.

Luke cocked his head sideways. He saw through the boy easily enough. Noah seemed to have aged twenty years in the time they'd been gone. Noah shouldn't talk this grown-up or care about Luke's empty belly. But he did.

"I'll be back later. So will Josie," he said. "I hope you'll be through with your nap by then."

"I will," Noah said, grinning. "I want to see the kitten."

Luke laughed. He'd just been replaced by a damn black cat.

Stoker slammed a fist to the table, rattling the dishes. "I want to ride over there and ask that whopper-jawed runt what the hell he thinks he's doing."

Luke took a seat in the breakfast room and calmly poured a cup of coffee. "That's exactly what you shouldn't do."

"Why the hell not?" Stoker pinned Luke with a gaze.

Houston strode through the door. "Because you'll get into a shouting match with Granger and there'll be no putting out the fire. Next thing you know, they'll shoot one or two of the ranch hands and we'll shoot back and this whole part of the country will be in a war."

"Houston's right," Luke said, taking a sip of coffee. He moved his elbow to let Cook slide a plate of eggs in front of him. Luke noticed the cat was missing and assumed Josie had put him in her room.

Josie's arm brushed his. "How is Noah?"

"Older. Haven't we just been gone two days or did I fall asleep for twenty years?"

She laughed. "Nope, it's just been two days."

"That boy's a keeper," Stoker said, propping his elbows on the table. "Smart as a whip." He chuckled. "I'm thinking of making him ranch foreman. He and I play checkers every evening and he whips the tar out of me. I haven't ridden down to the gate once since he's been here either." A faraway look came into Stoker's eyes. "I think William Travis would've turned out a lot like Noah." He gave a mournful sigh.

Who was William Travis? Luke crooked an eyebrow at Houston.

"He was Sam's and my kid brother," Houston explained. "He didn't live to see two years old."

"I'm so sorry," Josie said, laying a hand on Stoker's arm. "I'm sure you must miss him."

Stoker gave her a half smile. "Every single day."

Boots struck the polished wood floor and Sam strode into the breakfast room. The silver star on his chest gleamed in the lamplight. "I came as soon as I could. What are we going to do?"

"That's what we're trying to figure out," Stoker said. "So far, Houston and Luke have shot down all my suggestions."

"With good reason, I'm sure." Sam pulled out a chair and grabbed the coffee, nodding at Josie. "I have a feeling this may be a three-pot meeting."

"We need to defuse this keg of dynamite, Pa, instead of throwing kerosene and matches on it." Houston rose and looked out the kitchen window. "If we don't play this right, we could end up with a bloodbath and still lose the Lone Star."

Stoker's glare was the kind to scald a person. "No one is going to run us off our land. Not that beady-eyed possum Newt Granger, not a herd of armed bullies, not anybody. This land is ours. This is Legend land, run by Legend men, and Granger can go straight to hell!" He set down his cup rather forcefully and stood so suddenly his chair clattered backward onto the floor.

Rowdy yelped as though he'd been shot and ran under Josie's chair. She lifted the shivering dog into her lap.

"Pa, think about our ranch hands and their families," Sam said. "We're obligated to them, and carting home a bunch of them dead…" He let the sentence trail off before adding, "Will we be able to live with ourselves?"

"Nope," answered Houston without turning from the window.

"Granger doesn't have the guts to kill a man outright." Sam stuffed a biscuit into his mouth. "But I can't say the same for his hired guns. Granger picked up two more gunslingers in Lost Point yesterday."

Stoker huffed. "Who knows how many he has now."

"I should be the one to go talk to him," Luke said. "If he recognizes me, I could say I've decided to cut ties with family and offer my services. I doubt he'd turn down help."

The fact that Granger probably didn't know him was one advantage to the few visits he had made to the Lone Star, Luke thought sourly.

Quiet up to now, Josie spoke up. "A woman would have an easier time talking to the man. I'll go over to his place."

"No!" All four men hollered at once and Luke seemed the loudest. He wasn't about to let her go into that kind of danger. If anyone hurt her, he'd not stop until he tore them limb from limb.

"Just listen." Josie had to speak louder to be heard over the yelling. Luke gave a shrill whistle, and when they quieted, Josie went on. "Being a woman, I'd at least get a foot in the door. That's far more than any of you'd do. I can be your eyes and ears." Her eyes glistened in the light and Luke realized she relished being useful. Hell, she'd probably be good at it.

"We need to know if he's all bluff," she went on. "Who knows? Maybe I can reason with him, get him to return the land in exchange for his horse—without bloodshed."

They were silent. Luke knew she spoke sense, but dammit, he didn't want her going into enemy territory. Especially if Kidd, Brenner, and God knows who else was there.

Josie leaned back. "Do any of you have a better idea?"

The men around the table fell silent.

After pondering a long minute, Luke said, "I don't like it. Not one little bit, but she's right. A pretty woman can find out what we need to know."

"Have you lost your mind, Luke?" Stoker's glare pierced him.

"She can pretend to be anyone or anything. Believe me, she can do this. I've watched her in action." Luke met the warmth of her gaze, and the secretive smile said she remembered the posse and the hot kisses they'd shared. He dragged his thoughts back to the current situation. "Put her in a frilly dress, squirt some rosewater on her, and Granger's bunch will fall all over themselves. They'll say things they never intended to say."

Houston swung away from the window where he was staring out into the thin rays of a pink dawn. "It's the best idea we've got. It just might work. At least for now." He sat next to her. "I have a feeling you're a whole lot tougher than you look, Miss Josie. You remind me of my wife. On first glance you don't see the steel underneath."

Josie blinked and Luke knew she was touched. "Your wife is lucky to have a husband like you. I'd like to meet her."

"You will. I'll bring Lara to meet you later today and introduce my Gracie." He chuckled. "Just watch out. Gracie will enter the terrible twos in a few months."

"That daughter of yours is a real heart-tugger." Luke remembered how the baby girl wound every drover around her finger during the trail drive to Dodge City last year. Men argued over who was going to watch her while her mama cooked for them. Luke's mind shifted to Lara's little brother. "How's Henry doing these days? He had quite a scare on that trip."

"Real good," Houston answered. "The boy's pretty resilient. He hardly talks about how close he came to dying with the attack of the wolf pack and then when Yuma Blackstone cornered him and Lara."

"He's a tough boy." Luke explained to Josie that Lara's

little brother was slow and that he'd come on the trail drive as Lara's helper. "Henry just wanted to be normal for once, like his older brothers."

"You all have such a closeness," Josie said with admiration. "I hope when I find my family, they'll be like you. But I really don't think they will. Or even that I'll find them."

Luke set down his cup. "Don't give up so easily. I've only gotten started."

"And if he doesn't find them, I will," Stoker promised.

"Thanks. To both of you."

"Back to Granger…with the road blocked, Josie will have to go by way of Medicine Springs," Luke said. "I'll go along. Since I won't try to hire on, we'll say I'm her escort." He rubbed his stubble. "The fact that I haven't shaved in days will make me look mean."

Before anyone could say anything else, the heavy knocker on the front door banged insistently. A minute later, Pony Latham, their ranch foreman, entered. He stood on bowed legs shaped by too many hours in the saddle.

"Someone to see you, Stoker," Pony said. "He won't take no for an answer."

"One of Granger's men?" Stoker asked.

Latham shot Luke a glance. "No, sir. He's a U.S. Marshal. Wants to know the whereabouts of Luke Weston."

Luke's blood froze. He'd brought the law here. Dammit, why hadn't he listened to what his head had told him? He'd known to stay away, but after the recent nightmare, the need for family had been stronger.

There was only one thing to do. He pushed back his chair.

Stoker's grip stopped him. "Stay here. I'll handle this. I've been expecting this moment."

Sam and Houston both rose and flanked their father. Luke watched with a heavy heart as they stormed from the room. He'd known this would happen eventually. They'd have to hide him—lie for him. Well, no more. He started to rise.

"Don't," Josie said, clutching his arm. "Your father

knows what he's doing. And if his brash defense of you gets him into hot water, your brothers will keep him in line."

"They didn't ask for this. I did." He tugged free. "Go up and show Noah the kitten. He's waiting."

Luke didn't wait for her reply, instead followed after his family. He almost made it to the parlor when he heard Stoker.

"Are you threatening me in my own house?" His father's thunder seemed to vibrate the windows.

"Just stating facts, Mr. Legend. We have it on good authority that Luke Weston is your son. If you're harboring him, an outlaw and a murderer, you're going to jail. Your money and power won't save you. You stand to lose everything you have." The visitor spoke matter-of-factly in a flat, emotionless tone.

"I didn't catch your name," Sam said.

"U.S. Marshal Orin Haskill. I know your fame as a Texas Ranger, Sam Legend, and although you've exchanged that badge for a sheriff's, I know you don't take the duty lightly. Talk some sense into your father."

"No one needs to talk sense into me, U.S. Marshal Orin Haskill," Stoker snapped. "My answer's the same. Once and for all, I haven't seen Luke Weston."

Luke winced and sagged against the wall. He'd tried like hell to keep his lawless ways from touching his father and brothers, praying every single day that he wouldn't bring shame to them. And now they were being forced to lie for him—deny him.

"Do you still say he's not your son?"

The silence seemed to say it all. Luke released a muted whimper, curling up into a ball inside. His father couldn't claim him. The truth hurt.

"Is he your son, Mr. Legend?" Haskill asked a second time.

"Dammit, yes, he is my son and I am proud to claim him." From where Luke waited, Stoker seemed to fling the words at the lawman like they were projectiles. Luke released his trapped breath. The secret was out and there was no putting it back.

Now, they'd make Stoker pay. Luke knew it as sure as the sun was shining. Why hadn't his father kept denying him, saved himself?

"We're going to find him," Haskill said in a grim tone. "Bounty hunters will kill him for that two thousand dollars. Do you want to see your son brought to you draped across the rump of a horse?"

Pain tore through him to have his father go against everything he stood for—integrity, honor, truth.

"It looks to me that you could stop Newt Granger from plunging us into a blood feud," Houston ground out. "He poses far greater danger than my brother. We're going to have hell like Texas hasn't seen in a whole lot of years."

The marshal huffed. "Give up Weston and we'll talk."

Stoker yelled, "Get the hell off my land! Get off or I'll throw you off. And if you come back here, you'd best not come alone. A man will see you to the gate and it'll remain closed to the likes of you. That includes bounty hunters too."

Luke headed down the hall. He wouldn't hide. And he wouldn't let Stoker take the punishment that was coming to Luke. He'd give himself up. Before he could reach the door, Houston rushed from the room. He froze when he saw Luke, then grabbed him, propelled him backward into Stoker's office, and flung the door shut.

Luke glared and jerked away. "Let me do what needs doing."

"If you think I'm going to watch you throw your life away, you're crazier than a liquored-up bedbug."

Boots pounded on the floor outside the office and the front door banged so hard it rattled the boards.

"Why do you three keep trying to save me?" Luke asked.

"Because you're ours." Houston shrugged. "You belong to this family." He grinned. "And because I like having you for a brother. We're bound by blood."

Luke met his stare. "Houston, I've been down a thousand

miles of bad roads when I didn't know if I'd make it out alive. Do you know what got me through those times?"

"Nope."

"A dream of mattering—to someone."

Houston growled, "You do a hell of a lot more than matter to me, to this family." He waved his arm toward Luke's mother's portrait on the wall. "You mattered to her."

"Yeah."

"We've all had our share of impossible roads. I'll stand beside you to the bitter end, ride the bad trails with you." Houston squeezed Luke's shoulder. "I'll die for you, brother. Never doubt that for a second."

Thickness clogged Luke's throat. "No one has ever said that to me before."

"Well, now they have."

Luke had found out today just how far Stoker and his brothers were willing to go for him and it went far beyond money and power. He found the insight sobering. He dragged air deep into his lungs.

Houston sighed. "Now that I've settled that, frankly, I'm a little tired of you wearing sackcloth and ashes." He jabbed Luke's chest. "So what if you've had a tough break? Lots of people have. Stop pissing and moaning, and do something about it."

Anger climbed up the back of Luke's neck. "You think I'm not trying? Hell, I've ridden over a thousand miles during the last two years trying to track down the man who'll clear me."

"Listen, I know all that. What I'm saying is—"

"What, exactly? Spell it out." Luke wanted to know what his brother thought. He loved and respected Houston and knew him to talk straight and back up his words with action.

"I know you would do anything for this family, Luke. You already have."

"Damn right."

Houston ran his fingers through his dark-brown hair.

His reply came as a soft plea. "Get it into that thick skull of yours that we'll do anything for you. Let us help."

Luke met the unwavering resolve in Houston's eyes.

Sudden realization struck him. At last, he had a real purpose for being alive. His family was about more than words. Stoker had claimed him, at huge risk to himself and the ranch he loved more than life.

Luke couldn't deny that he mattered to them, really mattered deep down inside where it counted most.

"I hope you know what you're asking for." Luke reached into an inside pocket and pulled out his book of sins. He stared at it a long moment before handing it over. Swallowing, he slid his Colt from the holster and stared at the name scratched into the handle—Legend.

Yearning rose up so thick it almost choked him.

One day, he vowed. One day.

Twenty-five

A god-awful racket came from upstairs. Luke and Houston rushed from the office, meeting Sam and their father in the hall. Without warning, a black fur ball streaked past and flew into the parlor.

Rowdy followed, barking fit to raise Methuselah from the grave.

Luke rushed after them and found Rafael, hissing and clinging to the top of the very expensive drapes. The cat's sharp claws had shredded the delicate fabric.

Sounds of laughter behind made him turn. He found Sam and Houston bent double. Even Stoker appeared amused.

Luke scowled. "What's so funny?"

Houston wiped his eyes. "Your face. You didn't know what to do. Probably for the first time in your life, the famed outlaw didn't know whether to hightail it or try to hide the evidence."

"Glad I can entertain you." Luke stared at the ruined drapes and then at the damn cat.

"This house hasn't seen this much activity in many moons." Stoker barked a laugh. He glanced at Sam. "Remember the raccoon you snuck inside when you were six or seven?"

That set off a new round of laughter. Luke wondered what it was about. He didn't see anything funny.

At last, Sam said, "Yep. Mother was fit to be tied when she saw the mess in her clean kitchen. Flour, sugar, eggs, cornmeal, and no telling what else covered everything."

"She grabbed the broom and started swatting at the coon," Houston said, picking up the tale. "She broke plates and lamps and everything else, trying to hit the thing. The coon fled up the stairs then fell into the chandelier below, clinging to it for dear life. I don't remember how we got it down and out of the house."

"I do. I had hell accomplishing that," Stoker admitted. "I had to bring in a ladder and pry the coon's hands loose."

Josie ran into the room, saw the drapes, and froze. She clasped a hand over her mouth. "What have I done? I didn't know they'd hate each other this bad."

Stoker laid an arm across her shoulders. "Don't fret, my dear. I've been meaning to replace those old curtains. This just gives me an excuse."

Somehow, Luke knew his father was fibbing and he found that tidbit at odds with his long-held notions about the man who'd fathered him. Maybe Stoker Legend wasn't as big a mystery as he'd thought. He was a man with a bigger heart. The more Luke stayed around him, the more the blinders slipped, giving him a glimpse of the man his mother had loved so much.

Sam picked up Rowdy and ordered the dog to hush. Rowdy promptly licked his face, growling at the cat between licks.

Houston looked at Luke. "One of us has to get the cat."

With a sigh, Luke gave up. "Where's your ladder?"

"I'm sorry, Luke," Josie said. "I thought they'd get along."

"I think this means you've never owned animals, at least ones so totally different. Cats and dogs have always hated the sight of each other." Luke moved to the door.

"I was sure they'd be friends," she moaned.

"When we first met, I thought Newt Granger and I would be friends too," Stoker said. "Now look at us. You never can tell."

Apparently about friends or fathers either, Luke thought as he went for the ladder. Some things surprised the hell out of a man.

Like Stoker no longer hiding the fact that Luke was his son—despite the ramifications sure to follow. That his father was willing to stand by his side made him struggle to find that hard, callous creed that had served him well.

That afternoon, following a long nap, Josie sat on the wide porch with Rafael in her lap. She gazed out over the ranch and wished she had something similar waiting for her. Only she knew she didn't. She didn't have to be blessed with a gift for knowing to realize that. Whoever her father was, he was nothing but a scoundrel. Sorrow filled her.

A soft, cooling breeze caressed her face. She loved it here and she knew Luke did too, even though he hadn't said as much. She'd seen the yearning in his eyes when they'd ridden beneath the huge crossbar. If only he'd take what they wanted to give, but something wouldn't let him.

Was it that his mother hadn't gotten the chance to live here? Was that why Luke would also deny himself?

Maybe accepting it would make him feel he'd betrayed her.

No more complicated, stubborn man ever existed on the face of the earth. She doubted she'd ever understand Luke Weston completely.

A wagon pulled to a stop and Houston took a little girl from a pretty, red-haired woman and helped her down. His wife and child. Josie was glad he'd brought them.

Josie stood and went down the steps. Houston put his arm around his wife's waist; her body had barely begun to thicken. "Meet my wife, Lara." With the beam still plastered on his face, he held up the child. "And this is Gracie Jewel Legend."

His pride and love clearly showed in the way he looked

at both wife and daughter. Houston had what Josie yearned for, but was beyond reach. The only man she wanted to make babies with didn't want her.

"She's adorable." Josie touched Gracie's soft cheek and the girl gave her a grin that revealed two glistening teeth.

Lara laughed. "Gracie's a handful. After trying to keep up with her all day, I fall into bed exhausted at night."

"She's telling the truth," Houston said. "Most nights my wife is asleep long before I am. To give her a break, I often take Gracie for a ride over the ranch. She loves being on the back of a horse."

"Horsy," Gracie said, squirming and pointing to the team.

"The ranch hands just love her." Lara wiped slobber from her daughter's chin. "If they're not too busy, they take her with them. They think she's the best thing to happen at the Lone Star except rain."

"Well, I can see why." Josie noticed a long scar running down one side of Lara's face. Though the line had faded, it must've been gruesome when it was fresh. What had happened? For someone to do that, they must've been crazed.

"Let's go inside," Josie said. "I'll make some tea."

"Nope. Cook will make us tea," Lara corrected, laughing. "She won't let us anywhere near the stove. I know. I've tried."

"Can I hold Gracie?" Josie asked as the kitten scampered around her feet.

"I thought you'd never ask." Houston passed the child to her and told Lara he'd be back to get them in a while.

Gracie twisted to see the cat. She pointed her finger at Rafael, jabbering something, evidently scolding him.

"Kitty," Josie said. "Can you say kitty?"

Lara held the door. "She hasn't learned that word yet. If it's not a horsy or her daddy, she pretty much babbles." Lara pushed back a gorgeous copper strand. "Lord, how she loves her daddy. And he worships her. I'm a lucky, lucky woman. I asked for so little and I got the whole world."

The baby squirmed, trying to get down. Josie sat her on

the floor with a cookie. Soon she was crawling fast, trying to catch Rafael. They shut the door so she couldn't get out and let her play. The kitten would keep her entertained.

As they waited on their tea, Lara briefly told Josie her own story, a sign of trust. A horrible outlaw had come to her father's ranch and caught her in the barn. When she'd fought back, he'd viciously attacked her and sliced her face.

"The folks in town turned their backs on me, saying I asked for it." The pretty woman's fingers drifted to the scar. "When Gracie was born, that gave the gossipmongers even more fuel."

Lara spoke of how Stoker had played a trick on Houston to get him to marry her—just to give Gracie a name. Listening to the story, Josie found herself fighting back tears. Though she'd deeply admired Houston from the first, now she saw inside and the depth of his huge heart. He'd not only given his name to another man's child, he loved Gracie with every fiber of his being.

Cook brought their tea and Josie filled their cups. "I can't begin to understand why you had to endure so much to finally get the man of your dreams."

"No risk, no reward." Lara accepted the steaming tea. "Houston told me how Luke found you. I think it would be terrifying to lose who you are."

"More than anyone knows. But Luke is so kind. Everyone is."

Lara ran her finger around the rim of her saucer. "Luke is a very special man. I saw that on the cattle trail. My heart breaks for him."

"Mine too. I wish he could find a bit of peace."

"He will. Houston thinks you can help with that." Lara got up to rescue poor Rafael from Gracie's rough clutches. The cat might not be the same after the babe got through with him.

Josie brought her focus back to Lara's statement. "I don't know how in the world I can possibly help. Luke has ideas I can't change."

Lara winked. "There are ways, Josie. I can tell he means a lot to you. I've learned what ignoring Houston can do—that gets his attention awfully fast. Try that. Make him a little jealous. Show him that other men find you interesting to be around. Just don't be afraid to reach for what you want."

Thankfully, Josie caught the snort in time. She wasn't the least bit timid in showing, or telling, Luke anything.

The problem, it seemed, was getting the damn man to pay any attention. She leaned forward. "Share more of your ideas."

After a good night's sleep underneath his mother's portrait, Luke spent the morning with Noah while he waited for Josie to finish getting ready to leave. Luke carried the boy down to the shade of the porch and began telling him everything he knew about the Lone Star.

"The tall flag's my favorite of all," Noah said after he finished. "I watch it from my window." He squinted at Luke. "I want to grow up to be like my pa and Stoker. I'll do my part someday to make Texas better. It's in my blood."

Luke reached to ruffle the kid's hair. "I believe that. Texas is in my blood too. I've ridden all over and there's nowhere better."

Only what good had Luke done other than ridding Texas of a few bad seeds? That appeared to sum it up. Far too little.

They talked more, and when Noah became tired, Luke carried him back to his room then returned to the porch to wait.

When at last Josie stepped from headquarters, Luke stood, his breath trapped in his chest. She was so beautiful it hurt to draw in air. Her dress, the color of a deep pool of spring-fed water, appeared spun from his dreams. With her honey-blond curls spilling down her back and shoulders, Miss Josie Morgan created quite a vision.

Memories of making love to her swept over him. The night he'd kissed and touched every inch of her beautiful body.

If only he was free to tell her what she meant to him. But for what reason? Things were best for them both this way. He remembered the nightmare and premonition so strong in his dream.

Striding to her, he drawled, "I've never seen you all decked out, Josie. Ol' Newt won't know what hit him. You'll have him tongue-tied and stammering like a schoolboy."

"I hope you're right." She glanced up at him and he found it difficult to keep his train of thought on the tracks.

Thick lashes framed her eyes, and something about the light made them a shade he'd never seen before. They reminded him of the sky at sunset. His attention drifted to her softly parted mouth, those enticing lips that could ignite searing flames inside him.

She continued as though she had no idea what she did to him. "I'll try to get as much information as I can for you and your family. Everyone has been so kind to me, even though they don't have to." She flicked her tongue across her silky bottom lip as though hesitant to voice her thoughts. "I wish you and I could go back to the way things were at Doan's Crossing."

Her soft plea, her hand clutching his arm, made it impossible to swallow. My God, how he wished they could. Memories washed over him of holding her in his arms, exploring her curves, and praying the morning would never come. They would remain with him for the rest of his life.

Instead of answering, Luke said softly, "I still think it's too risky for you to go. You need—"

Anger flashed in her eyes. "The list of things I need is lengthy—to remember who I am, to know where I belong, to feel you lying next to me, holding me while I sleep." Her voice broke. She glanced away for a second. When she turned back, her eyes bore a layer of frost, as did her tight words. "Don't try to pretend you care about me. You don't get to have things both ways. I'm not some toy to fill your time with and then toss aside when you grow tired."

The tilt of her chin warned him to keep silent. Yet, anger colored his words as well. "I'm doing the best I can, giving all that I'm able to at the moment."

Her hand flexed and for a second he thought she'd slap him.

"Don't expect me to wait around, Luke Weston. I'm not going to moss over waiting for you to figure out if I'm worth having." The maddening woman whirled, snapped open a white frilly parasol, and marched toward the one-horse buggy that would carry her to Granger's land. Her back was as stiff as her resolution.

She'd ride into danger over his dead body.

Luke strode to his saddled gelding. And for the record, he wasn't *pretending* to care. That wasn't something he could fake. Not by a long shot. He'd tried.

Knowing Josie Morgan had wiggled under his skin was one thing. Doing something about it was quite another.

Stoker waved as they rode out. Luke nodded back and set his horse into a trot beside Josie. His worst secrets wouldn't be safe if he let his father get close, he told himself.

What would Stoker think of having a jailbird and opium freak for a son? It would kill Luke to see his father's eyes harden to hate, especially now after saying that he loved him. Stoker and his brothers were his last chance at something meaningful.

Even so, the cash Stoker had given him for the trip burned in his pocket, reminding him that he was again beholden, that he had nothing to offer Josie or any woman.

To rid himself of his dark thoughts, Luke rode alongside the buggy. Even if Josie vented more anger and hurt, it was better than this.

But he couldn't recall her ever being so quiet. She didn't

utter more than a few words during the ride. Wouldn't even look at him directly. Guilt weighed him down. He called himself every name he could think of, and when he ran out, he made up a few more.

It was well past dark when they reached Medicine Springs. A dog barked when they walked the horses past the Lucky Lady Saloon. Luke noticed the way Josie caught her bottom lip between her teeth and stared at the Lucky Lady. She still must have felt a connection with the establishment. Heaven help her if she did anything foolish.

He saw only one half-decent hotel in the whole blamed town. He dismounted. "Hold Major John's reins tight and wait here. I'll ask about a room. Don't loosen your grip for a moment or I'll never get the horse out of the saloon."

"Don't worry." Josie wrapped the reins around her hand and dabbed her weary face with a lacy handkerchief.

As he moved away, she said, "Luke?"

"Yep."

"Thank you. I'm glad you came with me."

With a nod, he strolled inside. The sleepy-eyed clerk said he had only one vacancy. "Fine. I'll take it for the lady outside."

After signing the registration book and clutching the key, he tied the horses securely to the hitching rail until he got Josie settled.

Luke juggled her satchel under one arm. With Josie's hand around the other, he escorted her up the stairs.

Moments later, he set her bag inside the door. "I'll take the horses to the livery. You'll be safe here." He gave her his sternest look. "Stay put."

"I'm too tired to do anything else. Where is your room?"

"Don't have one. I'm sleeping in front of your door."

"No. We'll share this room," she insisted.

The images that flooded his mind brought sudden hunger. How in blue blazes could he sleep only feet away, listening to her soft breathing, smelling her fragrance, seeing her form beneath the sheet in the dim room? Bad idea. He didn't possess the kind of strength it would take to resist her pull.

"We'll discuss it when I get back." He quietly closed the door behind him and all he wished he could claim.

Twenty-six

Luke shouldn't have been surprised to find the room empty when he returned. Still, finding her gone sent shock through him with the speed of a bullet. He tried to still his rapid heartbeat.

He'd really thought she'd listen this time.

Where could she have gone? One place leapt to mind.

He stormed downstairs, waking the clerk, who gave him the evil eye. He'd apologize later. Right now, he needed to head off trouble.

Josie in pants with her hair up under her hat was far different from Josie in a beautiful dress, her silken hair curling around her face. He fought to breathe. A man would give anything to run his fingers through that hair and down her body.

Sweat broke out on Luke's forehead. Dammit to hell.

The Lucky Lady was even busier than it had been before, cowboys spending hard-earned money on a lucky throw of the dice or maybe cards. The liquor was flowing freely from what he could tell as he pushed through the doors.

He started on one side and worked his way around the room that reeked of unwashed bodies, filthy clothes, and sour beer. He didn't spy her anywhere. A glance upstairs turned his feet in that direction. He weaved through the kissing couples and reached the landing. A narrow hallway revealed rooms on each side.

Luke started down the row, stopping at each to glance in. They were all occupied with men and their partners for the night, doing what came natural.

A struggle seemed to come from the room on the right. He opened the door and found a man looming over Josie with his fist drawn back.

Her pretty dress was torn.

Red streaks blinded Luke's vision. He grabbed the piece of walking cow dung and slung him into the hallway, then hauled him up by the shirtfront, driving his fist into his belly. The man grunted and doubled over. Screams from the fleeing couples echoed through the confined, airless space.

The man launched to his feet and landed a blow to Luke's jaw. He reacted with an uppercut that knocked the man backward into the room they'd started in.

Luke had drawn back to hit him again when the man suddenly crumpled to the floor. Josie stood over him, holding a whiskey bottle by the neck.

A glance at the unconscious man had Luke doing a double take. He stared into the face of one of Reno's men. A wide sombrero rested on the floor nearby. Had the bully recognized Josie and been trying to snatch her for Reno?

He had to get her out of here. Luke pulled her dress together. Holding her close to his side, he located the back stairs and stumbled out into the starry night. He didn't stop until they reached the hotel and the safety of Josie's room.

Neither spoke a word as he handed her a wet cloth. She looked at him with unseeing eyes, her thoughts somewhere else.

He scrubbed the blood from his hands and sat next to her. "You scared me tonight," he said quietly. "Probably the worst I've been in a long, long while. When I saw that no-good two-bit drunk about to hit you...and your pretty dress torn..." Words didn't exist to describe his anger. His hands still shook. Although he couldn't claim her, no one was going to hurt Josie.

"Why did you go back there?"

Josie met his gaze. "I had to. I know I lived there at one time and I wanted to find some proof so I wouldn't think I'd gone mad. So you'd believe me."

"Did you discover anything?"

She pulled from her pocket a length of black velvet with a cameo attached and handed it to him. "Turn it over."

He did and found the word *Josie* scratched into the silver back. "What do you think this means?"

"That I was there. Beyond that, I haven't a clue."

Or maybe the necklace belonged to another Josie. Other women had the same name. Luke couldn't bring himself to point that out. He couldn't destroy her hope.

"Where exactly did you find it?" he asked.

"That was rather odd. I heard voices outside the door. When I pressed myself against the wall, I stepped on a loose board. I pulled it up and found the cameo underneath." Josie laid her head on his shoulder. "Who am I, Luke? I can't bear to think I lived there. I hate that place. It's dark and dirty with such horrible people inside. That man grabbed me and almost..."

She shuddered, apparently picturing what she narrowly escaped. "If you hadn't come along, I don't know what would've happened to me. He might've killed me."

Luke put his arm around her. "But I did. If I hadn't found you in the saloon, I'd have torn this town apart looking for you."

"I'm glad." She rested her head on his shoulder. "I'd have searched for you too. We've shared so much in a short time."

"Did the bastard say anything to you?" he asked.

"Just something about how glad he was to find me."

So, it wasn't a random thing. Reno was looking for Josie.

"It's late. We'll talk about this in the morning. I'll go so you can get ready for bed," he said.

Panic filled her gaze. "I don't want to stay here alone."

"I'll be back in a bit." He moved to the door.

"Luke, I'm sorry I went to the Lucky Lady after you'd asked me to stay put." Her voice was barely louder than a whisper. "I thought I could handle whatever came. I learned differently. But I'm not sorry I went. I have what I sought."

"I know. Maybe you can rest easy tonight."

Maybe he would too—if he found Reno Kidd. He'd turn this town upside down this night. Ridding Josie of that scum would bring pleasure.

He closed the door but stood there lost in thought, wrestling with himself, wondering if she knew he'd sell his soul for another night with her.

Back at the Lucky Lady, Luke strolled around the room full of drunks and gamblers, looking for Sombrero, a man with a shot-off ear, or Reno.

A saloon girl clung to his arm, pressing herself against him. She tugged the dress that was already riding off her shoulders even lower. "I can show you a good time, cowboy."

Luke stared into eyes lined with something thick and black, saw her red lips that nature had taken no part in. Lost hope was etched on her face and in her lackluster eyes. She could be any age. Saloons aged a woman fast. Whatever her story was, whatever had happened to land her in this predicament, all her dreams had shriveled to nothing. The woman was dead inside just as Luke had been until a chance encounter had brought Josie into his life.

"Sorry, ma'am. Just looking for someone," Luke answered.

She shrugged. "Maybe I can help?"

Luke fished a shiny gold eagle from his pocket, pressing it into her hand. He described Reno and his men. "Have you seen them?"

"Sure. All three. But you just missed them. They lit out of here about ten minutes ago. They're a mean bunch. The yellow-haired bastard hurt one of our girls bad."

Disappointment burned a path through him.

"What's your name?"

"Alice," came her soft answer.

"I appreciate your help, Alice." Luke took out two more coins.

"No," she said, refusing. "I can't take more."

He reached for her hand and dropped the silver dollars onto her palm. "Buy yourself something pretty. And use the rest to buy a ticket out of here on the next stage."

"That's real kind, but it's too late."

"Take it from me, it's never too late for second chances." Luke turned and bumped into Clay Colby of all people. The gunslinger looked worse than the last time Luke had seen him a month or two ago. Memories washed over him of how he'd fought by Clay's side when they'd helped Houston drive a thousand longhorns up the trail to Dodge City. Men didn't come better than Clay.

They found a corner and sat down to talk. "What are you doing in Medicine Springs?" Luke asked.

"Passing through." Loneliness haunted Clay's eyes as he rolled a cigarette. "One place is as good as the next. Don't dare find a good woman and settle down. Tried that. Didn't work. Men won't let folks like you and me have a minute's peace."

"I'm going to keep fighting for better to the last breath. We're not quitters, Clay."

The gunfighter tugged his hat low on his forehead and dragged his attention from a hard-faced man who'd just entered the saloon. "Why are you here, Weston?"

Luke filled him in on Josie—her memory loss, and the attack a little while ago.

The bones in Clay's face seemed to turn to stone. Dark anger glittered in the famed gunslinger's eyes. "Nothing makes me madder than someone hurting a woman or child. I'll help you find the bastards if they're still here and we'll get some justice."

With Clay's help, Luke spent the next hour searching for

his quarry. Finally, he woke the livery man, who said Reno and his men had just ridden out.

After parting company with Clay, Luke stood in the deep shadows outside the hotel until the light in Josie's window went out. He should sleep in the loft of the livery, he told himself. That was the wise thing to do.

But he and smart thinking seemed to have parted ways.

Josie's plea not to leave her alone tonight pulled him inside.

Somewhere around midnight, Josie awakened, reaching for Luke. Finding the bed empty, she realized she'd only dreamed of him lying next to her, his muscular arm across her stomach, his breath ruffling the hair at her ear.

His scent had been so vivid in her dream, that of leather and wild Texas sage, swirling around her.

She rolled over and gave a start. Luke sat unmoving in a chair by the window. He'd tilted back in his seat, his feet propped on the windowsill, staring out into the night.

In the moon's rays streaming through the open window, his face seemed to have been chiseled from granite.

Gone was the sensitive, caring Luke, replaced by someone she didn't recognize. A man forged of rock and steel rather than flesh and blood.

Although she would never be scared of him, she could see why others feared him. The mere mention of his name shot terror into men's hearts. She recalled Reno's accomplices right after Luke found her and how they'd reacted to his name. Josie smiled. They'd stumbled over their own feet to get far away. And she'd seen both fear and respect at Doan's Crossing.

Hoarse, whispered curses reached her and she knew Luke was quietly whipping himself over some failing. Or perhaps blaming himself for not protecting her from the attacker at the Lucky Lady. The man who'd made love to her so expertly was haunted by the past, the present riddled with demons, and a future he couldn't see worth living. She ached for her Texas outlaw.

Only he was no longer hers. Unshed tears filled her eyes. Luke had been hers for just a short while. But probably never again.

Lara had been wrong. Ignoring him, telling him how she felt, loving him—nothing Josie did made any difference.

What they'd once found was over with only a few memories to treasure—the time she'd lain in his arms and he'd murmured *princesa* in her ear, as though she was someone he cherished.

Josie swallowed the lump in her throat, wishing she could go to him. That he'd welcome her if she did. But he was more than likely to turn her away and she couldn't take being spurned yet again. So she lay still, clutching the cameo from a place in her past. Another piece to fit into the puzzle.

Would she always be a cluster of tiny pieces, never a whole again?

She watched Luke with an aching heart until the long night ended and dawn filtered into the room like a silent thief.

When he tiptoed from the room, she rose. Her gaze landed on her blue dress and her stomach plummeted. In the light of day, it looked even worse than she'd thought. Somehow she had to salvage it. To look like Luke's princess one last time would be worth anything.

She'd go talk to Newt Granger to repay the Legend family's kindness, then ride away and never look back.

If she could just manage to save the Lone Star, maybe… just maybe she had the strength to save herself too.

Twenty-seven

Josie eased the buggy carefully toward a group of armed men blocking the road. Thankfully, these were not the same ones who stopped them before. She glanced at Luke, dressed this time in the fancy clothes of a Mexican vaquero, riding beside her. Thanks ran through her that he'd insisted on coming. His confident nod bolstered her courage. She said a silent prayer that their visit with Newt Granger would end well.

If it didn't…she didn't want to think about failure.

The dangerous visit would test her. She still didn't know what she'd say, and hoped something came to her.

Thank goodness for Luke's scruffy look. He'd traded his fancy trousers with the conchas for a plain pair this morning, and now, he tugged his black Stetson down low with a thumb and forefinger to further shield his eyes.

She glanced down at the bodice of her pretty blue dress. No one would be able to detect the mend. Luke had left the hotel early this morning and returned with needles and thread. While not an exact match, the shade of thread worked well enough and she'd completed the repair in no time.

Josie adjusted the large, white-plumed hat that Luke had bought her that morning. She'd arranged her hair in a style befitting an elegant lady, a few loose tendrils floating around her face, and felt beautiful and self-assured. Not someone who had no memory, no past.

A surly man with a rifle hollered, "Turn back around!"

Pasting on a bright smile, Josie pleaded, "Please, I came to speak to Mr. Granger. My name is Josie Morgan. It's a matter of great importance."

Another of the group stepped forward, swinging his Winchester toward Luke. "Who's with you?"

Luke adapted a relaxed pose and propped his arm on the pommel. "I'm Rafael." He quirked an eyebrow at her before finishing. "Montoya. Her escort."

The man squinted and showed his yellow teeth. "Did Granger hire you too?"

"Not yet."

Josie flashed her very best smile and batted her lashes. "I wired Mr. Granger that I was coming."

"He don't get telegrams out here." The surly man spat on the ground.

"It's just that I came so far." Josie sniffled and dabbed at her eyes with a handkerchief. "All the way from St. Louis." She released a sob. "I simply can't go back without speaking to Mr. Granger. It would break my heart."

"Wait here." The guard huddled with the others in a discussion, and after a minute, he spoke. "Come ahead."

"Oh, thank you, sir. This is good news." She dabbed her fake tears with the handkerchief and turned to Luke. "See, Rafael? I told you everything would work out."

"Yes, you did, Miss Morgan," Luke replied, not looking at her. He stared intently at the armed group. Josie prayed again that no one recognized him.

A grim-faced man on horseback led the way. Josie fanned the dust from her face and glanced at the rocky, inhospitable land. It didn't seem good for much of anything. No wonder Granger wanted the Lone Star. How did he make a living? She saw no cattle or anything—just dry, withered-up land.

About three miles up the road, they came to a stop in

front of a sprawling, white adobe dwelling. Three men with rifles stared at her and Luke.

Newt Granger was livid as he stormed out. "What are you doing, Fisher? I told you no visitors."

The surly rider motioned to Josie. "She said it's important that she talk to you, boss. I thought you'd want to see what she's gotta say. A pretty lady like her don't just come calling without a reason."

Josie studied Granger from beneath her lashes. Stoker had hit the nail on the head—the man *was* a sawed-off runt. Granger probably had to stretch to reach her nose. The louse would probably stare at her bosom instead of her face. He snapped his suspenders, sticking his thumbs in them and stuck out his chest as he hurried toward her. The breeze made his wavy red hair stand up straight.

"Miss, I'm very busy," Granger said. "You'll have to come back after I whip Stoker Legend—"

Josie widened her eyes, blinked several times, and flashed a smile. "Hello, Mr. Granger," she purred. "I didn't know you'd be so sinfully handsome. I'm Miss Josie Morgan of the St. Louis Morgans. Perhaps you've heard of us," she purred, trying to take in all the details to include in her report to Stoker. It was laughable how quickly Granger accepted that she came from people of importance when nothing was further from the truth.

A quick glance caught Luke rolling his eyes. If he could do better, he was welcome to take over.

Granger took her hand. "Morgans, Morgans," he muttered. "Oh yes, I know them well." He beamed. "I'm a very lucky man today indeed, Miss Morgan. Please come inside."

"I don't want to interrupt. I know you're quite busy." Josie found that protesting what she most wanted seemed to make Granger dance to the music even more. She filed that fact away to maybe use another time.

"I'm never too busy for a pretty lady. No, sir." He helped her from the buggy and flicked his gaze to Luke. "Who is this with you? Please don't say he's your intended."

"Oh, good heaven's no. He's my escort." She saw the man comparing her fair coloring with Luke's light brown and quickly added, "My father hired him." Josie sighed deeply. "This country is simply too dangerous to travel alone. Outlaws everywhere just waiting to ambush an unsuspecting lady and steal her valuables. Rafael insisted on escorting me."

As she'd predicted, Granger's eyes never raised from her bosom and the low neckline of her dress. "What a shame to have harm come to someone with your beauty, Miss Josie. Getting waylaid is scary. I'm glad you didn't have trouble."

She walked through the door he held open. "Oh, but I did, Mr. Granger." She clutched a hand to her chest. "I came face-to-face with outlaws brandishing weapons. It was most distressing."

Newt patted her hand. "I'm sure. A delicate flower such as you shouldn't have to cope with such lawlessness."

"It appears you have a war going on here, sir. I've never seen so many armed men." She took in the peeling wallpaper, the broken chandelier in the entry, and discolored floors. She knew exactly how to appeal to him.

"I regret that Stoker Legend has made all this necessary," Newt murmured.

"Let's not discuss these horrible subjects any further. It's most upsetting." After checking to make sure Luke followed, she strolled into the parlor on Granger's arm. "Oh, what a lovely room. Your wife has exquisite taste." She stretched the truth, of course. It had the same peeling wallpaper and floors in need of a broom.

"My dear, there is no missus. I'm quite available should the right woman come along." Granger winked and smiled bigger. He released his hold to spit into his palm and smooth his hair down. She sat on the sofa, spreading her voluminous skirts around her, desperate to keep away from his disgusting hands.

"Now, Mr. Granger, you're such a charming devil." Josie shot Luke a glance, grateful he was there as Granger moved her skirts aside and sat next to her.

Luke stood in front of the fireplace with his hand resting on the mantel. His grim expression darkened the lines of his face and made him appear even more dangerous. And she knew that *he* knew how threatening he looked. Damn the scoundrel! But the good news was that Newt didn't appear to recognize him.

"What's the size of your spread, Ranger?" Luke asked casually.

"That's Granger, with a G," Newt corrected.

Josie tried not to laugh. Luke seemed determined to ruffle the short man's feathers. He was more like Stoker than he ever dreamed. She wouldn't dare tell him that, though.

Unperturbed, Luke brushed a fly from his short black vaquero jacket that accentuated his lean waist. "My mistake. The size of your ranch?"

The despicable little man reached for her hand but she warded him off by fussing over her skirts. "I have a thousand acres." He finally glanced at Luke. "But I'm about to increase that considerably. Soon, I'll own everything around here."

Josie squealed. "You'll be very important. I just knew I came to the right place."

The besotted Newt finally caught her hand and left a slobbery kiss on the back, which made Josie squirm, wishing she could wipe it off.

Luke shifted. "Legend has this area all sewn up, senor."

Granger smirked. "Not for long. I'm going to take him down. He sits up there in his big house, acting like some damn king or something." He leaned closer. "But enough about the lying, cheating thief. Miss Josie, what is the purpose of your visit?"

"I'm very concerned about this feud of yours with the Legends." She scowled at Luke when he coughed and jerked his head toward the window where a group of riders had gathered. Were they trapped here? Momentary fear swept up her spine, then she glanced at Luke and everything settled. She was as safe as a baby in its mother's womb.

Newt jerked back. "Did that cheat send you?"

"No, in fact, he tried to keep me away." She slowly drew a fingertip down Newt's chest. "I have a proposition, just for little ol' you." Josie watched greed glitter in his eyes. She dared not glance at Luke because she could already sense the anger rising from the top of his Stetson.

Dust in the room suddenly made her sneeze.

Newt removed a handkerchief from his pocket. Before he handed it to her, he noticed it was dirty and stuffed it back into his pocket. Luke stepped forward to offer his.

"What sort of proposition?" Newt reached again for her hand. His grimy palms were harder to escape from than sticky molasses. Luke had moved away from the mantel. Josie had to conclude this quickly, before Luke took things into *his* hands.

"The fact is, Mr. Granger, no good can come of this feud. Decent folk can't even travel down the road. It's time to end this blockade of yours." Josie widened her eyes and made her voice breathless. Where she'd learned to do that she didn't know, but it seemed natural. "Before I or others get hurt. Or killed."

Newt frowned. "Legend is finally taking me seriously. He's not laughing now. I'm not ready to end this."

"Granger, you can be the big man here," Luke said. "You call the shots, so you can get a few things you want."

Josie threw him a smile. "Newt," she purred, "you can be the most important man in the area if you play your cards right. You'll be far more famous than Stoker Legend." She squealed. "He'll envy you."

"Imagine that." Granger's eyes glittered with greed. "Him envying me after all these years."

"Oh, yes indeed." Josie cringed but leaned closer. "You just have to be willing to bend—like a sapling in the wind. Feuding with your neighbor has got to stop."

"Or else what?" Newt stared at her palm. If he spit in it, she'd wallop him good.

"If you don't settle this, you'll wind up with nothing." Josie stared into his beady little eyes, trying to find some hope she could draw from. "You could lose every single thing unless you play your cards right."

Granger scowled. It hit her that he liked fighting with Stoker. Maybe it made him feel powerful somehow.

Josie held her breath. This was the sticky part. "Now, I've already spoken to Mr. Legend and he's agreed to return your beautiful racehorse. All you have to do is let him have his land back."

"Give up the land?" he squeaked.

She fought to seal the deal, trying to grab at anything. She just prayed Stoker wouldn't kill her when he found out she was changing the plan. "Oh, I didn't tell you. Mr. Legend is prepared to help build you a town. Just imagine. You could own"—she searched for a name—"Grangerville."

"Grangerville?" He brightened.

"You belong in town, not living out here on dead land. You could be mayor, someone important, someone people look up to. How does that sound?"

Granger looked ready to cry. "I don't keep the land?"

"Now, Newt, you know it belongs to Stoker." She fixed him with a hard, piercing stare. "Admit you manipulated those cards."

"I just want that land so bad. I had to have it. He's got everything."

"Picture this—an annual horse race here that would bring folks from all around. And it would provide a way to show off the beautiful racehorses I heard you've acquired." She gasped. "I see Grangerville packed with people who come to take part in horse racing, shooting matches, and other events. You'll make it famous." Josie prayed this did it because she was out of ideas.

"It's mighty tempting." Silence spread in the room. Finally, Newt Granger turned to her. "No, I won't do it. I'm keeping Stoker's land. I'm going to show him a thing or two."

Bitter disappointment swept over her. She thought for sure the town would sway the greedy little man. Apparently, nothing would. Well, on the bright side, at least

Stoker wouldn't kill her. Yet, she'd failed. Josie had nothing else left to say. Her silk dress rustled as she pulled her hand from Granger's. She set her chin and stood.

Luke moved to her side and placed his hand on the small of her back. "Then our business is concluded. Let's go, Miss Morgan." He shot Granger a look of scorn. "Newt doesn't even know when he's hit a gold mine."

They left Granger sitting in the parlor. There was no sign of the men who had gathered while they talked. But this was no time to dawdle. Before Luke could get her to the buggy, a rider galloped up to the house. She froze at the sight of the white man wearing a wide sombrero.

In an instant, she was back upstairs at the Lucky Lady, fighting to escape. She could still feel his dirty fingernails digging into her skin, smell his putrid breath, all the time knowing that Luke couldn't save her.

Now the man stared at them from his discolored face. The bruises and split lip were the result of tangling with Luke. Josie could tell by his puzzled expression that he hadn't placed them yet. They needed to hurry.

Luke stiffened. "When the shooting starts, duck."

She clasped her hands together as he strode toward Reno's henchman. If something happened to Luke, what would she do? With the road barred, the Lone Star was too far away.

If only she'd stuck her gun in a pocket. Hell! Look what trying to be a lady got her.

She'd failed in her mission and now she couldn't even help Luke.

Twenty-eight

Before Luke was halfway to the outlaw, Granger hurried from his adobe dwelling. "What's going on, Artie? Why aren't you guarding the road like I pay you to do?"

Artie's eyes never left Luke. "Fisher sent me, boss."

Granger stood waiting until finally snapping, "Well, spit it out. I don't have all day. Leave Miss Morgan alone. They need to get going."

Luke tensed, waiting for Artie's move. *Just wound him*, he told himself as he moved closer. He needed the man alive to get answers to the questions he now knew to ask. Failing that, he needed Artie to lead him to Reno. Or Brenner. A little voice inside told him someone wasn't going to walk away from here.

The memory of Josie's torn dress swept across his vision. *No one harmed her and lived.*

"This man is wanted. He's Luke Weston." Artie licked his split lip.

Granger took a step back. "Are you sure?"

"The man's sure, *Ranger*," Luke drawled, his attention riveted on Artie's eyes. "You won't have to pay him. He's about to die."

This time Granger didn't correct him on the name. The little man didn't seem to be able to utter a single sound.

Shoot at me, Artie. Just draw and shoot. Don't go wide and hit Josie.

Movement behind Luke barely registered, so intent was his focus.

"You're about to pay for what you did to the lady," Luke spat, flexing his hand. "Only one way to save yourself."

"How's that?" Artie snarled.

"Tell me where Reno is." Luke's brittle words offered no room for compromise.

"I only followed orders last night."

"Yeah, well, that's going to send you to hell." Luke read fear in Artie's ugly face.

"Look here, Weston, or whoever you are," Newt Granger sputtered but at least found his voice. "You can't come onto my land and kill. Are you Legend's hired gun? Did Stoker send you?"

"I'm a person's worst nightmare. I can be whatever, whoever, anyone wants me to be." Luke stared at Artie. "Give me Reno Kidd."

A horse galloped into the yard, making the hair on Luke's neck rise. "Who is it, Josie?" he asked without turning.

At her sharp, startled cry, Luke turned enough to make out the rider who leaped from his horse, but not enough to identify him.

"Well now, it seems the lady's having trouble talking."

The cold voice sent familiar waves tumbling through Luke. He moved so he could see both men. Reno Kidd clutched Josie tight with his filthy hand over her mouth. Fear filled her beautiful eyes.

Darkness rose up, drying the spit in Luke's mouth. He had to keep Reno calm until he could gain Josie's release.

"Been a while, Reno. I see you still wear my scar," Luke said almost casually. "This time I'll aim for the jugular."

"You won the last fight but this one is mine." Reno's eyes glittered as he placed his pistol against Josie's cheek. "The lady's also mine. I saw her first."

"She doesn't want you, *compadre*. The lady likes a gentle

hand and you play too rough. Let her go." Luke caught Artie judging the distance to his horse. The underling apparently didn't want to be anywhere near them. Luke had other ideas. Artie could bring back the third one of the group—the one with a half-missing ear. "Take another step, Artie, and it'll be your last."

A closing door told him Granger had taken refuge inside the house. But would he get a rifle and start shooting? The thought crossed Luke's mind.

Reno shifted, freeing his gun hand. The outlaw was getting ready to make his play. Luke waited, praying that he'd be a second faster.

If not, Josie would be at Reno's mercy. Luke had seen what remained of women after Reno got tired of them. "Reno, I wondered what happened that night at Doan's Crossing. Why did you attack Brenner and Walt Preston?"

The outlaw shrugged. "Thought they might be worth robbing. I didn't recognize Brenner McCall at first. The stupid fool looked all dandified. Glad I shot him."

"He's still alive and kicking. Seems you don't shoot that straight anymore, *amigo*," Luke taunted.

"Maybe you don't either, Weston." Reno's mouth curved in a smile, showing his rotten brown teeth. Keeping his eyes locked on Luke, he licked Josie's cheek. "You and me, we only live until we die anyway."

The crazy outlaw seemed to enjoy rubbing Luke's nose into the fact that he couldn't do a blessed thing without risking Josie's life. Hell!

"What's good about living only half a life, Reno? Surely, you'd like to buy a few more days. Everyone wants more time. Hell is a hot place, I hear."

"Don't need to go—I'm already there. I was born in hell. My father was the devil."

In unison, Josie bit down on Reno's hand with her teeth, stomped his foot, and ducked. "Shoot him, Luke!"

Reno raised his gun as Luke fired. The bullet hit the outlaw square in the chest, freezing the gruesome grin in place.

From the corner of Luke's eye, he saw Artie yank out his pistol. Luke whirled and fired. His bullet sped through the air, hitting the man between the eyes, propelling him back into his horse. The animal reared up in alarm before galloping off.

Through the smoke, Luke saw Josie kneel beside Reno, wiping away the blood trickling from his mouth. Luke squatted next to her. Reno was working his tongue, trying to speak.

Luke got some water from his saddlebag and placed the canteen to Reno's mouth.

After drinking, most of which dribbled out, Reno clutched Luke's vest. "McCall is the…one you…want. He planned your death with…politician."

"What are you saying?" Luke asked. "You're not making sense."

"Watch. Back." Reno's grip was starting to loosen—he didn't have much time left. He glanced at Josie. "You're his." A gurgle came from his throat. Reno's eyes rolled back into his head as he took his last breath.

"What did he mean, Luke?" Josie shivered. "I'm his what? Who's what? Who was he talking about? I need to know."

Luke shook his head, reeling. He was still trying to figure out what Reno had said. Brenner and Walt Preston planned his death? His old friend, Brenner, had betrayed him? And Josie was what? Brenner's daughter? Or Walt's daughter? Or had Reno meant something else? Wife, lover? Dammit! All he had were questions.

Josie clenched Luke's shirtsleeve as she stared into the distance, that look on her face like she was caught in another memory.

The sudden rifle blast from a window of the house told him to get her out of there. He threw her over his shoulder and ran for the buggy.

"Make yourself small." He rushed his gelding to the back and tied it.

Hot lead fell around him. Though Granger was a poor shot, the noise of the blasts would bring his men.

Luke jumped in next to Josie and whipped the horse into a gallop. "Hold on." No one was going to make him take the long way around. Not this time. He set his jaw and headed toward home as fast as he could make the buggy go.

A hail of bullets suddenly struck around the buggy. Luke glanced up on a hill and there sat Brenner McCall with a rifle. Urging the horse faster, Luke jerked out his Colt and fired. McCall swung around and galloped off.

Luke's hunch had been right. But he was still no closer to Ned Sweeney.

A quick glance behind assured him no riders were upon them. He hoped their luck would hold. Yet, five miles from Newt Granger's house, where his land butted up against the Lone Star, five gunmen blocked the road.

Luke pulled the buggy to a halt. He gripped the handle of his Colt and got out, leveling the gun barrel at the man in the center.

"I'm coming through, however I have to do it," Luke ground out. "Step aside or I'll litter this road with dead bodies."

A man on the end hollered, "We got orders not to let anyone cross."

"Are you willing to die for Granger?" Luke asked.

Josie's voice rang out. "Weston's killed more men than a dog's got fleas. Want him to add five more notches to his gun? I'd take him very seriously. Believe me, I've seen him shoot. No one can beat him. Five are no odds for him."

The armed men glanced nervously at one another.

Luke knew he was running out of time. "I'm out of patience, gentlemen. Who wants to go first? You? You?" He aimed his Colt from one to another down the line.

At last the men moved aside, giving them room to pass.

Satisfied, Luke climbed into the buggy, handing his Colt to Josie. "Keep an eye on them."

"Don't worry." She glared at Granger's men. "You move a hair and I'll put a damn bullet in your heart. If you think a woman is too soft, I can assure you this one is not."

Pounding hooves sounded behind them, coming from the direction of Granger's house and gaining ground. Luke lifted the reins and set the buggy in motion. Granger's men galloped behind at a frantic pace, getting closer and closer.

Lone Star headquarters lay too far away.

Shots from the riders' rifles rent the air as hot lead crashed around them.

Yelling blistering curses, Josie leaned out to return fire.

Closer and closer the pursuers came. Luke could hear the sound of the horses' hooves thundering along the ground behind them.

They weren't going to make it.

Luke searched for a place to take cover and fight them off until help arrived but the flat land offered little. He didn't give any thought to himself—he'd been in worse messes. It was Josie who drew his concern. He was going to keep her safe or he wouldn't be able to live with himself.

The buggy was too slow. They could never outrun the men on horseback. He whipped the horse until they careened ahead at an unsafe speed, the buggy threatening to tip over.

Then, just as Luke's hope faded, ranch hands rode to meet them, Sam and Houston leading the charge. Luke breathed easier. Josie was safe.

He slowed the buggy. "Thanks for helping."

Josie shrugged. "It was both our necks on the line. Had to do my part."

After a moment's quiet, she said, "Luke, I had a flash of memory when I stood over Reno. I saw a sick woman, I think my mother, in a bed. She told me to be careful and not to trust the captain." She twisted to look at Luke. "Noah said I went to visit his farm with the man his pa called Captain."

Luke covered her hand. "I may have figured that out. But I'm not certain, and I don't want to say. I could be wrong."

"Reno mentioned a name. Who is McCall?"

"An old outlaw I used to ride with, used to be a friend." Brenner had shown his dark side before, but if what Reno said bore truth, Luke couldn't afford to trust him. And Brenner had just shot at them back there. That said it all.

Why would Brenner McCall and Walt Preston plan to kill him? As far as he knew, he hadn't done anything to either.

"Could Reno Kidd have been delusional?" Josie asked.

"Anything's possible." Luke patted her hand. "I wouldn't worry. Maybe he made up the whole thing."

Except dying men staring into the flames of hell tended to speak the truth. Something about getting ready to stand in the face of judgment brought out honesty.

"I felt sorry for him in the end," Josie said softly. "I think he must've had a horrible childhood. I wanted to cry when he talked about his father."

Luke nodded. No telling what had happened to make Reno the way he was. Must've been bad, just like the things Luke had gone through that had turned him into a callous outlaw. Only one difference—he was willing to change. He only needed a chance. He glanced at Sam and Houston coming alongside. And Stoker riding hell-bent toward them.

His family had his back.

They were giving him his chance.

Twenty-nine

SILENCE ENVELOPED THE GATHERING ON THE PORCH, WHICH appeared to be the official place for most discussions. Luke and Josie had just given the others a rundown on their visit to Granger's place. Luke glanced at Noah, sitting nearby playing with Rowdy, then scanned the faces of his brothers and father. These family powwows made Luke feel a part of them and his opinions welcome. It was what he'd dreamed of years ago when he'd sneak up close and watch them, wishing they were his.

At least Stoker hadn't exploded. That was a plus.

The big man steepled his fingers beneath his chin. His face was pensive as he digested the information. At last he spoke. "That's damn good thinking, Miss Josie. I think you hit upon an excellent idea. I don't know why I didn't think of it."

"Because you were too busy fighting with Newt," Sam said. "You wanted to win at any cost, to prove you're the best."

"That's right, Pa." Houston leaned forward. "I have to agree with Sam. You taught me a long time ago that compromise gets the best results. We have the money now to build him a town. It's a small price to pay for peace with the man. All we have to do is try a little harder to convince him. Even though he turned Josie down, I think this will work if we stroke his ego some. Assure him that he's important."

"Whatever we have to do." Luke studied Stoker, who was deep in thought. "Otherwise, we'll have to go all the way down to Medicine Springs every time. It'll take days."

Noah glanced up. "I think you should do it, Papa Stoker. Fighting all the time just makes you grouchy and tired."

Houston barked a laugh. "Kid, you hit the nail on the head."

"How did you get to be so smart?" Luke ruffled the boy's hair.

Noah shrugged. "I just figured it out myself."

"I think you must have too much time on your hands," Stoker growled. "But I said from the first, kid, you'll be running this place one day."

Josie idly stroked the kitten in her lap. She'd been silent until now. "Newt Granger is a sad, lonely man. He just wants to be important and a town would give him a purpose for once in his life. And running Grangerville will take so much time he won't fight with you."

"I'll give him 'important' if he ever touches you that way again." Luke fixed her with a stare. "The way he looked at you with those bug eyes, he'd have undressed you if I hadn't been there."

And then there'd have been hell to pay.

"I knew I was safe because you *were* there," she said softly.

Luke's gaze lazily wandered over the luscious curves that he'd already memorized, his eyes caressing her. She looked so soft and feminine in the pretty blue dress, in that fancy hat that made her appear like a woman of the world. Only he knew differently. Josie Morgan had shown how vulnerable and scared she was inside. But she was also God-almighty tough. A hell-raiser when she had to be.

Each side of her intrigued him. She drew him like a magnet and twisted his insides into tight knots that he couldn't untie.

Yet, he couldn't have her, couldn't allow himself the luxury.

She definitely wasn't a toy for him to fill his time with. His feelings for her ran deep. Somehow, he had to get her out of his mind, his heart. Because he couldn't let her shoulder his burden too.

All of a sudden, Rafael leaped from her lap. The hair on Rowdy's neck stood and a growl rumbled in the dog's throat. Rafael arched his back and hissed, then streaked off the porch with Rowdy giving pursuit. The last Luke saw was a flash as the two animals raced down through the little ranch town.

"Rowdy, come back!" Noah hollered. "Here, boy."

"Go after Rafael, Luke, before Rowdy eats him," Josie begged. "Please?"

Luke got to his feet. The damn cat was going to disappear one day when no one was looking.

But he'd kiss its ugly butt if Josie asked him to. He'd do whatever she asked...except tell her he loved her.

Josie's gaze followed the tall figure of the man she loved. Tears lurked behind her lids. She'd made up her mind; she would leave come morning. Tally Shannon would take her in until she decided where to go.

And if Josie didn't find a place, she'd live out her days with the women of Deliverance Canyon.

Luke might come to visit once in a while, and she could remember the one night when they'd shut out the world and he'd made love to her. She could savor the huskiness in his voice when he'd called her *princesa*, and made her the happiest woman in the world.

She remembered Reno's words, telling her she was someone's something. It didn't matter anymore. Nothing did. She didn't care if she never learned the meaning of the cryptic statement.

The only thing she wanted to be, she never would.

Stoker and his boys stood to watch a long column of riders coming down the road. She glanced at the horsemen. They seemed to ride with a purpose, stiff in the saddle. As they approached, she noticed the silver stars on their chests.

Lawmen!

Her heart stopped. Trouble rode toward them. She had to disappear. Oh God, they'd come for her! Or Luke. She prayed he stayed where he was.

She stood on trembling legs and slipped inside the house. Upstairs in her bedroom, Josie grabbed her gun. Whatever came, she'd be ready. Anyone who came to take her to jail would have a fight on their hands. She hadn't killed Preston at Doan's Crossing. And if they'd come for Luke, she'd be ready to help him escape.

With the pistol in her grip to bolster her courage, she went down to the parlor to watch from the window. Hopefully, she could listen to the conversation. She peeked through the curtains. The group had halted in front of the porch with their weapons drawn.

"How may I help you, gentlemen?" Stoker asked without inviting them inside.

Sam and Houston flanked their father with their legs apart—a solid, impenetrable wall of strength.

Josie breathed a prayer that Luke would stay out of sight. She trembled, knowing she wouldn't be able to bear the sight of lawmen binding him, taking him to hang. She might not know her past, but she knew the fate of men who were accused of murder. At least he wouldn't suffer the kind of imprisonment that nearly destroyed him before. For that, she was grateful. Although a grown man would fare much better than a fourteen-year-old.

"Howdy, Mr. Legend."

Stoker nodded. "U.S. Marshal Orin Haskill. Nice weather."

"You told me to bring an army when I came back." Haskill waved an arm at the others. There had to be around fifteen. Most appeared to be ordinary citizens that the marshal had pressed into service. "If this isn't enough, I can get more."

All those to arrest one man?

Over half of the posse appeared to recognize Sam. They murmured among themselves and fidgeted in their saddles, seeming to rethink the wisdom of the job they'd signed on for.

When Sam and Houston started down the steps, Stoker put a hand out. "No, boys, this is my fight."

The little Josie could see of Stoker through the curtain showed the fierce determination in the set of his jaw. She imagined those green eyes had flames flashing in them as well.

"Are you going to turn Luke over?" Haskill rested his arm on the pommel.

"Put those weapons away," snapped Stoker. "There's no need in trying to intimidate me. You'll soon find scare tactics don't work with me. This land was wild when I came. Others tried to take it by force. They discovered, as will you, that I may bend a little but I don't break—and I don't scare."

Haskill straightened and glanced at his fellow lawmen. With a nod, they holstered their guns. "Now, respectfully, sir, I want Luke Weston and I want him now."

"Then you'll have to leave wanting!" Stoker thundered.

The marshal offered a thin smile. "If you refuse, I'll have to take *you* in, Legend."

"Whatever you have to do is fine with me," Stoker snapped.

"How far are you willing to go for your murdering, thieving son?"

Sam apparently had enough. He clenched his fist and Josie could tell he itched to yank the young lawman into the dirt. "Haskill, there's no need for name-calling here. You owe me—all of us—professional courtesy. We're peaceful, law-abiding people and Luke *will* clear his name of all charges."

Haskill's face reddened at the dressing-down. Josie read the posse's worried faces as they glanced at one another and appeared ready to turn and ride out. Their nervous expressions seemed to suggest thoughts like *Oh shit, I don't want to get in the middle of this.*

"We stand as one," Houston added. "You take one of us Legends, you'll take us all."

Josie watched the marshal glare at the three big men. If she were him, she'd be wondering if she'd brought enough help. And that would be a legitimate thought. The fearsome line of Legends would give anyone pause.

"Me too." Noah rose to stand next to Sam. "Leave my Papa Stoker alone. I did whatever it is you said he done. Luke saved my life. I'd be dead if he hadn't found me. He is *not* a bad man. He's good and kind."

That the sick kid would stand tall beside the Legends brought a lump to Josie's throat. She suspected everyone to a person on the Lone Star felt the same loyalty to the family and to Luke.

"Thank you, Noah, but I can handle this." Stoker rested a hand on the boy's head and squarely faced Haskill. "You asked how far I'm willing to go for Luke. Here's your answer. I'll go to the ends of the earth. For him as well as these other sons of mine. I take it you don't have any children."

"No, sir."

"I pity you. My sons are my life and a bright hope for the future. They'll carry my dreams forward for generations. My blood flows through their veins, and yes, I'm willing to die for them. So, do whatever it is you must. But understand, only to me."

"Pa," Houston protested. "They'll take all of us or none. Sam and I are just as guilty."

"No." Stoker turned to the marshal. "I need my horse."

Marshal Haskill gave him a cold smile. "You won't require a horse. We're going to hold you right here on the Lone Star until Luke gives himself up."

"That's good," Sam said. "That way you'll be here when I get a telegram from the governor. He's not going to stand for this."

Again, the posse seemed ready to bolt. They wanted no part of the Texas governor's wrath.

"Nice try, Sam," the marshal replied. "You and I both know it's a long ride to a telegraph office."

"No ride at all. We have one just across the way. Stoker installed it a few years ago for just such an emergency. And don't even think about trying to stop me. You won't stand a chance."

Josie watched the marshal's face fall. The man glanced up at the telegraph lines overhead, then back at the hardness on Sam's face. Haskill wasn't so cocksure now.

"And Pa will get to sleep in his own bed." Houston grinned. "I'm feeling better about this already."

"I'm afraid you're wrong." Haskill leaned over to a young lawman beside him. "Find us a suitable jail to commandeer. One with an upper floor that Legend won't escape from. One with a window that Luke will see his father from. I know he's hiding somewhere on this land."

"Sounds good." The man smiled. "I'll find a place."

Houston stepped forward. "I might be able to help. My old house is empty. It's two-story. It's large enough so some of the men can stay there too."

What was Houston doing? Josie gave a silent groan. Had he lost his mind? They didn't need to *help* the posse. They were doing enough damage all by their lonesome. From the way the men were looking at one another, some of them were just as confused.

Surprise crossed Haskill's face. "Why, that's mighty nice. Which one are you? Your name escapes me."

"Houston."

"Ah yes. I recall now. Someone once said you were your father's right-hand man, that you know as much about this land as he does."

"I doubt that." Houston glanced at Stoker. Josie saw the admiration on Houston's face and she knew he wasn't faking his regard. "You'd have to travel mighty far to find anyone as smart and tough as my father."

"Do whatever you have to, Houston, to protect the ranch from attack. Keep that bastard Granger and his hired guns off this land." Stoker leaned to murmur something to Sam. Though Josie strained to hear, she couldn't make out any of the words.

Sam somberly nodded and turned to Haskill. "Excuse me. I need to get that telegram sent to the governor."

The entire posse fidgeted in their saddles as they watched Sam saunter toward the makeshift town. Josie scanned what she could see of the compound from the window but saw no sign of Luke. She prayed he'd stay hidden. Hopefully, Sam was going to warn him. Coming to know him like she did, she could see Luke turning himself over to these lawmen.

One thing she knew—no matter his bumpy relationship with Stoker, he wouldn't sit idle while his father was locked up.

And then her tall, honorable outlaw would swing from the gallows.

Thirty

Luke ducked behind the telegraph office, clutching the damn cat. Removing his worn black Stetson, he peeked around the corner at the column of lawmen.

He grimaced, watching them snap handcuffs on Stoker.

The worst had happened. His father was paying for his son's crimes.

But why were the lawmen riding to Houston's old house? That puzzled him. What were they up to?

A noise alerted him and Luke had his Colt out before he realized it was Sam who slid up next to him. "You're lucky I didn't shoot you."

Sam's face was grim. "Came to warn you."

"What are they doing?"

"They've arrested Pa, but they're going to keep him at Houston's place. Gonna try to draw you out. They know you're somewhere close." Sam eased around where he could see the goings-on.

"Well, they're right. No way can I let Stoker take the brunt of my mess." Luke settled his hat back on his head and pushed away from the side of the building.

Sam grabbed him. "No. Pa said he'll handle this and for you to stay out of sight."

"If you really think I can do that, you don't know me at all." Pain ripped through Luke's heart. His family hadn't asked for this. They shouldn't pay for this. Luke jerked free.

"Sorry, Luke. This is going to hurt me worse than you." Sam drew back and slammed a powerful fist into his jaw.

Luke crumpled into the welcoming darkness.

He didn't know how long he was out. When Luke came to, he lay on a bed, staring up into Josie's eyes. She wore her cowboy disguise, complete with a gun belt and pistol.

She pressed a cold cloth to his sore jaw. "There you are," she murmured, like he'd been missing somewhere and she'd found him.

Someone else stirred nearby. Luke shot a glance toward the sound and saw his brothers. He pushed Josie's hand aside and sat up, glaring at Sam. "I owe you for that."

"Yeah, well, I owe you a lot more for almost hanging me two years ago," Sam growled.

Houston rose from a chair. "We finally managed to get you into one of our beds. It might take us some time, but Sam and I always succeed in whatever we undertake."

"Luke, now you know they have your best interests at heart," Josie lectured. "We all do. Listen to them."

"Why?"

"Because you're a stubborn cuss who doesn't have sense to come in out of the rain sometimes." Sam strolled to the door and eased it open enough to look out. He chuckled. "Word travels fast. The ranch women have lined up with their arms full of everything you can imagine to make Stoker comfortable. I see one with a pie and steam is still rising from the crust. The old man never had it so good."

A glance at the sparse room with nothing in it except a bed, a washstand, and a long chest brought Luke's question. "Where am I? This isn't headquarters."

"It's an empty house we built for a ranch family."

"Safer here," Josie said. "I have to be careful too. They

still have a warrant out for me for Walt Preston's murder at Doan's Crossing."

The posse could take Luke but they weren't getting her.

Sam shut the door and turned. "They took Pa to the second floor of Houston's house. We were able to talk to him for a minute. He wants to have a word before you do anything foolish."

Luke snorted. "So I just stroll in, like I was going to do in the first place, and those lawmen will let me talk to him out of the kindness of their hearts. Because we all know how forgiving they are of a wanted man with a price on his head."

"This is serious, Luke." Josie planted her hands on her hips, his warrior angel ready to avenge. "Please listen."

"There's a large elm beside the house," Houston said. "You can crawl up there and talk to Pa through the window." He scowled. "You can climb trees, can't you?"

"I've climbed a few," Luke answered, rubbing his sore jaw. "I just don't know what this will accomplish. Stoker and me—we can't reach an understanding."

"All we ask is that you listen to him. Then if you want to turn yourself in, go right ahead." Sam glanced at Houston. "We did our duty. Let's go. Pa needs us to keep the ranch running."

His brothers turned to the door before Houston stopped. "I've taken care of those names in your black book. You're clear of those. The murder charge is only a matter of time."

Anger—and shame—rose inside. Taking a handout rubbed against the grain. Luke knew he had to say something, but what? When he finally lifted his eyes, he saw something in Houston's face he never expected—admiration, love between brothers.

Luke stood and crossed the space. "I don't deserve it. You don't know what I've done, the men I've killed when it was me or them. I doubt I can ever wash off all the blood on my hands."

"Houston and I have some too," Sam said. "A man can't live in this lawless land without dispensing a little justice."

"There's a difference in killing because you like it and killing to civilize Texas." Houston glanced at Josie, who leaned against the wall. "I think she wants to talk to you." He gave Luke a heavy scowl. "Be nice. Sam and I will be back to bring you food. We'll talk more about tonight then."

"Thanks. A man couldn't ask for better brothers." Luke narrowed his eyes at Sam. "You've hit me twice. A third time and we're going to have a bad problem."

Sam grinned and lightly patted Luke's jaw before following Houston out.

With the closing door, Luke quietly turned to Josie. "When are you leaving?" An ache shot into his chest that she'd soon be gone from the ranch and from his heart. His legs tried to buckle under him.

"How did you know?"

"I recognize the look."

"I'll head out at dawn," she answered. "It's time. I'll not stay for the necktie party." Her voice broke. "Besides, I need to find out who I am. Failing that, I'll make a brand-new life for myself somewhere."

"Don't go back to Medicine Springs alone," Luke warned. "That's a rough place. Too rough for a pretty lady." He read the stubborn tilt of her chin. "I know. You think you can take care of yourself. But you're not as tough as you want people to believe." He lowered his voice. "I've seen the woman underneath the hard surface. I held her in my arms and made love to her. Kissed the daylights out of her. *Mi princesa.*"

"Please." Her tortured cry filled the small dwelling as she backed up. "This is hard enough."

Luke took one step toward her. "Would you stay if I asked?"

"Are you?" Hope filled her eyes "Can you say you love me?"

He tried to control his ragged breathing, the air working its way through the thickness in his chest. To lose Josie would be the end. Without her, life didn't seem worth living. He'd turn himself over to the law come morning and be done with the running and hiding. He had no reason to keep looking for Ned Sweeney.

"I have no right to say those words, Josie. I wish I could be what you need. I do hope you find a better man somewhere out there and have those children you yearn for." Another ragged breath forced its way from Luke's mouth. He did love her. He loved her enough to let her go. He had no choice but to release her. "Would it be too much to ask that you think kindly of me from time to time?"

A little sob escaped her. "I'll always have tender thoughts of you, Luke Rafael Weston. Time will never change that."

It took every bit of willpower to curb the hunger to keep her with him. He caressed the dainty curve of her cheek with his eyes, swept down the long column of her throat, skimmed her sinful curves. Suddenly, he discovered he hadn't curbed a damn thing. All the longing and yearning for her rose up and overpowered him.

He covered the space separating them and took her face between his large hands. "Here's something to remember me by."

Before he could stop himself, he lowered his head and crushed his lips to hers. Fire raced through him and made his groin ache with a hunger he'd never felt before—the kind that made it impossible to breathe, to think, to see.

Josie's breath hitched as she leaned into him and wound her arms around his neck. She returned every bit of hot passion and desire. He groaned. *Dios mío*! He wanted her.

His hand slid around her and splayed across her back. Everything inside him cried to hold her and never let go.

With a harsh cry against his mouth, she pushed away from him. "Please."

Luke watched her stumble to the door and then she was gone, leaving him nothing but silence and emptiness. His aching heart felt worse than the fire from any bullet wound. He'd gladly take hot lead over this searing pain that seemed to rip him open.

"*Estúpido.*" Why couldn't he just let her quietly walk away? Why make things worse?

Because he loved her. And God knows he did.

It had taken so long to see the truth.

Now he'd lost everything that mattered. Tightness closed the air to Luke's lungs as tears filled his eyes. He slumped onto the bed. A broken man.

A man without a heart.

Thirty-one

STRUGGLING TO QUIET THE SOBS, JOSIE CREPT BACK TO headquarters using the buildings to shield her. Luke's kiss burned on her lips, his touch branded on every inch of her body. She cried for what she could never have.

A deep ache pierced her heart, making it impossible to breathe. She knew she'd carry the memory of the tall outlaw's special scent with her no matter where she went.

Yet, there was nowhere else she wanted to be than here.

Would she stay if Luke asked? In a heartbeat.

But he wouldn't. He couldn't tell her he loved her. He couldn't say the words she longed to hear.

Instead, he'd sent her to find another man to make a life with. That would never happen. She'd remain a spinster for the rest of her days. To marry someone else, to speak to him of love, would be a lie.

She slipped in through the kitchen door. Cook glanced up, shrugged, and returned to the vegetables she was chopping.

"Sorry, ma'am," Josie muttered and kept walking.

Taking care to avoid the windows, she turned to the stairs and discovered Noah sniffling on the bottom step.

"Hey there." She sat next to him. Joining him seemed a good idea. She had no need to ask the reason for the boy's tears, just sat silently with her arm around him.

Finally, Noah glanced up. "What are we gonna do, Josie?"

Good question. For Noah, that is. In her case, it was a bit clearer. She was going to run, ride out before daylight and never return. There was nothing left for her at the Lone Star. But she couldn't tell Noah that.

"I think you should march yourself over to that house and demand to see Papa Stoker."

"Do you think they'd let me?"

"Of course." She winked. "Those tough marshals are scared of kids. Kids can throw temper tantrums and if that doesn't work, kick their shins. It's against the law to hurt a kid. Why, they could even go to jail for it."

"I wouldn't ever be mean, even if I don't like 'em much. My mama told me to always be kind. If I don't, she frowns at me from heaven. I don't want to make her sad."

"Then kind you shall be. Go into the kitchen and see what Cook has baked today. I'll bet you'll find something to tempt those nasty marshals with. Kill 'em with kindness, I say." And she hoped they choked on whatever Noah found to take them. She thought about sneaking something sharp inside.

If she had a mama in heaven, hers probably would share her views, for she must've been a hell-raiser like her daughter.

"What about Luke?" Noah asked. "I need to see if he's okay too."

"Honey, I think Luke is very sad." She hugged him tight. "But he'd feel a lot better to see you."

She told the boy she'd take him to Luke's hiding place, cautioning him. "We'll have to be very careful and leave Rowdy here. He'll bark. We don't want anyone to know where Luke is."

"Nope. We have to keep him safe. Luke is my family now."

"Yes, he is." For however long he lived. Determined, she fought back the tight pain in her chest and gave Noah the biggest smile she could. "Now go and see what Cook has. I have to go to my room to check on Rafael. I'll meet you here."

"Okay." The boy moved toward the kitchen.

Noah would be good for Luke right now. The outlaw needed a friend.

And he'd made it clear he didn't want her.

Darkness had fallen and Luke's jitters made it difficult to sit, so he paced the room of the small house. In a few short hours, Josie was riding out of the Lone Star and out of his life.

He'd always keep her locked in a special place deep inside him.

What worried him most was that he couldn't protect her and keep her safe. Everything in him knew she was riding straight for Medicine Springs, and into the worst trouble of her life.

Talking to Stoker wasn't going to be easy either. He dreaded that.

Luke felt a bit better after spending a few hours with Noah, but the kid was too bright. He'd seen through the causes for Luke's dark mood.

"Listen to Papa Stoker when you talk to him," Noah had said. "Tell him you love him, because papas need to know that kind of stuff."

Then the kid had startled him when he said, "Sometimes when we find something, we don't know how important it is until it's gone. Don't let Josie leave, Luke."

He wished to God he could.

A slight rap sounded on the door. Luke let his brothers in. It was time. Sam told him the plan and Houston said Stoker would be at the window.

"Whatever you do, don't get caught," Houston growled.

Luke glared. "I wasn't born yesterday."

"We'll distract the marshals, raise hell about the nerve of them taking over the ranch and interrupting everything," Sam added and clasped Luke's hand.

A few minutes after his brothers left, Luke slipped out

the door and melted into the darkness. One way or another, this would end tomorrow. Either he'd head to the gallows or Stoker would do what he did best—bulldog his way over the top of everyone.

Thirty-two years of practicing stealth proved useful as Luke made his way to the elm. The starless night was like trying to see through a bucket of tar, but the barrel was right where Houston promised. Luke climbed onto it and shinnied up the tree, nothing but a dark shadow.

Everything had gone too well. When he made it to the limb he needed to reach the window, he found the branch wasn't as sturdy as his brothers had thought.

The wood cracked, threatening to snap any second. Luke carefully inched onto the limb and stretched out, not moving a muscle, clinging for dear life.

The ground was quite a ways down. Falling would hurt, if not kill him.

Luke held his breath. Sam and Houston should be raising that hell they spoke of by now, but only silence greeted him. Great. Without noise to provide cover, the marshals would hear the cracking wood. He waited for what seemed an hour. Finally, he heard the yelling and threats. He heard them shout that they'd wired the governor about the unlawful use of the ranch, holding their father, and the marshals would find marching orders by morning. His brothers were sure giving the marshals hell. Luke's mouth twitched. They'd evidently stolen a page from Stoker's book.

Luke inched out along the branch, fearing he'd plunge to the ground any second.

His progress was slow and with each inch gained, his weight dropped the limb a little lower. At last he made it to the window.

Only there was no Stoker.

He glanced inside the lit room and didn't see anyone. The weak branch dropped still lower. If this continued, he'd be *below* the window soon.

The minutes ticked by. Luke was ready to return to the

main trunk when Stoker appeared. Though his father was fighting mad, the fire was gone and he appeared weary. Luke could see the strain written on his father's face. Guilt surged over him. Stoker wouldn't be in this mess if not for him.

His father raised the window. "Had to wait until my guard left."

"Sam and Houston said you wanted to talk."

"I know what you're thinking and hope I can change your mind, son." Nearby light in the room revealed deep lines in Stoker's face that hadn't been there yesterday.

"What difference does it make? I've heard it all. I know what I have to do." And Luke would make everything right come morning.

Stoker spoke low. "We only have a few minutes, so listen. You are not to turn yourself in. You're innocent of that judge's murder."

"Yeah, well, everyone *swears* I did it. They've produced witnesses." Ones who'd sworn on a stack of Bibles they saw him holding the gun with smoke curling from the end, even though he'd never fired it. "I can't let you give up everything for me. Your whole life is this ranch. It flows in your veins like blood. You've worked yourself to the bone to make it what it is."

All while Luke squandered the same years, living the life of a renegade outlaw.

"Listen, son." Stoker's voice cracked, sending more guilt through Luke. "I'd gladly give up every single inch of this land to save your life. I failed you and my beautiful Elena and I want to make it up. I'm a tired old man." Stoker wearily wiped his eyes. "I've done and seen just about everything. You have your whole life—a good life—ahead of you."

Stoker leaned from the window and stretched out his hand. Luke stared at it a minute before he reached, straining, to touch his father's fingertips. The contact brought suffocating tightness to Luke's chest. A vice squeezed around his heart. He'd yearned for this so long.

Now the mere brush of their fingers had cemented their relationship.

He struggled to breathe. His father would give up all he had...for him.

That Stoker would sacrifice everything for his son's love sent waves of guilt over Luke. He'd brought Stoker nothing but shame, while he'd clung to his bitterness. He didn't deserve such a father. He realized and accepted that he did love Stoker.

But he didn't know how to say it.

Stoker broke the silence. "Think long and hard about what I said. Think before you act. Lay low and keep trying to find the man who'll clear you. Let me do this one thing," Stoker rasped, his voice thick. "For you."

Maybe it was time he trusted his father. To put aside the bitterness he'd carried. "I promised you never to bring trouble to your door, but I failed miserably. I can't let you take on my fight."

"Everyone needs—deserves—a second chance. A father doesn't just love his son when everything is rosy. I love you even when the storm clouds darken the sky. I'll stand beside you to the very end." Stoker leaned out so far, he was about to fall. His father closed his whole hand around Luke's.

Their skin touched for the first time and the shower of his father's love washed over Luke. He'd never known anything like this before. This was different from his mother's and she'd loved him with every bone in her body.

"We're all in this together, son." Stoker withdrew his hand and moved back. "If you think I'm afraid of lawmen or gunslingers, you don't know me. I don't intimidate."

His father's vision blurred and Luke wiped his eyes. He couldn't let him go to prison. "I knew that even before Sam brought me here. I used to sneak up here when the night shadows fell and watch you and my brothers. I always wondered how it would feel to be included."

"And?"

"I wouldn't have missed it for the world. I'll think about

what you said." But Luke already knew he couldn't let his father take his punishment. A man had to stand tall or he couldn't look at himself in the mirror.

Stoker turned at a noise. "Someone's coming. Get down from there, and for God's sake, don't break your fool neck."

"I hope you know what you're doing," Luke said.

"Trust me, I do."

"I'm learning"—Luke managed in a hoarse whisper—"Pa."

But Stoker had already lowered the window and hadn't heard him.

Awash with love that he could finally allow, Luke began the slow crawl backward. He discovered that getting off the branch was as tricky as climbing out on it. He'd almost reached the main trunk when the limb broke off completely, crashing to the ground. Luke dangled, clutching onto the jagged piece sticking from the trunk.

Using all his strength, he swung his body up to safety and stared down at his narrowly missed fate.

Two of the marshals rushed from the blackness. Up above, Luke hugged the bark while they argued about what had just happened to cause the break. Hopefully hidden by the leaves and dark shadows, he took slow shallow breaths. The marshals stared up, trying to see.

"I wouldn't be surprised if Sam and Houston haven't tried to help their father escape," one said. "Who would put a barrel here otherwise?"

"Climb up there and see if you see anyone," urged the other.

The first one snorted. "Are you crazy? I'm no organ grinder's damn monkey."

Finally, they rolled the barrel around to the front of the house and disappeared.

When it seemed safe, Luke shinnied down and jumped to the ground. He returned to his hiding place. He had lots to think about.

Houston and Sam were waiting at the empty dwelling for a report.

"Well?" Sam asked once Luke got inside.

"Stoker talked. I listened for the most part." Luke plowed his hands through his hair.

"And?" Houston pushed.

"I don't know." Luke sat down. "What kind of man would I be to let him lose everything he's worked like hell for? They'll confiscate this ranch and throw him in jail. I tell you what kind of man does that...the sorry kind." He dragged in a lungful of air. "I'm not that low-down yet."

"I'm sure Pa told you to sleep on it. You can make a decision come dawn," Sam said at the door. "A few hours won't make any difference. By the way, we brought some things in case you need a disguise. Put them on, and with all the ranch hands milling about twenty-four hours a day, coming and going from guard duty, the marshals will have heck trying to pick you out."

With their leaving, the silence in the room pounded against Luke's head. He slid his Colt from the holster and ran his thumb over the word scratched into the wood.

Legend.

The name was etched on this raw land as well. It spoke of everything he wasn't. Luke didn't know if he had what it took to wear the name. He couldn't even say the right words to keep the woman he loved from riding off into danger, or tell his father how he felt, until it was too late.

He called himself every name he could think of. Was he worth anything, least of all saving? Death and blood riddled his soul. Bodies lined the trail behind him. Their ghosts rode in his saddle. He yearned for a refuge, a place to think, and only one came to mind.

After slipping on spurs, chaps, and a long, black duster, Luke hung a coil of rope over his shoulder and emerged from the house. He moved quietly, mixing in with the milling ranch hands. No one paid him any mind. Everyone seemed to focus on guard duty both at the gate and on the western edge of the property. He boldly walked right by a group of the marshals with his head down low. Though they glanced at him, none called out his name, and they resumed their conversation.

Thanks to the lack of pictures on the wanted posters, none of them knew what Luke Weston looked like. Once by them, he glanced up at the thick clouds that had moved across the moon. The night seemed perfect for his needs. When he reached the end of the row of the town's establishments, he moved against the side of headquarters.

He pressed into the deep shadows of the big house and settled down to wait, taking note of the time between the patrolling marshals. They rode by every hour on the dot.

As he waited, a fog rolled in and turned the night into a thick soup. Now, there was no way anyone could see him. Satisfied, Luke removed his spurs and sauntered to the huge bronze star on its thick chains. The star had a ghostly appearance in the dark shadows, almost like it was a friend waiting just for him. The heavy chains were outstretched like arms, reaching to draw him into an embrace.

He stretched out in the damp grass. What was he going to do about this mess?

If Stoker could risk everything for him, Luke would do one last thing for his father and brothers. It would be his contribution to the family who'd taken him in.

To sleep beneath the star was supposed to reveal his worth. Slowly, peace filled him. Soon, his eyelids grew heavy and he relaxed, safe in the knowledge that no one could see him in the dark, soupy fog.

He slept, and dreamed of his mother. She told him not to turn himself in, to keep trying to find Ned Sweeney. "Stoker Legend can take care of himself," she said. "Your father knows how to escape trouble. He has powerful politicians and lawyers at his beck and call. They'll make sure he doesn't go to jail. Trust this man we both love. And, Luke, never think you have no worth. From the moment you were born until I closed my eyes in sleep, you gave me joy and made me the proudest mother in the world. You have a rare combination—sensitive caring and toughness.

No one is smarter or has more courage or determination to right wrongs."

He drifted, seemingly on a fluffy cloud. Sometime later, he felt soft lips pressed to his, and the feeling of Josie's presence surrounded him. He loved this dream.

She whispered, "I hope you discover the worth we all see inside you. I love you so much, Luke. I always will. I pray I have your child growing inside me and you can be with me forever."

Josie smoothed back his hair, soothing his ragged spirit. "I wish we could've held on to the treasure we found. My love for you will never die, but spread across the heavens. When you gaze up at the stars, you'll find me there."

Josie's sadness matched his own. He tried to reach out, to pull her next to him, but clutched empty air.

Sometime before dawn, certain truths filled him. He mattered. He wasn't the bad son he'd believed. He'd done a lot of good in his life. He'd helped the poor, given shoes to orphanages, saved Noah—other children too. Luke Weston was respected and welcomed in countless homes.

Another truth hit home that shook him to the core and a weight lifted from him to admit the truth.

He didn't just love Josie Morgan, he worshipped her. She was embedded deep into the fabric of his soul and she mattered more to him than anyone since Angelina. So much the reality made him tremble.

He wasn't supposed to care for anyone.

He wasn't supposed to let anyone in where the darkness dwelled.

He wasn't supposed to love again.

But heaven help him, he did. He loved Josie Morgan with all his heart, even with her strange quirks and headstrong ways.

The thought wound through him like a clinging vine. He was a fool to have fought her. She was his light, his world, his everything. And he'd tossed her aside.

Light had begun to filter through his eyelids when Luke

felt someone lie next to him. He opened his eyes to see Sam and Houston spread out on each side.

His *hermanos*.

These men were so much more than brothers. They were his best friends. They shared more than blood, more than a name. They shared a heart.

He now knew he was worthy of saving. Most of all, worthy of being loved. For however long remained, he'd spend it with them and Josie. If she'd still have him. Hell, she might shoot him on the spot and he deserved a bullet for being a fool.

One thing was as clear as the fragrant air of the Lone Star—he could not live without her.

Whatever came, they'd face it…together.

An urgency gripped Luke to find and tell her before she left. He propped himself on an elbow to stand when he noticed a cameo laying on his chest. He knew without turning it over that Josie's name was etched on the back.

He shot a glance at his brothers. "Which one of you put this here?"

Sam rose. "It wasn't us. Josie laid it on you."

"I thought she was a dream." Oh God, she'd already left. Panic raced through him. Luke jerked his head toward the huge crossbar, narrowing his eyes, straining for a glimpse of her. He'd go after her. He'd ask her to stay. He'd tell her he loved her. Just give him one more chance.

"Nope, not a dream," Houston said. "We saw her."

She'd been real and had come to say goodbye.

Josie was gone.

Thirty-two

A SOB TORE THROUGH LUKE. HE'D LOST THE WOMAN HE loved.

Luke leaped to his feet. He couldn't waste precious time. "I've got to bring her back."

"First things first, brother." Sam stood and pulled Houston up from the damp grass. "We caught someone sneaking onto the ranch last night. Claims he came looking for you."

"Who is it?" He didn't have time to humor someone hoping to make a name for himself. He had to find Josie.

"Calls himself Brenner McCall," Houston said.

What the hell did McCall want? Luke had to ride out, not spend it with a man who'd tried to kill him, who'd lied and pretended to be a friend when he felt no loyalty to anyone. Luke had a lot to say to him, but not now.

"I know him." Luke bit back a curse. "Where is he?"

Sam shifted. "We tied him up in a horse stall until we could decide what to do with him."

"Well?" Houston asked.

"Well, what?" Did his brother want an answer about Brenner or Josie?

Houston punched his arm. "Quit playing dumb. Are you turning yourself in or not?"

"No." Luke filled both lungs with the fresh morning

air and stared out over Lone Star land that stretched as far as he could see. Then he turned his gaze to the Texas flag fluttering overhead. "No, I'm going to find the man who calls himself Ned Sweeney and beat a confession out of him. I'm not going to hang for *his* crime."

Sam draped his arm around Luke's shoulder as they strolled to the back door of headquarters. The sky was beginning to lighten, but it was still dark enough to escape the attention of the marshals. "Exactly what we were waiting to hear. We'll go with you and scour every inch of this state. We'll find the slippery murderer."

There it was again—family loyalty. For a moment, Luke struggled to speak. At last, he managed, "Thanks."

But he wanted to say much more. That one word was inadequate for what he felt. He inhaled a shaky breath as they reached the kitchen door.

"This McCall fellow, he came to ask for your help in finding Josie Morgan." Sam turned the knob.

Luke froze. Of course. But what was the damn connection? He doubted McCall would tell him. "Afraid I can't help him. She's long gone. And why I'm standing here talking to you instead of saddling Major John, I don't know. I've got to go after her." He whirled to find his horse.

"Hold on. Wait just a damn minute." Houston turned him back around. "Josie is still here."

"Houston, I heard her tell me goodbye," Luke argued. He opened his hand that held the cameo. "She left this."

"Did you fall from that tree and crack your thick skull?" Sam asked. "Listen to us, dammit. We stopped Josie from leaving. We locked her in the tack room in the barn."

All the pain, sorrow, and frantic need to race after her left. He'd gotten another chance.

"Well, why didn't you say so? All this time you let me believe I'd lost her. I oughta whip you both to within an inch of your life." Anger then relief swept through Luke. She was going to be one mad *señorita*. He didn't want to be in his brothers' shoes. "Does she have her gun?"

Sam's face froze. "I didn't take it. Did you, Houston?"

"I thought you did," Houston answered.

Great. She was mad *and* she had her gun. Plus, she could draw and shoot almost as well as Luke.

"One question—why did you stop her from leaving?"

With a shrug, Houston said, "We know you love her. She loves you back."

It appeared Stoker wasn't the only one with tricks up his sleeve.

"You two better lay low until I can calm her down." Hopefully, saying he loved her would help her forget how mad she was. He'd say it anyway. He'd say it a thousand times and maybe she'd forgive him. Luke took a step and turned. "Which stall is Brenner in?"

"Very last one on the right. Oh, and, Luke, the ranch hands fed your horse enough beer to float a ship and Major John isn't feeling too good." Sam went through the door. "I smell coffee."

Hell!

Luke slipped into the dark barn without making a sound. Once inside, he paused to listen. He heard nothing but the rustle of straw. In the dimness, he saw a few horses sticking their heads from their stalls.

Brenner could wait. Everything could wait—except Josie.

He moved to the tack room and placed his ear against the door. No sound came from inside. Maybe she'd fallen asleep. Or maybe she was lying in wait to shoot whoever opened the door.

"Josie, it's Luke," he said low. "Don't shoot."

Still nothing. He turned the key sticking from the padlock. When he swung the door back, she burst out at him with the gun raised.

He caught her hand and pried the weapon from her fingers. A shot would've brought every marshal on the place.

"Dammit, Josie. I told you who I was. I had nothing to do with locking you in here."

"I know. That was for letting me ride away, if your brothers hadn't stopped me." She sniffled. "I thought you had some feelings for me. At least a little."

"Does being in love with you count?" he asked softly. "I want you to stay."

Josie's hair was tangled and in disarray and dirt covered one cheek, but she was the most beautiful woman he'd ever seen. She stood with pants-clad legs braced apart, her breath heaving. He'd never wanted her more.

He pulled her lush body against him. The gun fell from his grasp as he folded his arms around her. He could feel her heart pounding.

Her mysterious eyes made Luke think of heaven. "I thought I lost you." Shaking with how close he'd come, he ground his lips to hers in a kiss that blazed with heat and raw need.

In that moment, he knew he'd never get enough of this wild and crazy woman.

Overcome with hunger, Luke backed her against a wall and deepened the kiss, letting his mouth relay the depth of his love. His hands slid down her body before returning to her breasts. Damn the layers of fabric that stood between them. He needed to run his fingers across her silky skin. Given where they were, he could only settle for this much. He raked a thumbnail across her swollen nipples that begged for attention.

Josie gasped, desperately trying to unfasten his pants.

A voice yelled, bouncing off the barn walls. "Hey, I need to take a piss. Come untie me."

Damn Brenner! Luke dragged his mouth from Josie's.

"Who is that, Luke?" she asked.

"We need to talk, but I have a problem to deal with at the moment." He nuzzled her neck. "Try to leave and I'll hunt you down. You belong to me, lady," he growled.

"Oh, Luke, you're a funny man. Don't you know by

now? You're my only love." Josie tenderly laid her palm on the side of his jaw.

He kissed her once more and picked up her gun from the floor, sticking it into her holster. "This won't take long." He patted her saucy bottom and aimed her toward the door. "Go get some breakfast."

Without glancing back, Luke strode down the row of stalls to the empty one on the right. With Brenner tied up, he wouldn't need his Colt.

Brenner McCall sat in a corner on the straw. "Weston. About time. What's going on here? Why was I trussed up like a Christmas goose?"

"Keep your voice down. Marshals have arrested Stoker and they're holding him not far from here." Luke cut the ropes. "I heard you were looking for me." Luke pierced the old outlaw with a stare. "How did you know to find me here?"

"Imagine my surprise, boy, to find out that you're one of the Legends." Brenner rubbed his wrists. "You could've told me."

"Not your business." How the old outlaw had found out, Luke didn't know. He grabbed Brenner's shirt front and yanked the man to his feet. "Why are you looking for Josie Morgan? Consider your answer carefully. I'm a hair away from killing you."

A thick cry came from behind. Luke turned to see Josie standing with her gun pointed at them.

"Hello...*Pa*." Thick sarcasm colored her voice.

Thirty-three

At first glance, Josie projected calm and control, but Luke noticed the quiver of her hand and chin. He wanted to go to her and take her in his arms, but she didn't appear to issue an invitation.

"Do you know Brenner McCall?" he asked.

"Sorry as I am to say it, I do know the bastard." Josie dragged in a breath. "He's my low-down father."

"I've been looking for you everywhere, daughter." Brenner tried to move forward but Josie stopped him short with a wave of the gun. "I feared Reno might've killed you," Brenner muttered.

Luke winced, watching Josie's soft features harden to stone. She bore no resemblance to the woman he'd held in his arms mere minutes ago. Hurt filled her eyes.

"As though you'd care a fig about that. You were only worried about shutting me up in case Reno didn't. I know plenty to tell. You're a sorry piece of shit. You know that?" Josie gave a sarcastic snort. "I just didn't know how rotten you were until that night at Doan's Crossing."

A rock plummeted to the bottom of Luke's stomach. Had her memory just returned? Or had it never left? Had she been playing him for a fool all this time? He knew her skill at playing roles. It's quite possible he'd fallen for a ruse from the outset.

"Josie, honey, when exactly did your memory come back?" Luke dreaded her answer but he had to know.

She must've seen the doubt mirrored in his eyes. "Oh no, not you too," she cried.

Memories flooded over Josie so fast she could barely make sense of them. Her knees tried to buckle. She braced herself against the side of the stall. She knew everything now. But seeing the doubt fill Luke's eyes hurt her to the core. She set aside her own need to process her returning memory for later. Right now, she needed to focus on the man she loved.

She couldn't bear for him to think that she'd tricked him but his sharp, narrowed eyes and the disbelief in his voice told her he did. Fresh rounds of pain doubled her over.

"I can't explain it, but when I saw him, it was like floodgates opened. Everything came rushing back, just like Doc Jenkins said." She licked her dry lips, begging him to believe her. "You know I never listen. Something told me to follow you down here. The minute I laid eyes on him, I found everything I'd lost. My name is Josie Morgan. My mother was Sable Morgan, and she owned the Lucky Lady in Medicine Springs. That is, until Brenner stole it," Josie spat at the man who'd taken so much from her.

She trembled and her voice shook. "Now I know why that place felt so familiar to me. It was home. Please say you believe what I'm telling you."

She silently pleaded with Luke to speak. To say something.

In the quiet, she could hear her pounding heart. "If you ever loved me, you must know I'm telling the truth, Luke."

As though sensing discord, Brenner wiggled into the opening. "He's a smart one, girl. You're just like your mother, always trying to bluff your way out of everything."

"Don't speak to me." She delivered the words with a

vicious snarl. "Luke, I pledge on my love for you that I had no memory of anything until a few minutes ago."

Luke yanked Brenner around and tightened the ropes binding him. The man who'd kissed her, made love to her so tenderly, began to loosen.

His gaze tangled with hers for a long moment until finally he said, "I know. I'm glad you have it all back."

Relief swept through Josie. She turned to Brenner. "Do you want to tell Luke what you and Preston discussed that night, or shall I? I dare say he's going to be all ears."

When he stayed sullen and silent, she spoke. "They planned to murder you, Luke. Planned everything right down to how Preston would display your bloody body in town for passersby to spit on. I heard every bit of their contemptible plan. Even though I'd never laid eyes on you, I was going to try to find and warn you."

Shock deepened the lines on Luke's face. He swung to Brenner. "Why? I thought we were friends."

"You were dispensable. Preston needed to get elected and he promised me that he'd appoint me as the highest judge in the state if I helped him. I wanted to be someone important. Someone people looked up to." Brenner's shoulders slumped. "I was finally going to be somebody."

"So the plan was what?" Luke asked tightly.

"You were supposed to meet Brenner at Dead Horse Creek the next morning," Josie supplied, glaring hate at Brenner. "They were going to ambush you there."

"Ned Sweeney." Luke muttered a curse. "Of course. You fit the description. You've been under my nose this whole damn time. I'm so stupid."

"I knew you wouldn't suspect someone so close to you." Brenner edged closer to Josie. "That's why it worked."

Not trusting him, Josie moved out of reach and kept a sharp eye on the man.

"It would've worked if Reno Kidd hadn't stuck his nose in it. Preston would've been a big man showing off the carcass of an outlaw with such a big bounty on his head. People would've elected him by a landslide." Brenner wagged his head. "Why couldn't you have just died? No one would've missed you."

Except his family. Josie couldn't imagine how Luke's death would've devastated them.

"My question is why you waited two damn years. Why so long?" Luke asked.

"Preston struggled to get the backing he needed to put his name on the ballot. Even after I got rid of Judge Percival for him, Preston had trouble with his image and the public didn't trust him. We sort of underestimated the judge's popularity. He had this state sewn up."

Josie clenched her teeth and kicked at the man who'd brought her nothing but pain. "You'd better thank God those lawmen are out there or I'd blow you straight into hell and give you a head start on shaking hands with the devil. It'd be worth going to jail for, and Luke is fast enough to outrun them."

"You're an ungrateful trollop, just like your damn mother," Brenner spat.

"Say that again, and I'll lay you on the floor." Luke's steely warning filled the air. "You'll show her respect."

"It's all right," Josie said sadly. "From the moment he walked into my life, he made it plain how he felt about me. I return the sentiment."

"All the same, I won't let him disrespect you. Seems I owe my life to Reno Kidd." Luke's mouth quirked in a wry smile. "Imagine that."

"The bastard!" Brenner released a string of curses. "I glimpsed him at Newt Granger's but he vanished before I could get to him. I'd put a bullet in his brain in a heartbeat."

"Reno's dead. I killed him." Luke narrowed his eyes. "With his last breath, he warned that you were plotting against me." He swung to Josie. "How did you get in Preston's wagon?"

Luke stood there so tall and strong, but she saw a frightened little boy who'd survived the darkness of prison. She saw how difficult it was for him to trust anyone. He'd been betrayed over and over. With so many lies and manipulations, it was hard for him to believe her totally, even though she could tell he yearned to.

Had he really said he loved her a few minutes ago? Or had she imagined that?

"I'm going to tell you the facts of that night and lay all your doubts to rest." She relived the scene in her mind as she told it. "Preston met Brenner at the saloon in Lost Point. They'd left me earlier at a boarding house to wait but I knew they were up to something bad, so I hid under a tarp in the back of the wagon. They never knew I was there until Reno attacked them. I jumped up and tried to stop Reno from killing Preston. The rest you know."

Josie glared at her father. She never thought she could hate anyone so much.

"I did grow up in the Lucky Lady." It was strange how she'd known that even with her memory gone. "And I didn't know my father's name until Mama died a year and a half ago. Brenner had swooped in, all loving and polite at first, but everything changed once they laid my mother in the ground. Within a few hours after burying her, he sold the saloon and the new owner tossed me out. Brenner promised to give me enough money for a new start if I came with him. But he's dangled that carrot all this time and never given me one blessed thing. He took me to live in Fort Worth and I saw every shady deal he was involved in—all the schemes, the lying, cheating farmers out of their land, and pretending to be a friend to those in need."

Why she had ever thought he'd keep his word to her she didn't know. He was the nastiest, slimiest kind of crook.

Thank goodness, he and Sable never married. Before her mother died, she'd warned Josie about trusting him. That had been the memory Josie had seen when she'd knelt over Reno.

A horrible ache washed over Josie. "I wish I could've stopped all this, Luke. When I hid, I didn't exactly know what I was going to do—just something. Then, Reno interrupted everything and I never got a chance."

Outside, she heard men talking. Soon cowboys would come for their mounts. They needed to finish. But what would they do about Brenner? Unless Luke had a plan that Josie didn't know about.

"Just one more thing." Luke turned to Brenner McCall. "Mind telling me who sent the posse after Josie? Who told them she'd killed her husband?"

"You might as well know everything," Brenner answered. "I did. I needed to find her, and putting her face on wanted posters was the easiest way."

Josie's kick connected with his shin. "You get sorrier and sorrier, you piece of shit."

Brenner let out an oath. "I knew I could get you off. I'm a damn good lawyer."

"Well, I just wish you were a damn good human being but I see that ain't ever gonna happen." She couldn't help wishing she'd aimed her kick a lot higher. Now, that's where it would really hurt.

In the dim light, Luke's eyes were hard, glittering stones. "Explain the part about Judge Percival to me, Brenner. That's what I really want to know. We played cards the previous night. You knew I had won enough money to buy amnesty." He jabbed Brenner's chest. "I told you I was going to see him."

Now they had him, if Brenner would just speak the truth. And Luke's long, desperate search would be over.

The old outlaw shrugged. "At the time, we didn't have any plans to kill you. We just needed someone to pin the judge's murder on. I went ahead of you and did the deed, then struck you with my pistol and left you to take the blame." Brenner sneered. "You played right into my hands. You and your talk about how you were going to clear your name and walk away from me. After all I did for you, you were going to walk away, you pissant. I should've left you lying in your filth."

"My God, are you listening to yourself?" Josie had

known the depth of Brenner's black heart but this truly shocked her. He'd tried over and over to destroy Luke—all the while pretending to be a friend to a lost boy. That was the cruelest part of all.

"Why didn't you just shoot me at Doan's Crossing?" Luke asked.

Josie watched her father's anger boil. He *still* burned with a need to have Luke dead.

"I wanted to. God, how I wanted to! But I was hurt and even if I pulled the trigger, I couldn't outrun the rangers camped nearby." Brenner's lips thinned into a cruel line.

"I watched your eyes and saw how little I meant to you. I was ready. But you knew you didn't stand a chance of outdrawing me. I wish you'd tried." Questions still filled Luke's eyes. He turned to Josie. "What were you doing with Brenner at Noah's parents' farm?"

"This sack of shit was trying to pressure Abel Jordan into helping with another job," she answered. "Brenner saved his life once and said Mr. Jordan owed him. Only, the man was smart enough to say no thanks."

"I took care of that later," Brenner smirked. "His wife too. Couldn't find the kid."

Luke glared at his former mentor. "I think all we have left here is to haul you across to the marshals."

Warm happiness surged through her. "This will wipe away the murder charge, Luke. After this hanging over you for so long, you'll be a free man at last. You can have your dream."

She let her gaze caress his tall, dark shape. God, how she loved this man!

Brenner suddenly lunged at her, the ropes he'd somehow worked free from falling uselessly to the floor, and snatched the gun from her hand. His fingers dug into her arm as he pulled her up next to him with an iron grip. "Get back," he ordered Luke.

"Take me. Let her go. She's done nothing," Luke bargained. "It's me you want."

Brenner's breath smelled like week-old fish. "She's done plenty, and she'll pay."

Josie glanced around for a weapon. "It's all right." She tried to smile at Luke but it didn't quite form. "I knew it would come to this, saw it the day I laid my poor mama to rest."

Her heart broke into a million pieces as Brenner jerked her toward his horse. Why did things have to go all wrong the minute they started to go right? Tightness burned her chest and dark foreboding filled her.

Either she or Brenner McCall would not return.

Her vision blurred. No matter the outcome, however this went, Luke would be her love for the rest of eternity.

Thirty-four

Luke stared after Josie, locked in the clutches of an outlaw he hated. He considered raising hell and letting the marshals shoot Brenner. But they could hit Josie. No, this job called for someone with a steady hand and sure aim—him.

With fear gripping like a vise around his heart, Luke hurried to find a horse, since Major John was in no shape to ride. He pulled the roan Josie had ridden out of a stall.

He had the roan saddled and was checking the cinch one last time when his brothers ran in.

"Brenner has Josie!" Luke hollered. "I'm going after her. You're welcome to come, but even if you don't, I'm going anyway. Brenner holds my future. He's Ned Sweeney."

Sam raced to his horse's stall. "We saw a flash go by the window. Thought I saw Josie on the back, hanging on for all she was worth but wasn't sure."

"I'm coming too." Houston yanked his saddle from a rail and stalked toward his horse. "He's not going to get away, Luke."

"I just want Josie. If he hurts her..." He wouldn't voice his fear, or what she meant to him. How could he explain that the world would stop turning without her? There would be no more sun or moon.

"I'm riding ahead." Luke grabbed the reins. "You two can catch up."

Without waiting for a reply, Luke turned to lead the gelding out of the barn.

"Wait," Sam called. He brought Luke a pair of chaps. "Put these on. The lawmen will think you're one of the ranch cowboys. Hopefully. And not start shooting."

Luke wouldn't let a bullet stop him. He'd get to Josie if he had to crawl through a pit of fire. He couldn't live without her. She was his air, his food, his heart.

"We'll be right behind," Houston hollered. "We'll chase the bastard to the end of the world. He won't get away."

Outside the corral, Luke vaulted into the saddle. He made it to the small town before he heard the order to halt. He raked the roan's flanks and the horse leaped into a gallop.

Bullets flew around him as he raced past the shooters. "Is that the best you've got?" Luke muttered as he flew under the crossbar.

If the lawmen gave chase, they'd have to have good horses. He leaned forward and patted the roan's thick neck. Luke scanned the rugged landscape ahead but saw no sign of Brenner McCall. He slowed and leaned from the saddle to look at the tracks. The fresh ones had to be the old man.

Hatred seethed inside him. Why in the name of all that's holy didn't he figure out who Ned Sweeney was? Damn Brenner! As furious as Luke was at his old partner, he reserved the biggest portion of scorn for himself. There was no excuse for him not putting everything together.

Rage burned a path through him. He'd confided in Brenner about his need to find Ned Sweeney many times over the years. Luke might as well have put the bullet in Brenner's gun.

He'd been betrayed and led down a crooked path like a bull with a ring in his nose.

"*Estúpido*!" Luke yelled. Why had he been so blind?

Well, he wasn't blind anymore. And he would right his mistake before the day was out.

But if luck wasn't on his side, he'd have to bury Josie in some grave out on the prairie. He wouldn't ride away and leave his *princesa* all alone. He'd lie right down beside her. And then, then he'd put a bullet in his brain.

He never thought he'd feel this way about any woman. His feelings for Angelina had been deep and lasting but it was nothing like this soul-piercing love he felt for Josie.

Finally, he'd gotten an answer to something that had puzzled him—Stoker's deep feelings for his mother. It wasn't that he loved Elena Montoya more than his wife, Hannah. But Elena filled a larger part of his father's heart. Elena had been fire and excitement. From what Luke heard his brothers say, Hannah had been rock solid and steady—the perfect rancher's wife.

Josie was like his mother. She grabbed more life in a day than most women did in a lifetime.

And she was his.

Luke grinned. He'd finally done something right.

Josie Morgan was going to be his wife; she just didn't know it yet.

As Luke rode, he thought about the depth of Brenner's betrayal. Greed and ego had eaten up the ruthless old outlaw. He'd wanted to be someone important. Sadly, now, all he was going to be was a murderer.

Suddenly, the whole scope of it hit Luke. He was cleared. As soon as he turned Brenner over to the authorities, Luke could stake his claim to everything he'd longed for.

He'd no longer be Luke Weston, the outlaw and gunslinger.

"I can finally be Luke Legend and I'll help run the Lone Star!" he shouted into the wind.

A rider emerged from a ravine ahead of him. It had to be Brenner and Josie. The need to cut off that horse exploded inside him. He urged the roan to go faster. They appeared to be heading toward Deliverance Canyon.

He froze. Brenner would catch Tally and her small band unaware.

Someway, somehow, he had to warn them.

Josie struggled to stay on the galloping horse in this mad dash from justice. She recognized the landscape and knew Deliverance Canyon lay directly ahead.

Tally and those ladies didn't know the hell that was riding toward them, and she had no way of sending a warning.

Maybe she could manage to grab Brenner's gun. She needed a weapon. The minute she got her hands on one, she'd put a bullet in Brenner's black heart.

Then she froze. No, she needed him alive so he could clear Luke. No one would believe them if it was hers and Luke's word alone.

She'd take Brenner back to the Lone Star and turn him over.

Then she'd shoot him!

A much better plan.

But first she had to get a gun.

Tally would help her—if Brenner didn't kill her first. She wouldn't put anything past Brenner McCall. Not one damn thing. The rotten man had made her life hell for the past year.

All Josie had wanted was a father to love her, hold her, and keep her safe. But Brenner was far from a loving parent. It was her mother, the beautiful and tough Sable Morgan, who had taught her to shoot. Dangerous men came through the saloon. Sable and Josie had lived upstairs and her mother wanted Josie to learn how to use a gun. For a year, Josie had practiced with some of the best marksmen around. The minute Brenner McCall came into her life, she ached to one day put a bullet into him.

No one except her mother had shown caring or offered safety until Luke rode up on his beer-drinking horse.

Josie turned to glance back and saw a rider gaining on them. It had to be Luke.

Her mind whirled. What could she do to help?

He wouldn't shoot with her on the horse. Jump off? She glanced at the ground skimming by. The fall would hurt bad. It might break her neck.

Nope. Only as a last resort. She thought some more.

A better idea would be to distract Brenner. Yes, that's what she'd do. She could bite and hit. Maybe she could push him from the saddle. She'd love to inflict pain, to pay him back for some of the mean names he'd flung at her.

Mean, hateful names and they'd hurt. Oh Lord, how they'd hurt.

Armed with a plan, she settled back with a smile on her lips. He'd never know what happened. She unbuckled her empty gun belt and let it dangle from one hand. She'd sling it as hard as she could at his stupid head. Then whip his back and shoulders. That'd knock him from the horse for sure.

She hoped the horse stomped on him. Serve him right.

Patiently, she waited, willing Luke closer.

Except Luke was pulling up for some reason. What was he doing? Had his horse gone lame?

Brenner entered a thick grove of mesquite and she lost sight of the man she loved more than anything on earth.

Somehow, she'd take care of her rotten father and ride back to him.

As sure as whiskey flowed like water in the Lucky Lady, Brenner McCall would face his fate.

Thirty-five

The roan suddenly slowed, limping. With muttered curses and a sinking heart, Luke jumped from the saddle, watching the riders grow smaller in the distance. Whatever was wrong with the animal, he had to fix it and in a hurry.

He just prayed he could figure out the problem. And not with a bullet. He couldn't lose the horse.

If he did, he'd lose Josie too.

An old saying flashed into his mind. *What cannot be remedied must be endured.*

Please, God, don't let this be the time for this lesson.

Luke's breathing was ragged as he ran his hand down the animal's left leg. Nothing. He raised the hoof. There was the source of the limp—a rock was lodged deep between the shoe and tender tissue. Jerking his knife from his boot, he dug it out and mounted back up.

Behind, two riders were coming up fast. The marshals? Or his brothers?

A muscle worked in his jaw. He couldn't let the marshals stop him from getting to Josie. No matter what he had to do, even if he had to kill them, he'd save her. Fear crawled up his spine. He had to do this. He couldn't be too late.

The gelding shook his head and snorted, then took off in the fastest gallop Luke had ever seen. The ground flew under his powerful hooves.

A mile across the landscape, Luke saw them ahead, thankful that a horse with two riders was slower. Brenner's mount had to be using a hell of a lot of energy and would soon wear out at this pace.

Slowly, bit by bit, Luke gained on them. They had almost reached Deliverance Canyon.

He made out Josie's ashen face as she turned to glance back. Maybe seeing him would reassure her and give her strength. He yearned to take her in his arms and keep her safe.

Like he'd promised. So far, he'd failed.

Suddenly, Josie raised something. Her gun belt? She drew back and began whaling on Brenner McCall with it. The man struggled to stay in the saddle. He slipped sideways and clung by his fingernails.

As Luke watched the fight, wishing he could help, Brenner's horse disappeared into a thick stand of mesquite. Luke was frantic with need to see Josie, to know she was all right. A minute later, he stopped short and got off. He'd flush Brenner out on foot.

Before drawing his Colt, Luke raised his hands to his mouth and gave the mournful howl of a coyote. This was the signal for danger that he'd discussed many times with Tally Shannon. At least they'd know trouble was near. A second later, he received an answering call from deep in the canyon.

Tally knew and would hide the women.

Now that he'd warned them, Luke slid the Colt from the worn, well-oiled leather and picked his way through the thorny mesquite.

Slow and steady.

His steps were silent.

Inch by inch.

Then he spied his quarry. Brenner held Josie in front of him with a gun to her head. Her torn, dirty clothes and the red mark on her cheek told him how the old outlaw had managed to regain control.

Something ugly and dark rose from deep inside Luke.

No one hurt Josie and lived.

Not while he had breath in his body.

He heard the faint sounds of other riders in the distance but he didn't turn to see how close. His thoughts and focus were riveted on the woman he loved in the grip of evil.

"Stay back, Weston," Brenner called. "You do anything foolish and she dies."

Josie hollered, "Luke, just shoot him! He's nothing but a rotten piece of shit."

Didn't she understand that he didn't have a clear shot? He wouldn't risk hitting her. Fear squeezed tighter and tighter until he couldn't breathe. This was Angelina all over again. A bullet was going to steal Josie from him.

"You know you're a dead man, Brenner. Turn her loose or I'll kill you where you stand then let the buzzards peck out your eyes." That was a promise Luke would keep.

The burst of Brenner's .45 spoke for the outlaw. A bullet struck a mesquite tree, splintering the trunk. Luke crept closer, using the undergrowth as cover, confident Brenner couldn't see him.

"Don't worry about hitting me!" Josie yelled. "I know what to do. Just shoot the bastard!" With that, she stomped on Brenner's foot as hard as she could and tried to elbow him.

Though Brenner called his daughter every bad name in his vocabulary and let out an oath that made Luke cringe, he held fast to her.

Luke moved in a circle. Closer and closer. He was set to tackle Brenner from behind when a couple of frightened ground squirrels rustled the brush next to Luke's foot. Brenner whirled, firing. Luke dove to the ground.

"Brenner, let's sort this out," Luke said. "Just tell me one thing—why do you want to kill me so bad? Just tell me what I did to you."

"I took in a snot-nosed kid that didn't know shit. I got you cleaned up and offered you a fresh start. Treated you like my own son. And what did you do?" Brenner barked a laugh. "You turned your back on me like I was dirt. Betrayed me and your own kind. You were going to get amnesty and change your life. You thought you were better than me. Besides, you know too much. I can't trust you not to turn me in, boy. Can't trust Josie either. Can't trust one damn person."

The truth struck Luke. By trying to do the right thing and straighten his life out, he'd wounded Brenner McCall. Outlaws were a strange bunch. Loyalty to them protected you. But try to get out and they'd kill you. Being an outlaw meant being one for keeps.

"I owe you, Brenner. I will to the day I die." Luke's voice trembled. "Like you said, you saved me. I'm sorry you thought I'd turned on you. Your secrets were safe with me. But something else burns inside me now. I need to do right. I need my family."

"I was your damn family!" Brenner yelled. "I'm going to blow Josie's head off and you're going to watch, knowing you can't do a blessed thing."

Cold terror washed over Luke. He had only one option. Josie would *not* die for him.

"Look, I'm going to lay down my Colt and walk toward you. I'll face you alone. Unarmed. Let Josie go. You can take your revenge on me. She's innocent in all this."

"If that's the way you want it."

"Luke, don't do this!" Josie screamed. "Don't sacrifice yourself for me. Don't!"

"It's all right, Josie. I've always known this moment was coming. I'll gladly give my life for you any day." Luke stilled his trembling hand, took a ragged breath, and laid down his gun.

It suddenly hit him that this was what Stoker had been trying to do for him. Everything was as clear as day. This was what you did for the people you loved. When Luke came down to it, his life didn't mean that much when Josie's was on the line.

Hands raised, he rose from cover and walked slowly toward the man he'd once thought of as a father. Brenner cursed, flinging Josie aside. Orange flame shot from his pistol.

Hot lead ripped into Luke's chest, sending fiery flames shooting through him. The pain was unbearable. The dream he'd had at Doan's Crossing had come true.

What cannot be remedied must be endured flashed through his mind. He'd endure whatever he must for the woman who'd stolen his heart. His all was not too much.

Gasping for air, Luke fell.

Thirty-six

"No! No! No!" Josie screamed and flew to Luke. She couldn't lose him now. Not when they were so close to having everything they wanted.

Not when he was within claiming distance of his birthright.

Sobbing, she dropped to the rocky ground and cradled Luke's head in her lap. His eyes fluttered and he worked his tongue but no sound came out.

Brenner McCall stood over them with his gun aimed.

Josie stared up into his strange, glittering eyes. "I hate you with every bone in my body. I hope you die a thousand deaths with each more miserable than the last. And then after that I hope you burn in the fiery pit below."

"Say your prayers, *daughter*," he spat.

She lowered her eyelids so she could no longer see Brenner's face. She'd die with the man she loved.

She'd heard it said that right before the end came, her life would pass before her eyes. Memories suddenly flooded over her. Of Luke's kisses, the nights when he'd held her next to his scarred, hard body, and the times they'd made love in the squatter's shack at Doan's Crossing. The sinful, crooked smile that put a sparkle in his eyes and showed his white teeth. The assurance he'd help fix her life. Even though she hadn't known who she was or where she'd come from, her heart had been light. Luke had driven out fear and replaced it with sure knowledge that she was safe with him.

She waited for the explosion of the gunshot that would end it all.

But the rustle, flurry of movement, and a deep grunt didn't sound like a bullet. She opened her eyes to see Tally Shannon and five of her small army holding Brenner.

"We heard Luke's warning call and came." Tally shot Brenner a glare. "Just not quick enough."

"Let me go!" Brenner shouted. "You're gonna pay, just like Luke and Josie."

"I'm afraid you're out of luck, mister." In a flash, Tally kicked Brenner's feet from under him and he landed with a thud on the ground. After instructing her ladies to shoot him if he moved a muscle, she knelt to inspect Luke's bloody wound.

"This is far worse than when we found him before and patched him up," Tally murmured.

Josie's breath froze as she met Tally's eyes and saw the unvarnished truth in the woman's blue gaze.

"I don't see how he can live." Tally covered Josie's hand with hers. "I'm sorry."

Luke gasped for air. "Listen to her, Josie. This is it for me."

"No. You're tough," Josie insisted brokenly. "We're going to be married and start a life together. You—you said you love me. No, I'm not going to let you die. I'm not."

A gurgle came from Luke's throat. He fumbled for her hand. "If you remember only one thing, remember that I love you and I…I cherish every second with you."

His faint words struck fear into her heart. She clutched his hand, willing her strength to flow into him. She couldn't accept this. She wouldn't.

"We'll have more times together, sweetheart. Listen to me, Luke Weston. You are *not* going to die, so get that out of your head." Holding back a sob, Josie tenderly wiped a tear trickling down the side of his face. "You're going to get well. We'll have a wonderful future. And you'll have the dream you've worked so hard for. I'm not going to let you give up, do you hear me?"

"Some things even you can't stop, *princesa*." He reached up to capture a strand of her hair between his fingers. "So beautiful. Go on with your life. Find someone who makes you happy."

"I swear, Luke, you haven't learned a blessed thing about me." She pressed her lips to his, drinking in his love.

She prayed that her words had made a difference. Something had to. The minute a person gave up, they were done for.

Luke was *not* done. He had so much to look forward to.

He could claim his place at last in the Legend family.

She heard riders coming as though from very far away, then seconds later, Sam and Houston knelt next to their brother.

Like ghostly shadows, Tally and the others disappeared below. She and her friends had gone back into hiding. When Josie glanced up, she saw the reason why—two marshals strode into view. Brenner was on his belly with his feet tied to his hands, a gag stuffed in his mouth. No wonder he'd been so quiet. Tally's soldiers had trussed him up tight. He glared at Josie with glittering eyes so full of hate. Satisfied that he couldn't hurt anyone, she turned back to Luke, willing him to live. She squeezed his hand to let him know she was there.

Sam held a canteen to his brother's lips. "Luke, we're here," Sam said. "Hang on and fight like you've never fought."

Luke worked his tongue to speak and finally managed to say, "Take care of Josie. Give her my land—home."

"Quit talking nonsense." Sam yanked open Luke's shirt and frantically pressed his bandana to the wound. "You're not going anywhere. You're going to pull through and make your home on the Lone Star just like you planned. Nothing has changed."

"It's only a scratch," Houston muttered thickly. "You're not going to let this get you, brother."

Another gurgle came from Luke's throat and blood dribbled from the sides of his mouth. His lips tilted up for just a second. "Funny."

Houston stood, towering over the two marshals. Josie watched fury flash from his eyes and felt the heat of his wrath. In that moment, he looked like the spitting image of Stoker. One of the marshal's Adam's apple bobbled as he struggled to swallow.

"You ride like hell back to the ranch!" Houston thundered. "Get my father. And Doc Jenkins. Anyone can show you his house. Don't bother to come back without both men—and a wagon. Got that? Return empty-handed and I'll have a bullet waiting."

"You can't order us around," a younger one replied hotly. "We're lawmen and this man is a wanted murderer."

"I don't care if you're President Rutherford B. Hayes." Sam rose and stood beside Houston. "If Luke dies, we'll hunt you down. I promise you that. Now ride!"

Without further argument, they hurried to their horses and set off at a gallop.

As the hoofbeats faded, Tally Shannon returned. "What can I do? Darcy and Holly Beth went for water and medical supplies." She pushed back her hair with a tired hand. "I'd offer my home, but I think moving Luke will kill him for sure."

Houston thrust out a large hand. "I'm Sam's and Luke's brother. I've never had the pleasure, ma'am. I overheard them talking once about you and the other ladies down in the canyon. Your secret is safe. I won't do anything to bring harm."

Josie watched deep emotion ripple across Tally's face. Though the woman was dry-eyed, her lip trembled. Luke meant so much to her.

Tally glanced at Luke, lying so still. "If turning myself in would save that man, I'd do it in a heartbeat. Luke kept us safe and fed. We owe him our lives. He's like family and I love him like a brother."

Sam put his arm around her and Tally clung to him. Josie watched how his gentle comfort slowly bolstered the stoic woman who'd weathered untold pain, heartache, and death. Minutes passed until Tally stepped away, her strength returned.

Josie envied Tally's ability to bounce back and do what needed doing. Luke thought Josie was strong, but he didn't know that inside she was a quaking mess.

She glanced at the bandana Sam had pressed to the wound. It was soaked with red. Luke's life seemed to gush out—the blood mixed with hurt and loneliness. She dashed away sudden tears. Though Luke lay with his eyes closed, he wouldn't see her cry. He'd see only the fiercely brave woman he thought she was.

Go on without him? How?

Darcy and Holly returned with blankets, water, and medical supplies. Josie washed the wound good and wrapped it with plenty of padding.

Frustration swept over her. When would they come back with the doctor?

Houston stood apart, staring toward the ranch.

As she fought impatience and fear, a strange thing happened. One by one, the women of Deliverance Canyon filed out and knelt to speak to Luke, telling how much they still needed him and thanking him for his care of them. Josie stepped aside, knowing they loved him just as much and had to be with him. Luke didn't know just how much he'd touched their lives, as well as so many others', in ways he never could've imagined.

He'd been so blind. Luke mattered. Dammit, he mattered to them all.

Sam retrieved the Colt from the dirt, unbuckled Luke's gun belt, and slid the gun into the holster. After wrapping the belt around it, he handed it to Josie.

She clutched it to her. How many times had Luke fired

this weapon to save someone's life? He'd saved Josie when he didn't have to. He could've ridden on to his meeting. But he'd stopped, and she would never forget the tenderness of his touch—even though he'd wanted to strangle her, both then and other times. Josie laid the gun belt and Colt next to him, just in case it helped him rest easier.

Brenner shifted, rustling against the ground by the fire, and she glared at him, willing him to disappear from her sight as he already had from her mind. At least Sam and Houston were keeping a close eye on him. He wasn't going to escape.

Night fell and the women sentinels of Deliverance Canyon disappeared to safety below. Sam and Houston built a fire. Having done as much as they could for Luke, they marched over to Brenner, leather chaps slapping against their legs, and yanked him up.

Sam pulled out the gag. "We're gonna have a talk. And you won't like what happens if you don't tell us everything."

"I'm a respected lawyer. You can't treat me this way," Brenner spat. "I'm going to be appointed judge soon."

"You know, Sam, I think McCall is right," drawled Houston. "We shouldn't treat him this way. It's much too nice and civilized." In a swift move, Houston jerked Brenner up by a hand around the man's throat. Brenner's eyes widened as he choked.

"The marshals are gone," said Sam, calmly testing the sharpness of his knife. "There's no one to see what we're about to do."

"When the lawmen return, they'll find your carcass a mile from here." Houston tightened his grip, lifting Brenner off his feet. "We'll tell them you got away and the animals feasted."

"So, you see?" Sam smiled grimly. "We've thought of everything."

Brenner's eyes pleaded for Josie to save him. Houston lowered him when she stalked over. She drew back a fist and drove it into his face. Blood squirted from his nose. Then she kicked him with the toe of her boot until her leg gave out.

"You never kept one damn promise you ever made," she spat.

"All right," Brenner screamed. "Get her away from me. I'll talk."

Sam glanced at Houston. "I think we should use her in all our dealings with outlaws."

By the time Brenner McCall had answered all their questions, an hour must've gone by. They tied him back up and warned if he didn't keep quiet, they'd gag him.

The two brothers drank coffee and stared into the fire as the shadows deepened and the black night closed around them. Josie sat by Luke's side, gently caressing his face. The dark stubble along his jaw made him look dangerous, even though his piercing eyes were shut. She washed blood from his mouth and leaned to kiss his lips, pouring her love into him.

"Wake up, my darling cowboy," she whispered. "Get well so we can plan our future."

His mouth moved. "Love…you…" The words were weak and she could barely hear, but she hadn't imagined them. He still felt her, knew she was there.

But was it his final goodbye?

Oh God, please don't let it be that.

Let it be a sign that he wasn't giving up.

Time dragged. Where was Doc Jenkins? He had to hurry. He had to save Luke. She didn't want to live without him; it would be impossible. Her heart beat only for him, for this lonely, scarred outlaw who'd burrowed into her thoughts, mind, and soul.

The fire crackled and popped. Then she heard what could be the faint sound of riders. She, Sam, and Houston jerked to their feet at the same time. She strained to hear, praying it was help. The sounds came again, closer and clearer.

Houston whooped and grinned.

Help had arrived.

Soon after, Stoker's big form strode toward Josie. Then she spied Doc Jenkins. Also the whole group of lawmen, but that didn't matter.

Stoker's long legs carried him to Luke's side. He knelt and took Luke's hand. "Son, I'm here. I brought Doc and he's going to fix you up in no time. You're going to be all right. Just trust me and hang on for dear life."

Josie watched him smooth back Luke's hair. Though his touch was awkward and rough, she saw love in each stroke.

Luke's eyes fluttered, then opened. His voice was weak. "I'm a Legend." He tried to smile but couldn't. "Luke Legend. For one day." He tried to wet his lips. "I love you...Pa."

Thirty-seven

Tears rolled down Josie's face. The father and son had finally found what each had sought. Luke had seen his dream of being a Legend come true. He belonged. And Stoker had gotten his third son into the fold at last.

Only...was it too late?

Josie glanced up at the stars and prayed as she never had. Surely God didn't need Luke yet, but Lord, how *she* did. Couldn't God wait longer for him?

Doc knelt and opened his black bag. Someone lifted a torch so the man of medicine could see. She hoped he had a miracle up his sleeve, because that's what it would take.

Everyone stood in a circle, barely breathing, waiting for the verdict.

Doc frowned as he inspected the wound. Finally, he addressed them. "He needs surgery—now."

"It'll take time to get him to the ranch." Stoker's glance swept to Luke's still form. "He's holding on by a thread."

Doc rose. "That's why I'm going to do it right here."

Josie gasped. "Isn't that too risky?" She thought of the dirt, the flies, the thousands of other things that made the conditions unsanitary.

"We're out of choices, Miss Josie," Jenkins answered. He turned to the men. "Back the wagon up real close, and carefully lift Luke into the bed. Don't jostle him or that bullet will move. Get me all the whiskey, clean cloths, and water you have. I'll need torches—as many as you can make." He swung to Josie. "I'll need an assistant."

Everyone—lawmen and all—scattered to put things in place for the doctor.

All except Stoker. His dark, angry features frightened her. The man was someone to reckon with. If Josie had any kind of softness in her heart for Brenner, she'd have felt sorry for him. Only she didn't. The man deserved his fate.

Stoker, his face a stone mask, stalked over to Brenner McCall, Marshal Haskill by his side. Stoker jerked the outlaw to his feet and swung a beefy fist into his jaw. "Give me one good reason why I shouldn't put a bullet into your brain right now."

Terror filled Brenner's eyes. "Luke ruined my plans. I only wanted to stop him. He always had too much conscience for his own damn good."

Marshal Haskill watched as Stoker backhanded Brenner. The blow would've knocked the outlaw ten feet if Stoker hadn't been gripping his shirt tight. "My son is worth a hundred of the likes of you. He wears honor and courage like a badge. I know you've already told your story to my sons but you're going to tell me and Marshal Haskill."

"I'm tired of talking," Brenner spat. "Take me to jail."

Josie quaked at the glassy hardness in Stoker's eyes. She prayed he never had reason to turn that frightening gaze on her.

"God have mercy on your soul if you don't!" Stoker thundered. "I've seen men stake their enemies out in a red ant bed. Have you seen what those ants do to a man after a week?"

Brenner gulped. "No need for that."

While Josie and Doc prepared for the surgery, Brenner came clean. She listened and sagged with relief when he cleared Josie of Walt Preston's murder, then detailed the night of Judge Percival's demise, taking the bounty off Luke's head.

She heard the marshal say they'd take Brenner to Fort Worth to jail come morning.

Stoker moved to Luke, and the rest of the men sat around the campfire. It finally hit Josie that Luke was free. But would it really make any difference now? If he died, he'd never know. The more Josie's thoughts tumbled, the harder she scrubbed her hands as Doc Jenkins instructed, scrubbing and scrubbing.

Anger that it had taken so many years to right that wrong washed over her.

The kindly doctor laid his hand over hers. She'd scrubbed her hands until they were raw. "That's enough," he said. "Let's go."

"Doc, be honest. What are Luke's chances?" Her voice quivered, barely louder than a whisper.

"I won't know until I get in there and see the damage. Hopefully, I can repair it. Another concern—his breathing is too shallow."

Doc Jenkins paused before he went on. "Miss Josie, I'm going to do my level best to save that young man." He patted her shoulder. "But will my efforts be enough? Only the good Lord has the answer to that."

It didn't do much to ease her mind, but Josie appreciated the honesty. "Thank you, Doc."

She went with him to the wagon where Luke lay on a thick, bloody bedroll. His eyes were open as he reached for her hand.

"If I don't make it through this—" When he paused to suck in air, a whistling sound came from his mouth. His breathing was so shallow. "Pa said…land is yours."

Stoker cleared his throat and laid a hand on her shoulder. "I'm going to take care of you."

Unable to speak for the sob lodged in her throat, Josie pressed her lips to Luke's. She couldn't bear to hear him talk of death. He was strong. She chose to believe that he was going to survive. He'd survived prison, and every other single thing the world had hurled at him. He'd get through this too. Brenner's wasn't the bullet he'd feared all his life. Somehow, she had to make him believe that.

"Luke Rafael Montoya Legend, hush with this kind of

foolish talk," she said over the roar of her fear. "You'll die over my dead body. So dammit, you better fight and fight hard."

"Trying," Luke muttered, his hand going limp in Josie's.

His pale-green eyes stayed locked with hers until Doc placed a cloth over his mouth and dropped some liquid onto it. Finally, freed of the searing agony, Luke slept.

Stoker crawled from the wagon and stood at the end.

Doc Jenkins told Sam, Houston, and the marshals with torches to gather close and give him light.

"The chloroform blocks the pain," Doc explained to Josie. "He won't feel a thing."

Yes, but would he wake up? That was the question keeping an iron grip on Josie's heart.

Thirty-eight

Josie turned her head as Doc put a scalpel to Luke's chest. She couldn't watch the loss of even more precious blood. Even a tough Texas outlaw like Luke had only so much.

Her hands shook and she prayed she could follow Doc's instructions. What if Luke died because she messed up?

Whatever she had to do, she'd just have to make sure that didn't happen. Josie took a calming breath of air and focused on the task.

The passage of time didn't register as she and Doc Jenkins worked in unison. She immediately handed him whatever he requested, without fumbles or questions.

Finally, Jenkins tied the last knot in the stitches and straightened. Lines in his face betrayed his deep weariness. Blood covered the fancy pinstripe suit he always wore. Josie suspected this didn't happen all that often. She glanced at Luke. His face was ashen and he barely breathed. Only the slight rise and fall of his chest said his heart still beat.

"I've done all I can do," Jenkins announced to the grim-faced men around the wagon. "The rest is up to the man upstairs. The next hours will be critical."

Stoker's voice rose. "I want to be with my son. I'll sit with him—me and Miss Josie."

She murmured thanks to Luke's father for including her. He knew she would not leave the man she loved. She stared at the blood covering her hands.

After washing up, she climbed into the wagon next to Stoker. Josie took Luke's palm and held it to her cheek. He would feel her presence and perhaps take some of her strength. She'd gladly give all she had to save him.

Stoker put his arms around her and told her everything was going to be all right. And who would dare dispute such a commanding man? He was Stoker Legend, so the words had to be true.

She sat by Luke throughout that endless night, touching his face, willing him to wake up. To tell her he loved her one more time.

Just to hear his voice again, to feel his arms around her would be heaven.

Sam and Houston never left the wagon, their gazes locked on their fallen brother.

In a touching show of the depth of their hearts, the marshals came one by one to ask if there was any change. Deep concern lined the face of each man.

Marshal Haskill assured Josie that his men had Brenner under guard and would transport him to jail at daybreak.

Josie would be glad. She wanted to finally be rid of him. His vicious hatred had possibly destroyed her chance at happiness. She felt nothing for the man who'd fathered her. What her mother first saw in him she didn't know, but Brenner must have been very different as a younger man, before greed and hate and meanness took over.

Filing that painful chapter of her life away, she turned her focus back to Luke, resting her hand lightly on his bandaged chest. She could feel the reassuring beat of his heart beneath her palm, steady and sure.

Stoker leaned to put his arm around her. "He's going to make it, Miss Josie. Luke's a fighter. I'd put my money on him, and I always bet on a sure thing."

Josie rested her head on his wide shoulder. She adored

this man who had seen endless trouble since establishing the Lone Star. From what Sam and Houston had said, it had taken every bit of strength and determination Stoker had to hold on to his dream. No question that he loved his land, his sons, and the women who'd borne them.

And Luke loved his father right back. He'd finally confessed what was in his heart.

She remembered the scene and her eyes welled with tears. Luke had endured so many horrible tragedies, and any number of them could've killed him. Stoker was right. Luke was a survivor.

As she borrowed from Stoker's strength, she clung to the knowledge that Luke would emerge even stronger and tougher.

Dawn broke with Doc announcing that his patient still held on to life. A loud cheer went up.

Josie caught Doc Jenkins. "When will we try to take Luke home?"

"I wish I could wait a week, but I don't think that's possible." Jenkins rubbed his bleary eyes and yawned. "I need things I don't have at my disposal here. We'll start in a few hours. We'll have to take it slow, so we'll sleep under the stars another night."

"That's good news. I want you to have everything you can possibly need." And Josie would feel a lot better being where she could take care of Luke properly. With all these eyes staring at her, she hadn't had a private moment.

She yearned to lie beside him and listen to his breathing, to feel him returning from this place he'd gone to.

A place she couldn't go.

As dawn broke, spreading color across the sky, Marshal Haskill and his men rode out with Brenner. It appeared to Josie that the air became cleaner with the outlaw gone. If Luke died, she'd find whichever jail they'd taken Brenner to and put a bullet in him. It didn't matter what they did to her after that.

Without Luke, her life would be over anyway.

Sam and Houston disappeared for a bit and Josie knew they'd quietly slipped away to relay news of Luke's surgery to Tally and her ladies—Luke's other family.

Over the next hour, she busied herself getting Luke ready to travel. She piled blankets that Tally's group had brought, as well as sleeping bags and whatever else she could find around Luke to cushion him for the ride.

If he could just make it to the Lone Star, everything would be all right. She just knew it.

Doc and Stoker discussed the smoothest route, with Sam and Houston throwing in valid arguments.

At last, they set out. Josie rode in the wagon with Luke and kept a close eye on him. Very frequently, she checked to make sure he still breathed. After each time, she sent up a prayer of thanks. Though he hadn't shown signs of waking up, or returning the squeeze of her hand, she was grateful for each second he still lived.

When twilight fell, they made camp. Sam and Houston hunted for game and they shared a quiet meal. With a pall hanging over them, no one felt like talking. They took turns sitting up with Luke. Josie was glad for a little rest, even though she dreamed of nothing but problems. One after another, various things prevented them from reaching the Lone Star. She'd never been so happy to see dawn.

After traveling all that day, they finally reached ranch headquarters about sundown. When she saw the tall Texas flag waving proudly, she breathed a sigh of relief.

She kissed Luke's still lips and whispered, "We're home, my love. You made it. You're going to live."

~

Josie met Mrs. Ross on the porch's bottom step and filled her in. Noah hurried out and insisted on crawling up in the wagon to see the man who'd saved him. The boy clung to Luke's hand and told him that he was a hero and heroes didn't die. Noah shed no tears, but his solemn expression showed plenty of worry.

The men had agreed that instead of carrying Luke up the stairs and putting him through untold torture, they'd set up a bed in the coolness of the office. Josie and Mrs. Ross hurried to ready the room. When Josie opened the door, she inhaled sharply in surprise. A striking portrait of a beautiful woman hung on the wall.

"That's Luke's mother," Houston said.

"This room is perfect." Josie stepped inside to take a better look. Luke would have to get well now, with his beloved mother watching over him.

Once they brought a bed down from upstairs, she made it up with Mrs. Ross's help. Then Josie stood for a moment, her glance sweeping the room. The tall bookshelves on two walls must have held hundreds of books. She ran her fingers across Stoker's mahogany desk, feeling the smooth wood. This room reflected Stoker's personality—big and powerful. While she waited for the men to bring Luke, she glanced at a framed letter on the wall.

Josie stepped closer. It was a letter signed by Sam Houston, thanking Stoker for service above and beyond in the fight for Texas independence. The general called Stoker a true patriot and an uncommon hero. Josie couldn't agree more.

The men entered with Luke and she quickly moved to get him settled. As they slowly lowered Luke to the bed, he winced, the first time since the surgery he'd given any indication he felt anything.

Maybe this meant he was waking up.

Josie crossed her fingers and helped Doc make him comfortable.

Luke was safe within the walls of headquarters with everything at hand.

And he had his mother's arms around him.

Now, she knew he had the very best chance.

When Doc stepped out to get something, she leaned over to kiss Luke's lips.

"I'll love you forever, my darling. Rest and gain your strength. Then come back to me. I'm waiting."

Thirty-nine

The next morning, Josie chose to wear the pretty blue dress that Luke had loved. Then she went down for breakfast with Luke's father and brothers. They celebrated the fact that he had survived the long trip and, though no better, seemed no worse.

The foreman, Pony Latham, entered, holding his hat in his hands. "Sorry to bother you, boss. Newt Granger rode up to the gate and wants to see you. He's waiting in the parlor."

Josie slumped into her chair, praying she wouldn't have to see the ungrateful little beady-eyed man. She might not be too civil.

Stoker lowered his coffee cup and scowled. "What the hell does he want? I don't have time for the sawed-off runt."

"He didn't say. Just that it's important and you should hear him out." Latham waited for a response.

"Hell!" Stoker pushed back his chair and strode out. Sam and Houston followed, probably to keep their father from strangling the man.

Josie wondered if Newt had come to declare more war or make peace. Or had he decided to accept their offer? Just exactly how much did it cost to build a town, anyway? Probably more than she'd ever see in a lifetime. If Stoker was out a whole lot more money than he'd planned on, he'd be mad at her for offering to give away so much without speaking to him. Finally, she couldn't stand not knowing. She rose and crept to the parlor. She'd pressed her ear to the wall beside the open door, trying to hear the conversation, when Sam suddenly strode out and into her.

"I came to find you," he said. "Pa wants you inside."

Josie's heart skipped a beat. "Is he mad?"

"Why should he be?"

"Having to build a town for Granger probably put your father in a bad mood. I never intended to offer that." Josie scrunched up her nose. "It just sorta slipped out."

"I think you should come and see for yourself." Sam took her arm.

Josie took a deep breath, stilled her trembling legs, and pasted on a bright smile. Filled with determination to own up to everything, she braved the lion's den.

The men stood when she entered. Stoker beamed and kissed her cheek. "I don't know how Luke ever found you, but I'm mighty glad he did. Granger is returning my land and making peace."

"And the town I promised him?" Josie asked weakly.

Houston grinned. "Granger and I are building it together since it'll benefit us both."

Newt Granger shook his finger at her. "You're one smart young lady."

Josie shook her head. "I just needed you to listen and end this feud."

"You sure gave me a lot to think about." Granger grinned. "You'll never believe this. A fellow came to see me about my horses and bought two. He already paid me sight unseen for the one Stoker is keeping here." Granger tried to reach for her hand, but Stoker batted it away. Granger frowned and went on. "Funny thing. The man proposed the very same thing you did about the annual horse race. He said it would put Grangerville on the map when we get it built." He cocked his head and squinted. "Was that your doing also?"

"No, I'm afraid not. I'm really glad for you." Happiness

spread through Josie. At least this part seemed to have worked out.

Stoker held up the deed to his land. "I told Newt he could take the horse back with him today. You, my dear, fixed a problem that had festered for a long time." He kissed her forehead. "You're a beautiful angel."

"Are you sure you won't marry me?" Newt Granger asked hopefully. "You'll be a mayor's wife. Won't that tempt you?"

Not in the least. Her heart was already taken. Luke wasn't a mayor but he offered so much more.

Josie shook her head. "I'm sorry, Mr. Granger. I'm spoken for." When the man looked ready to cry, she added, "One day you're going to find the perfect Mrs. Granger and she'll make you the proudest man in all of Texas. I guarantee it."

A firm belief had formed when she had lived in the Lucky Lady. All kinds of different men gathered there, and loneliness dripped from the faces of so many. Some of them yearned so deeply for a woman to share their life with. She knew that somewhere in the world a woman waited for every man. He simply had to look hard.

Belief that it would work the other way too had provided many months of speculation. She'd scoured the face of every man she met. One time she'd danced with a handsome, young gentleman and was certain he was the one she was waiting for. But he'd left town in the middle of the night, and she'd never seen him again.

Whether Luke survived or not, Josie had found her perfect mate. There was no other in all the world for her.

While the men finished their business, Josie wandered down the hall to the office. The ranch's new preacher was with Luke. He turned when she entered. "Do you know if his heart is right, Miss Morgan? Mr. Stoker didn't tell me much about this son of his."

Josie stared at the ruddy-faced young man. He was so young; he couldn't have been shaving long. Luke's heart was just fine. It was the hole in his chest that was the problem. "His heart is strong," she murmured.

"That's a relief. So many men and women go unprepared to meet their Lord and Savior." He held out his hand. "I'm Timothy Crutchfield."

"Josie Morgan," she muttered, shaking his hand.

"I'll be going, but call me if he gets worse."

Once the preacher left, she took the chair beside Luke and curled her fingers around his. He didn't appear to be breathing. His chest wasn't rising.

Oh God, had he passed? Terror struck her.

In a blind panic, she leaned to place her cheek to his mouth. Nothing except a small wisp of air let her know he still clung to life. But just barely. He was slipping away fast, moving alone where she couldn't follow.

If only she could've married him. They'd have been happy for a short time, at least.

In the cool quiet, she brokenly whispered a vow to him. "I promise to stay by your side in sickness and in health, 'til death do us part. I'll love you always, Luke. Now and forever, in this life and the next."

She thought about adding something about obeying, but Luke would never believe that, so she didn't.

Doc Jenkins entered and she moved aside, watching, hoping, praying. He muttered to himself as he examined Luke, then without a word, he left.

A short time later, a rough voice spoke from the doorway. "I have something to discuss with you," Stoker said.

Josie wiped her eyes. "Sure. Can we talk here? I don't want to leave Luke. He's worsened and I'm terrified he'll die alone. I can't let that happen. He needs someone with him."

"Here is fine." Stoker sat in a chair next to her and took her hand. "I'm worried Luke won't survive, and it shatters everything inside me. But I have to be practical. I have a rather delicate question to ask and I'm not sure exactly how to go about it."

"It's all right," Josie said softly. "Just go ahead."

Stoker cleared his voice. "If you don't want to answer, I'll respect your privacy." He paused. "When and you Luke were alone... Uh, when you... Were you...uh, together?" Red streaks climbed the man's neck and colored his face.

When Josie realized what he was asking—without asking—heat rushed to her cheeks. Oh goodness, this was embarrassing. Yet, she knew he had to know if he'd be a grandfather. She just prayed he wouldn't look down on her for the happy times she'd spent in Luke's arms.

"Yes. I could be with child." There it was. She lifted her chin, feeling no shame in loving Luke.

"Then we'll have to do whatever we can to protect that life." Stoker looked very relieved as he rose. "Let me talk with Doc and I'll know how to proceed."

With that he strode from the room. Josie had no idea what Stoker could do, if anything. Everything hinged on Luke waking up, but now the likelihood of that seemed very remote.

She was still clutching Luke's hand when Stoker, Sam, and Houston came in. Their grim faces struck fear deep inside her.

"What did Doc say?" she whispered.

Stoker sat beside her and patted her hand. "He'll be lucky to see tomorrow's sunrise. Doc's done everything he can. We're losing the battle."

Josie's mouth quivered and the words she needed to say were stuck inside her. This was it. In a matter of hours, Luke would be gone.

She'd never feel his touch moving over her body, his lips on hers again. Never see the sinful smile once more that promised heaven and made her heart flutter like an army of butterflies. Oh God! How could she bear to lose him?

"What Pa is trying to say is that we need to move fast," Houston said. "We've sent a man down to get Preacher Crutchfield. We want you to marry Luke before he passes."

Forty

Josie sat in stunned silence. Surely she'd mistaken Houston. She couldn't marry someone in a coma. She knew they were all upset and their hearts were breaking, but couldn't they see Luke's condition?

Things were in bad shape if she was the sanest one.

"What are you talking about?" Josie asked. "Luke can't even speak."

"Marriage by proxy," Stoker explained. "It's when one party or the other is unable to be present and someone stands in for him."

"I see." Only Josie didn't. Not really. She had a lot of questions, such as who would stand in and if she'd want to say the vows burning inside and professing love to someone other than Luke? That would make her feel very uncomfortable.

And what would Luke say? Not that he could say anything now, nor, according to Doc, would he be likely to again.

Still, she had to put aside her feelings and think of Luke's child that could be growing in her belly. It would need a name. She'd shoot anyone who said a word against the innocent babe.

Her mother had faced a similar problem when Josie was born, but the men who frequented the saloon had protected them both. No one said a disrespectful word with them near. The Legends would do the same with her child. Her heart swelled with love for this family.

Sam touched Josie's arm. "We think you should do this. It'll protect both you and Luke's child."

It occurred to her that being a widow was a sight better than an "almost wife."

Josie stared into their faces. "All right, I'll do it."

"Excellent." Stoker draped an arm around her shoulders. "I can't imagine how hard this is for you. It's bad enough being Luke's pa, but to be the woman he loves… I admire your strength and courage." He pulled her into a hug.

"You're family, Josie," Houston said in a strangely husky voice. "Here's what's going to happen."

He explained that she and Sam would stand together. Sam would announce that he acted on behalf of Luke. Reverend Crutchfield would then ask her and Sam to take the marriage vows. Simple enough.

But was it? Even simple things could go awry.

An hour later, she stood beside Luke's bed with her heart breaking. She loved him with every inch of her body. She was only half-aware that Sam was the one next to her holding her icy hand.

Stoker, Houston, and Noah were in attendance. They'd explained to the boy what was going to happen. Noah appeared to sense her uncertainty and slipped his small hand into hers.

"Luke would want you to do this, Josie," he whispered.

"Are you sure?" she asked.

"Yep. He likes you a whole bunch and he'd marry you if he could wake up." Noah glanced up at her with worried eyes. "Will he ever quit sleeping?"

Josie pondered how to answer. She couldn't steal his hope. That wouldn't be fair to the kid. "Sure. He's going to open his eyes and everything is going to be just fine." She prayed God would forgive her for lying. Surely it wasn't a sin when it was to comfort a scared kid.

Crutchfield cleared his throat and tried to act twenty years older, pushing back his shoulders and trying to turn his boyish voice into a deep baritone. It didn't work. Stifling laughter, she idly wondered if he was a real man of the cloth. Or was he like Luke and had stolen his identity off a dead man?

In the minutes that followed, she repeated the vows, trying not to think it weird that she uttered them to Sam. When Luke's brother bequeathed all his worldly possessions to her, she pinched herself to keep from laughing, sternly reminding herself that Sam was a stand-in. Nothing more.

The moment she'd dreamed of and waited all her life for seemed to be nothing but a joke.

Just get through this, she lectured herself. She could do anything for Luke's child.

Was this how Houston's wife, Lara, had felt when she'd had to marry an utter stranger? The woman had been incredibly brave. And so would Josie.

When Crutchfield concluded the ceremony, Josie twisted the little emerald ring on her finger—a gift from her mother on her sixteenth birthday. She laid her hand on Luke's chest. She prayed he'd forgive her for vowing to love Sam.

Noah leaned over to whisper in Luke's ear. "I'm sorry I can't save you like you saved me and Rowdy. If you're ever lost, just ask God to show you the way like I did. He'll bring someone to help you. Please try to wake up. I miss you. So does Josie and Papa Stoker."

Stoker laid a big hand on Noah's head. "We have to let him go, son. It's the way it has to be."

"No! I can't." Noah stumbled from the room.

When Josie tried to go after him, Stoker said, "The boy needs some time alone. I'll check on him in a bit."

Everyone filed out, leaving Josie with Luke. They all might've given up waiting for a miracle, but not her.

Josie planted her fists on her hips. "Now you listen here,

Luke Rafael Legend. I didn't just say my vows to Sam for the fun of it. You and I are a team. The least you could do is quit worrying me and wake up." She paused. "Furthermore, I need you. I don't know the first thing about taking care of land, raising cows, or being Josie Legend."

That responsibility scared the daylights out of her.

"And you just can't walk away from everything you always wanted. You have your dream now. Even a shiny new name that will protect you from glory seekers. No one will bother Luke Legend."

She kissed his lips gently. "I'll give you one more day to sleep. But you'd better open your eyes come morning or I'll...I'll run off with your brother Sam. We're married now, you know."

A steady stream of visitors went in and out of Stoker's office all morning. Everyone saying last goodbyes to the man who'd touched their lives.

Sam and Houston told Luke how much they loved him and what it meant to them having him for a brother.

Noah crept in and perched on the bed. He kept up a running dialogue about Rowdy and Rafael the cat and the latest trouble the animals had gotten into. "It's a hard job trying to take care of them," Noah said, sighing, then left.

Doc Jenkins came in after lunch to check Luke. He raised his head after a minute of listening, wonder in his eyes. "Well, I'll be thunder. His breathing is stronger and color is returning to his face."

Josie jerked up from the chair in which she'd been dozing. "Are you sure, Doc?"

"Of course. I'm positive. Don't count Luke out just yet." He patted her shoulder. "He's not out of the woods yet by any stretch, but he's improving."

"When do you think he'll come around?" she asked.

"If he keeps on this way, it could be soon." Doc scratched

his head. "Now I wonder what in God's name swung the pendulum to our favor?"

Josie shrugged.

Maybe laying down the law to the mule-headed outlaw that she loved more than anyone else on earth?

That night, Josie slept soundly in a real bed, the first good sleep she'd gotten since she couldn't remember when.

She dreamed of dancing with Luke. He wore his black trousers with the shiny conchas up each leg, and a short Spanish jacket that showed off his lean waist. With hunger in his eyes, he strolled to where she sat, bowed, and asked her to dance. His arms tight around her, Luke swung her about a floor made of soft, fluffy clouds. He called her his *princesa* and stared deep into her eyes. He spoke of his everlasting love for her and how much she'd changed his life.

When Josie woke, it was still dark out. She lay there, hugging herself, trying to recapture the feeling of the dream, and Luke's words of love.

Rafael meowed and jumped from the bed as she threw back the covers and swung her legs over. "Sorry about that," Josie muttered, lighting the lamp. "Poor kitty."

Picking the kitten up, she gently laid him in the cushion of covers. Josie threw on her clothes and hurried downstairs.

In the soft light of the office, Stoker rose from the chair beside the bed and stretched. "Now that you're here, I'm going to change and get coffee. Would you like some, daughter?"

"Yes, please. That would be wonderful. How's Luke?"

"He stirred a lot the last hour or so. Seemed restless. I think that's a positive sign, though he never opened his eyes."

"So do I." Josie smiled. Luke was getting better.

Stoker left and she leaned over and traced Luke's mouth with a fingertip. He had the most beautiful lips. Not thick or thin, but just right, decidedly masculine and perfectly formed. She imagined a sculptor carving them from clay. After studying his mouth and running her finger across his lips, she kissed the man she loved, long and deep. Josie poured all the passion she had into it.

Ending the kiss, she whispered, "Luke, sweetheart, it's a fine, beautiful morning here on the Lone Star. The Texas flag is flying and the birds are singing. Don't you want to see? You're missing out."

Though Luke's eyes fluttered, they didn't open. Disappointed, she filled the chair Stoker had left. She should sing to him. Maybe he'd like that. She searched for a song. Growing up in a saloon hadn't exactly given her a wide variety and none of the songs she knew belonged in a church. The only tune that came to mind was "Betsy Barlow, the Calico Queen." Not exactly appropriate, but the music was pretty.

Besides, Luke was asleep. He wouldn't mind.

As she began to sing, she raised her voice higher and higher.

Way down in Texas where the tumbleweeds blow
Lived the Calico Queen, pretty Betsy Barlow
Men blazed a wide trail to the Buckhorn Saloon
Jus' a glimpse of her charms, the cowboys did swoon
'Mid cards 'n' rye whiskey they fought for the harlot
Longin' to win the fair lady in scarlet.

Nimble 'n' quick, Betsy gave 'em a tumble
Their henrys wore smiles—

Josie stopped mid-chorus and stared in amazement.

Luke's legs and arms twitched. A grin teased the corners of his mouth. He opened one eye then two.

He woke up!

She leaned over him. "You're back. It's a miracle."

"Hey." His voice was weak and a little rusty.

"Hey yourself, cowboy." She slanted a kiss on his lips.

"I have a lot to tell you. Brenner's in jail and will probably be hung. I'm glad. I don't even feel pity for the man. He tried to destroy both of us and almost succeeded. Luke, you're cleared of everything now. You can start fresh and live your dream."

A scowl darkened his face and anger flashed in his eyes. "Why did you marry Sam?"

Forty-one

Dark despair shot through Luke's heart as he struggled to rise only to collapse against the pillows. Josie had betrayed him. She was the only woman he wanted and she'd married his brother—who was already married, or had Sam divorced Sierra? How long had he lain like this? It stung to the quick that Josie didn't wait for him. She just went right on as though his love for her didn't mean squat.

"Luke, I didn't marry Sam," she protested.

"I heard you, Josie."

She stroked his jaw. "You lunkheaded man. Read my lips. I married you. Only you. I thought you were dying. Doc gave no hope, and your father said this was what I needed to do, so I married you." She took a deep breath. "Don't you want me?"

Hell yes, he wanted her. That was the problem.

"So you said your vows…to Sam…except you meant them for me…while I was fighting to come back to you and couldn't do a damn thing. I had no say in the matter."

Why was he so angry, anyway? This was what he'd wanted. From what she seemed to be trying to explain—not very well, he might add—Josie was his wife. Luke raised a hand to wipe his eyes. Maybe his brain was scrambled. Thick sludge filled the cavity up there, blocking coherent thought.

"Hold on there, Luke. The hasty marriage was Stoker's and your brothers' idea," Josie said hotly. "I needed a name for our child."

A child? What else had happened while he was unconscious?

Luke narrowed his eyes. "Exactly how long have I been asleep?"

"Three or four days. I lost count, but it seemed an eternity. I thought I'd lost you forever," she whispered brokenly. "I was terrified."

"Then how can we have a child? Please explain that."

"Well, you start with a man and woman and they—"

"No, not that! I know how it *starts*," he said impatiently. "Do you think it's possible?"

"I don't know yet, but it is possible. Stoker wanted to protect Luke Jr., in case." Josie's gentle touch as she stroked his hair felt like the caress of an angel's wings. "I'm sorry I didn't wait for you, sweetheart. I tried to do the right thing. The quick marriage seemed best at the time." She stood straight, frowning. "I'm puzzled how you heard all that, anyway. What else did you hear?"

He grinned. "The song you were singing. At first I thought it was an angel, but then I knew no holy being would sing such a bawdy tune. You're a bad, bad girl, Josie."

She returned his grin. "I know. But it was the only one I knew all the words to. Every night cowboys in the saloon would belt out 'Betsy Barlow, the Calico Queen.' The song would echo up and down the street of Medicine Springs. I thought you might like it."

Though moving took all his effort and made his chest burn like a raging fire, he made room and patted the empty spot. "Come here, wife. I want you next to me. I'm as weak as a day-old pup but I can still run my fingers over your skin."

She lay on her side, facing him, and cupped his jaw. "You scared me."

"Sorry. I never meant to cause you worry." Luke fell

into the depths of her hazel eyes. "You're even more beautiful than I remembered in my long sleep. Never doubt my love for you. It's the strong and lasting kind." He frowned. "But, don't ever marry Sam again."

As she leaned in to kiss him, he caught a tendril of her hair between his fingers. Silky, just like he remembered. Though he was much too weak now, he couldn't wait to get Josie into a real bed and make her crazy with need. Luke touched her cheek, still bruised from Brenner's hand. He was going to make that, plus a lot more, up to her.

He'd make her love being wife to an outlaw.

Except, apparently, he no longer had that title. Luke grinned. It would take some getting used to. He'd been hunted and reviled for most of his life.

Josie kissed the hollow of his throat. "You're not angry I married you when you were unconscious, are you?"

"*Mi corazón*, I'll take you any way I can get you. I still have questions, and I want you to start at the beginning and tell me everything. But not now. Right now, I just want to talk about us."

Josie wiggled, fitting her curves against him. "I love you, Luke. I didn't exactly know how much until faced with losing you."

"I can see a forever in your beautiful eyes." Luke laid his hand over her heart, feeling the wild beat beneath. He'd never known such contentment and love. But also fear. He vowed not to fail Josie like he'd done Angelina and his mother. He finally had a chance to get this right, and he'd not waste it.

"I can see heaven in yours," Josie murmured.

"Do I have all the answers? Hell no. But I can promise you this, my pretty wife. I'll wake each morning with one purpose—to make life as good for you as I can."

"That's beautiful but more than I ask, sweetheart. I just need you to simply hold me, love me, and never leave me. That's all. The rest we'll work out as we go. You're going to be the best husband and father."

This new chapter of his life was a far cry from the lonely existence he'd known. It would take some time not to look over his shoulder and startle at every sound. His new life would have new challenges, but he looked forward to starting.

He grinned. "I'm glad you really might be in the family way."

"It's too early to tell, though."

The door swung open and Stoker strode in with his coffee. He stopped, staring in disbelief. "You're back, son. By God, you're back."

Josie swung to her feet, straightening her hair and looking guilty. Luke didn't know why women did that. As though patting on their hair was going to make one iota of difference.

He turned his attention to his father. "Pa." The word was still unfamiliar on his tongue but Luke liked it. He liked the belonging it brought. And to think a bullet to the chest had broken down all his defenses and let the feelings inside.

"This is truly a day to celebrate." Stoker sat down. "Your brothers will be grinning from ear to ear."

"Tell me about my marriage to Josie that I wasn't at, Pa. Is it legal?" But as his father began to explain the proxy thing, Luke drifted off, with the warmth of family and home surrounding him.

He jerked awake to Noah touching his face. He stared up into the boy's worried eyes.

"Me and Rowdy had to see if you're really alive." Noah held his wiggling dog.

"I'm alive, son. Sorry to scare you. I'm glad you're doing better."

"Doc says I can ride soon. Papa Stoker is going to show me the ranch and start teaching me." Noah grinned and leaned in to whisper, "I think he likes me."

"No thinking to it. He does a lot more than like you." Luke smiled. "So do I."

"Do you want to pet Rowdy? He missed you."

"Sure." When Noah lowered the dog, Luke ran his hand

over the soft fur. Rowdy licked his appreciation. "How is he getting along with the cat?"

"They're making do. Sometimes they hate each other and sometimes not. I don't think they'll ever be friends but that's okay." Noah shrugged. "We don't always have to like everybody, so it's the same way with dogs and cats. Papa Stoker says that's the way of things."

"He's a wise man, your Papa Stoker." It just took Luke so long to see it.

He glanced up at his mother's portrait. If only she'd told Stoker about his son when she came to the ranch. Luke didn't fault her, though. She'd done what she thought was right, and had refused to put a wedge between Stoker and his wife, Hannah. Elena's sole thought had been Stoker's happiness. Luke wondered if she'd have made different choices had she known the hard life she'd lead. No one would ever know.

Josie stepped inside the office and his breath caught. Her golden hair glistened, framing her face, and a new dress the color of a purple Texas sunset brought a glow to her cheeks.

How on earth did he get so lucky?

His wild and wonderful and unpredictable wife had shown him what living really meant. She'd swept away all the ash inside and replaced it with fertile soil so new dreams and plans could grow tall.

He was no longer Luke Weston, outlaw and gunslinger. He was Luke Legend, husband and rancher—part owner of the enormous Lone Star ranch.

And God, how he adored Josie Legend.

His wife.

Forty-two

A MONTH LATER, THOUGH STILL WEAK, LUKE SAT ON THE porch enjoying the beautiful morning. Fluffy summer clouds drifted overhead. Josie glanced up from where she was arranging shaving essentials, letting her gaze caress the man she loved. It was time for Luke's beard to go; she preferred him without all that hair. She'd already cut the beard short with the scissors and came at him with a sharp straight razor, ready to complete the task.

"We don't have to do this." Luke gave her a nervous look.

"Don't tell me I scare you. I know how to wield one of these." She lathered up the soap and approached.

Luke narrowed his eyes. "Just how many men have you shaved?"

"Well, none, but I know it can't be that hard." She applied a thick lather to his face.

"Can you hold it while I write a will?"

"Oh, for heaven's sake! I'm not going to cut your throat. Unless you squirm. Or the razor slips. Or—"

Luke grabbed the white cloth she'd draped around him and tried to get up. "My brothers can do it."

Josie blocked him with a quick arm. "I swear, Luke, you're acting worse than Noah. I'll be careful." She'd rather hurt herself than harm one hair on his head.

With the sharp razor in her hand, she slowly proceeded,

making careful strokes. By the time she finished, he didn't have one nick. Her heart beat wildly. No one was more handsome than Luke. In her opinion, which was the only one that counted. She loved her new husband with every fiber of her being and couldn't wait for him to recover enough to show him.

After putting everything away, she scooted next to him on a wicker settee. A gentle breeze lifted her hair as she threaded her fingers through his. "I'm so happy, I'm about to burst."

Luke's pale-green eyes darkened. "Why's that?"

"My husband is getting well, you don't have to hide, we're here safe and sound, and life seems just about perfect. I feel like singing."

Luke grinned. "Not the Calico Queen. Do you know any others, Mrs. Legend?"

Josie widened her eyes in mock horror. "You don't like my song?"

"I love it, but the cowboys might hear and come running, thinking we've opened a saloon. Then Stoker...Pa... and Houston would get mad about losing in poker." Luke nibbled her neck. "Sing it to me in private."

Josie released several buttons on his shirt and slipped her hand inside, avoiding the bandage covering the wound. She loved touching his skin. Biding time, waiting for him to get well, was killing her.

Luke had spent the past month resting and growing stronger. The days were filled with long talks with his father, and the nights... Oh, the nights were for Josie. The minute the sun went down, she and Luke would lock themselves in their bedroom. They spent hours exploring each other's bodies, but there had been no lovemaking yet. Doc strictly forbade that pleasure, saying they had to restrain from strenuous activity. It frustrated her to no end.

Still, Luke knew how to build a raging bonfire inside her with his hands and mouth until the explosion would bring relief and leave her as weak and trembling as a day-old calf.

Yet she yearned to show her husband the value of a wife and make him hoarsely cry her name.

Josie ran her flattened palm down the sides of his chest. "Luke, I want to make love to you until I wring every drop of passion from your body."

His voice roughened. "Tonight, you get your wish."

She searched his eyes. "Are you sure it's all right?"

"We're making love tonight," he growled, adding, "I don't care if it harelips the governor."

Anticipation swept the length of Luke's body and hardened him like a randy bull. He was done with waiting. He'd have his fill of Josie before morning. Doc could get glad in the same shoes he got mad in. Luke had to get on with living.

Josie laughed and pointed to a basket at the end of the porch. There, curled up together as cozy as could be, lay Rowdy and Rafael. Hated enemies making a truce at last.

Two riders came down the road, catching Luke's attention. From the wary way they rode, Luke knew they weren't ranch hands. His eyes narrowed as he rose and leaned against the post.

Josie stood and slipped her arm around him. "Who do you think they are?"

"Not sure yet." Luke felt naked without his Colt and wished he'd strapped it on. If these men had brought trouble, he couldn't handle it.

A few minutes later, they reined up outside the headquarters and Luke recognized their faces. Happiness spread through him to see Clay Colby again. His partner was Jack Bowdre, an ex-lawman turned outlaw.

Luke grinned. "You're a sight for sore eyes. Get down and make yourselves at home."

"Howdy, Luke." Jack Bowdre pushed back his worn Stetson and dismounted. "We were told we might find you here."

"Jack, it's been a while. I've wondered how things were going."

Clay swung wearily from the saddle. "Not in jail, so must be pretty darn good. Did you ever find Reno Kidd?"

"I did and I'm glad to say he won't bother anyone ever again." Luke pulled Josie close. "Gentlemen, I'm not riding the outlaw trail anymore. Married now and settling down for good. This is my wife, Josie."

Both tipped their hats respectfully to her and called her ma'am.

"You're welcome to cool off on the porch," Josie invited. "I'll get some refreshments."

"Mighty nice of you, ma'am." Clay glanced longingly around the ranch where he'd once worked. "We won't stay long. Just need some advice, Luke."

Advice? Luke didn't know if he had any, except never to stop giving up reaching for their dream. Luke waved them to empty chairs. "Tell me what this is about while my wife gets some lemonade."

Noah opened the door and sidled up to Luke, eyeing the visitors cautiously.

"Is he your boy?" Jack asked.

Luke ruffled the kid's hair. "If he wants to be. Up to him. Name's Noah."

"Luke found me and I live here now with my dog," Noah said quietly.

"Lucky boy," Jack said.

"You sort of remind me of Henry," Clay said quietly. "How's Lara's little brother doing?"

"He seems to be all right after his ordeal on the cattle drive," Luke answered. "He and Lara ask about you every time I see them. Houston got a good drover when he hired you."

They caught up on all the news. Luke told them he'd cleared his name and was a Legend now. "Heard Brenner McCall drew a prison sentence for life," Luke said. "I'm fine with that. I didn't want him to hang." He turned when Josie came out the door and helped her with the tray.

She filled the glasses with cold lemonade. She was the perfect wife—gracious and charming. Luke burst with pride and put an arm around her. Jack and Clay watched her with envy as she and Luke sat down on the wicker settee.

Luke had something few men did, and gratitude washed over him. He'd never envisioned this life. Never in his wildest dreams had he pictured a woman like Josie, full of love for him.

Rowdy jumped from his cozy basket and stretched, sniffed Jack and Clay, then hopped into Noah's lap where the boy perched on the top step. Noah threw a stick for Rowdy to fetch, and Luke watched them play.

Was Noah his boy? Did he want to be? Luke meant to make a home for the boy if he stayed. They needed to have a talk soon.

Jack took a long drink of his lemonade. "Luke, remember our old hideout, Devil's Crossing, in the Texas Panhandle?"

"Nothing but a dangerous outlaw den, best I remember." Luke had holed up there for a while when things had gotten too hot.

Clay Colby leaned forward. "Jack, me, and a few like-minded outlaws have this dream of cleaning it up. We'll root out the bad seeds and turn it into a respectable town with a new name. We want to make it a place for families and bring in businesses. I want to give settling down one more try before I give up for good."

The yearning in Clay's face tightened Luke's chest. Jack Bowdre's too. Like him, they wanted more. "If I can help in any way, I will. I just don't know what I can do. As soon as I heal, I'm going to start working this ranch alongside my pa and Houston."

"We just want you to tell us we're not loco." Clay took out his sack of Bull Durham and rolled a cigarette.

"You're not crazy to want this, Clay. But towns won't thrive without families to occupy them. How will you make that happen?" Luke saw the huge chore ahead of these two. "And you'll need law and order to keep them safe."

Clay lit his cigarette and inhaled. "Jack and I will handle that part. We'll run rotten killers like Montana Black clean out of the territory."

"I did some carpentry on the side when I sheriffed." Jack picked up Rafael and scratched him behind the ears. "We also have Ridge Steele with us and he's tired of running too."

"I met him once. A good man." Luke leaned forward. Their plans excited him. Ridge Steele was an ex-preacher who carried a large pistol inside a hollowed-out Bible. He and Ridge had once fought their way out of a town full of vigilantes.

"We recognize we need wives and families to make this town happen. But no decent woman will marry an outlaw." Smoke from the cigarette curled around Clay's head.

Josie poked Luke in the ribs. He frowned. What the hell? He ignored her and shot the men a look of admiration. "I see you're serious about this." Josie poked his ribs again. "Would you like to say something, Josie, or bruise me up worse than I am?"

Her eyes burned bright as she leaned forward. "I have the perfect solution. Luke and I know where to find wives for you."

"We do?" He wondered what had been in that lemonade.

"Remember? Tally Shannon?"

Oh. Well, maybe. But even if he could convince Tally, and that would be a tall order, how would they get the two groups together, never mind talking to each other? Still, Josie might have something. It would sure help those women find their way out of Deliverance Canyon and get themselves a place where they could really live again.

"It's a possibility," Luke admitted. He turned to the outlaws. "Communication would have to be in secret. Josie and I could hand-carry letters back and forth so you could get to know each other before anyone moves anywhere."

"And find the perfect match," Josie insisted. "A marriage won't happen unless it's right." She giggled. "We'd have the start of an underground mail-order bride service. Discreet and safe. We might just be on to something, Luke."

Good Lord! The only thing he wanted to be "on to" was her naked body.

That night, Josie lowered the lamp to a just a tiny flame, removed her shoes, and got set to put on quite a show for her husband. He sat propped up with pillows against the headboard, looking like the dark, dangerous outlaw of old. Bare-chested, the white of the bandage contrasted with his light-brown skin.

The gleam of hunger in Luke's eyes made her heart flutter and her mouth go dry. Lord, he hadn't been a bit shy about telling her how much he wanted her. And she him. But not just yet. Tonight, she'd drive him crazy with desire before she fell into his arms. She was already burning hot, for beneath the sheet draped over his lap, she knew he didn't wear a stitch of clothing. He was ready for her. By the time she finished undressing, neither would want to waste one second.

With her eyes locked on his, she unfastened her bodice, one button then another with a pause in between. Very slowly, she opened one side, teasing him with a glimpse of what lay beneath.

With excruciating slowness, she drew the fabric down her arms, dangling it by the barest of fingertips before dropping it.

Luke grinned, quietly singing "Betsy Barlow, the Calico Queen."

She joined in and ran her fingertips across her lacy chemise, untying the satin ribbon. But instead of removing the undergarment like she knew he yearned for her to do, she slid her hands to the waist of her skirt, releasing it to puddle around her feet.

Giving him a flirtatious smile, she tugged down each

stocking and offered her legs to Luke to pull the bit of silk off.

"I always said you have the prettiest legs this side of heaven," Luke murmured, tracing their curve.

Tingles sashayed up her spine like shameful dancehall hussies and her heart hammered against her ribs. She hurriedly retreated from reach to finish her performance. Except she couldn't escape his smoldering, dark gaze that seared her.

One by one, she dawdled over each bit of clothing until she stood at last in only her chemise. She raised the hem of the thin fabric, teasing him with skin.

"I'm a very lucky man," Luke drawled. "You do have the most beautiful body of anyone alive, Mrs. Legend." His eyes darkened to a dangerous shade. "But if you don't get over here, I'm going to get up and rip that damn thing off you."

Heat flared in Josie and she issued a breathless dare. "Oh, you will, will you?"

"Faster than you can whistle 'Dixie.'" His eyes glittered with raw lust and sultry heat.

"One. More. Little bitty. Piece." Josie lazily let her fingertips drift across the swell of her breasts and each pebbled tip. She lingered over the satin ribbon that nestled in the deep valley between her breasts. Her knees went weak with desire for Luke and she was tempted to abandon her plan entirely and quench the fire blazing inside her.

Opting to continue a bit longer, Josie drew the fabric aside, one inch at a time, revealing more and more hot, aching flesh to Luke's gaze.

Before she could pull the chemise over her head, he leaped naked from bed and grabbed for her. Josie yelped and sidestepped his reach, scurrying behind an overstuffed chair. Her gaze swept appreciatively over his lean body, pausing on his jutting need.

The throb between her thighs told her she had to end this playtime. She had to have what he alone could give. And soon.

Luke's eyes smoldered as he gripped the arms of the chair, growling, "Do you know what happens to naughty little girls who tease the big bad wolf?"

Her eyes widened innocently as her breath hitched. "Does she get eaten, perhaps?"

"Nibbled on, devoured." Luke lunged for her again.

Josie squealed and made a break toward the bed. He caught her a second before she reached it. She twisted free, snatched up a pillow, and launched it at him.

Luke again grabbed, holding her fast to him. She tilted her head back, trying to calm her pounding heart as he crushed his lips to hers.

The kiss sent a scorching flame through her body. Josie slid her arm around his neck. Breaking the kiss, he swept her into his strong arms.

"Luke, put me down. You're still healing."

"I refuse to be an invalid a second longer." His lips moved down her neck. "*Mi princesa hermosa.* You've driven me out of my mind. I'm ordering you a scarlet dress in the morning as soon as the mercantile opens."

Josie trailed her finger along his jaw. "What'll happen when I get fat with your child?"

"I'll love you even more, Mrs. Legend."

When he lowered her to the bed, she held up her arms. He yanked the chemise over her head and pitched it into a corner.

He was inside her in an instant, filling her with his love. The vigorous rhythm couldn't be good for him and Doc was sure to pitch a fit, but she had no breath left to even whisper a warning.

Luke was back and she took everything that he gave.

Life with him would never be mundane or boring. He'd rescued her, and she liked to think, in a way, she'd saved him too.

He was her love, her dream, her future all rolled into one.

Maybe love was nothing more than two people saving each other and spending their days making one another happy.

Here on the Lone Star, where a man found his true worth sleeping under the bronze star, a dream had collided with life.

Josie snuggled against Luke's side, taking care not to hurt him. The day they'd met, she'd run screaming after those outlaws, begging them to tell her who she was. Now she knew.

She was Josie Legend, Luke's cherished wife.

Epilogue

Three months following Luke's escape from death, Stoker Legend met a slow-moving wagon under the crossbar. His heart smiled. They had brought his lady.

The wagon stopped. "Where would you like us to go?" the driver asked.

"I'll lead you." Trembling, Stoker tied his white horse to the back and climbed up. He kissed the freshly hewn coffin and wept. "You're finally home, my darling. Welcome to the Lone Star."

He wiped his eyes, reached into his pocket for a pencil, and scrawled the words *I Love You* on the wood, then laid a single red rose on top.

"Head where those people are gathered." He pointed the way to the little hilltop cemetery where a crowd waited in silence. When the wagon stopped, Luke helped his father down.

"Your mother is here, son." Stoker gazed into the eyes of his firstborn. "This won't make up for all the years when I didn't know about you, but maybe it'll help."

Luke nodded. "I know she's happy here, Pa. I feel her presence and I'm sure she knows she's loved."

Josie slipped her arm around Luke's waist. "We're all together now, sweetheart. Your mother is at peace."

Sam and Houston strode forward to help Luke and

their father carry Elena Montoya to her final resting place. Stoker's vision blurred. He longed to grab those lost years. Except he couldn't. Life had to go forward, not back.

A short time later, Elena lay next to where Stoker would one day. Both of his loves, resting on either side. Two remarkable, unforgettable women and he loved them both with all his heart and soul.

Luke moved the tombstone into place and quietly knelt alone beside his mother.

Though Stoker itched to go to him, he refrained. Luke needed a private moment. Maybe Stoker had learned something after all these years. Now wouldn't that be something? Even so, a man his age had learned certain truths.

He couldn't fix his sons. They alone had to do that.

He couldn't fight their battles or protect them from every hurtful thing, only ride beside them and help.

In the end, he could only love them.

And Lord, how he did. No man ever asked for better.

Noah Jordan stole up beside him and slipped a hand into his. "You made Luke happy."

"No, son, he made himself happy. I only helped." Stoker met the boy's upturned face. "Are you going to live with Luke and Josie when they finish that house they're building?"

The orphaned kid shrugged his bony shoulders and his brows drew together. "Do you need a little boy, Papa Stoker? Maybe I can stay here."

Something pierced Stoker's heart. He loved this kid, whose worldly possessions only amounted to a chewed-up mutt. Stoker knelt to eye level and worked to swallow. "I sure do, and it would put a big ol' smile on my face if you'd be my youngest son. Mine are grown and married now, and they don't need me anymore."

"Nope. I need you, though. Maybe you need me, too, just a little bit."

"Noah, I always said you were one smart boy." He winked and rose, putting his arm around the kid. "You know, a man should have a lot of sons. And dogs."

"Yes, sir." Noah seemed deep in thought. An old man in a young boy's body. At last, he raised his eyes. "Papa Stoker, my pa would've liked you. I wish you could've known him. He loved me a whole bunch." A troubled sigh followed. "I miss my ma and pa real bad sometimes."

"I know, son. But you have your memories and no one can take them away. Guard them and hold them in your heart."

"Yes, sir." Noah drew his eyebrows together. "Can I ask you a question?"

"Always. Shoot."

"What is a harlot?"

A bolt of lightning couldn't have delivered more of a jolt. "Where did you hear that word, son?"

"Josie was singing to Luke. It was something about a calico queen and a harlot."

"Well, I'll tell you what." Stoker winked. "In five more years, we'll sit down and I'll tell you all about those ladies. Deal?"

"I reckon I can wait. I ain't goin' nowhere."

Sam's son, Hector, ran up and asked Noah to play. Stoker let out a sigh of relief when the two scampered off, Rowdy chasing after them.

Stoker gazed out over the land he loved. It was rugged, inhospitable at times, and a bit untamed. Like him. His attention shifted to the tall flag fluttering proudly, high above the ranch. He'd fought for that piece of material, held men in his arms—his brothers and others he called friends—who'd died for freedom.

His Texas.

Stoker's gaze returned to his family. His sons, their wives, and their children. Each had found the perfect mate. Although Houston had needed more than a little shove. But what were fathers for?

His eyes misted as he glanced at Sam, and the scar around his neck from the hanging rope. He and Sierra almost hadn't gotten to declare their love. Their two beautiful children—Hector and Sam Jr.—were welcome additions.

Next came Houston, Stoker's spitting image, and his wife, Lara. Houston held sweet little Gracie, who was squirming to get down. Stoker bet the farm that she'd grow up to be a spitfire of a woman. She'd make everyone in sight toe the line.

Stoker shifted his attention to Luke and Josie, who'd married in such an unusual way. It was fitting for that pair of strong, unusual people. A few days before, they'd announced that another little Legend would join them before long.

A smile curved Stoker's mouth. He loved his daughters as much as his sons. No tougher, more courageous women lived than Sierra, Lara, and Josie.

He thought back over the last few years, and the dramatic changes they'd brought to the ranch. He and his sons had worked hard to overcome evil, heartache, and death, and they'd emerged victorious.

The Legends were survivors and dreamers...tamers of a raw land.

Pride swelled in his chest and a mist blocked his vision.

In Texas, some Legends were made, some were born, and some were created by destiny.

This was the way of things.

This was his legacy.

This was the mighty Lone Star Ranch.

Keep reading for a sneak peek of the next book in the Texas Heroes series by Linda Broday

The Cowboy Who Came Calling

Santa Anna, Texas, 1881

Often the elders spoke in hushed whispers about a long, painful night of the soul. How the wind visited, carrying problems as thick as a biblical plague. It's also said that impatience dries the blood sooner than age or sorrow.

Surely this must be such a time.

In twenty years, Glory Marie Day had come to know more about injustice and patience than most women twice her age. She hadn't asked for any breaks, only a fair shake, and fate hadn't seen fit to deliver even a sliver of that.

Truth of the matter, she hadn't overly complained of the lousy handout she'd gotten. She made her own luck and became tougher for it.

Whatever it took she'd do. Though the difficult task at hand might scare off a person of lesser grit.

Glory's fists curled in a ball. Somehow. Someway.

Reverend Matthews's sermon yesterday merely gave her added determination. "When Saint Peter marks against your name in the great Hereafter, you'd best make sure you have enough scratches on the plus side."

Papa always bragged about her being whip-smart. Good thing, because she'd need everything she had to solve this problem. At least more pluses than minuses at the end.

Snooty Bess Whitfield's snickers brought her thoughts back to the present. For a Monday afternoon, Harvey's Emporium held a good many patrons. Across the room, Bess gave Glory's faded breeches an imperious frown, then whispered behind her hand to her companion, Amelia Jackson.

Though not close enough to hear, Glory knew the slurs by heart. "Poor homely Glory. Dressing like a boy, she'll never have a beau. Her father's a rotten jailbird. Better stay clear of those good-for-nothing Days."

A woman's voice interrupted her thoughts. "Here you are, Glory."

"Thank you, Aunt Dorothy." She accepted the box of cartridges she'd requested. Except for her aunt, Uncle Pete, and a few others, she would've compared life in the Texas town of Santa Anna as something akin to hell.

"Going huntin'?" The woman she loved as a second mother propped an elbow on a big jar of pickles.

Glory's mouth watered for one of the juicy pickles. Lord knew she loved them better than candy. The sign read five cents. Cheap enough, she reckoned, if a body had a nickel in her pocket. The eggs, milk, and butter she'd just sold her aunt barely covered the ammunition for her Winchester.

"Yes, ma'am. Better see what game I can scare up for supper." Without a doubt, if she hadn't stepped up to fill her father's boots... Well, she didn't want to dwell on that.

"You're the strong one, Glory. Your ma, God bless her soul, is too frail to see to the needs of you children. I love my sister-in-law to death, but Ruth wears my patience down to a nub. Right alongside Pete Harvey. I swear, those two were carved from the same block of wood."

Allowing a half smile, Glory slipped the cartridges inside her pocket. "Where's Uncle Pete today?"

Although the man suffered from flights of fancy, what the polite ones called it, Glory worshiped him. Pete Harvey's eccentricities added a certain flavor to her existence. She had to marvel at anyone who marched as he saw fit, taking whatever paths his imagination led to. If ever she should be so free.

"The fool is out dowsing for water. Cut himself a peach tree limb as a divining rod and declared he'd find water or bust a gut trying."

"This drought has everyone in a bad way. Paying Mr. McConley twenty-three cents a barrel is highway robbery. If Uncle Pete can truly find water, he'll have every family in Coleman County bidding for his services."

"Hmph! If is a big word." Aunt Dorothy straightened, reached for a long feather duster, and flicked it over the nearly spotless counter. "I'm mighty thankful I don't have to depend on his crazy notions to put food in our bellies."

Depend on Dorothy Harvey to look on the bright side.

Bess and Amelia sauntered to the counter. From the way they brushed tightly against Glory, the aisle might well have become a narrow strip of dry ground in a mud pit.

"Afternoon, Mrs. Harvey."

Did they speak in unison like that just to irritate a body?

"Girls, what'll it be for you today?"

Glory headed for the door but stopped when Aunt Dorothy called, "Oh, wait a minute, I have a letter for you, dear."

"We'll take one of these new toothbrushes and a jar of this paste to go with it." Bess gave Glory a sidelong smirk. "Clean teeth is as important as bathing regular."

The implication that she did neither had Glory fuming. A daily rubbing of soda powder kept her teeth shiny and clean enough. Thank goodness proper customs weren't limited to those who could afford it. But, it sure seemed as if good manners ran in short supply.

Amelia plopped down a bar of perfumed toilet soap. "Can you put these on my daddy's bill, Mrs. Harvey?"

"I suppose I can. Will this be all?"

The Persnickety Twins nodded their heads again in unison.

While Aunt Dorothy wrapped the items in brown paper, Glory cast the jar of luscious pickles another longing stare. Even should she suddenly by some miracle possess a nickel, her sense of honor would kick in. She didn't want anything if her sisters couldn't have the same. Just wasn't right.

All of a sudden, the pickle jar doubled. And tripled. Then her vision dimmed as if someone had extinguished the oil lamps hanging on the store walls. She shook her head, closing her eyes for a minute. When she opened them, she could make out her aunt's form, a decided improvement.

Perspiration dampened her palms. This loss of vision had come and gone over the last few weeks. At first the episodes had been shorter and farther apart. Now, she experienced two or three a day. Still, she refused to let her worst fears take root. Nothing worse could happen...could it?

The tinkle of the bell over the entrance seemed far in the distance. It was the deep tenor that broke her trance.

"Afternoon, ladies."

Bess and Amelia tittered, nudging each other. Curious, Glory turned to see the cause of such a stir.

The tall stranger smiled and sidestepped past. He'd not paid her any attention. No, the two girls bedecked in fine dresses took his eye. No reason in the world why he should notice a girl in faded britches and mule-eared boots. No reason whatsoever.

She watched him head for the coffee grinder. Hmm, coffee beans. Yep, the brown strands nestling against his collar were the exact shade of those beans he poured into the grinder.

Nice.

From beneath lowered lids, she took in the rest of him. The dark-blue shirt added breadth to his shoulders. The polished silver concha on the button-down cavalry bib spoke of pride. Slim waist, long legs that stretched from here to yon, and a finely shaped behind. A figure that could easily climb atop a horse—or a...

A flush crept from her toes upward. Where had that thought come from? Her mind deserved a good scrubbing. Besides, he'd never give her the time of day.

For a split second, bitterness bubbled to the surface like

fermented yeast. She didn't want to be the provider, the strong one, the head of the family. For just one day, she'd like to worry about her teeth instead of feeding hungry stomachs. She'd like to wear dresses and act a lady. And for once, she'd like to have a man look at her with warm desire in his eyes. Someone besides Horace, Simple Simon, most folks jeered, who moon-eyed over her whenever she came near. Not that anything was wrong with Horace. She'd just like to have the attentions of a man like this stranger for once.

"Here you are, girls." Aunt Dorothy handed over the wrapped parcels before turning to the stranger. "Can I help you, mister?"

"Yes, ma'am."

Glory knew a moment of jealousy when he nodded and cast the fashion queens a brief smile. "Ladies."

Still, she quickly averted her gaze when he swung back to her aunt. She watched Bess and Amelia sweep regally toward the door, all the while whispering behind their hands and giggling. Prim and proper as they pretended, they sure acted stupid.

"I'll take some of this coffee and a bag of flour. Throw in beans, some jerky, and cartridges. That'll do it, I reckon."

"You passing through or plannin' to stay awhile?"

The paper Aunt Dorothy bundled his purchases in rattled loudly, forcing Glory to concentrate to hear his answer. Not that anyone would speak her name and busybody in the same breath. Mere interest—a slight but distinguishable difference.

"Depends, ma'am. I'm camped just outside town for the time being."

The length of his stay in the area probably depended on whether the Miss Prisses invited him home to meet their daddies.

Besides his being easy on the eyes, the man's polite manners fit snug about him. His resonant voice created tightness in her chest.

Her own papa had such a way of speaking. The lump in her throat refused to budge. Would she ever get to hear that sound again?

She quickly ducked when the man favored her with a glance and became intent on a handbill lying on the counter. Now that the store had emptied, she couldn't remain part of the woodwork. Being noticed was one thing, pitied another story altogether. For two cents, she'd not wait for the letter Aunt Dorothy mentioned.

She forced her mind back to the crisp paper in her hand.

Hell's bells! The words leaped off the page. Mad Dog Perkins, a five-hundred-dollar reward for his capture. Why hadn't she paid attention to it before? That was enough to hire a real lawyer. Not one of the shyster varieties.

"Oh, yes, your letter." Aunt Dorothy reached into a wooden slot and handed her an envelope.

Worry forced all thoughts of Perkins from her mind as Glory recognized the flowing script. They'd received similar ones from Dr. Fletcher, the physician who treated Jack Day at Huntsville State Prison. Each one had brought pain and made her ever mindful of the racing clock.

Terrible foreboding knotted her stomach. Dark smudges stained one corner. Blood? Her chest constricted. Her daddy's?

"Hope to goodness it's not bad news, dear," her aunt remarked, noticing her reluctance, and then her eyes lit on the handbill. "You know, this very morning, Mr. Harvey told me over his cold eggs and burnt biscuits that he got a gander at a man lurking around Bead Mountain. That man's cooking is worse than his forgetfulness, if that's possible."

Glory tried to curb the impatience others had warned would dry the blood. Truth or not, she darn well knew it didn't help her nerves. "What did he say about the man he saw?"

"Swore he resembled Mad Dog Perkins. Course, that old coot sees things few other folks do. I think his mind's took to wandering worse than ever."

The stranger's head whipped around. The new pocketknife he'd admired must have lost its shine. Glory caught the slight shift in his feet as he leaned forward. Maybe she was a bit hasty in bestowing attributes he didn't possess.

A lower tone of voice and turning her back would fix him. "Too bad we don't have a sheriff either here or in Coleman City. Not enough pay to develop a fondness for bullets. Did he mention his suspicions to the U.S. Marshal in Abilene town?"

"No need. Everyone from here to the Mississippi knows my Pete. Say he's tetched and don't pay him no more mind than if he was a flea."

Bead Mountain. The old Indian burial place would provide excellent cover for a wanted man, since most folks shied away from there. Haunted, the rumormongers whispered. Not that she believed such herself. Nothing but the howling wind could make her bones shiver.

"Thank you for the letter, Aunt Dorothy." She kissed the woman's cheek, slipping the letter next to the box of cartridges. "I have a hundred things to do and I'm wasting time."

She whirled—right into a rock-solid chest. The collision sent the handsome stranger's purchases flying.

"Sorry, mister." Mortified, Glory snatched up the items from the floor and stuffed them back into his arms before he had a chance to blink twice.

That's when she made her second mistake. Both steamy and dark, his gaze pulled her into a murky pool where she foundered helpless as a scuttled ship.

"No harm done, miss." The twinkle and lopsided grin held her spellbound. "Name's McClain. Luke McClain."

Tongue-tied under his scrutiny, she couldn't make a squeak. Before she made the worst mistake of her life, she fled.

The sun beat down as Luke crept silently in the tall grass. Beads of sweat ran into his eyes, burning worse than an eyeful of cayenne. Momentarily blinded, he wiped his face with the sleeve of his shirt.

With sight restored, he spied his prey.

The figure squatted on his haunches just ahead. Mad Dog Perkins, as he lived and breathed. After months of looking, he'd finally found the slippery man. Before the day ended, he'd learn who and why someone had stolen his life.

Perkins knew—Luke bet on it. He eased his Colt from the holster and inched close enough to spit on the man who'd holed up at the foot of the small mountain. Thick brush at the base of a natural overhang offered an excellent hiding place. Destiny must've put that girl in the emporium that morning. Otherwise, he wouldn't have found the man so soon.

Luke crouched, ready to spring into the camp. But before he could make his move, a slim figure appeared from nowhere.

The newcomer yanked the lever of his rifle down and up in a snapping motion, startling Mad Dog Perkins.

What the...? Luke watched the scene with a knot in his belly. Who had beaten him to the prize? He shrank into the tall brush.

"Don't even think it, mister." The shadows of a floppy hat concealed the wearer's face, but the voice sounded way too young for this dirty business. "Throw your pistol over here nice and easy. No tricks."

Perkins growled like the rabid animal his name implied and tossed his weapon within inches of the rifleman.

Unable to watch someone steal what was rightfully his, Luke scrambled to his feet and into the small clearing. "Just a cotton-pickin' minute."

He skidded to an abrupt halt when the slim figure swung the lethal rifle his direction.

"No, you wait. Mister, I don't know what your business is here, but you're lucky I didn't part your hair."

Surprise curled inside him at sight of those delicate-shaped eyes. Those didn't belong to any boy or man. Ricocheting surprise gave him a pleasing taste. A cajoler at heart, he figured taking candy from a babe couldn't present that much of a challenge.

"What're you doing? If I'm allowed to ask, ma'am?"

The Winchester remained pointed at his heart while she nervously eyed Perkins. A streak of dirt across her nose and cheek added grit to the stubborn tilt of her chin.

"Stay out of my way. I'm taking this man to Abilene town and collecting the reward."

His breath caught at the back of his throat. The unusual blue gaze seemed lodged in his brain. Her eyes reminded him of polished stones worn smooth by the timeless flow of water. That was exactly what they resembled—stone-washed. Yet, his memory of their meeting refused to yield the place.

"It's my duty to take charge of Perkins. No job for a lady." If he gave her the wrong impression, wasn't any fault of his. Didn't need a tin star when the callin' pumped in a man's veins as thick as life-sustaining blood.

"Over my dead body! I captured him fair and square."

Mad Dog shifted his stance from one side to another, seeming to gauge the distance to the rifle. The young woman sensed his movement and swung sharply.

"I wouldn't, Perkins. It would be a mistake to test my temper." She clearly meant business.

But so did Luke. He wasn't about to relinquish the desperado now that he'd found him. And not before he had a chance to get those answers he desperately needed. Yet, how could he make the interloper see she'd stepped in the middle of something where she had no right?

"Weeeell, I do declare. I must be sumpin' to have folks fightin' over who's gonna fetch me to the marshal." Perkins grinned, giving them both a good view of his brown, rotted teeth.

"Begging your pardon, miss. Tackling wanted criminals is a man's job." Luke used his most reasonable tone, the one he used when cajoling troublesome fillies. "Not meaning any disrespect, but I've dogged Perkins's trail for the better part of two months."

Her chin jutted farther. "I saw him first and he's mine."

"Y'all mind if I sit a spell while you dicker over—"

"Keep standing!" he and the woman answered together.

"Move one muscle and I'll shoot you," she added.

Luke didn't know which of them she meant. Judging from the fire-breathing glare, Mystery Lady might shoot both simply for the heck of it.

Although she was a tad on the slim side for his taste, he admired the way she filled out those britches. His gaze traveled upward to her heaving chest. Yep, her curves were certainly in all the right places...and then some.

By some quirk of fate, her hair chose that particular moment to spill from beneath the floppy hat. He could only hold his breath at the spectacle and watch the glimmering strands slip one by one from their hiding place. They teased, they dallied, taunting him in a slow, sensuous dance until the golden mass caressed her back and shoulders.

Have mercy! For a moment, he was afraid the thick lump he'd swallowed had been his own tongue.

Then it hit him. Harvey's Emporium in Santa Anna. His thoughts had been more on the handbill than who held it. No mistaking though—this was the girl who'd knocked the supplies from his hands. No one else in the whole state of Texas had eyes that color.

"If you're through staring, cowboy, you can holster that pistol and ride back where you came from."

A hot flush rose and crept toward his hairline. "I'm not going anywhere, miss, except to take this man—"

Perkins chose that moment to jump, knocking the girl to the ground.

Luke renewed his grip on the Colt, springing forward to help. Midair of his leap, an orange flash spat from the end of her Winchester. A deafening blast followed.

The bullet tore through flesh and muscle. A white pain enveloped Luke as he fell. Through the dizzying haze, he watched helplessly as the man who'd helped destroy him vanished from sight into the brush.

Now, someone's plan to ruin him was complete.

He might never again be this close to the truth. Despair twisted in his gut. His hand went limp. The revolver made a quiet thump as it fell.

Two

GLORY PULLED HERSELF SLOWLY TO HER FEET. THE DRY brush crackled in the wake of Perkins's escape, seeming to mimic her crumbling hopes and dreams. Sick at heart, she glared at the meddlesome stranger who'd thwarted her plans. If he hadn't interfered, she'd be well on her way to town, along with the means to solve all her problems.

The man sprawled, clutching his right leg. Despite deep aggravation, her stomach plunged when she saw red oozing from between his fingers.

"Dear heavens!"

"You shot me!" He struggled to sit up.

She pulled a kerchief from her back pocket as she ran to him. "I didn't mean for that to happen. You saw it, didn't you? Perkins, I mean. It just went off."

Kneeling, she tied the kerchief high on his leg above the wound. That meant working awfully close to his...uh... unmentionables. Her hand trembled so badly she could only hope her jerky movements would limit the blood loss.

"Why did you let him grab your rifle? Blew half my fool leg off here."

"Oh, and I guess you'd have done any better?" If he could complain, he wasn't hurt too badly. She hid her relief behind a frown. "Besides, you're exaggerating. The wound can't be all that serious. Now, if you'd have been closer, and

I hadn't loaded this Winchester with buckshot, we might've been contemplating amputation, McClain."

"How'd you know my name?" Luke grimaced as she gently eased the afflicted limb back to the ground. "I don't rightly recall the introduction."

All manner of strange pinpricks mocked her outward calm as she tried to avoid the face that stirred her fancies. The stranger could certainly charm the pitchfork from the devil himself. Fighting the war on both fronts, she focused on putting from mind the firm hardness of his leg and the close proximity of the other...part as she worked. Wild flutters of panic beat their wings against her rib cage.

A deep breath might steady her nerves. Yet, when she managed to gulp a large portion of the heady air, it merely made her realize nothing short of putting distance between them would solve the problem.

His name? Truth told, she didn't seem prone to forgetting it.

"You made your acquaintance to my aunt, not me directly, this morning. I may be a lowly female and therefore unworthy of capturing a wanted criminal, at least in your estimation." She gave the kerchief a yank, tying the knot a teensy bit tighter. "But I am not the least bit deaf."

"Ow! Damn, lady." The pasty white of his face warned that he teetered on the brink of blackness.

"Sorry. I need to get this down to a trickle or there'll be no need for me to haul your carcass anywhere. Else, might as well let the buzzards have you."

"A man truly lives for the moment when he can place his life into the hands of such a caring, compassionate woman." McClain's words came from between clenched teeth.

"I suppose you'd have better luck with the Miss Prisses then?" The sting of remorse came instantly. Rudeness went against her nature. She treated everyone with kind respect, even poor Horace Simon.

It boiled down to letting the answer to her desperate plan slip through her fingers. Her father depended on her. The whole family looked to her for their needs, and the question remained as to how long she'd have before she lost the skill to do so.

"Am I delirious? Who, pray tell, are the Miss Prisses?"

"Forgotten so soon? You certainly ogled them this morning in the emporium."

"Oh, those ladies. I was merely being polite. Nothing wrong with that." He cocked his head. "Do I detect envy?"

"You'd be wrong if you did." His assumption hit a layer of hard rock. She wasn't jealous of what Amelia and Bess had…it was more the things they could have that bothered her.

When she risked another fleeting glance at McClain, she fell headlong into that smoldering gaze. To say she became taken with him would've been an understatement.

"Not fair, Mystery Lady. I still don't have your name."

Glory blew a tendril of hair that'd fallen close to her mouth and wished the day hadn't turned so blasted hot. Or that the curve of his mouth that accented a white scar just below his bottom lip didn't make her heart race. Or that his arresting brown eyes didn't make her wonder what secrets lodged behind them. Although for the moment, a grim line held the lazy grin at bay.

And furthermore, she wished his study of her didn't turn her legs to jelly.

"It's Glory…Glory Day," she murmured.

Before he could further wilt her self-confidence, she stood, retrieved her Winchester, then scanned the rugged brush for signs of McClain's horse.

Common sense told her she was obligated to take him home with her. After all, she did shoot him and couldn't just leave him hurt, however much she so desired. But, once there, she'd turn over his care to her mother and sisters. Her duty done, she'd make certain she stayed well beyond reach of any magical spells the charmer tried to weave.

A horse's whinny off to the left alerted her. She pushed through the tangle of briars and thistle.

"An Indian pony. Might have known he'd not ride

a nag." She untied the light-colored paint, admiring the ripple of muscle beneath the tan-and-white hide. Good horseflesh. She doubted any in the area could rival it.

The stranger's face brightened when he spied her leading the animal.

"Saints be praised! The thought crossed my mind you'd left me for buzzard bait." McClain tried to pull himself up, but pain clearly evident on his face sent him back to the hard ground.

"I have to admit, the plan had merit." She bent and, trying to keep his nearness from her mind, slipped an arm around his holstered middle. "If you grab around my neck and push up with your good leg, we might get you on your feet."

"I'm game if you are, Miss Glory."

The man's solidness surprised her. For all his lean, lanky build, it taxed her strength to raise him. His body pressing tightly against hers sent rampant thoughts of the entirely inappropriate variety swarming through her head like flies to hot apple pie.

Her pulse and ragged breath were neck and neck in a horse race. Which one would win? And in what shape would it leave her?

By the time she got him vertical, she knew she probably would never be the same. Then came the job of boosting him into the saddle. One slight problem—where was she supposed to boost him from?

A quick survey up and down his trim form left few options. She'd simply have to put her hands on his backside and imagine pushing Bessie from a mud pit. She looped the paint's reins around her arm.

It wasn't as if his finely sculpted behind was bare. No sirree, his britches covered it, outlining it perfectly.

"When I count to three, pull yourself up, Mr. McClain." Why in tarnation did her heart pound like this?

"I'm hardly in any position to object."

Glory stooped slightly to give herself leverage. "One."

Her hands rested on each side of his posterior. "Two."

"You know, I don't mind getting shot quite so much," he murmured.

She closed her eyes. He surely didn't feel much like the milk cow. And it hadn't rained in so long she couldn't even remember a mud hole.

"Three."

Up he went, sliding onto the horse.

"Don't mind my saying so, Miss Glory, but you sure have a heck of a system." He flashed her a crooked smile as he reached down to give her a hand.

"No, thanks, I have my own mount. I hid him down in a little wash not too far from here."

A rush of excitement swept over her when his grin slipped. Obviously he'd expected her to ride behind. Even anticipated perhaps? Who was she kidding? A man with heart-stopping grins wouldn't be interested in a pants-wearing female.

Jumbled thoughts clouded her head as she led the paint to the gully where she'd stashed her mule. Once the glow of besting him faded, disappointment set in. McClain's trousers resting snug against the inside of her thighs might not have been so bad. She'd never know now.

When she gave a fleeting look back, it was merely to see if he still sat anchored in the saddle. For no other reason, she assured herself.

Old Caesar brayed loudly when he saw her. Though the white mule had serviced the family well, for once Glory wished the animal were a horse. Nothing, except a donkey maybe, spoke of worse circumstances than a mule.

No sooner had the wish formed than her conscience berated her. She should consider herself mighty lucky to have what they did. Her poor father struggled for a bite of bread.

And at least she owned a saddle. The animal skittered as she placed her foot in the stirrup and swung onto the leather.

"Are you all right, Mr. McClain?" The man's ashen color didn't reassure her.

To his credit, McClain sought to put on a brave front. "Fine as frog's hair. Where did you say you're taking me?"

"Didn't say." She lifted the paint's reins.

"Well, if you don't mind, would you like to share that piece of information? A man has a right to know."

"You're a mean-tempered old cuss."

"Well, pardon me for breathing. Hobbling around with holes in a fellow's leg tends to sour a man's disposition. And what did you mean by old? I'll have you know I'm far from ready for an undertaker yet."

She thought it strange that the part about his age drew the biggest objection. "I'm taking you home."

"Sounds good to me—if I knew where home was."

He slid sideways. Glory grabbed him before he fell and pushed him back in the saddle.

"Hang on, cowboy. I'm taking you to our homestead."

"Don't wanna be a bother. If you'll just point the way to Santa Anna, I'll head over there."

"Too far, and besides, they don't have a doctor. Guess it's me or nothing."

"If'n you say so." His trailing voice warned her he was slipping close to unconsciousness. Blood now stained the right leg of his soft denims a dull red from thigh to knee.

Damnation! The wound might be worse than she thought. Here she was gabbing with the man when she should be more concerned for his welfare. She flushed. He'd tangled her emotions worse than a slipknot. The harder she struggled to get loose, the more bound she became.

She gripped the Winchester tighter and urged the animals to a faster pace, keeping an eye peeled for a possible ambush. Though she assumed Mad Dog's first thought would be to hightail it out of the country, she also knew he would be after revenge.

Tumbleweeds blew from the west like silent, gray ghosts spooking the animals. She dodged what she could while toying with the idea of resuming the search for Perkins. The likelihood of sneaking up on him a second time would increase the danger tenfold. Dare she let that stop her?

Their destination rose into view while she weighed the pros and cons. Mama topped the con list. That she'd raise a fuss was a given. And who would see to putting food on the table?

They waded into the Red Bank Creek, which meandered through the Day property. The con side grew longer. Glory couldn't shirk her duty. She sighed. Going after Perkins again was out of the question. Their means for survival had vanished into thin air. And she laid the blame on the stranger slumped in the saddle. No choice but to take him to the Day household, dearly as it galled her. Caesar plodded up the slope on the other side.

From a distance, there was something majestic about the stone house where she had come into the world. A body couldn't see the missing porch step, the hole in the roof, or the tear in the screen door. This far away, the tangle of wild honeysuckle covering the entire east side gave it a stature worthy of a castle. Her grandfather had constructed the dwelling half a century ago from natural limestone he quarried and hauled down from the mountain. The durable structure had withstood Texas twisters, drought, and spring floods. She tried to wet her dry mouth, but nothing came—not enough moisture for spit. The godforsaken heat had sucked the life from the land. Nothing thrived but tumbleweeds, wild honeysuckle, and broken dreams.

She patted Caesar's neck and gave him a nudge with her knee. "Get along, you flea-bitten bag of bones. We're home."

Her youngest sister came flying out to greet them, letting the screen door slam shut behind her.

"Glory, guess what!"

The ten-year-old's enthusiasm evoked twinges of jealousy. Patience didn't have to worry about food supplies or meeting the payments on the banknote. In fact, the pigtailed youngster had few things to disrupt her sleep. Like it or not, Glory meant to keep it that way for however long she could.

"What, Squirt?" She halted at the stone fence that surrounded the house and dismounted. "What happened today?"

"Miss Minnie had kittens. Four of 'em. They're so cute." Patience squinted against the sun. "Who's the stranger, Glory?"

"Name's McClain. Don't rightly know more than that."

"He's bleedin'. How'd he get shot? Huh? Stage robbers shoot you, mister?"

"Patience Ann Day! Where are your manners?"

McClain roused. "This jabber-jaw your sister?"

"Afraid so. Can you get down?" Oh, Lord, she hoped so. She didn't need to get close to him again. He'd ruined her breathing and turned her brain to mush once already.

"Think I can make it. If nothin' else, I can fall—"

Before he could complete the sentence, he slid from the paint and crumpled to the ground in a heap.

"Go get Hope." She pushed the girl toward the house. "I need help."

"Hope, come quick!" Patience shrieked as she ran to the house. "Glory's brought home a man."

The statement brought a fluster on which she had no time to dwell. She touched his forehead. Cold and clammy.

"What's wrong?" Hope's hurrying stride whipped the skirts about her ankles.

Glory met her middle sister's worried gray eyes. "Please help me get him into the house. I think he's in shock."

With McClain between them, each draped an arm around her neck. He roused again and helped relieve their burden somewhat by hobbling on his good leg. Patience held the door and they maneuvered him inside.

"Where's Mama?" Glory peered into the tidy parlor.

"Lying down. She had one of her headaches."

"In that case, let's put him in my bed." She shifted the weight, ignoring sharp needles that shot through her neck. "I'll sleep in the barn."

"You can share my bed." Hope panted under the load.

"We'll worry about that later."

Half dragging him, they dropped McClain onto the bed in a little alcove off the kitchen. Glory exhaled sharply.

"Who shot him?" Her mother's voice came from the doorway. Ruth Day leaned against the wall, holding one hand to her forehead. The ruckus had evidently awakened her.

Not sure what or how much to tell, Glory stared silently at the circle of faces.

"Sorry for the noise, Mama," she said gently. "Go lie back down. We'll take care of him."

"Who is he and what is he doing in my house?"

Her mother seemed determined to have answers despite her frailty and ill health.

A wince and a deep breath later, Glory wished she could soften the blow. "Name's McClain, and I shot him."

Shocked gasps flew around the small, windowless cubbyhole.

"You what? Why on earth?"

"An accident, Mama." She rubbed her eyes wearily. "Mad Dog Perkins grabbed my Winchester and it went off."

"Mad Dog Perkins, the outlaw?" Her mother struggled to comprehend. Worry creased Ruth's forehead. "Glory Marie, I think you'd best explain yourself."

The man called McClain groaned and opened pain-clouded eyes. "Mystery Lady?" he asked, his voice soft as a whisper.

"I will later, Mama. But first I need to tend to our guest before he bleeds all over my feather mattress."

"It's not proper to have a strange man in our house." Ruth twisted her hands nervously. "Whatever will folks say now?"

"Sorry, ma'am. Don't mean to cause no harm." McClain tried to sit up. "I'll just be on my way."

"No, you won't." Glory held him down firmly. "I shot you and I'll patch you up." She gave her mother a clipped answer. "Besides, since when did it matter to us what others say?"

Hope quietly added her opinion. "I don't think they can spread worse rumors than they already have."

"Elevate the man's legs. I once saw a doctor do that," her mother cautioned, swaying and holding her head in both hands.

"Patience, take Mama back to her room, then put some water on to boil." Glory lifted a pair of scissors from a sewing basket beside the bed before turning to Hope. "We need bandages."

"What're you planning to do with those, little missy?" McClain's eyes held more than a hint of nervousness as his gaze centered on the scissors.

"I can't pick out these pellets through your clothing. Now lie still."

"But...but, you can't just strip a man of his pride without a never-you-mind. Don't I have a say-so in the matter?"

"No." She snipped the material while he continued to object.

"Ain't there any other choices here? Can't I—"

"No."

She kept her mind on her task, ever mindful of the closeness of the wound to his important...stuff. Bothersome thoughts tripped over each other inside her head. Things like how firm his flesh was and how the muscles twitched just beneath the surface. The downy hair on his leg brushed against the back of her hand and she jerked back.

Dear Mother Mary! Her palms grew sweaty and her pulse raced as if she were running for her life. Or in this case—away from trouble in the form of a stranger on a paint horse.

"I did what you said, Glory." Patience skipped into the room, her reddish-gold pigtails bobbing.

"Asked. You did what I asked," she corrected, quickly jerking the sheet over the man's naked leg. "You don't need to be in here right now. Run along. Go see what's keeping Hope."

"Oh, phooey. I'm not a baby, you know. When I grow up—"

"Scoot!" This time Glory added a firmer tone and reached for the tweezers, ignoring the familiar pout.

"Anyone ever tell you what pretty eyes you have, miss?" It seemed as if McClain willed her to meet his gaze, for he stole her power to do otherwise. "Your ma's right, me being here is gonna cause..."

Inky-brown depths pulled her into a place of mystery and odd contentment. Breath left her in a sudden rush.

Three

"Let me worry about that. You focus on breathing."

Buckshot had peppered his thigh. Engrossed in her task, Glory lost count of the small pieces of lead she coaxed from the soft tissue. An eternity later, she wiped her brow and dropped the tweezers into the metal bowl, satisfied she'd gotten them all.

McClain's closed eyes gave her hope he'd drifted into oblivion again. A blessing for sure.

Not that she knew firsthand, but having metal fragments dug from your flesh must severely test a body's courage and will. From what she'd seen, McClain wasn't short in either department. He'd handled the ordeal with considerable fortitude.

Lord knew her own had been severely stretched.

A rustle in her pocket reminded her of the letter she hadn't had time to read. She finished binding the wound and adjusted the sheet over the man's long form.

With as much quiet as she could manage in light of her clumsy boots, she tiptoed out of the alcove and into the kitchen. Patience sat cross-legged on the floor, trying to tie a frilly piece of cloth on Miss Minnie's head for a bonnet.

"Hi, Glory," the girl said, looking up. "I'm making Miss Minnie real pretty. Hold still, you darn cat."

"No swearing in this house. You know Mama would have a conniption fit if she heard you."

"I only said darn. An' it ain't cursing. Uncle Pete says it all the time."

"Isn't. It isn't cursing," she corrected automatically. "And 'darn' is not ladylike language. You can't repeat things that Uncle Pete says. I've heard him cuss a blue streak."

She watched her little sister play with the cat and four new kittens. It wouldn't be long before the girl would have each newborn wearing tiny doll clothes. Much to Miss Minnie's irritation, Patience had dressed her in all kinds of garb from the moment she showed up on their doorstep. Not that the scraps of fabric stayed on long. Somehow, the calico always found ways to get the ruffles and bows off.

It wasn't right that Patience had to resort to playing with animals instead of children her own age or even dolls. And it didn't sit well in Glory's mind that her sister should suffer the sting of the town's rejection.

A precious thing, a child's innocence. Too bad the loss of it had to come at any point in life, but far better when one was older and equipped to deal with hate and prejudice. The townspeople's taunting and ignorance had been harsh taskmasters for Glory and her younger siblings.

Hope struggled through the kitchen door with a bucket of water from the creek. "We used all the water, so I went to refill it before dark. Sorry to leave you to finish by yourself."

"That's all right. It's over and he's dozing."

"Glory, have you thought about supper?" her mother asked, joining them.

"No, Mama. I've been pretty busy." She tried to keep the annoyance from her voice. There was only so much she could do by herself. And there was still the matter of the letter.

"Well, I'm sure you'll think of something, dear." Ruth Day plopped down in a chair at the kitchen table. "Don't think I've forgotten the explaining you owe me either.

Bringing a strange man into our house. What do you have to say for yourself?"

Hope set the bucket of water on the sideboard and took a chair beside Glory, an expectant look on her pretty features.

"Not much to tell, actually. It began with a handbill I saw at Aunt Dorothy's this morning." Glory related the details of her confrontation with Mad Dog Perkins, and the wounding of McClain.

Patience came to her feet, her eyes wide. "You really tried to bring in a wanted outlaw? He could've killed you!"

"I don't ever want to hear of you trying anything that dangerous again." Ruth's anger ended any thoughts of resuming the chase. "Do you hear me, young lady?"

"I think we should commend Glory for what she did." Hope cast her older sister a look of admiration. "Had it worked, it would've answered all our prayers. Just think, we could've brought Papa home to be with us before..."

The miserable catch in Hope's voice rekindled Glory's frustration. McClain had ruined everything. He'd stolen her father's last chance to die in his own bed on the land where he had come into the world. She pulled the soiled envelope from her pocket and handed it to her mother.

"Aunt Dorothy gave me this letter today. Never had time to read it."

"Oh my." The woman's slender fingers trembled as she held the news from her husband. "I know your father will be home soon. I just know it."

Though Glory ached to tell her mother that it was hopeless, that Jack Day would die far away from them in a hateful, forbidding place, she held her tongue. She couldn't bear to snip the one thread of hope that kept the woman from slipping forever into her own world. Ruth had always hated Texas. Said the hot sun drained a person's soul.

Not that Mama hadn't hit upon a vein of truth. The unrelenting heat had surely withered her hopes, dreams, and lost innocence, turning them to parched, dry dust.

Patience and Hope sensed their mother's fragile state, for they both put a protective arm around her shoulders.

"Read it to us, Mama. Tell us the news from Papa." Hope laid her cheek softly against her mother's.

"Dear Mrs. Day, I regret to inform you that your husband has taken a turn for the worst. He asks for you every waking moment. Is there any way you can see your way clear to coming? Time is short and swiftly fading. Your humble servant, John Fletcher, M.D." The letter dropped from lifeless hands while a quiet sob broke from Ruth's lips.

"It'll be all right, Mama. That doctor's wrong. Papa's gonna be well soon. You'll see." Tears filled Patience's blue eyes. "Glory can fix it. Can't you, Glory?"

Glory kicked a rock and sent it skittering. "Glory can do this, Glory can do that," she mimicked. "When are they going to see I can't solve all our problems?"

Cursing the sickening whirl in her stomach, she shook her head impatiently. "I have needs, too."

The underbrush rustled to her right, bringing her attention back to the task at hand—supper. Could be an animal. Or it could be Mad Dog Perkins. She gripped the rifle tighter. Thank goodness she'd pumped a cartridge into the chamber right from the start, because she dared not risk making noise. The importance of stealth lent quietness to her feet.

Before she crept a couple of yards, a wild turkey took flight, landing on the low branch of a post oak tree. The succulent meat would sit mighty nice on their table. She held her breath and took aim, the bird clearly in her sights.

Then a second away from squeezing the trigger, her vision blurred. Now two turkeys sat on the branch and she couldn't distinguish the real from the illusion. She took her best guess and shot. The frightened bird skimmed just above the ground and over a small rise out of view.

Her heart sank. Two months earlier, she'd had no trouble with accuracy. Today, she couldn't hit the broad side of a barn.

The thought niggled her brain as she hurried after their escaping supper. Two months back seemed about the time a cougar had scared Caesar, causing the mule to kick Glory's head. Gave her a powerful headache, though she recovered after a day in bed.

"I wonder if that had something to do with…no, it couldn't. Not possible," she muttered to herself. Whatever the reason, she wished to high heaven it'd go away. Her shoulders weren't broad enough to deal with any more complications.

About an hour later, approaching darkness forced her to trudge home empty-handed. The turkey that had teased her taste buds had vanished. Two hawks, a porcupine, and a puny prairie dog were all she'd seen.

The fact that they had another mouth to feed further weighed on her heart as she pushed through the kitchen door.

Patience chattered like a magpie from the alcove where they'd taken McClain. Hope glanced up hopefully from her task of making biscuits. It brought an uncomfortable lurch to her chest. They could blame her for a bare table.

"Did you…?" The light from Hope's face left as she quickly read Glory's dejected posture.

"Nope. Nothing. Guess it'll be whatever we can scrounge from the garden or root cellar." She hung her serviceable hat on a peg beside the door. "Lord knows there's pitiful left. This heat's burned up everything. Including our will. Mama's right. Maybe there's no use."

"Don't say that, Glory." Hope wiped the flour on her apron and gave her sister a hug. "We'll manage. We've had hard times before and lived through them."

Glory envied her sister's eternal optimism. Their parents couldn't have bestowed a more appropriate name on her. Unlike her own. Glorious? Far from it. The Greek name Hydra would fit better. The name of a dragon killed by Hercules.

"Besides, what choice do we have?" Hope added softly.

"None, I suppose." She took a ragged breath. It'd been a long, disappointing day all around.

"Rest for a bit. Sit down and I'll see what I can find."

Too tired to resist, she let Hope push her into a chair. "Mama still lying down?"

"No, in fact, Aunt Dorothy stopped by. The two of them are in the bedroom talking."

"Wonder what about."

Hope disappeared out the door without answering. Whatever it was, Glory prayed it brought Mama out of her doldrums. Busy sorting through the list of possibilities, she overheard Patience from the next room.

"My sister didn't mean to shoot you, Mr. McClain. She's truly a nice person. Even when she yells at me sometimes, I still love 'er."

"I'm sure you do," Luke said.

"Doesn't it hurt something awful to get shot?"

"All in a day's work when you're a lawman, little 'un."

A lawman, huh? He'd not so much as breathed a word of this to Glory and he'd had ample opportunity. She smelled a rat.

"My name's Patience. How many times have you been shot?"

"Reckon if'n you count arrows and bullets both, might near ten or twenty times."

Glory shamelessly listened. You could learn a lot about a man not so much by what he said, but how he said it. Not that she cared a piddly poo about unearthing personal details. Other than making sure he wasn't the sort to kill them all in their beds, that is.

The braggart truly didn't suffer from shyness. His exaggeration—and she had no doubt that described McClain—was a feeble attempt to glorify himself in a little girl's eyes.

Well, that sure fit what she knew of him so far. Plus, his drawling slang spoke of rustic living. Most likely, he didn't even know his letters or how to cipher.

"Where'd your sister go?" he asked.

"Which one?"

"The crack shot. Miss Glory."

Her heart seemed to stop when he spoke her name. Evidently, neither had heard her come in. She should put a stop to his meddling. Still, she wanted to eavesdrop a little while longer.

"She went to find us some supper. Glory takes care of us since our papa got put in prison. She can shoot real good."

"I've gotten a taste of her shootin' skills." McClain's tone rivaled the dry Texas wind.

The nerve of him! She hadn't shot him on purpose.

"My sister can kill anything if she wants. That's why you're not dead, mister."

Hurrah for Patience. Glory almost wished she had put the braggart out of his misery. Or else have shot a different part of his anatomy. Now there was a tempting thought. An inch or two higher would've changed his deep baritone to a soprano.

"Appears I owe you an apology, Miss Patience. Didn't mean to hit a tender spot." Did her ears deceive her? McClain almost sounded sincere. "Why's your pa in prison? That is, if you don't mind my asking."

"Wasn't his fault. Glory calls it a case of ignorance on account a ol' lady Penelope being blind as a bat. She says that old sow cain't find her backside with both hands."

Glory leaped to her feet, shocked at her baby sister's language. It never entered her mind that Patience would repeat her rantings. Didn't matter that hurt and disappointment had driven those words from her mouth. The damage had been done. She had to stop this conversation and silence Patience.

The house filled with McClain's laughter. A step from the alcove, she paused when her mother appeared with Aunt Dorothy. Ruth's chalky face set off alarms.

"Dorothy's brought some news from town."

"What is it now, Mama?"

Ruth Day pursed her mouth, trying to form the words. Finally, she said, "Mr. Fieldings at the bank might call in some of the notes he holds."

"Aunt Dorothy?" Glory swung, fixing her aunt with a stare.

"I'm sure it's just a baseless rumor, dear. Might not be a smidgen thing to it."

"You must have thought different, to come all the way out. Did you hear how soon or which property?" Hell's bells! Maybe she'd been the one to take a load of buckshot the way she hurt inside. Despair riddled her thoughts. Losing the land—their home—would be the final straw.

"Are you behind on the payments?" Dorothy was asking Ruth as if her mother had an inkling of their financial state.

"I don't know." A blank look swept over Ruth. "Glory?"

"We're a little past due, but I was hoping to catch up come next week." She sank into a chair at the table.

"Well, perhaps it's merely harmless speculation. You know how folks get in a tizzy over the smallest whispers. And even if it turns out to be true, I'm sure he wouldn't take this farm." Dorothy gave them a helpless smile. "Oh, dear me, look at the time! I must get home before dark."

"Yes, Jack will be home soon, too. He always comes riding in after dusk." Ruth's childlike statement startled both Glory and her aunt.

"No, Mama. Papa won't be coming home. Not now, not ever." She refused to let her mother think anything but the unvarnished truth. But the facts wouldn't keep insanity at bay. Ruth appeared to be slipping further from them.

"Yes, he is! I don't know why you want to hurt me."

Aunt Dorothy caught her eye and shook her head in warning. Pain and remorse played hopscotch up Glory's spine.

"I'm sorry, Mama. Why don't you go lie back down so you'll be fresh as a daisy when he gets here?"

"I'll put Ruth to bed," Aunt Dorothy told her. "Then I'll let myself out. If you need me…if your mother gets worse, send Hope for me."

"Thank you. I will." At least she had her aunt and uncle to depend on. They weren't entirely alone.

Through a haze, she watched Aunt Dorothy steer her mother toward the bedroom.

What else was going to happen? She couldn't help her father, couldn't put food on the table, and couldn't save the farm if there was no money to pay the banknote. What else? Oh, yes, she couldn't half see and her mother was losing her mind. Heaven forbid if her plate overflowed!

In the quiet stillness, Patience continued to chatter up a storm to their wounded guest.

"Papa's not well. The doctor don't give him much time. That's why Glory tried to capture that mean ol' outlaw."

"You don't say."

"And, she could've, too, if you hadn't stopped her. With the reward money, we could get Papa outta prison and he could come home, and then Glory wouldn't have to be the man o' the house."

This time nothing would deter Glory. Patience seemed intent on airing their family laundry as well as her lungs. Four purposeful strides took Glory to the door of the small bedroom.

"I like you," Patience said. "For a stranger, you're awfully nice. Would you marry my sister, Mr. McClain?"

About the Author

Linda Broday resides in the panhandle of Texas on the Llano Estacado. At a young age, she discovered a love for storytelling, history, and anything pertaining to the Old West. There's something about Stetsons, boots, and tall, rugged cowboys that get her fired up! A *New York Times* and *USA Today* bestselling author, Linda has won many awards, including the prestigious National Readers' Choice Award and the Texas Gold Award. Visit her at lindabroday.com.

Also by Linda Broday

Texas Redemption

Bachelors of Battle Creek

Texas Mail Order Bride
Twice a Texas Bride
Forever His Texas Bride

Men of Legend

To Love a Texas Ranger
The Heart of a Texas Cowboy
To Marry a Texas Outlaw

Texas Heroes

Knight on the Texas Plains
The Cowboy Who Came Calling